Also by J. A. Collignon

ARROWMOUNT BOOKS SERIES
A Second Story
A Little Luck

CONTEMPORARY ROMANCE
(UNDER JENN COLLIGNON)
Merry and Bright

A Favored Fey

J. A. Collignon

Book cover art and design by Tessa Brenan, @roguecorner on X, @roguescorner.bsky.social on Bluesky

Interior maps and illustrations by J.A. Collignon

Print ISBN: 978-1-7388682-8-5

Ebook ISBN: 978-1-7388682-9-2

A | ARROWMOUNT PRESS

AUTHORS NOTE

Author's Note: this book has depictions of chronic pain and pain flares, anxiety, injury, minor stalking, gaslighting, and pregnancy (mentioned right at the end, and no, it's not a main character or surprise pregnancy, I can promise that). If any of these affect you, please proceed with caution, or come back for another cozy fantasy I write at some other time.

For those of us who want to find our place in this world

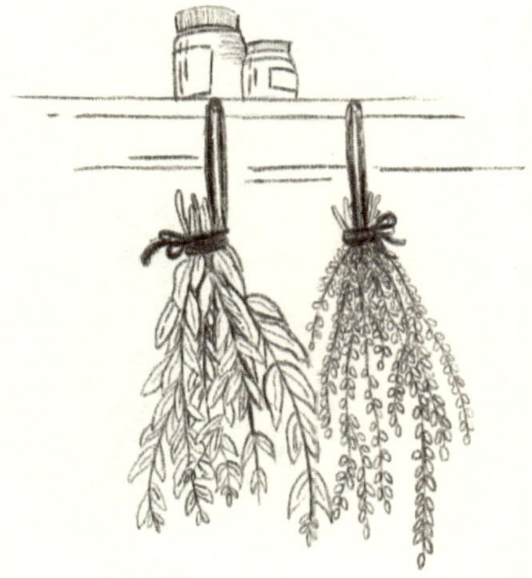

CONTENTS

RAVAR
NERIAN EMPIRE
BRENEM EMPIRE
MANID EMPIRE
CASPASIAN ISLES
CASPASIAN SEA
THE DEAD SEA
DUNNALOCH PASS
Malgail Wastes
ADARLAN PEAKS
BLACKSHELL FOREST
Antosar
Antovers
Tua Outreach
Glasrock
Frelun
ENSGÅRD
Törduu
Ardnablane
Dunnaloch
Malgård
Blackshell Reach
Falenroch
Northdenn
Underthall
Charteau
Grenne
ALIEWETH
Deliar
Narveil
Crestborne
Claymore
Ironcoast
Basingrove
Tage's Reach
Shadyside
Feycross
Silver Creek
Kharan
Reat
PRALON
Tanju
Hutton
Boarsrest
Notton
Riverspoke
Arrowmount
Quhar
NARAKAMI
Lilleby
Kenmar
Wolf's Pack
Mosfell
Ryefeld
ZIDIEN
Almcir
Talimar
Taimen
Rath
Sarisan
Meadon

ARROWMOUNT
1. Town Gate
2. Town Center
3. A Second Story
4. May's Cafe
5. Zanve's Apartment
6. Old'n Narrow
7. Meri's Cottage
8. Caelynn's Apothecary
9. Glass Smiths
10. Eldar's Wall
11. Barracks
12. Lord's Manor

Part One

The Keeper of the Lines

THE KEEPER OF THE LINES

Meriwen

Strangeness flocked to Meriwen. Take, for example, the bottle-green wyrmling that clung to her shoulders making a noise in the back of his throat like an anxious grandmother fussing over the amount of salt she put in her soup.

"Don't like," he crooned to Meriwen. He peered over her shoulder at the stone currently nestled between stems of unseasonably fresh lavender. His voice always came out like he had sand stuck in his throat.

Meri shifted back onto her strong leg as she took a half step away from the garden bed. "You don't like anything, Hemlock."

"Mmmm." Lock curled his tail tighter around her upper arm. "I like you."

"That's only after I've fed you, you beast," she said, smiling as she pulled playfully at the tip of his tail.

The two of them looked at the stone in the lavender, quiet. It had an odd aura about it. If she was looking at a creature, Meri would have said it had an awareness to it; but this was a stone. In her fairly extensive experience of the material realm, she had yet to come across one that was sentient. Sure, there were earth elementals that were made of stone, but that was different than something this small and seemingly insignificant.

The surface shone like an oil slick on the ocean in the thin, late winter morning light of her garden. Roughly two handfuls big and pitted like raw granite, the stone looked as if it should have been quite heavy; but when she had picked it up at the Magic Goods stall in town when she'd purchased it, it was surprisingly light. Some odd sensation had come over her when she had walked by the stall; it was as though someone had pinned her with a stare, drawing their eyes physically over her skin. But when she looked back at the stall, the proprietor Cecily Little was deep in conversation with someone else.

Then Meri had noticed the stone, innocuous amongst the other odds and ends Cecily sold. The moment Meri's fingers had grazed the surface, her heart knew it had to come home to her cottage with her.

Meri ran her fingers gently over the pitted surface. It looked good out here, in the lavender. She'd been moving it around her small cottage and garden, trying to find the right place for it for the past two weeks. This was only another attempt to see where it would remain, as nothing had felt quite right yet.

Something incorporeal brushed up against her consciousness. She froze, fingers lingering on the stone.

"Mmmm," said Lock in her ear, shocking her out of her thoughts. Whatever the feeling was vanished as she tried to focus on it, leaving her feeling bereft and aching, right below her ribs.

"Stranger things have happened," Meri said quietly to herself before turning away. It had been quite some time since she'd experienced an oddity in her day to day life, despite being rather used to them. Last time it happened was when Lock had shown up in her garden, a tiny wyrmling out of his element. Wyrmlings were more commonly found deep in the Blackshell Forest, staying mostly away from any population that may disturb them; or up in the mountains near the Nerian Empire. Seeing one this far south east near the coast had been quite the surprise.

The oddities came with being the Witch of the Woods, as the towns-folk of Arrowmount called her.

Or, in the case of her actual title, the Keeper of the Lines.

High Fey, many centuries ago, created the position by choosing specialized folk to be stationed throughout the fey realm where nexuses of ley lines appeared. These nexuses needed to be watched over, as the knots created immense possibilities of incredible power. Keepers like Meri treated the ley lines ritualistically when the seasons changed to keep the magic flowing safely through the realm around them. They kept it in balance.

No one in Arrowmount knew that she was a Keeper. For the most part, the townsfolk that populated the seaside town carried on thinking of Meri as an oddball who lived by the edge of town, tucked away in a cottage, staying mostly to herself.

Meri preferred it that way. It allowed her to go about her life exactly how she wished to.

"I'm off to gather a few bits, Lock." Meri played with the wyrmling's tail as she moved slowly back through her garden and to her little stone cottage. "Be nice to the birds, no matter how much they bother you."

The chattering birds that usually occupied Meri's kitchen counters had taken to messing with Lock's bed, which was under her kitchen cabinets. They seemed to find it funny, or perhaps were just hunting for any soft bits to build their own nests with — poking and prodding at Lock's blankets until soft fuzz and material would come away in their beaks. The wyrmling had taken to trying to eat them.

"And do not touch my stone."

The last bit came unbidden, but the feeling, the *need* to protect it, was suddenly overwhelming in her gut. Lock crawled up her shoulders and head a little higher, slithering through her two towering antlers so he could peer upside down into her eyes.

"I mean it," Meri said, raising her eyebrows.

Lock grumbled in response, the vibration shuddering through her skull from the weight of his body. He wasn't the tiniest of creatures; from snout to tail tip, he stretched the length of a small child laying down. Thankfully, even with his concealed wings, he was rather lithe, and was mostly tail and neck.

"Fine. No touching stone." Lock wrinkled his long snout as much as his scales would let him in annoyance. "Or birds," he added at her glare.

"Thank you." She tickled his nose.

"Mmmm." He huffed and straightened out of her vision, sliding back on her head to rest in his usual position on her shoulders. "Meri makes fuss over stone."

Meri sighed. "I simply don't want *you* to make such a fuss, okay? For me."

"Why go into town?"

"Supplies, Lock." They argued about this regularly, no matter when or why Meri headed into town. The wyrmling simply did not like when she was gone.

But, she needed to go into town to check if Caelynn had any Tanju violets on hand. She'd run out in her preparations for the ritual tomorrow — if Caelynn didn't have any, Meri was going to have to resort to regular violets, which wasn't going to achieve quite the same effect.

Tanju violets were precious and quite rare to acquire, seeing as they are harvested from the north-western tip of the Manid Empire mountain range, and only grow during the dead of winter for two months at a time. Their season was just ending; so, if anyone had some on hand, it would be Caelynn.

As Meri was inventorying her supplies last night, double checking if she needed to refill on anything else, she also noticed that a meriwen plant had been vandalized. Tiny, meticulous bites had been taken from the stems, as though something was testing the plant. She'd have to start looking around her property for mice or a similarly tiny creature that had started to nest without her knowledge.

Meri let out a long, slow breath, trying to ease the anticipatory nerves clawing at her insides. She was always nervous at the change of seasons, despite having done this for countless years now. If something went wrong, if the ritual failed in some way...

She had grown up with her grandmother telling her over and over again to ensure that no matter what, the ritual was to be done. Because if a Keeper failed in their job, they failed the town they were protecting.

The High Fey had decided to implement Keepers around the fey realm due to the danger those nexuses put on the people in the realm. As a girl, Meri had been taught a lesson all Keepers were of a town that had a particularly large knot of magic where many ley lines knotted and crossed. It had gone unsuspected and unbalanced for a long while — until the magic there began to twist the townsfolk around until they were nothing more than a hard existence of shadow and darkness that tore itself apart.

Keepers ensured that this was to never happen again.

Meri had never failed, not once, since moving to Arrowmount after discovering the two nexuses: one that lived in the middle of her garden, and one in the middle of town.

Lock wrinkled his snout in an approximation of a frown as Meri lifted him from her shoulders, depositing him on the old garden chair she had stationed outside her kitchen door. A low noise of anxiety sounded at the back of his throat.

Meri grabbed her old garden coat from the hook that hung above him; it was weather-beaten to a light tan and eaten away along the cuff by a pesky moth, but worked in a pinch to keep herself warm.

Lock curled his tail in around himself and glared at her reproachfully as she bent over the lower half of her heavy oak kitchen door to retrieve her bag, casting a quick eye around the inside of her plant-filled, sunlit kitchen, seeing if she had forgotten anything or if a stray creature had gotten in without her permission. They had a knack of doing that, especially the birds that she'd find tottering and bouncing playfully around the many jars scattered on her counters and windowsills.

Meri eyed her old cedar staff, wrought by a woodworker from the Kingdom of Alieweth long ago, leaning against the doorframe. She shifted, gauging briefly if she would need it for her walk down to the town. No, today was a good day. Meri thought about her route briefly, marking two points — one at the edge of the trees, and one more in town where there was a small rocky stoop against a building she could stop, organize her basket and rest without looking too conspicuous if need be.

Meri shut the upper half of her door with a firm snap, and slung her bag across her chest, feeling the gentle clink of empty jars against her hip.

Lock frowned at her from his perch on the rickety old chair before he turned his snout in the direction of the lavender.

"It's *just a stone,* Lock.".

"Mmmmm. Both know it's more than that."

Meri hesitated, taken aback by the low, cryptic voice that had just come from the tiny wyrmling. What in all the realms could he mean?

She tightened the grip on her bag and frowned back at him. "If it makes you feel better, you're in charge, okay?"

Lock lit up and sat up straight, becoming all at once attentive and happy. A thin wisp of smoke escaped his nostrils.

"That does *not* mean you get to boss everyone away from the house just so you can get your beauty rest in my bed," she said quickly, stopping to pick up a basket seated beneath the chair and hooked it over her arm.

Lock's spine dropped a touch and he flicked the end of his tail around himself resentfully.

A soft breath of mist puffed out around Meri in the chilled air as she stepped onto the path leading from her garden, the last dregs of winter still clinging to the world. Meri took her time ambling down toward Arrowmount, taking a looping track through the towering trees that lined her property. They were wonderful beings, ones that Meri had come to know almost as well as the gardens she'd planted. Both the plant life and the creatures that surrounded Meri's little cottage were more friends to her than any living person was.

The trees stood sentinel over the town, acting as a natural barrier that Arrowmount hadn't truly needed for centuries. All the same, they grew thick and tall, and were Meri's constant companions.

Over the years she'd spent living in this realm, Meri had learned that plants and the natural things around her deserved just as much love and attention as the living beings that moved through that natural world. Thankfully, along the shores of Arrowmount, the people here seemed to be content with what they had, and were not interested in destroying more of that natural world than they ought to. It was one of the many reasons she'd chosen to settle here.

Trailing her fingers along the bark of a particularly lovely, enormous oak that had wrapped itself into knots with its neighbour long ago, Meri smiled at the trees. Sunlight dappled down amidst the bare branches that swayed in a light breeze, teasing Meri's long, curling hair and skirts.

"Good morning, ladies," she called upward, a gentle knot of tension easing from her shoulders. The boughs rattled in response as they whispered their greetings to her, the morning sunshine leaking through their bare branches and starting to melt away at the thin layer of frost coating their bark and the grasses around them.

It wasn't quite enough to relieve the anxiety coursing through her, the gentle background thoughts of *"what if regular violets are all I have, and it's not enough, not strong enough for the ritual to take? If Caelynn doesn't have the violets, then..."*

Meri pulled her coat tighter around her, and continued on, stepping out of the tree line and onto the winter trampled earth.

This late in winter, there wasn't a lot to look at in this stretch from the edge of the forest to the town gates, other than the occasional squashed patch of grass that was starting to come back to life. Soon, though, this expanse would be positively riddled with an entire rainbow of colors as flowers and bugs alike spent their days dancing under warm sunshine.

Meri stepped eventually onto the road that bisected her path toward town and followed it the rest of the way to the two figures standing sentinel at the entrance to Arrowmount.

"Good morning," she said softly, her voice barely louder than a murmur of birds' wings as she tilted her head toward the two guards. One of them, the shorter of the two, snapped to attention as she approached. His eyes trailed her from the slightly soiled hem of her skirt, up over her tall frame to her pair of antlers, towering up from her head. His mouth dropped open as he stared at her, rather rudely.

Surely these two had seen her coming. It shouldn't be *this* much of a shock to see her here, walking up to the gates.

"Morning," said the other guard, his voice pleasant and deep. She turned her attention to him, meeting his grey-eyed stare. His eyes shifted in the sunshine, taking on a bit of the golden warmth. He began to smile, but before she could fully appreciate it, she dropped her gaze and nodded to both of them before continuing on through the gates. She didn't want to linger overlong in case the second guard, the one still rudely staring, found his voice.

Meri had come through the town gates enough to recognize the taller guard, the one with the grey eyes, though she knew next to nothing about him. She only knew that he was kind to her, and never gawked at her like the other guards did.

The shorter guard, the black-haired rude one, said something under his breath and began to chuckle as though he'd said the joke of the century when, she supposed, they thought she was out of earshot. The taller one, the kind one, grunted in reply.

Meri shook her head and continued on, slowing her gait to careful long steps, not too fast or slow. She thought, perhaps, that years of walking sure-footed through the forest would aid her in the uneven surface of the cobblestones, but no matter how many times she came into Arrowmount, she continuously failed to adapt to them.

The townsfolk milling about at this hour were early morning workers going about their business and mostly ignored her as she walked through the town. *Mostly*. She could feel the gaze of some locking onto her, the antlers sprouting from her head and her height drawing curious looks.

Arrowmount was a place of odd folk; she was not the only one around here to appear slightly out of place. Rather, no one was really out of place here, because how could one be if everyone was a little odd? That was another reason she liked this little seaside town: it was a place where beings of all walks of life connected, making it rather normal to see those who may not be considered normal elsewhere.

Still, some townsfolk considered her strange and otherworldly, which wasn't entirely wrong. She was from the fey realm, not the material realm, after all. She knew of the rumors that swirled in Arrowmount about her. Some folks went as far as to call her the Witch of the Woods. Passing whispers of children often told stories about her having wings that shone with the power of the sun.

She wasn't as powerful as that, of course. She was just Meriwen.

2

CAPTAIN LUDRU'S SPECIAL

Zanve

Zanve grit his teeth, controlling the urge to hit Damian square in his face as the man chuckled under his breath, making a lewd face at him.

"What?" the sorry excuse for a man had the audacity to say, wiggling his eyebrows. "She's really something, isn't she? What do you think the Witch of the Woods does all day cooped up in that tiny cottage? Maybe she runs around naked—"

"Shut up," snapped Zanve, his usually calm demeanor shortening dramatically. Gods, he hated this man. Damian got under his skin in a way that sent Zanve over the edge, no matter what day it was, and no matter how much Zanve tried to talk himself down.

Especially when they'd just spent an entire night shift together and their shift replacements were behind schedule. He was itching to get out of there, out of his uniform, and into bed.

Though, he couldn't complain about being able to catch a glimpse of the woman who lived in the woods. She was her own kind of mystery, one that vaguely intrigued him.

"Oo-hoo-hoo," said Damian, settling back against the stone wall behind him and lifting his chin. The weak morning sun made his pale complexion positively incandescent, hurting Zanve's eyes. "Our little Zanve has a crush, does he? You want the big bad Witch all to yourself? Whatever will everyone say?"

Zanve repressed the urge to throttle him with a heavy sigh. He didn't dignify the man's comments with an answer.

Damian chuckled. "Just think about what she'd be like in be—"

Zanve closed his eyes, sending up a silent plea to the gods to give him the strength to complete this shift without biting Damian's head off.

Easy, Einar, he told himself, drawing back and turning away from the man. He knew what kind of man Damian was. What he'd witnessed every day he'd known the man — which was far too many days, in his opinion — showed him that Damian was not worth his time or energy, despite his uncanny ability to get under Zanve's skin.

Their shift replacements, Adrias Waylan and Nisri Frosthelm, arrived moments later. Adrias' short and stocky dwarfish stature stalked along next to Nisri's lithe, tall and dark elven form, Adrias taking three steps to Nisri's one. Nisri lifted a hand in greeting.

"Morning gents," said Adrias, his voice crackling with sleepy grit. He nodded to them, bags under his eyes a gentle purple as he sipped from a rather large tankard that steamed around him.

"Where've you been?" said Damian, turning his lewd attention on them. "Sleeping in? Showing your woman a good—"

Zanve's patience snapped. He took that opportunity to shove Damian off balance, sending him a touch more forcefully than he should have into the wall. Damian went sprawling, his usually perfectly slicked back pitch black hair falling askew. Adrias snorted into his coffee and tipped the tankard to Zanve in appreciation.

"Morning." Zanve nodded to the two of them.

"Zanve," said Nisri, narrowing their piercing rich brown eyes at him as they neared. "Are you alright?"

"Yes, just..." he tilted his head in Damian's direction. "Long night."

Adrias chuckled as Damian took that moment to stalk off into the town with his cheeks blazing a mottled pink. "Ah, go ahead and run off, you sniveling little rat of a man. As a matter of fact, I *was* with my lady last night, who I love very deeply and truly," he said, turning to wink at Zanve before pitching his voice louder to follow Damian. "Something that that little pale rat doesn't know the feeling of."

Damian stiffened but did not turn around and instead lurched off into Arrowmount toward the guard barracks, looking rather like a crow who just had an embarrassing fall from a tree.

Zanve grinned, his mood having lifted immediately at the sight of his two friends. "He has a way about him that just gets under my skin." He gestured to the purple bags under Adrias' eyes. "Did you sleep okay?"

"Like a baby," answered Adrias with a smile. "Just these early mornings, you know how it is."

Nisri frowned at Adrias as they leaned against one of the salt-covered walls surrounding Arrowmount, the warming early morning sun bathing their golden skin. "Don't you have to get up early on the farm, too? Shouldn't you be used to it?"

"Yes, well. It is always a bit harder to get up when you have your beautiful soon-to-be-wife in your arms." Adrias' face crinkled into a beaming grin so bright that Zanve couldn't help but smile along with him. The Waylan family ran one of the more profitable farms surrounding Arrowmount, where Adrias himself traded weeks on and off with his brothers. On the weeks he didn't have to work the fields, he was here in town, living with his partner.

"The Witch was rumored to pass through here," said Nisri, with a slight twinkle in their eyes. "Did you happen to see her, or was that just town gossip?"

Zanve nodded and suppressed a yawn. "She did, actually. Too bad you two weren't actually on time, or you would've seen her and been able to wish her good morning." He shot a knowing look at Nisri. "I know how that thrills you whenever you get a chance."

"Oh, shut it. She's just..." Nisri waved their long, slender fingers in an all-encompassing movement, a soft smile on their face.

"She's a woman, that's all. Which is probably more than our Nisri can handle, eh?" The other guard laughed and knocked an amiable fist into Nisri's thigh. "You should've seen them last night at the Narrow, Einar. They were trying to talk to Briar and was red as a tomato, stumbling all over their words."

Zanve cackled. Even he had learned, years ago when he was more outgoing with men and women alike, to steer clear of the barmaid. Briar was incredibly wonderful, but didn't take to that kind of advancement.

"I don't turn red, in case you haven't noticed," Nisri gestured at their dark complexion and rolled their eyes, though Zanve was fairly sure that Nisri's cheeks deepened in color. "But... gods, something about curvy women. And mysterious women. Like the Witch."

"It's all women, my friend." Adrias cackled and raised his tankard of coffee toward Zanve. "Go get some rest, Einar. I heard Captain wants you back on duty again tonight. We've got it from here."

Zanve groaned. He was going to have to check the schedule before heading off home to grab some much-needed sleep.

Zanve passed through the guard barracks only to confirm the schedule, seeing his name penned in alongside a newer recruit's name for the second nightshift in a row. He didn't mind these later shifts, since they allowed him to drift off into his own mind or bring a book to read, but having them back to back was harsh.

At least it wasn't with Damian again, he mused, yawning wide. He walked through the tight building once more, nodding to Amalin, Captain Ludru's second in command. She was seated behind the criminally tiny desk that the Captain had crammed into the left-hand corner, looking only half awake.

"Einar," she muttered, sniffing heavily.

"Yikes, even I don't look that tired and I was up all night," he answered, teasing. "What on Ravar did you get up to last night?"

Amalin groaned and lifted a hand to her brow. "Captain Ludru wanted to celebrate my birthday."

Zanve blinked. "Your... birthday?"

"Yes."

"That was a month and a half ago, wasn't it?"

"Yes."

"So..."

"The Captain forgot," she said simply. "Until last night. And he insisted. I bet he'll come waltzing in here like he doesn't feel a thing in a few hours."

Zanve snorted. "Honestly, yes. Want me to grab you some coffee?"

"Not from the pot," she said as he shifted to a tiny counter that was piled up with papers that hadn't been moved in months, and a half-filled crusted over coffee pot. Amalin turned a gentle green, her stone elemental visage wincing in nausea. "Not from *that*."

Zanve grimaced in agreement. "I'll have someone run over a coffee from May's, then?"

She sighed and nodded, going even more pale.

Zanve left, heading toward May's Cafe. He ordered one of her best brews and a large egg and bread bake that he often enjoyed after a late night out with his friends and one too many ales. He winked at Andrew, the young gnome behind the counter, and flicked him a gold coin.

"Mind taking that to Amalin, at the barracks? And maybe, uh. Wear your apron."

Andrew nodded, grimacing. "Ah, hangover?"

"One of Captain Ludru's specials."

The gnome whistled and nodded, eyes widening, before he stepped out from behind the counter. "May, I'm going to go deliver this, I'll be back in a bit!"

A beautiful half-elven woman turned from her seat beside a studious giantkin, glasses perched on the ends of both of their noses as they peered over a parchment between them. May nodded, tucking an errant curl behind her long, pointed ear. "You've got it."

Andrew and Zanve left together, walking up the cobbles of Fetterly Place before parting, Andrew speeding off toward the barracks and Zanve toward home.

3

QUHARIAN MEADOWSWEET

Meriwen

Meri stepped carefully over the threshold of Caelynn's apothecary, ducking her head to avoid the copious amount of low hanging plants and dried herbs. The shop itself was so fragrant that for a moment, Meri's nose couldn't distinguish between anything at all, as though she'd run into a wall of scent. She breathed out and wrinkled her nose, casting her gaze around as she acclimatized to the darker, claustrophobic space, eyeing the tightly packed shelves.

Caelynn, the sweet older giantkin who was serving the only other customer in the apothecary with a smile, turned toward Meri's entrance. Her soft, kind face melted into genuine glee as she saw Meri, the other customer ducking out with a wave.

"Meriwen! It's been a while, darling. Welcome, welcome!"

The giantkin beamed and slid out from behind her small counter, herbs brushing along the top of her head as she moved to wrap Meri in a warm hug. Meri smiled, all the while trying to ensure that her antlers didn't tangle in the honeysuckle plant hanging above her. "Are you in for some of that Tanju violet? Or just your regulars?"

Meri blinked at her. "How did you know?"

Caelynn's eyes sparkled as she winked. "I catch on, you know. I'm not as old as I look. I've just had a shipment in from the Manid Empire today, and the last of the Tanju's were in there, I made sure. Come on through to the back."

Meri followed Caelynn through a cramped back door and into an attached greenhouse at the back. Caelynn had transformed the space herself to grow her own supply of herbs. Meri felt as though she'd stepped into her own greenhouse, recognizing the same glasswork and framing that the Miirthgroves had done in hers. It was the reason Caelynn and Meri had become friends; Caelynn had come up to her cottage on the advice of the Miirthgroves to see how Meri's greenhouse was set up.

Once again, Meri's senses were drowned in an array of scents from the countless exposed pots of powdered spices and open boxes of fresh herbs that were piled along the back. Half of them were still fresh or partially dried, splayed out in meticulous chaos over the many tables and shelves that Caelynn had crammed inside the tiny space.

The main apothecary was pungent, but nothing compared to the smell of fresh plants. Meri paused to inspect a few of the pots.

Caelynn's attention trickled through a pile of well wrapped packages set in front of her. "Take a whiff of this!"

She handed Meri a package, which Meri immediately breathed in. Something about the dusty, heat-filled scent immediately transported her back decades and across the continent of Ravar.

She closed her eyes, remembering the heavy, oppressively dry heat that had dug into the back of her eyes, the sand that had swirled around grating along her skin as she held onto her mother's hand. Elestren had pulled her along through crowded markets in Narakami, the capital city of the Manid Empire. Meri had never experienced such a bustling, busy place. Back then, as a much smaller person than she was now, all she could see were various shades of dust layering the pants and skirts and furred legs that surrounded her.

Scents rich and bitingly fragrant had wafted to her through the scalding heat of the sun, drawing her attention up and around as Elestren steered her toward a shop folded in between what felt like a million other shops. Bursts of color had been hung around the entrance with what Meri had thought was magic until her vision cleared enough to see they were beautifully wrought scarves and blankets decorating the shop.

Inside were scents so divine and entrancing that Meri had stood in the middle of the space, mouth agape, as her mother's hand had slipped from hers, letting go for only a moment. Meri had gazed around at the hanging herbs and flowers, the towering thin baskets of spices so full that Meri marveled at how they didn't topple into one another, spilling their beautifully colored contents all over the floor.

"Scents really do trigger the most interesting memories, don't they?"

Meri blinked back into Caelynn's greenhouse as the giantkin chuckled.

"I..." Meri cleared her throat as though there was sand lodged there. She hadn't thought of that market trip with her mother in years.

"Here we are," said Caelynn, unearthing a number of colorful, familiar bundles. She handed Meri a sprig of minuscule burnt orange flowering stems, tinged brown with lack of moisture. "I always ask for extra meadowsweet, because I know how much you love it."

Meri clutched the sprig carefully and held it to her nose. "Quharian?"

"The very stuff."

Meri inhaled the sharp, almond-like smell, the faintest hint of honey mingling through the nuttiness, barely discernible in the overpowering greenhouse. "Incredible."

Caelynn gestured to the half-opened packages around her as she picked one up and withdrew some particularly long pitch-black tendrils that wiggled freely in the air. "Feel free to open whichever and poke around. I've forgotten what I've ordered this go around."

They worked for a few minutes side by side, unwrapping the plants and herbs, discarding the wrappings beneath the table in a large bin.

Meri gently thumbed the leaf of a particularly large mint plant, releasing the sharp, clean smell into the air. She hunted for a moment, wondering where the package of precious Tanju violets was. She reached for a smaller bundle wrapped in brown paper, before Caelynn's own cracked and worn hand came into view, holding out a half-opened package of the flowers.

"I always wondered why they call them violets, when they're so violently pink," she mused, winking as Meri beamed at her. "Sometimes us old witches know, eh?"

"You know you can have any pick of my garden, whenever you like."

Caelynn hummed happily under her breath before shifting again, a small hitch in her throat. "I should, I should. It's been too long. Your rosemary does something special with bread that none of mine ever has."

Meri hesitated, taking a better look at the aging giantkin, noting the soft lines that were creasing along her softly furred grey face, and the gentle lean, a familiar pose that Meri herself adopted when she was trying to hide pain.

"If you do, I'll have a pot of meadowsweet tea ready for you."

"Oh, wonderful!" Caelynn chuckled. "Your teas always work wonders with my aches."

"I'm going to bring you some next time," said Meri, straightening with a bundle of herbs in hand, the precious Tanju violet bundle folded carefully alongside some of her new meadowsweet. "A lot, so you can brew it whenever you need."

Caelynn sucked her teeth with a soft smile. "You are too kind. I simply like when you brew it, darling. It is so much more special to have tea with a friend."

"Yes, well." Meri glanced down at the giantkin's hip, slightly concerned. "If you really need any help with that, I'm sure the clerics here will—"

"You worry too much," chuckled Caelynn, leading the way back into her apothecary. "I am just fine, it's simply aches and pain that come with age. I'm not as young as I look, you know." She burst into a positive guffaw of laughter, which Meri couldn't help but mirror with her own chuckle.

After a few more moments poking through Caelynn's apothecary before gathering up her purchases into her basket, Meri waved goodbye to Caelynn and set off toward the town center in search of Cecily Little and her market stall.

After returning home, Meri spent the evening prepping the final bits for her upcoming ritual. For easy assembly, she carefully laid out most of everything on the various tables and shelves in her greenhouse.

She stretched, turning this way and that as she stepped away from her stool, relieving the tense muscles along her neck and back from bending over for so long. With a quick motion, she dusted off her hands, scattering plant debris.

All was ready.

Momentary relief spread through her, erasing a tiny bit of anxiety from her limbs. Being prepared helped most to quell the pre-ritual anxieties, as now she knew nothing was missing or left to do before tomorrow.

Most of her spring planting was complete, too. The air still held that gentle crispness of winter and the ground was solidly frozen, but Meri's cottage — thanks to the ley line nexus in the middle of her garden — was quite a bit warmer, and the soil ready to plant in. The bubble of warmth also allowed her to walk around barefoot as the snow around Arrowmount was still melting, which she appreciated. She preferred having her feet connected to the earth whenever she could.

It was nearly dark now, the sun having long since sunk behind the forest lining her property. The magic around her from the ley lines and the earth beneath her bare feet thrummed over her skin, nearly at its most active as the change of season came ever closer. She wiggled her fingers through the air as she walked back toward her cottage, feeling her way through the invisible power, pulling on a bit of it to help remove most of the dirt from under her nails.

Even with magic, though, there was always some that lingered. That was the consequence of gardening.

Come.

Meri froze, instantly on alert. It wasn't quite a full word, whatever had gone through her mind, but she understood its meaning all the same. Something foreign, entirely outside of herself, pulsed at the base of her ribs with so much raw emotion she almost burst into tears.

She swallowed a sob and listened, pushing out her senses to try and hear if a person or a creature was approaching her property, if they could be doing this to her.

Whatever it was reached out toward her and pulled, drawing out an incorporeal tether from her core, drawing her toward her garden beds.

Toward the lavender. Toward the stone, she realized with a jolt.

She took a few halting steps toward the stone nestled between the lavender and placed her hand atop its surface. Heat radiated from within, as though it had been baking out in a summer sun all day. It coursed up Meri's arm and filled her whole body as the feeling below her ribs, the connection, expanded through her.

Images, flashes, completely nonsensical, filtered through her mind in a blink, before the stone — or whatever this thing was — narrowed in on that specific almost-word again, pushed into her mind with a yearning to join her. A *yearning* to exist.

Open. Something deep inside that feeling in her gut pushed at her limbs, wanting to take over.

Meri hesitated, pulling herself back from the stone. Out loud, because she didn't really know how else to address it, she said, "I will not be your puppet."

The presence, the consciousness, whatever it was, pulled back, wary.

"But if you need my help, you need only ask."

A relaxing of muscles echoed through her mind, a sensation that reminded her of a tensed creature ready to spring away from a predator realizing that it was not in danger.

Help?

Meri nodded, letting her hand fall back to the stone. "Okay."

The connection that was spread through her limbs heated, and she was nudged into action. It wasn't a full puppeting of her body — instead, it was a suggestion, a nudge, a question.

Even with this, Meri couldn't quite recall what happened as she moved around her garden feverishly, gathering ingredients and supplies from her kitchen. It was as though she was watching herself from far away, noting moments when she picked up rosemary before replacing it and going for the bundle of her fey herbs instead; or when she nearly broke a nail as she used her mortar and pestle to grind an unknown combination of herbs to such a fine powder that it dusted away in the air as she transferred it to a small glass jar.

Lock, annoyed at having been awoken from his nest of blankets in one of her kitchen cabinets, crouched on the counter in front of her and frowned, watching her carefully. She was sure he probably was groaning in his anxious way the whole time, but she couldn't recall hearing him, or hearing anything for that matter.

As the first few stars dotted the sky above, Meri gathered a veritable treasure trove of things in her arms before she started out into her garden once again.

Here? She thought, the first fully formed thought she'd had in a while, voiced toward the connection. Her hands scooped up the stone, nestling it close to her chest, even as dirt clung to her hands and shirt from her raised garden beds.

No. Further.

She let her feet take her where the connection, where *the stone*, wanted her to go. She let it take her out of her garden and into the forest, in the opposite direction from Arrowmount.

If she had been in her full mind, she would have questioned this tenfold. She grew up in the fey realm, she knew better than to let strange consciousnesses tell her to do anything, let alone take over her body and mind in any way. But whatever this was, it felt... *right*. It felt safe.

Something in the connection gave her back a little more of her mind, then, leaving her standing in the middle of a clearing not overly far from her place. The ground beneath her bare feet was much colder and harder, and the air around her condensed with cold as she walked away from her protected garden.

Open?

Meri breathed out and began her preparation. A perfectly formed ritual spell unfurled in her mind, an answer to all of the elements in her arms, but it was completely unknown to her. Her grandmother had taught her many rituals when she was a girl, preparing her for her role as a Keeper, but nothing had ever come close to being as complex as this. There was an ancient, underlying strangeness to it as she started to place her prepared ingredients in the clearing in an exact pattern that she couldn't quite picture.

The presence was excited now, its attention fully on Meri and her movements, urging her silently on.

Her chest vibrated, but no sound reached her ears. Her mouth worked over words she wasn't entirely sure were in common or in any language she knew, but the shape was almost familiar, as though brushing an old, childhood memory of something long forgotten.

She blinked and found herself in the middle of the clearing, the stone placed at her feet, with a sprig of the herb that was her namesake in her hand.

Her mind churned with questions, wanting to study what she was doing, wanting to understand, but the connection, the presence, didn't let her dwell. It swelled, pushing her forward.

Meriwen is not an herb of protection, she thought, trying to understand. Something in her recognized an aspect of the larger ritual, seeing the layered protection spells she had cast, weaving into the fabric of whatever she was doing under the stars.

No, agreed the presence, but it did not elaborate. Meri wondered briefly what her namesake herb had to do with anything, but the presence didn't let her linger on the thought.

She sucked in a breath, the presence leaving her fully, leaving just that soft pulse at the base of her ribs.

The little stone that had seemed so innocuous in her garden only hours before started to glow. In the bright, blueish green light, Meri saw the pattern she had drawn out with each element of the spell in the clearing, laid out all around her. She suddenly became aware of Lock's claws digging into her calf, and the sounds of the night around her.

The pattern was a gateway.

4

TOO MUCH THIGH

Zanve

Zanve gazed into the middle distance as exhaustion pulled relentlessly at his eyelids. It was a particular cruelty, to have to do both night shifts less than 10 hours apart. He'd had maybe three hours of good sleep before his neighbor had started to bang pots and pans around outside, for a reason Zanve would never know.

He huddled tighter into his coat, the night air cold and biting along his neck as it wound around the stone wall surrounding Arrowmount.

Cadoc, a new recruit who had been hired a few weeks ago, was nodding off as their shift inched forward. No one had come in through the gates since Adrias' father had led an empty cart back out to the Waylan farm an hour ago, waving goodbye with a yawn as his horse slowly clopped up the road.

Zanve had forgotten his book. He had purposefully left it out on his kitchen table to take along, but he'd been so bothered by the neighbor and their godsdamned pans that he ran out, leaving the little paperback behind. So, instead of having the next instalment of his favorite series to pass the time with, he was staring into the distance, trying not to fall asleep.

The soft calls of birds and creatures far off in the forest drifted over to him, mingling with the distant wash of waves from the ocean that was becoming increasingly audible as the sounds of Arrowmount quieted. It lulled him into a trance, marked only occasionally by the gentle snores from the now-sleeping Cadoc.

Rather than wake the boy, Zanve simply leaned back and let him snooze, figuring that tonight was going to remain slow and devoid of anything he needed to be awake for.

He blinked, trying to refocus his eyes, letting his gaze travel off toward the dark trees surrounding Arrowmount. Tomorrow, he'd be able to sleep in and actually have a day to do things around his apartment. His kitchen was woefully dirty, dishes stacked up in his washing basin — and he should visit Wyn at some point before she got irritated at his depriving her of the opportunity to feed him.

He should visit Kaius and Jay, too, come to think of it. The past few weeks his shifts had clashed with his friends' schedules, always falling when they weren't busy. And—

A light flashed in the distance.

He sat straight up with a jolt, eyes snapping with sudden attention on the darkness expanding from the trees. He honed his ears, letting himself slip ever so slightly into his other form to heighten his senses.

Everything around him shifted into better focus, the darkness receding a touch, the hum of bugs and gentle movement of far off creatures becoming almost deafening. He breathed in, smelling nothing out of the ordinary.

Zanve glanced at Cadoc, tracking the slackness of his jaw and the deep, slow breathing, knowing that he wasn't going to wake for a long while.

Perhaps it was nothing. Perhaps it was just a trick of his eye, seeing things appearing in the dark. Everything was still and quiet, too, like nothing had happened. Maybe Zanve himself had fallen into a dream without realizing it—

Blueish-green light flashed again, deep in the forest, just barely illuminating the trees.

Zanve was up on his feet, shrugging off his coat and moving toward it before he had taken another breath. He'd almost fully shifted into his other form before he remembered he was wearing his guard uniform and was currently walking away from an unfinished job and came to a halt.

"Gods," he hissed to himself, looking over his shoulder toward Cadoc and the softly glowing lantern lights illuminating the small opening in the Arrowmount town wall. Was he really going to do this?

He had, in his years as a town guard, become rather good at his job. He never got in trouble, never stepped wrong with the Captain, and had honestly taken his job rather seriously. He wouldn't step away from his post for nothing.

And this could be nothing. It could have been a complete trick of his eyes, seeing things in the darkness, or—

The light flashed again.

His fingers started to make the decision for him as they fought with his buttons and trousers. Whatever it was, he had to go investigate. What if it was something dangerous, coming toward town?

Before Zanve could completely strip naked in full view of the front gate and stables, he hurried off down the side of the wall a few feet where the wall started to curve until he could no longer see Cadoc asleep on the job. There, he quickly undressed and left his guard uniform balled up in the grass — he had destroyed one too many pieces of clothing in his life and did not want to have to explain to Captain Ludru about needing *another* uniform — and started to run toward the forest.

In between strides, he let the animal in his chest expand out, his limbs heating with the delicious warmth he had come to know and love. He fell forward onto all fours and pushed faster, his lithe panther body fast and agile in the night.

He blended in perfectly with the dark trees as he took off toward where he'd seen the flash, darting through the underbrush until he came upon a well-trodden path.

The scent of nighttime assaulted his nose as he slowed, inhaling deeply, trying to discern where the disturbance had come from. He turned his head this way and that, trying to use everything at his disposal to track where he was and where he needed to go.

He was a town guard, after all, he tried to convince himself, ignoring the guilt in his gut at leaving his post. It was his duty to protect the town from whatever was happening outside of it.

There was a soft sound from far off, almost as though someone had just exclaimed out loud in surprise.

The Witch, he thought, a small jolt of panic thrumming through him. Meriwen, as some people knew her in town. Cecily, one of Zanve's friends, did business with her at Cecily's Magic Goods stall in the town center. From what Cecily had said, Meriwen was often quiet and soft-spoken, and had a penchant for bringing Cecily herbs and plants from her garden.

Zanve followed the path until Meriwen's cottage appeared between the trees as though it had been folded away by magic. One moment, it wasn't there, and the next, he was blinking slowly at the dim light leaking from a few of the windows, illuminating the slumbering garden. The tiny cottage looked like something straight out of a fairytale, built partially with old brick and plaster, vines and plants already crawling up the sides, despite the chilled air still clinging on to the end of winter.

The scent of herbs, sharp, warm, and mingling with the richness of freshly overturned earth filled Zanve's sensitive nose as he slowly padded through the Witch's garden. He paused, taking in an old rickety wooden chair resting next to the open door, with a rather large, ancient looking coat hanging above it. There were mud-covered boots resting outside of the door, next to what looked like a well-loved woven basket.

He snuffed loudly and bounded off through the trees, following a trail of candles, until he came to the edge of a clearing.

Slowing to a halt, he waited, still hidden in shadow. A soft bout of conversation echoed from the other side of the clearing, where he could see the back of a tall, antlered figure, bathed in orange flickering light from the countless candles that had been arranged. The figure motioned with an arm and hissed something under their breath to someone that Zanve couldn't quite see.

"Enough, Lock, I—"

Even in his panther form, he almost lost his breath at the sight of her. She turned and was lit by the soft, flickering candlelight, a breeze that he could not feel puling at the long, curling strands of her hair, casting her in a soft ethereal glow.

The incredibly bright blueish green light flashed again, before a deafening *CRACK* echoed through the space. Zanve blinked rapidly, trying to clear his sight, to see what had caused it. He started to wind around the clearing, carefully padding through the underbrush of the forest to stay as quiet as he could.

Meriwen rocked back a few steps as something in front of her scrambled away from the clearing and up along the trunk of a tree opposite, looping a long curling tail around itself as though terrified.

A nondescript rock rested on the ground in front of the Witch, a number of steps away, pulsating a dull blue-green, marred by a long crack. It didn't look as though it had cracked from a fall — no, it looked like something was cracking it from the inside.

Zanve crept up around the side, using his powerful hind legs to launch himself into a large tree nearby as quietly as he could, giving himself a better vantage point. He nearly missed, his claws gripping into the bark as he slipped a few inches, causing the entire tree to shake with his weight. The sound caused the figure in the clearing to snap her attention to him.

At that moment, the stone shifted, almost as though it had vanished from its spot on the ground and reappeared a few inches to the left, before a second deafening *CRACK* sounded around them.

Light scattered out around them in beams, shards of rock flying in a wide arc. Meriwen turned on her heel as the small creature with the winding tail let out a terrified shriek.

And then something... *else* was there with them.

A small, cat-sized shape hurtled toward the Witch on all fours, knocking her off her feet and into the trees. With an unpleasant thud, everything went dark, candles across the clearing snuffing out.

Blinking furiously to erase the white spots bouncing in his vision, Zanve dropped down from his tree. Meriwen was lying motionless, her hair somewhat over her face, limbs askew.

The sounds of the forest around him were dreadfully silent in the wake of the explosion of magic. He glanced around for both creatures but couldn't see them in the darkness.

A soft snuffling sound came from the winter-crumpled grass by Meriwen's head. Zanve tensed, curling down lower to the ground, preparing to pounce.

In the dim light of the moon filtering through the trees, Zanve could just see the outline of what looked like a ball of feathers standing up at all angles, reminding him immediately of a baby that had got stuck in something messy and needed a bath. Every ounce of danger drained out of him, despite Zanve still not knowing what this little thing was. The creature looked up at him with shining black eyes, timid and wary as he approached slowly, carefully, so as not to startle it.

That creature did just knock out Meriwen, he mused as he snatched it up in his mouth the moment he was close enough to it. Maybe it was more dangerous than he could tell.

Zanve tried to keep his jaws as gentle as possible around it, but the creature's feathers were slick, and the creature was so surprisingly light that Zanve had a hard time holding onto it as it wriggled in his grip. It weighed next to nothing, as though it was mere skin and hollow bones, like a bird.

What was he going to do now? Should he trap it somehow? He had to get it away from Meriwen, that was for sure; but bringing it all the way to Arrowmount to his superiors was immediately off the table. Thinking about an unknown creature — at least, Zanve didn't know what it was — in the walls of the town he was supposed to protect was a nightmare.

The creature squirmed again, almost slipping out of his mouth.

The Witch probably knew what to do with it, he realized, looking at her once again. For now, he had to find a spot he could keep it, just until he could make sure that Meriwen was okay. He started back toward her cottage at a run, jaws locked around the creature.

Her house wasn't a very good option, since he was planning on bringing Meriwen there. What if the creature hurt her again, more seriously? Not as though he had had an actual chance to check in on her and her injuries, but if it did anything *more...*

Ilmater's mercy, he was messing all of this up. He had to move, fast. She was the priority.

He raced back to Meriwen's cottage and garden, casting a quick look around. The creature in his jaws made a strangled, panicked mewling sound, which caused the other animals — gods, how many were there? An absolutely astonishing number of forms scattered from around the garden and nearby trees as he approached, vanishing further into the darkness and safety of the trees.

The movement pulled his attention to another building on the property, back directly across from Meriwen's cottage, sunk into the trees. He made a snap decision to throw the little thing into it and lock it inside. At least there, it would be contained to one room and would be out of the way.

Zanve shifted back to human form within the space of a heartbeat, tossing the creature up into his arms — the creature was so shocked that it froze, staring up at him with shining black eyes — before he deftly unlatched the door and deposited it inside, before closing the door once more.

A chill ran across his naked skin as he turned on his heel, half positioned to shift again and run back to Meri.

Godsdamn it, he thought to himself, knowing he had to keep his human form if he wanted to do anything helpful for her — but he was 100 percent, entirely, completely naked, standing in the middle of the Witch's garden.

If she woke up as he carried her into her cottage, he was going to probably give her a worse scare than the whole spectacle in the clearing had. She'd think he was trying to prey on her in her vulnerable state, or—

Zanve, breathe.

Right.

Nothing good ever came from panicking.

He caught sight of the well-worn jacket hanging outside the half-open back door to the cottage, waiting on a hook as though it was meant for him.

It was better than nothing.

A tiny brown tabby cat, the lone animal that hadn't run from him when he arrived in the garden, sat atop a raised wooden plant box and narrowed its eyes at him.

Zanve shifted back into his panther form and reached for the jacket with his jaws, before turning back to the cat and chuffing deep in his chest.

The cat, to her credit, simply blinked at him.

He raced back to Meriwen and shifted back to human a few steps away, keeping just a touch of his heightened eyesight so he could find her in the dark, and slid the jacket on. Surprisingly, it was quite long, even for him, and covered most of his most offending bits. Though, if he had a choice, he wouldn't be showing this much thigh to anyone, let alone the unconscious Witch.

A small, angry little creature was sitting across her chest, its tail coiled so tightly around itself that it gave the appearance of an incredibly irritated snake. Zanve recognized it as the shrieking creature that had wrapped itself around a tree trunk, vanishing into the darkness when the stone had exploded.

"Hello," he said quietly, approaching slowly, hands up.

"Mmmmmmmmmmm," the creature said, the sound low and grating. "Get away."

Zanve, already at his limit for weird shit that he'd seen tonight, simply laughed. He'd heard many rumors about the Witch that concerned a familiar — some that claimed she had transformed a man into a lizard to keep him at her beck and call, among others, but whatever this creature was, he'd not expected to find it capable of talking.

Nor did he expect to see it puff itself up in defense, much like a cat would, despite its lack of fur.

"I'm here to help." Zanve took a few steps closer, slowly with his hands up, wondering if this tiny dragon look alike was capable of spitting flame or other substances like its much larger counterpart. "I want to make sure she's okay."

Meriwen was most definitely not okay, seeing as she was currently unconscious on the ground. Zanve bent, now at her side, and moved the hair away from her face. This close up, he could tell that one of her legs was twisted oddly under her skirts, her bare foot sticking out at an odd angle.

Bare feet? In this cold?

The tiny dragon creature made a nervous sound in the back of its throat and lifted its head up to stare at him, extending its neck toward Meriwen's face, watching Zanve's every movement.

"I'm going to help her, I promise." He gently laid a hand on her knee, before speaking directly to her, in case she could hear him somehow. "Meriwen, I'm sorry to do this, but I need to move you inside. I'm just going to make sure you're okay, that nothing is broken."

"Mmmmm." The creature looked at Meri with a distinct flash of concern on its face. The end of its tail flicked, in what Zanve thought was probably a worried way. "Mmmmm."

It eyed him with suspicion, but didn't say anything to stop him as Zanve slowly started to move his hand up Meriwen's leg, inspecting to see if it was bent or snapped in any way. Zanve kept one eye on Meriwen's face, watching to see if she had any reaction. She stayed motionless, serene in her unconsciousness, her face expressionless and still.

"Well. I need to bring her inside, to make sure she's not hurt. Back where there's light." He straightened out her leg as best he could, eyeing the creature. "What do you say?"

"Man carry Meri?"

"Yes," he answered without hesitating. Though Meriwen was quite tall, Zanve was a touch taller and rather strong. He knew he would be able to carry her to safety without issue.

The creature gave the slightest of nods, which was all Zanve needed. Honestly, he was halfway to picking her up anyways, but it was nice to know the little creature was at least somewhat compliant. He scooped her gently up into his arms and stood, the creature clinging onto her chest.

Meriwen was surprisingly warm as he hurried her through the clearing back to her cottage, as though she was running a fever. Her head lolled into the crook of his neck, her breath soft against his bare collarbone, and in that moment, he felt more naked than he was, jacket notwithstanding. The gesture was so intimate it stripped him down to his bones.

Focus, Einar, he chastised himself, shifting her soft body in his arms to have a better hold on her as he stepped sideways into the dimly lit kitchen pockmarked by candles. The dragon creature made a concerned, anxious noise in the back of his throat again as Zanve took a moment to glance around the space. He was startled to see an adult deer standing in the middle of Meriwen's hallway, staring intently at him.

"Follow," said the dragon creature, its voice crooning.

He followed the deer inside to the kitchen, where it stopped and seem to gesture with its long neck toward an open doorway. He took a moment, marveling at the deer being *inside a building*, before he carried Meriwen into the room and set her down on a bed positively overflowing with pillows. He walked out briefly, hunting for another blanket to lay over her, before coming back with one in hand and passing the deer once again.

"Uh," he said, not quite knowing what to say or do to get the deer out of the house. He was fairly sure that Meriwen wouldn't want a random deer inside — though, now that he thought about it, who knew what she would want, perhaps she knew this creature and it was a common occurrence for it to come inside, but still— "T-thank you?"

The deer let out a soft huff of air from its nose and clopped back outside, flicking its tail at Zanve as he stared after it.

What a strange evening, he thought, hesitating on the threshold of Meriwen's room.

A soft chorus of twittering came from nearby, alerting him to a couple of birds who were bundled together amidst a number of jars on the countertop of the kitchen. Soft candlelight emanated from various spots, casting an ethereal warmth around the place, almost as if he had walked into a spell.

Zanve breathed in deep, taking in the space. He caught the gentle scent of salt and innumerable herbs that he couldn't quite differentiate, and sharp clean lemon. He made eye contact with one of the little birds, who looked at him with what he swore was a soft quizzical frown, as though the bird was saying, *who are you*? Despite the light being nearly too dim to see clearly by, he could've sworn the bird was unnaturally pink.

He felt a surreal calm settle over him. What kind of place *was* this?

He ducked into Meriwen's bedroom, blanket in hand, and draped it over her feet.

The room was barely big enough to be called a bedroom. Half of it was filled with a bed squashed between the walls and a windowsill. The other half was open, except for a sturdy shelf at hip height that ran along the entirety of the room. There was no other furniture in sight.

He was about to reach over and start to carefully check Meriwen for injuries when she murmured under her breath, moving ever so slightly.

The dragon creature curled up higher on her chest, its snout almost coming into contact with her nose.

"Meriwen?" Zanve asked softly, not wanting to scare her.

Her eyes flickered open.

5

MALADIES AND CURES

Meriwen

Meri woke with a weight pressing down on her chest. She sucked in as much air as she could before she opened her eyes, only to find herself staring at the shadows of Lock's irritated face, his snout very close to her own nose.

"Lock," she groaned. "What..."

She slowly moved her hands, recognizing the soft surface she was laying on. How on Ravar had she gotten back to her bed?

"Mmmm. Meri." Lock shifted until his nose touched hers, as though he needed to be as close as he could be to make sure she was alright.

She blinked a few times and sighed heavily, trying to pull together two thoughts that weren't just *how did I get here* and *what happened?*

"Give her space."

Meri's heart slammed into her throat. The voice that spoke was much deeper than any of her creatures — though, of course, none of her creatures spoke at all, besides Lock.

She jolted upward, sending Lock tumbling off her chest with a shocked squawk. Deep, bone rattling pain thrummed through her hip and leg, causing her breath to hitch. Every nerve in her body stood on end, holding her still as the full realization of how much pain she was in washed over her.

Root and ruin, not again.

"Woah," the voice said, before the owner of it came into view. The tall town guard with the grey eyes was by her side, hesitantly extending two hands, just close enough that he could steady her if need be. "Easy."

There was a man in her house. This man, with the grey eyes. He was *in her house.*

She blinked at him, frowning.

He was in her house and wearing her old gardening jacket?

She shook her head, trying to consolidate the events still churning in her mind, her head cloudy from pain.

"What?" she said softly, her voice nothing more than a crack of sound.

"How are you feeling?"

She breathed out long and slow, trying not to wince, keeping herself as still as possible. "What's going on?"

"You were thrown," explained the guard, moving a touch closer. "I saw the light from the gates — are you hurt anywhere? Anything broken?"

Meri slowly took stock of her body, trying to push down the nausea in the pit of her stomach. It kept growing in the waves of constant, deep pain pushing through her. She assessed her hands and arms in quick succession, no pain present whatsoever — just a little bit of dirt under fingernails that she continuously forgot to scrub clean. When one had a garden to tend to and lived mostly outside with creatures, dirt under your fingernails was a standard.

She ran her attention down her spine, assuring herself no new pain echoed through the bones along her back. Satisfied, she focused further down.

She slowly, achingly, started to move her toes, then her feet, until she was flexing and gently moving her legs beneath the blanket, ensuring that nothing was broken. This kind of pain was not from a broken bone.

"I don't believe so."

"Okay. Good." The guard looked at her for a moment, then looked down at himself. "Listen, I know this is a lot, but if you give me ten minutes, I can explain everything."

"Ten minutes."

"Yes."

Meri narrowed her eyes at him, confused. "Okay?"

"I'll be right back. Don't — don't move."

The guard was up on his feet and out of her bedroom before she could grasp what she was seeing, but as he left, she was fairly sure she'd just caught sight of a *lot* of thigh.

"I..." she looked at Lock, who had crawled up in the folds of the blanket draped over her and let out a soft groan. She was in so much pain, she needed to assess whatever damage there was.

"Meri," Lock crooned as she gently pushed him out of the way and adjusted herself on her bed, leaning back on her bed of pillows. "Pain."

"Oh, yes. Pain," she said, gritting her teeth and swallowing down the nausea that was climbing higher. A lot of pain. It was deep, familiar, and unsettling pain that ran all along the right side of her lower body, pulsing and throbbing as though the knotted skin there had been recently split open down to bone. Sure, her leg occasionally flared up and made every-day life a chore, but the last time she had felt pain like this? It had been at least a decade. "What happened, Lock?"

"Mmmm. Stone open, bad thing come out." A snort of smoke erupted from his nose angrily. "Bad stone."

"The stone opened," she repeated slowly, putting her memories back in place. She groaned, rubbing the back of her head slowly.

She remembered the pull of the stone in the few hours that she had been home from town, and the unexplainable need to be outside with it when the sun went down. She remembered the protective spells she'd cast, and the slow churning ritual that had uncoiled in her mind as though being fed to her from somewhere else. The way it had been built in some kind of gateway. And how the seemingly innocuous stone lit up brighter than any magic she'd seen before.

When it burst apart, cracking in pieces, it unleashed... *something*. Something that was much larger than the stone that held it.

For some reason, she also remembered a very large whiskered animal, looking at her with brilliantly yellow eyes.

"Lock... was there... a really big cat here tonight?"

Lock snorted again. "No. No big cat."

"Alright." Must have been her imagination, then, having knocked her head, she thought.

Meri tried to breathe through another wave of pain. She must have twisted her leg when she fell, she thought, wincing through the pain of slight movement. It wasn't anything she couldn't handle, though. Meri had been through worse pain before.

This was close, though.

Meri moved back, achingly slow, until she was settled against her pillows. It was only as she was starting to wonder what had happened to the guard when she heard hurried footsteps outside, crunching slightly on the gravel path that lead up to her cottage. A soft fluttering came from a flock of startled birds in her kitchen as the guard came back into her room, panting slightly. His fingers worked at the front of his shirt, which was put on wrong. He was now fully dressed in his guard uniform, looking *slightly* more put together.

"Hi," he said, sounding only slightly winded as he stood at the threshold. "Sorry about that."

"That's... alright?"

"How are you feeling?" The guard came in hesitantly, eyeing her now sitting up amidst her pillows, and the wyrmling curled up in her lap like a protective guard cat.

"I've been better," she answered, rubbing the back of her head again. Doing so granted her a discovery of a lump swelling that twinged with pain when she pressed it. "My head's a little fuzzy. What happened?"

"I came to investigate when I saw a bright blue light," he said, clearing his throat, before he knelt again at her bedside. "It was rather odd, to see something that bright more than once coming from the forest."

A small bolt of panic shot through Meri. "Did anyone else see?"

"Not that I know of," he answered, a bemused expression crossing his face. "My partner on duty was asleep when it happened, so unless someone was atop the wall or out walking that I didn't see, but... why would that be an issue?"

"Apologies, it wouldn't," she said quickly, looking away. "I... I'm a little jumbled."

She breathed out, controlling her expression. *Would* it be an issue? She couldn't quite explain the anxiety in her gut at the thought of the town knowing something went awry with her garden. Not like they would kick her out, but... well, would they? Tell her to leave, if something dangerous was to spawn in her garden?

She wasn't actually sure. If they made her leave, she would have to somehow get word to the fey realm so that they would send another

Keeper here, just to make sure that Arrowmount didn't suffer in any way. And where would she go, then?

The thought of leaving made her deeply sad, so she pushed the thought from her mind and brought her attention back to the guard in front of her. "You came to investigate?"

"Just to make sure that everything was in order," he said quickly, "that the town wasn't in danger. I've never seen anything like that before."

"Nor have I," said Meri softly. He was protecting the town. That made sense. But did that mean he was going to have to report what he saw? Root and ruin, this was a mess.

"Right." The guard's cheeks flushed. "Anyway. I came by just in time to see that thing, whatever it was, come exploding out of that rock and knock you backward. You were out cold, and I didn't want to just leave you there."

"You have impeccable timing, it would seem. Thank you for that." Meri shifted slightly on her bed, trying to suppress a wince. Lock crooned worriedly until she patted him on the head. "It's okay, Lock."

"Lock?" The guard looked between them curiously.

"You didn't introduce yourself, you silly wyrm?" Meri rolled her eyes at Lock and immediately regretted it as her skull thudded in response. Lock peered at her with particular disdain. "Yes, this is Lock. Hemlock in full, if he's being particularly nasty. He is a wyrmling, though where he originated from, I'm not entirely sure."

"You didn't conjure him?"

Meri felt her lips start to crack into a smile but held it back. It was one of the more popular rumors about the Witch of the Woods that ran through Arrowmount. Something about her conjuring a man from her past to shrink him into a lizard. Conjuring was not part of her skill set.

"No. He simply arrived one day, not long after I finished building my house. And he never left." She scratched Lock under his chin briefly. "He's become my companion, unofficially."

"I'm, uh, pleased to meet you officially, Lock," said the guard, rubbing the back of his neck before sticking out his hand in her direction. "I don't believe I introduced myself — to either of you. I'm Zanve Einar, part of the Arrowmount town guard."

Zanve. That was his name. It had taken all these years of seeing him stationed at the entrance to Arrowmount, giving her soft, welcoming smiles, to finally learn his name. It suited him.

She reached out and let him wrap her hand in his. Before she let go, Lock shifted on the blankets and reached up with his tiny clawed hand to place it on top of Zanve's. A thin wisp of smoke curled from Lock's left nostril before he let out a soft, "Mmm. Zanve."

Meri shook her head. "And I'm Meriwen, but Meri is just fine."

"It's a pleasure to properly meet you, Meri, now that you're not unconscious or just passing through the Arrowmount gates." His eyes twinkled softly at her in the low candlelight. Meri couldn't help the small smile that broke across her face, then, as he continued to *twinkle* at her. There was no other word for it, to describe this utterly charming town guard.

Town guard. Oh, root and ruin, he was duty bound to the town! He was probably going to take the creature from her and bring it to Arrowmount, hand it over to authorities before she could properly figure out what it was or what it was doing here.

"What happened to the creature?" she asked worriedly.

"Oh. Ah." He glanced down at his feet as though he expected it to be sitting there and shook his head. "I locked it up."

Meri blinked slowly, her heart dropping into her stomach. "You — you *locked it up*? Where?"

"I didn't want it to run away, or get into more trouble," he said quickly. "It wasn't an overlarge creature. It looked like a baby, but I couldn't be sure. What even is it?"

"I have no idea. I didn't even know that was going to happen at all." She strained her ears, wondering if she'd be able to hear the creature in her house somewhere. Please, please let it still be here in her cottage or garden, and not already in town. "Where?"

"The building at the edge of your property."

Meri's heart squeezed at the thought of a creature locked inside her greenhouse, at what kind of trouble it could get into with all her stores and plants, and the fact it was still here. Hopefully it couldn't climb. Meri shifted slowly on her bed, moving to get up.

"Where are you going?" Suddenly Zanve was right in front of her, reaching out a protective hand. "Are you sure you want to get up this quickly?"

"I'm fine," she said, ignoring his hands and pushing herself to standing. Dizziness rolled through her as her pain in her leg escalated, making it very *very* clear that she was not going to be able to walk unaided, if at all.

Zanve cleared his throat awkwardly, but didn't move away. Instead, he only watched her warily. "You didn't know that rock was going to break apart and hatch a creature."

"No, I only... it is rather odd to explain."

"I have time."

She eyed him carefully. She wasn't entirely sure what this man wanted, sticking around here and asking her questions. Shouldn't he be wanting to get back to the gates, or taking the creature in for inspection or whatever it was they could do?

His expression was open and kind, his eyes locked on hers, mouth tilted down in the softest concern that matched the tiniest crinkle between his eyebrows. He seemed genuine enough.

Meri pushed herself up using her hands and her good leg, but she nearly passed out from the agony that ripped through her. Instinctively, it seemed, Zanve's hands were on her hips, steadying her as she swayed on the spot.

"You really don't look well. Are you in pain?"

"Not much worse than normal," she said, blinking through a wave of dizziness, as she waved him off, "aside from a small headache."

She didn't want to get into it. It was odd, having someone be this visibly concerned about her. Meri was practically a stranger to him — he shouldn't care any more about her than a passing bird did.

Well, no, that's cruel on the birds. She happened to like the little family of birds that had taken roost around her cottage. It wasn't their fault that they didn't seem to care much about anything other than themselves and their own little world.

Zanve frowned at her. "Any pain isn't normal. You look like you're going to be ill."

Meri bit her tongue. She lived every day in pain, as did countless others in the realm. This *was* her normal.

"Do you mind grabbing the staff in the kitchen, leaning up with my broom?" Meri put a hand out and steadied herself on the wall, gently extricating from his hands. "I would like to go and see the creature in my greenhouse."

Zanve frowned and mouthed *greenhouse?* but he went all the same, stepping quickly out into her kitchen. Meri began maneuvering herself round her small room, using the sturdy shelving that ran along the wall, right at her hip's height. She listened to the guard's soft footsteps as she moved toward her kitchen, before hesitating just by the door. She could picture him looking around the space, searching for the broom and staff tucked out of the way.

He returned a moment later, eyeing the beautifully wrought wood with interest, before passing it to her. "That's a beautiful staff."

"Thank you. I've had it for a long time." She steadied herself with it, the soft curving groove of the grip familiar in her hand.

She teetered her way out of her room with difficulty, trying to keep herself upright as much as she could so Zanve couldn't see her wince with every step she took.

By the time she made it to her closest kitchen counter, though, a cold sweat had broken out across her entire body.

"Meriwen?"

"Just a moment," she said, leaning against her counter and breathing heavily. Lock jumped up next to her.

"Mmmmmmm," he said anxiously. "Meri."

"I know, Lock," she breathed. She knew she shouldn't be on her feet.

"See, this is what I mean by not normal," said Zanve, moving in a little closer, as though readying himself to catch her.

"Pass me that clay jar just there, if you don't mind," she said, pointing to her collection of teas just out of reach, gritting her teeth at having to ask him for help yet again. She frowned at the things she'd left in her kitchen earlier, but didn't move to clear anything up. She didn't have the energy. Her spell book was open with a dusting of rosemary laying across the pages for her usual ritual tea that she drank, a fresh bundle sat ready next to it for tomorrow, and a mug and a rather haphazard amount of crumbs were laid out from the dinner she had eaten carelessly over the counter.

Zanve followed the direction of her finger, eyeing her stash of innumerable jars and small boxes of ingredients, before handing her a small clay jar.

"What's this for?"

Meri didn't answer. She slid the cloth atop the jar off and reached in for a pinch of the leaves inside. Usually, she would brew this into a tea to wake herself in the morning, but desperate times called for desperate measures. The tea didn't help at all with her leg pain, and would probably make it a little worse with her soon-to-be-heightened awareness, but she needed a little help getting rid of the fog in her head, and a little oomph to help her head out into her garden.

"Meri?"

She stuck some of the leaves beneath her tongue and held them there, their bitter, slightly tangy taste zinging through her mouth. "Right. Greenhouse."

"Are you—"

"I'm *fine*." She sucked in a breath, having snapped a little bit harder at him than she anticipated. "I have dealt with this for most of my life. Thank you, but I can handle myself."

Instead of being cowed, Zanve simply tilted his head and frowned. "Most of your life?"

"Yes," she sighed heavily before deciding to give him the quick version. "I was injured as a child and it never healed right. Some days are better than others, but some days I need my staff to get around. Now if you don't mind. My greenhouse?"

"Right. Okay."

To his credit, Zanve took her attitude in stride, and lead the way out into her garden. In the past, if Meri had to tell others of her injury, they would croon and peck at her like overly worried chickens until they themselves were satisfied. It did very little for her to accept their pity, except for making her annoyed that she had to go through this over and over with people.

The moment Meri's feet touched the hard, packed earth outside, she breathed in, bringing a swell of magic up into her limbs from the ground. She thanked the gods that she'd not put on any boots earlier that evening, leaving her feet free to connect directly with the earth. The pain in her head muted as the small bit of magic went to work, pairing with the leaves beneath her tongue, to quell the dull ache behind her eyes.

With every slow tap of her staff, she felt the earth beneath her feet singing through her bones, trying its best as it always did to right the pain in her leg. But Meri knew better. Some pain, some maladies, were never going to be cured by magic, and that was just the way life was. Just having the magic there, singing in her bones, was enough to keep her stumbling forward.

The closer she got to the greenhouse, the stronger a pull right below her ribs became. She'd completely forgotten about the connection to the stone in the ocean of pain she was wading through.

A soft whine became more audible the closer they got to the door.

"It's still in there," said Zanve with a soft sigh.

Then he twisted the handle of her greenhouse and pushed it open.

6

SHATTERED GLASS

Zanve

It was an absolute massacre. Zanve's heart sank as he took in the interior of Meri's greenhouse. It was as though an errant wind elemental had thrown a full-on tantrum, tearing the plants to shreds and scattering them across the floor so violently they were practically mulch. The closer he looked the worse the damage got: plant pots shattered, dirt shunted up the base of the walls and glass window panes, and the tables and shelving snapped like twigs. He hadn't had a proper look inside the greenhouse when he tossed the creature in, but he was fairly sure that it hadn't looked like this.

Meri reached into the space with a graceful hand as though plucking a fruit from a tree. Light burst into being from a few arcane lanterns strung along the center ceiling beam, illuminating the greenhouse in a soft golden glow that felt totally at odds with the carnage.

"Cover your nose and mouth," said Meri over her shoulder as she stepped past him, her bare feet crunching on debris. "I don't know what

54

kind of combinations could have been... oh, all my *work*."

Meri reached out of sight and withdrew a large cloth that she wrapped shakily around her face, covering her nose and mouth. Zanve raised the neckline of his uniform to cover his own, eyes watering slightly.

Herbs and glass mixed together, wilted and broken, and a soft dust tinged the air. Dirt and water mingled in the middle of the space, water still dripping from an overturned bucket. Zanve narrowed his eyes — it looked as though the corner had been gnawed through. Another substance that Zanve couldn't name was splashed up the wall, glittering softly as it caught the dust hanging in the air, coating the glass walls and roof around them.

Zanve watched as Meri's hand grasped for the wall, the other gripping her staff so tight her knuckles were white. The ache in her eyes as she took in the space hurt him more than he cared to admit. She was still pale; *too* pale, for his liking. She really shouldn't be on her feet after what had happened.

"Skies above," he swore lightly, his boots crunching as he stepped toward her. "Meriwen, I am so deeply sorry. All of this — this *wreckage*. That can't... that can't possibly be from one little creature, could it?" He hesitated, casting his eyes around the space again. "Where is it?"

"It's hiding there," said Meri, her voice brittle, as she pointed to a back corner beneath an overturned piece of table. The creature had balled itself up so tiny it looked like a shadowy smudge against the glass it was pressed against.

"Hello." Meri cleared her throat and readjusted her grip on her staff, cautiously stepping forward. "You've gotten yourself into a mighty mess, haven't you?"

Zanve followed after her, wanting to be ready in case the creature attacked her again. There was no world in which a creature this tiny could have done *this* much damage. Even dogs who are anxious trapped in a room could eat through a wall — but *this* level of destruction? He was having a hard time believing it.

"It's alright," Meri cooed to the creature, starting to bend at the waist. Pain flashed across her expression before she straightened again, face tinged slightly green. She pulled her scarf down so the creature could see her entire face, and placed a hand on her stomach. "You know you're safe with me."

At first, the creature only raised its head to look at her, then at Zanve behind her, with caution; then, as though deciding it was okay, it scrambled out of its hiding spot with a speed that sent Zanve's heart into his throat. He took a half-step forward, ready to protect Meri from whatever this creature was about to do—

But the creature stopped at Meri's feet, gazing up at her with what Zanve could only call reverence.

In the soft light of the arcane lanterns, Zanve got his first proper look at the thing. It didn't quite fit into any profile of any animal that he had ever seen before — certainly, it was the *size* of a cat, but it wasn't quite the right shape. It was as though someone had taken the idea of a dog and a cat, dreamed them together with a falcon, and then decided to twist the resulting shape until it also had bear-like qualities about the face. The creature was covered with fine, dark glittering feathers that shifted color in the light.

This wasn't a creature of their world, he was certain. But where could it have come from?

"What is that?" he hissed under his breath. Meri jumped slightly, as though she'd forgotten he was there. She reached a hand down to the creature, only for it to jump up into her hands, making hardly a sound.

Zanve watched Meri's shoulders swell with a sigh. Standing amidst the scattered remains of her greenhouse, she turned a look on Zanve that almost pinned him to the wall behind him. Her eyes shone bright, as though she had a fever.

"Why are you still here, exactly?" she asked, her voice thin and quiet. "I am fine, as you can see."

She was lying. He could see very clearly that she was *not* okay.

He scoffed. "You were knocked out, woke up, ate some raw herbs, and look as though you're about to keel over because of some mysterious pain or fever."

"I am fine," Meri snapped, pulling herself up to her full height. He hadn't quite realized how imposing of a figure she posed, with her antlers cresting nearly to the ceiling, until that moment. The creature in her arms cowered further into her, its two eyes staring at Zanve. "I am not a damsel in distress you need to rescue, town guard."

He raised his eyebrows at her and opened his mouth to respond. If he hadn't been here—

"I am sure you meant well," she said, interrupting him. "But I must ask you to leave. I have too much to do here, and you will only get in my way."

"I'm not leaving," he said. "Not before—"

"This is *my property*, and you are not—" Meri stopped, closing her eyes in a grimace as she took a step toward him. The creature in her arms let out a soft chirrup, gazing up at her.

"Let me at least see you back to your cottage, so I can call you a healer. The sheer destruction that this thing caused — I'm sure you need someone to take a look at you just to make sure—"

"I am *fine*," she repeated, her eyes snapping open with such ferocity that Zanve hesitated.

He cleared his throat. Despite how much he wanted to throw her over his shoulder and march her back into her cottage to make sure she was safe in bed; he knew that it was probably not a good idea. For one, he might hurt her further, and he hated lording his strength over others. Plus it was rather impolite, he figured, to pick someone up without their consent.

Slowly, he swallowed his pride and conceded. "Right. Well, I am deeply sorry again for my intrusion. If you need anything..."

Meri simply glared at him.

He nodded to her and stepped out of the greenhouse, feeling the weight of her eyes on his neck.

7

CAVORTING WITH THE WITCH

Zanve

Zanve's mind was a whirlwind of thoughts as he rushed back to the gates of Arrowmount. Was Meri going to be okay? She shouldn't be out there alone after that kind of an accident. What if she got sick, or fell unconscious, or—?

"Einar."

Zanve's stomach dropped at the sound of his captain's stern voice, wrenching him out of his spiraling thoughts. He groaned inwardly, looking down at himself, hoping he wasn't overly disheveled. He also noticed immediately how cold it was, now that he was beyond the magic of Meri's garden.

"See, sir? I told you he was off cavorting with the Witch," said a second voice that Zanve would have rather pried both his eyes out than to hear right then. *Of course* Damian would be here, a witness to his missing-in-action on the job. Quinlan, another member of the force and

59

one of Zanve's better friends, winked at him, looking all too amused at the circumstances. Zanve groaned inwardly, knowing that Quinlan was going to be begging for a story later.

Zanve looked up to find Captain Ludru standing where he himself usually stood guard, arms crossed over his impressive chest, expression dark and stormy.

"Is what he says true, Einar?" Captain Ludru eyed him carefully.

"Is what true, sir?" he answered, trying to keep his voice calm and collected.

"That you were out fu—*finding* your way through the Witch's house, if you will," said Damian, side-eyeing the captain. "We all know you have a soft spot for her, we were just waiting to see—"

"Enough, Briggs," snapped Ludru. Zanve's feeling of pleasure seeing Damian's cheeks turn pink with embarrassment lasted only seconds as the Captain turned his ire on him. "Einar. Why were you not at your post when I came to ensure that Cadoc was receiving the proper introduction to our service? I expected to find my best soldier here, standing guard, as he should have been, modelling the way that our town deserves to be treated. Instead, I find Cadoc asleep on the job and my best guard missing."

"Right." Zanve cleared his throat and caught Cadoc's eye, who looked sincerely scared not only for his job, but his life, too.

"Explain." Captain Ludru crossed his arms and raised a stern eyebrow at him.

"I was out doing rounds, sir, and became caught up in a trouble that needed my aid," he said, trying to think on his feet.

"Doing... rounds."

"Yes, I was stretching my legs, checking parts of the wall as I usually do, to ensure all was well on the sides that are not overly clear to see from this vantage point." Zanve motioned over to the left and the right, where the tree line became obscured by the wall surrounding Arrowmount. "I happened to catch sight of a disturbance in the trees, and was caught up with helping until now. I deeply apologize for my unprofessionalism, sir."

He was apologizing deeply for a lot of things today, it seemed.

Captain Ludru eyed him with a deepening frown. "And you thought to just leave young Cadoc here, is that it? Unaccompanied? *Sleeping*?"

"He was not sleeping when I left," Zanve said, shooting Cadoc a look, hoping he would catch on. "We agreed that he would stand watch, as I believed him capable of on such a quiet night, while I did the round."

"Is that right," said Ludru, sounding very much like he wasn't asking a question. "Cadoc, why did you not say so?"

Cadoc let out a soft sound that almost sounded like a whimper.

Zanve tried to force a look of calm on his face, trying not to laugh at the lad's expense. "I believe, sir, he is rather intimidated by you. As we all were, once. It is my fault I was not here to entertain Cadoc to keep him awake, and I apologize."

Captain Ludru sighed heavily and shook his head as Damian snorted. "It will not do to let your intimidation get in the way of your job, Cadoc. You are an adult, so stand up and act like one. Tonight will not cost you your job. However, I do expect you to try a little harder in the future." Ludru snuck a wink at Zanve, acting the ever stern Captain. Zanve knew that Ludru had found many of them asleep on the job more than once in the past.

Cadoc nodded and saluted Captain Ludru, stammering his thanks. The boy looked at Zanve rather sheepishly before passing him his coat. Zanve slid it over his shoulders gratefully.

Captain Ludru turned on his heel, causing the rest of the guards gathered to stand a little straighter. "Well, what are you all standing around for? Shift is to change, Einar and Cadoc are done for the day. Einar, if you would come with me."

Ah, skies. The Captain wasn't quite done with him.

Zanve briefly laid a hand on Cadoc's shoulder in farewell before falling into step with the Captain. The further they walked away from Cadoc, who was being harassed amiably by Quinlan, the more Zanve started to feel the exhaustion of being up two nights in a row itch behind his eyes. Dawn was cresting around them, the sounds of early morning birds in the surrounding trees mingling with the sharp clacking of their boots.

"You know, Einar, I should be harder on you," said Captain Ludru, his voice now much softer, more friendly. "Sneaking off to see a woman on the job."

Zanve immediately shook his head. "I swear, sir, that is not what happened. There really was a disturbance. You know I wouldn't abandon my post for nothing."

"That's an incredibly vague description." They came to a stop as the Captain looked around, ensuring they were alone. "I trust you, boy. I always have. You're a good lad. A hard worker."

"I promise you I am telling the truth. I... I feel wrong telling you any more than that, since it not my business to tell." Something, he didn't quite know what, was keeping him from divulging what the night had wrought. Perhaps he was wary about sharing Meri's private workings — or perhaps it was something in his soul that knew, somehow, to keep the little creature quiet. "Nothing to worry the town, of course. Everything was dealt with. But I promise you, I did not sneak off to see a woman."

Captain Ludru inspected Zanve, eyeing him up and down. "And your disheveled state?"

Zanve knew the Captain's keen eye wouldn't miss how his normally pristine uniform was rumpled, shirt unbuttoned at the bottom, the back sticking out. He swore under his breath. "I had to shift, sir."

Very few people knew of Zanve's abilities, and it had been a choice long ago to let his employer in on that secret. It would have been rather difficult to explain away multiple ruined uniforms — shredded, torn, in pieces — if he hadn't. Plus, he trusted Captain Ludru more than he did many people he knew. The captain was a good man through and through.

"Ah, I see."

"I didn't want to ruin another uniform."

"Sure, sure." Captain Ludru chuckled. "Whatever it was, I'm sure whoever you helped were thankful you did."

Meri's angry glare came to mind. He suppressed a wince. He wasn't entirely sure about that. "Thank you, sir."

"I hope you know that you will be doing double shifts for the next few weeks to make up for this."

Zanve groaned inwardly. "Of course, sir."

Captain Ludru clapped him on the shoulder. "And, if you must go see a woman at night, do it on your own time, not when you are being paid, eh?"

"Yes, sir. I'll keep that in mind."

8

THE FEY REALM GREENHOUSE

Meriwen

Meri coughed, tasting a layer of plant dust in the back of her throat. She ran a hand along the edge of the doorframe, finding the small groove she'd had installed, and pressed. Each of the windows, once by one, began to fall open, gently thunking into place, letting the cool nearly-spring breeze filter out the tainted air.

The powder that still hung in the air shimmered, reminding her of the fairytales told to children about minuscule pixies that would leave behind magical dust as they flew. Most pixies that she knew of were much larger than that, ranging from a hands-height to the height of one's forearm, and definitely didn't leave behind a glowing magical dust.

Meri sucked in an unsteady breath as she leaned heavily on her staff, looking at the wreckage of her greenhouse. She placed the bird-boned creature on the floor where there was the least amount of debris. Tears burned at the back of her eyes, but she refused to let them fall.

"Meriwen, remember; no matter what, if you are sick, if you the rain is pouring down, if the world is covered in white from a blizzard, it does not matter — you must *do the rituals,"* her grandmother's voice pierced her mind, bringing with it the image of her grandmother's face leaning in, eyes imploring. *"It is imperative that they are completed on time, each time. If you don't, you do not know what the power will do."*

She'd learned that lesson first: never, ever miss a ritual. They were to happen with every change of season, when the magic pulsing through the ley lines was at its peak, and the fabric between the worlds and realms was thinnest. Once you started the rituals, you never missed one. If you did, the power that usually went balanced could spin out of control, endangering the town and people nearby.

"If you miss a ritual, you fail as a Keeper."

Now, looking at her ruined preparations scattered into unusable detritus across her greenhouse, Meri had very little time to try and rectify the fact all of her preparations were destroyed.

Her eyes traced the space, trying to place where everything she needed was, but everything was in such a chaos she couldn't make heads or tails of it.

"Lock?" she called, tilting her head to look out at her garden. "I need your help."

Lock scurried over from the old garden chair, hopping from garden bed to garden bed.

The second he crossed the threshold of the greenhouse, though, he came up short; his entire body curled up in an arc, and a low gurgling growl echoed from his chest.

"Lock, leave it be," she said, utterly exhausted. "Come help me."

Lock narrowed his eyes at the creature before letting out a low, uneasy *mmm* as he inched by it. The feathery creature simply looked at him, then up at Meri, as though entirely confused at whether or not it should be scared.

"Can you—" Meri motioned at the ground where the most of her ritual stores were scattered, "I need to know if anything is salvageable."

Lock cast a glance sideways at her before he started to scoop the larger bits together, handing them up to her so she didn't have to crouch down all the way.

Soon Meri was holding little more than a loose bit of twine, a barely recognizable lump of herbs, and finely ground herb dust that she'd spent so long churning with her mortar and pestle, infusing with magic as she went. Now it was mixed with dirt and other herbs, ruining her intentions and rendering it inert.

Everything in her hands was limp and empty, destroyed. Not only were her ritual preparations gone, but the stores she had meticulously spent years growing were gone.

She had nothing left to redo the prep for her ritual with.

Herbs and powders that lasted for near decades once dried properly were scattered and crushed, unusable; fresh ones that were ready to be prepared into various tinctures and salves were damaged and bruised beyond their lifespan. Everything she'd stored in her greenhouse, which was most of her ingredients for all her spell work, was destroyed. Plants, too, that were on lower shelves and tables had been tossed from their resting spots only to shatter on the ground, stems and leaves pulverized by whatever the creature had done.

Lock poked around, using his tail to somewhat scrape together the mass of debris. "Mmmm. Meri."

She breathed in deep and long, one tear escaping and rolling down her cheek, leaving a hot streak of shame behind.

Her wyrmling curled his tail around her ankle gently.

Before she completely fell apart, she turned to the back of her greenhouse. She hadn't wanted to look when the town guard was here, because back there folded between window panes, was a small portal she'd had installed that directed to a separate greenhouse, one full of fey realm plants. If those remained, she would be able to substitute some of them for the plants and herbs she used from this side, the mortal realm side, of the greenhouse for the ritual. It wouldn't be perfect, but it would be something.

They should be fine, she thought — they were in a different part of the greenhouse, and shouldn't have been affected by whatever the feathered creature had done, surely.

Unease spread in Meri's gut.

Moving achingly slow, Meri stepped across the debris, bringing Lock with her; she pointed to a few of the plants whose roots she could see, having him lift them carefully up to her. She had nowhere to put them except to cradle them in her hands, like broken child's dolls. Hopefully they would be able to regrow, but only time would tell.

She continued forward, the pain in her leg so intense it nearly sent her to her knees, but she kept going. She had to check.

A thin sheet of magic warped around her as she passed between two window panes and stepped through to her little pocket of the fey realm.

Deep rooted memories swelled in the slightly unsettling smells; the surroundings changing from rich earth and growing things to mists tainted with magic that bubbled like sour apple wine. The air smelled faintly of citrus and burnt cinnamon, and the temperature rose to one not unlike a warm summer day spent with your waist submerged in a lagoon. Meri blinked the thoughts of the fey realm away before they could consume her, as they usually threatened to do when she stepped into this part of her greenhouse.

"Root and ruin," she swore, slipping momentarily into an old language she'd long thought her tongue had forgotten.

Pieces of pottery and soil and strange vine-like plants crushed under her feet as she stepped carefully into the room, her breath catching as she swayed on the spot.

"No, no no…"

She leaned against the wall and began to sink, all of it too much. Somehow, this little creature had got in here, too, completely decimating her stores and any hope of completing the ritual tonight. Meri rocked back on her heels and crumpled to the floor, not caring that she was seated in soil and sediment, and dropped her head into her hands. Lock slid from her shoulders and curled into a ball around her feet, looking up at her with concern.

Tonight.

The ritual was tonight. There was nothing she could do. Caelynn wouldn't have the herbs, because she didn't stock any fey realm plants herself — regardless, there was no way Meri could walk all that way into town to check. Not with her leg as it was.

Meri began to pick through the soil and pulled at the plants buried in the wreckage as her eyes swam with tears. The leaves, vines, spikes and weird glutinous bits of plants that she needed, the live elements that held the magic of the plants, fell limp her hands as she sifted through the carnage.

She placed the broken plants lined up one by one as though they were about to go to sleep.

For the first time since she had arrived in Arrowmount, she was going to *fail*. Meri was going to miss the ritual, failing her duties as Keeper. Failing her grandmother's lessons and rules.

She was going to fail the town, rendering it helpless to whatever the magic was going to do when it went unbalanced. Without the ritual, Meri didn't know what was going to happen to Arrowmount. She'd been balancing the ley lines for decades, ensuring everything remained in order.

A fresh wave of anxiety rushed through her as tears began to fall. What was she going to do?

A soft sniffing echoed through the mortal realm greenhouse behind her, announcing the feathered creature, searching for her. Meri tilted her head, watching the portal in the corner with one bleary, tear streaked eye, wondering if the little creature was going to find its way back in here again.

The barrier rippled as it poked its feathered head through. Its eyes brightened when it saw her, but it hesitated. It watched her as though not entirely sure what to do or how to react at seeing her sitting there, crying. Instead of chastising it, though, Meri simply reached out to the creature, offering her hand.

He was just a baby, after all, she thought, the pronoun coming to her unbidden. A soft rightness flooded through the base of her ribs as the creature saw her. Meri wondered at the feeling for a moment, the emotions she could feel outside of her own mind.

Something had happened last night, as that otherworldly voice took over Meri's body — something had created a connection, tying her to this creature, and this creature to her.

She could feel it, now, thrumming with warmth as the creature stepped closer to her.

He leaned into her fingers and cooed, the sound oddly bird-like. He crawled over to her, sidestepping Lock without a second glance, and settled in her lap. As she carefully threaded her fingers along his feathers, petting him, Meri let the tears fall, feeling more useless than she ever had.

9

THISTLE AND TEA

Meriwen

When she eventually made her way back out of the greenhouse, Meri watched the little creature poke around her garden with interest. He lifted his nose into the air and tried in vain to see atop some of her garden beds. He was particularly intrigued by the bed of lavender that Meri had rested his stone in.

Meri leaned up against one of the raised beds, near her destroyed greenhouse, unable to move much more than she already had. She was going to have to somehow make it back to her house, to the soft surfaces and partial remedies she had stashed inside; but for now, she was ignored the boiling panic in her gut at the state of her greenhouse, the heart crushing grief trying to pull her to the ground, and her pained leg.

"Careful," she said, reaching out a hand but being entirely unable to go toward the creature as he tried to jump on two hind legs and ended up sprawling backwards. "You're not that coordinated yet, silly thing."

He made a soft sound of annoyance in the back of his throat and turned his attention toward the nearest patch of grass, crouching low as

70

though he was about to hunt something. Meri watched, half a smile on her face, as she saw what had entranced the creature — a long blade of grass was swaying heavily back and forth, a brilliant blue beetle hanging onto the end of it. The creature wiggled his little behind in the air and pounced, the beetle fleeing in a deeply panicked buzz. Instead of chasing it, the creature sat next to the bit of grass and pawed at it.

The more she watched the creature, the more fascinated she was by him. He could walk into her fey realm greenhouse with ease, and he arrived in a burst of ritualistic magic through a stone that had acted as a doorway. There was no denying he was most likely fey — unless there was some other kind of magic or realm that birthed creatures with the power to pass through magical barriers of the fey variety — but what kind of fey, she had no idea. Meri had very little knowledge of fey realm creatures, only that there were countless kinds, just as in the material realm across Ravar.

This one, this feathered creature, had come already attached to her. The bond that sang beneath her ribs thrummed. Meri pressed a hand into her stomach, and the creature peered at her, his little eyes bright and attentive.

Meri let out a steadying breath and pushed herself to her full height, trying to ignore the pain ricocheting through her leg and hip. Nothing would do for just sitting around worrying and complaining, she thought.

Instead of running into her, the creature approached carefully, waiting just a little way away for permission to come closer.

She bent slightly and held out her arms once again. He jumped into them without hesitation, immediately nuzzling into her neck.

"Root and ruin," she sighed, holding him in close. He smelled like fresh growing things and a mixture of herbs that slightly burned the back of Meri's eyes.

"Mmmmmm," came Lock's annoyed mumble from behind her. Meri peered over her shoulder and raised her eyebrows at him.

"I know what you're going to say," she said to the wyrmling as he crawled up the nearest garden bed and carefully stepped around the rosemary. "You don't like him."

"No," said Lock, coming in closer to peer at the little ball of feathers in her arms.

"You'll get used to him," said Meri. Gently, she placed the creature on the ground once again, letting it trot off. "Besides. He's not our biggest problem right now."

Lock huffed nervously, gazing at Meri's greenhouse.

"I don't blame him," she said, grabbing hold of her staff once again before holding out an arm to the wyrmling. She couldn't really even say the guard — Zanve — that had come by, either. He had no idea what he had done, locking the creature up to keep him safe and tucked away.

"He's a baby. You can't blame a baby for not wanting to be trapped."

Lock frowned, as much as his little scaled face could frown. But, instead of saying anything, he carefully climbed Meri's arm and shoulder, settling into his favorite spot on her back.

"Careful," he said into her ear as she started back to the house, leaning heavily on her staff. "Careful."

"I *know*, Lock."

The wyrmling considered for a moment before he did something he had never done before: instead of curling around her shoulders tighter for a better grip, he slid off her back and walked next to her instead, easing her of his weight.

"Thank you," she breathed, trying to pull whatever little magic she could from the earth around her to help take the last few steps. Fresh tears burned at the back of her eyes and escaped down her cheeks.

Daylight finally broke over the trees as she rested her staff at the door, shuffling inside. The air changed, the spring equinox beginning.

Meri hesitated at her threshold, drawing in a breath, filling herself to the brim with the sparkling, special sense of magic that came only with the change of seasons. How much more was it going to grow, without her to balance it? What would it do to the town?

She turned from her garden and stepped inside, letting all of the ley line charged magic fall from her, unspent.

With a soft grunt of effort, she leaned heavily on the shelving that she'd had installed all around her house, starting at the door. It sat at perfect hip height and helped her haul herself around, keeping her weight off her leg. In the past few years, she'd started to fill the shelf with bits and bobs, having not needed to use it as much. She navigated around before using her counter to move fully into the kitchen.

Many of the birds housed among her jars chirped happily at her appearance, hoping, she figured, for dropped crumbs and seeds from a morning toast or muffin.

"Not today," she said, her voice like a croak. They all kept hopping around her as she hefted herself around the space using her hands and one pain-free leg, making herself tea.

She let herself cry silently, over the pain, the state of her greenhouse, and the knowledge that she had failed for the first time since she started doing the solstice rituals in Arrowmount, as the water boiled softly.

"You can always cry over things," said her mother's voice in her head, *"but don't let that take over your life. Heal, take that time you need, but tomorrow? Tomorrow's a new day, with a new sun, and new energy in the world outside. Tomorrow, you can put on a new face, my love, and try again."*

But today, Meri thought as she opened up a cupboard just to her right, pulling down a nearly forgotten mug at the far back of her eclectic stash of drink ware. Today is when she should have been perfect, should have done her ritual just as she always did. So today, she was an utter failure.

From the back of her tea cupboard, Meri pulled out a small clay jar she hadn't cracked open in months. The minuscule bubbles and pits in the soft, dull green glaze were familiar against her fingertips. Even before she removed the lid, she could smell the mixture of meadowsweet and valerian root that had dominated much of her childhood.

"It'll help!" her mother would say every time she brewed her a mug of the tea, no matter how many times Meri would answer that no, in fact, it did not help the pain. "It's shown to help ease pain. Trust me, my love."

At this point, Meri only continued to make the tea for herself for the nostalgia of it. It had a relaxing agent in it, and was rumored to help relieve inflammation and pain, but it rarely worked on anything more severe than a light headache. Nothing, she'd found, ever worked on her pain.

But the tea reminded Meri fiercely of her mother. In that alone, it helped, as it eased her heart a little, and right then, she needed that comfort desperately.

Her hands moved without much conscious thought, having done this so many times she had, in fact, done the steps in her sleep once. As the water boiled on her small stove, she starting to shake. *Focus on the tea, Meri. Just get it done.*

The bright blue kettle sang as steam billowed out. A tablespoon of the dried herbs into a mortar, sprinkle in a dash of fresh ginger if she had it; then five churns of her pestle, no more, no less.

White hot flares started to spread out from the knot of old scar tissue, echoing through her hip and lower back.

The tea, Meri.

All turns of the pestle clockwise, and while she did so, a soft pull on the magic in her to emphasize the ingredients' properties.

The ground tea then went into one of her well used thin linen tea bags, and pour the boiling water over in counter clockwise turns until the mug is full. It usually took a few minutes for the tea to fully steep, but that was Meri's favorite part — waiting for the scent of the tea to wash over her, sharp and comforting all at once.

She closed her eyes, agony causing her to bend her head back, holding her breath, trying to ride the waves of pain. Just a few more minutes.

"Meri?"

The little wyrmling's nails pressed delicately into the top of her foot, alerting her to his presence.

Wiping her cheeks free of the tears that had escaped, Meri shot a glance out of her windows. The feathered creature stared at her house forlornly from the garden as it sat amidst a patch of thistle and wild grass.

With shaking hands, she used a spoon to press the tea bag into the side of her mug, leaching out as much of the concoction as she could, before she removed it and plopped it on her counter without care.

"Lock—"

The wyrmling stood up on his hind legs next to her, extending his thin, clawed hands, knowing immediately what she wanted. She carefully moved the steaming mug of tea from the counter into his waiting grasp. He waddled off with practiced ease toward her bedroom, holding the tea carefully aloft for her, the scalding hot mug not bothering him in the slightest.

Meri took a second, gathering herself as much as she could before she made her way unsteadily across her kitchen.

She cast one last look out her front door, only to see the little feathered creature looking in at her. He tilted his head, feathers shining. Some of them were sticking up at the back, like a cowlick of hair.

"Well, come on in if you like," she called, immediately feeling a soft tug in her chest as the creature burst into movement. He gamboled over the threshold and into her kitchen, looking around curiously.

Eyeing the creature as he rose up on his hind legs to peer at the raucous chirping of the family of birds living on her counter, Meri sighed.

"If you're going to make a home here, you're going to need a name, aren't you?"

The creature turned to look at her expectantly, Meri's ribs warming from their bond. The image of him sitting amidst the thistle flashed into her mind once again.

"How about Thistle?"

The creature let out a noise halfway between a bird chirp and the sound that Lock made when he accidentally caught his tail on something, before he hopped around her in happy little jerks of his back legs.

"Okay," she said through the tears rolling down her cheeks. "Thistle it is."

10

A PACKAGE DEAL

Zanve

Once Zanve had successfully rid himself of his uniform at the barracks and returned to his much more comfortable civilian clothes, he began to weave his way through Arrowmount in the gradually brightening morning light. He shivered beneath his coat, tugging it tighter around his neck to block the chilled wind from biting at his skin.

This past winter, Arrowmount had suffered under a brutally cold and snowy few months, the sea kicking up nasty storms that pummeled the coastline. Soon, if he believed the way the snow had begun to melt properly now, spring was on its way. Zanve couldn't wait for the sunshine-filled weather, the beginning of life all around.

Zanve was simultaneously exhausted and fully awake from the night he just had. He kept battling a sense of guilt and regret, telling himself over and over that it was good he had gone to check what that bright light was; if he hadn't, who knew how long Meri would have lain there unconscious. But, if he hadn't gone, then he would never had locked the little creature in her greenhouse, destroying everything inside.

Why Meri had kicked him out so quickly, without letting him *help* her was beyond him. It was his fault her greenhouse was in the state it was. He should have at least swept up the dirt for her. And helped her back to her cottage, despite her protests. And—

Well. I am glad I was there, either way.

In his distraction, he found himself walking up Wyn's street, headed toward her welcoming front door. Her house — *their* house, he corrected himself, shaking himself mentally for still referring to the place as only hers; Jay and Kaius lived there too — faced a small courtyard, the buildings multi-storied and leaning inward as though they were discussing the latest gossip.

Wyn's front door was painted a bright sky-blue and detailed with tiny vines and flowers, all hand painted by Wyn herself. Last summer, after Arrowmount had been bombarded by a terrible sea storm that had left many buildings in need of repairs, Wyn's old front door and frame had been entirely replaced by Kaius, who'd just moved in with her.

He'd installed a beautiful grouping of glass panels along the top half; they were dappled and tinted a light yellow so as to bar vision into their house. The window often caught the light in a thoroughly magical way in the later part of the day.

Kaius had spent an entire day on it, taking his time to ensure the panels were just right; and it had paid off. It was his most beautiful work, in Zanve's opinion, which was saying something; Kaius' family ran the glass forge down by the water. Kaius had a knack for perfection and beautifully wrought designs, though, which Zanve recognized in some of the glasswork around town.

During that project and subsequent painting of the door, Kaius and Wyn met Jay, who was doing a bit of volunteer gardening work around

Arrowmount to help clean up the mess from the storm. And of course, like every good story goes, they all fell in love. It hadn't taken Jay very long to move in with them, as well, filling what had once been just Wyn's home perfectly.

Jay usually kept the front stoop of their home filled with flowers and beautiful plants. Now, though, Zanve approached the door to a rather drab and empty bit of space, most of the perennial plants laying limply on their sides, waiting for winter to officially come to a close.

Zanve knocked sharply, wondering if Wyn was awake yet. He squinted at the sky, trying to think back to what he knew about her schedule this week, as the door opened.

"Good, you're right on time."

"On time for—?" he blinked at Wyn's retreating back as she spun on her heel, kicking up a whirl of skirts around her. She rubbed her hands down the front of apron, padding barefoot back toward her kitchen. In her wake, Zanve got the first waft of a deliciously rich scent of melting butter and also something greasy and salty.

Wyn's thick, ever unruly dark auburn hair was tied up in lumps all over her head in a way Zanve recognized from back when they were younger, best friends working on various projects or traipsing around Arrowmount on the next adventure they had cooked up. She often shoved it up out of her way in whatever way she could, sticking hairpins or the various quill into it, keeping it in place.

Her hair also had bits of flour in it.

"Good morning, Wyn," he said after her, stepping inside and closing her door. He slid off his boots and left them at the door, relishing in the feeling of his feet being freed from their confines after the night he had.

Wyn herself simply waved back at him in response. "Say hi to Tiny."

He crossed through her tiny front living room, pausing only a moment to pet her ancient cat, Tiny, that they all assumed was immortal. Tiny — whose given name was Percival, but they all agreed that that was too fancy of a name for him — was laying across the back of one of Wyn's well-loved emerald green high backed chairs as usual, his ginormous grey body poised just precarious enough to make Zanve worry he that he would go tumbling over.

"Pet tax paid," Zanve murmured as the cat glared at him, all the while purring so loud it practically shook the pans in the kitchen.

"Taste this." Wyn appeared next to him as he turned toward her golden kitchen, some kind of pastry in hand. In here, too, Kaius' yellow-tinted glasswork continued, casting the kitchen in an effervescent golden glow.

Finally getting a good look at Wyn, Zanve started to grin at the streak of flour that marred her rich, golden skin, right across her forehead. Which prompted Wyn to shove the pastry into his mouth.

"Ah, hot," he said, mouth burning. He sucked in air around it, trying to chew at the same time.

"What do you think?"

Beyond the scalding heat, he started to taste the butter and something oddly... floral. Then came the warm sweetness he recognized as honey.

"Wow," he said around the pastry, "that's something."

Wyn narrowed her eyes at him.

"Sorry, right." He swallowed and nodded, trying to make his exhausted mind work. Wyn loved when you gave her actual feedback, not just exclamations. "That's delicious, Wyn. You can really taste the honey and the... lavender?" he guessed, seeing her nod, before continuing on, "but nothing overpowers the other. They pair really well with that pastry."

Satisfied with his answer, Wyn finally smiled, letting him into her kitchen with a one-armed hug. He hugged her back, her smell wrapping itself around him like a soft, familiar blanket. Everything about Wyn spelled home for him; from the butter lingering in the air to her soft curves and warm embrace.

Zanve headed toward the small table and chairs in the corner, running a hand along the back of his usual chair and settling into it.

"Don't mind the mess," she said, motioning to what she considered to be a mess — and honestly, Zanve couldn't see a single thing out of place. There weren't any dishes left out from what had obviously been a morning full of baking and cooking, the entire kitchen rendered spotless before Zanve had entered.

The absolutely divine smell of the kitchen made his stomach gurgle, reminding him he hadn't eaten in a long while.

"Have you—"

Before he could fully form a sentence, Wyn produced an enormous plate of breakfast food, including bacon and eggs and toast.

"Ah, Wyn, you're a goddess."

"I somehow knew I'd need to make more than usual, even if Kaius and Jay are at work," she said, sitting across from him, setting both the plate of breakfast food and the hot lavender-honey pastries down on the table between them. She picked at a bit of dough that had stuck to one of her fingers absently. "What brings you out this way this morning? Didn't you just finish your shift?"

"Yeah," answered Zanve, picking up one of Wyn's pastries and taking a careful bite. Again, he sucked in air around it to cool the scalding hot as he chewed, savoring the incredible taste. "Gods, this is really good."

"Thanks." She eyed him, tucking a wayward auburn curl above one of her long, pointed ears. "Are you going to tell me what's wrong, or are you going to make me wait?"

One thing that Zanve had learned early on about Wyn was that she had a knack for knowing exactly what people were feeling, no matter how hard they tried to hide it. The more they tried to hide it, the more suspicious and insistent she became.

He swallowed the mouthful of pastry. "Ariawyn, you won't believe the night I had."

She smacked his hand. "Don't call me by my full name, you know better."

"This is worth it."

Wyn leaned in, biting into her own bit of toast. "A busy night at the town gates?"

"Not at the gates, no. I ended up paying a visit to Meriwen, the Witch."

Wyn's eyes went wide. "What?"

Zanve told Wyn everything he felt was necessary — much more than he had with Captain Ludru, but tried to keep himself a bit censored when it came to Meriwen's private life. As much as he trusted Wyn, he knew Meri would rather keep her pain a secret — it was hers to share, not his.

"And so I put the creature, whatever it was, into her greenhouse for safekeeping until I could make sure that she was okay," he explained between bites of bacon and eggs. "When we went back out there a bit later, the greenhouse was absolutely destroyed on the inside."

Wyn shook her head solemnly. "I know what Tiny can do when he gets angry, and he's as old as I am. I can't imagine him in his prime. Little creatures often are incredibly destructive, even when they don't mean it."

The two of them looked over at the cat, who was still sitting in the same spot, eyeing them both as if to say *as if I'm not in my prime now, you heathens.*

"But this was different. That greenhouse looked as though something had exploded inside of it — it wasn't just an animal panicking and breaking things. Something's... different about that creature."

"I wonder what kind of creature it could be," mused Wyn. She tilted her head, contemplating. Then, her eyes snapped to his, a playful shine twinkling as she started to smirk. "So, you were naked that whole time? That's a bit forward, Zanve Einar."

Zanve threw a bit of pastry at her as his cheeks started to warm. "No, no. I mean, I was, but she had an old jacket that I put on when I was carrying her inside, just in case she woke up before I could do anything about it. And then when she did wake up, I ran back to the gate to grab my uniform, because I knew it was probably going to shock her twice over if she properly got a look at me inside of her house and I was stark naked. I think I got back before she noticed."

Wyn snorted and stole a piece of bacon from his fingers. "I can picture it. You have some delightful thighs, but my goodness Zanve. Next time take your uniform with you when you run off into the woods to see the Witch."

He waved away her delighted smile. "Don't get any ideas. There probably won't be a next time, anyway."

"Of course there will be," she said, pointing at him with the bacon. "You, my darling friend, are too kind for your own good. So am I, for that matter. You're going to go back out there and apologize again for ruining her greenhouse. And then you're going to offer your services to fix the space back up."

"She definitely did *not* want me to be there any longer than I had to be. I don't think she's going to want me coming back."

"You underestimate what a few good lavender and honey pastries can do for a person." Wyn shoved the bit of bacon into her mouth before pushing up from the table, grabbing a number of the pastries from the plate in front of them and turning toward her cupboards.

He watched with growing apprehension as Wyn withdrew a small basket, wrapping the pastries in a soft, bright yellow towel and placing them inside, before adding in a couple jars of her homemade jam. She reached for a fresh loaf of bread resting on her counter, and a jar of honey that Zanve recognized from the Bickertons, who lived to the south west of Arrowmount.

"Wyn, please, there's no need—"

"If only I had known,' she said, cutting him off. "I would've made some of my soup. You know the one, with the ginger? I should do that today actually, it's the perfect late-winter meal anyway. And this gives me a good excuse to make some, because I've also been meaning to bring something down to the Venthroths, Kael is ill with a cough."

"This is perfect as it is," said Zanve, standing and putting a hand on the basket's handle. "I don't want to scare her away."

"Food will never scare someone away," Wyn scoffed, as though the idea was impossible. "I should come with you, that way I can—"

"No," interrupted Zanve as he shook his head and put both hands on her shoulders, making her stop to look at him. "I'll go. I'll take this to her."

Wyn frowned at him. "You don't think she'll like me?"

Zanve very much did not think Meri would have a good reaction to Wyn showing up in her garden unannounced, filled with sunshine and energy and bringing gifts. Wyn was wonderful, his favorite person in the realm, but he knew that some folks were a touch overwhelmed on first glance.

"I think she'll love you, if she ever gets to meet you. You're like the sun, Wyn, you know that."

"If?" Wyn poked a finger into his chest until it hurt. "If you're inserting yourself into her life to be the helpful human I know you want to be, then I'm going to be right there next to you. We're a package deal, you and I. Oh, and Kai and Jay, but." She waved her hand dismissively.

Zanve snorted and rolled his eyes. Her partners were her entire heart.

"Let me just see how going back and offering help goes with Meriwen, okay? I don't know her well enough to really make a snap judgement, but she doesn't seem overly open to new people. Kind of like a cat, you know."

"But — fine, fine!" Wyn threw up her hands at Zanve's glare.

He kept his sigh to himself, knowing that Wyn was probably not going to let up on this until he had a definitive "no" from Meriwen on his offered help. He didn't really think that she would accept his help at all, gift basket or no.

She'd been quite clear when she banished him today.

Zanve watched Wyn with a soft expression, perfectly happy. Now that his belly was full of good food, the edges of exhaustion were finally pulling on him, calling him to sleep.

Wyn fussed with the basket she'd made up. "I really should be off; I have a new order of jams to bring down to the market, and a new loaf of bread to pick up from Gable."

Zanve rubbed at his eyes. "I need to head home."

"Then back to the Witch's place," said Wyn with a happy smile on her face, pushing the basket into his hands. "So that she can have these, fresh."

Wyn turned, withdrawing a much larger basket from a lower cabinet absolutely overflowing with her handmade goods. It looked enormously heavy, laden with glass jars freshly sealed with her jams and spreads.

"Do you need help with that?" Zanve moved and quickly cleaned their remains of breakfast from the table, wrapping the bits of food left with different beeswax wraps she'd sourced from the Bickertons' apiary.

"No," she answered, hefting it onto her hip, resting it perfectly there, "I am quite strong, Zanve Einar. Let a woman carry her own basket. Plus, I got it specially magicked to redistribute the weight so it's much easier to carry. I'll walk with you."

He felt rather silly, holding the tiny basket of select goods as Wyn hefted the much larger one full of her goods, but they made their way through town all the same. She waved him off as they neared the town center, him diverting off toward home, and her continuing on with an important air toward the regular stall that helped sell her goods.

Zanve decided he was going to give Meri a day, at least, without him appearing on her property again. It was only kind, he figured. A day, then he'd go apologize.

Any longer and Wyn would have his head over letting the bread go stale.

11

RETURN OF THE GUARD

Meriwen

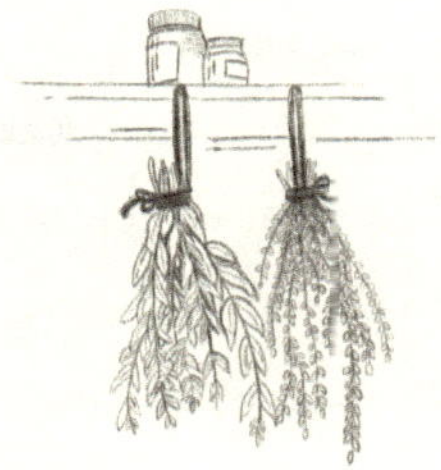

Thistle gamboled around the garden in the evening sunlight. The grass was wet with dew; frost creeping in beyond the border of her garden as the sun sank behind the trees. Meri was halfway through her third mug of meadowsweet tea, standing in her open kitchen doorway, watching the evening crawl toward night.

For the entire day, she'd been unable to get out of bed. She had, finally, about an hour ago, and only managed to make it to her kitchen to make her tea and stare at the garden outside.

Meri tried to keep herself planted firmly on both feet, but the pain that radiated through her twisted, scarred muscle refused to let her. She tilted to one side, left shoulder pressed into the doorframe to stay upright. She closed her eyes, sipping the cooling tea, hoping above all else that it would start to soothe the ache in her chest.

If you miss a ritual, you fail as a Keeper.

All day, she kept looking out through her bedroom window, wonder-

87

ing what the magic was going to do, now that it was unbalanced. She could feel it, tense, waiting.

Whatever happened, it was going to be her fault. She missed the ritual. She failed her job.

With a gentle breath, Meri pulled a touch of magic from the ground, through the planks of her cottage and to her hands. She heated her mug back to the best drinking temperature.

Lock was seated with his tail wrapped around her ankle as a soft trail of contented smoke rose from his nostrils, watching the garden with her. She noticed that every so often the direction of his gaze would travel to Thistle, his tail tensing before he looked away, toward the tree line where birds sang away into the evening air, and he would relax once more.

Meri wondered why this wyrmling was always so wound up. She had never really figured it out, despite Lock having been with her for decades now. He'd been with her the longest out of all her creatures; most of the woodland ones around her phased in and out as the years went on. It pleased her beyond anything that the creatures decided that her cottage and garden were safe to spend a little of their lives here, sharing the space with her.

A few months after she'd decided to make herself comfortable in a cottage of her own making, hiring out a number of contractors to help build it to her specifications beside the nexuses of the ley lines, the creatures started to come.

Day after day, Meri would sit outside in her soon-to-be garden and watch. Slowly, the birds and deer and other creatures of the forest joined her, warily looking from her to the people making noise in their beloved home, but the more they watched her and she watched them, the more comfortable they became.

After the woodland creatures came the cats, of course, because no matter how much cats wished that they appeared aloof, mysterious beings, they never wanted to be left out.

Then came Lock.

He was the first of a few magical creatures, though he was the only one that stayed. The others would come and go, occasionally stopping by for a quick rest, but Lock never left.

When he arrived, he was the length of Meri's forearm and could barely string a couple of words together. It made her smile, the way he had fearlessly nosed his way onto the edge of her skirts on that cold winter morning.

Meri remembered the way Lock's tiny body heated her feet as though she'd put them up on the edge of a fire. He had slowly made his way up her leg, as though trying to find the warmest spot to sit in the chilly morning air. His tail, then thin as a whip and no longer than Meri's hand, tried to wrap itself around her. She gently lifted the tiny wyrmling close to her chest.

"You can stay here, if you like," she had said to him, bringing him into the cape of blankets that she had wrapped around herself. His big, lamp-like eyes had shone up at her, drinking her in, as a soft *mmmmmm* sound stirred up from his chest. Then, as though he had decided he was safe, he had wrapped his tail as best he could around her wrist and curled into her.

Lock in the present grumbled, bringing her focus back, her perfectly warmed tea wafting a curl of steam thick enough to rival Lock's. His tail tensed hard around her ankle, before he leapt up onto her shoulder.

Meri watched him curiously before noticing Thistle was now also on alert. The feathered creature bounded toward her and stood at her side, all his feathers standing on end.

Lock, for once, didn't protest at another creature coming in close to her, and instead kept his eyes trained on the edge of her garden.

Through the slowly darkening evening sky came a figure, walking tentatively up toward her line of garden beds. She blinked a few times before her eyes focused on the face of the town guard, Zanve, who had supposedly rescued her earlier.

And destroyed her greenhouse. Meri narrowed her eyes, suspicious. Why was he back?

He walked with his head slightly down, as though to keep track of where his feet were. Something swung by his thigh, held fast by a long curved handle. He was no longer wearing his guard uniform from that morning, and instead wore what looked like rather comfortable, well-worn trousers that hugged his thighs and calves. His shirt, too, Meri noted, hugged the muscles of his chest rather well. His gaze passed once over her garden, scanning, she assumed, for her, before he eyed her little house. He had the funniest expression on his face, as though he was trying to both keep his expression neutral and drink in everything that was around him.

A curious one, she decided, right at the moment that he saw her in her doorway.

"Oh, hello," he called, running a hand through his slightly unruly hair. "Sorry to barge in again."

She raised an eyebrow.

"I wanted to make sure that, uh—" He approached slowly, closing the distance so that they weren't calling to one another from across her garden and cleared his throat, "that you were okay after yesterday. And apologize again for being the cause of your greenhouse's demise."

"Alright."

The two of them stared at each other, silent for a moment. Meri watched as Zanve rocked slightly on his heels, a basket swaying slightly by his side. Despite her irritation at this man, the gentle fear that he was here to take Thistle away again, she couldn't help but relax slightly. He didn't look malicious at all.

"You're not here to take the creature away, are you?"

He blinked at her. "Why in all the realms would I do that?"

"Because you're a town guard. You're... duty bound, or what have you."

"Oh." Zanve frowned, as though the thought hadn't occurred to him. "No, no I won't take him away. I never planned on doing so, either. You seem to have things in hand."

Before she could stop herself because she was not in the shape for company or hosting anyone and really desperately was hoping that this mug of tea would finally be the one to help her fall asleep, she said, "do you want to come inside?"

Zanve looked at her, relief passing across his face. "I don't really know if your two guard animals — guard creatures? will be happy with me if I do."

"Don't mind them," she said, wiggling her toes slightly to try and shift Thistle. "Lock is harmless, and well. Thistle..."

"You named it?"

She blinked at him slowly. "What else is one supposed to do when they take in a baby animal? You give a place to sleep and a warm meal. Of course I named him."

"Him." Zanve looked down at the creature, his face blank, before he nodded, a smile breaking across his face.

Thistle whined softly before shifting off of Meri's feet. She handed Lock her mug of tea so that she could maneuver around her kitchen, grabbing hold of her shelf once more.

"You're moving around quite well," said Zanve, ducking into her kitchen. He looked around, a soft color rising in his cheeks. "Are you feeling any better?"

"I have my ways," she answered his first statement, gesturing to a spot along her countertop where she knew she had a stool for him to sit on. With a soft one-legged hop, she pushed herself up onto her counter to sit amongst the jars. She wondered briefly where the birds had gone. Honestly, those birds had an entire little world much more interesting than her own.

Lock reached up toward her with her mug extended, which she took gratefully, before he curled up in the corner, eyes latched on Zanve.

"This is from my friend Ariawyn," said Zanve. He placed the basket on the table between them, then cleared his throat, looking down at Thistle, who was smelling his legs tentatively. "Wyn. She, uh, made up a basket when I went to see her today, to help me apologize."

Meri eyed it, immediately noting the gorgeous load of bread. She knew it was from Gable's baked goods stall, with the angled leaf cuttings along the top. They had the best baked goods in all of Arrowmount, and it looked as though this loaf was one of their coveted herb loaves.

She tried to not show how eager she was to dig into it. Then she realized what Zanve had actually said.

"You told your friend about yesterday?"

"I didn't tell her about you or anything personal, just the events that happened," he said quickly, looking slightly pained.

"But you told her about Thistle."

He cringed slightly. "Ah, yes. Was I not supposed to? She won't tell a soul, if I ask her to. I had to fight her pretty hard to keep her from coming with me. I didn't really know how this was going to go, but I figured bringing someone else wasn't the right move."

Meri bit the inside of her lip, gently worried. The more people who knew about Thistle, the easier it could be that he could be found out; potentially taken from her and harmed in some way. But, this Wyn person sounded nice enough.

Without her, Meri wouldn't have fresh bread.

Zanve cleared his throat again and ran his hand through his hair, drawing her eye. His eyes flickered a soft yellow-grey in the candlelit kitchen. "Also. About your greenhouse."

Meri's stomach clenched, remembering the damage. "What about it?"

"I feel the need to fix it."

"You *feel the need*—" Meri let out a choked laugh. Was this man some sort of hero-wannabe?

"No, sorry, I said that wrong — I don't feel the need, but I also do? Sort of?" He shook his head, rambling on slightly as the color in his cheeks deepened. "What I'm trying to say is that it is my fault that your greenhouse was destroyed, and so I would like to help you put it back together. Since, well."

He stopped talking, looking as though he had overstepped.

Since you can't yourself, she finished for him in her head.

"On the contrary, I very much can," she said, feeling a slight waspish tinge to her words sneak out. She tried to bite it back. Was he just being kind? Or was it pitying? "I do not need your help, but I thank you for offering."

Zanve's cheeks reddened and he hurried on to say, "I didn't mean to upset you in any way, I just mean that — well, I know the carpenters in Arrowmount quite well, and another who works with glass at the port but is also is an absolute wizard when it comes to building things, who would most definitely be able to lend me the materials and tools to get whatever was needed done, and..."

It didn't surprise her that this charismatic, rather beautiful man had lots of friends. But, Meri thought decidedly, that didn't mean she wanted him to bring them all *here,* into her space and her life. She was perfectly fine on her own.

"I know you are probably more than capable to fix it back to what it was," he continued on, holding up both his hands carefully as though he was placating a cat. "I am simply offering my services to help you get it done quicker. Since I'm the reason it's in the state it's in."

"Again, I thank you, but I can manage on my own."

A small voice in the back of her head made a sound much like Lock did. *Are you sure about that? He looks incredibly capable, perhaps you could use the extra hand.*

She couldn't help but size Zanve up, from the strong arms that currently were resting beside Wyn's basket to the stool he was sitting on that was obviously too small for him. Meri took a moment, noticing how much room he took up in her kitchen, and wondered how she hadn't seen it the moment he walked through the door. The man was built like a mountain.

Yes, well, she could still do it without his help, she thought venomously. Eventually.

Meri shifted on the counter, trying to hide her wince of pain. *Could* she get it done herself? Yes, but most assuredly not in time to be ready for the summer equinox in three months. By then, she would hopefully have enough of her plants revived, but the greenhouse itself... she had already resigned herself to working out of her kitchen.

Meri thought wearily about the weeks to come, imagining having to suffer working in her kitchen and dealing with her chronic pain. The greenhouse would be fixed, but not for a long while.

She wasn't going to be able to walk properly for a while, if her old flare-ups were any indication. If she was being entirely honest with herself, she could use the help.

"Well, I won't say I didn't try," said Zanve amiably, before adjusting the basket in front of him on the counter slightly. "I do sincerely apologize. If you want more of whatever goods Wyn snuck into that basket, please let me know. I would be more than happy to bring whatever you wish."

If you have his help, you may be able to get everything else ready for the solstice, her thoughts argued with her. *You should take his offer*!

Thistle snuffled slightly from his spot next to Zanve's feet. The creature seemed to have finished his very thorough inspection of Zanve's legs and feet.

Zanve glanced down at his feet and chuckled in soft surprise. "So you're Thistle, are you?"

He lifted the little feathered creature. Thistle looked no bigger than a loaf of bread in Zanve's arms.

"Thistle, this is Zanve," Meri said softly. And, because she still felt a little bit angry about the whole thing, she added, "he was the one that put you in the greenhouse."

Zanve shot her a look as the little creature froze, eyes wide as they locked onto his face. "Yes, but that was only to protect Miss Meriwen, you understand. I didn't want you to run off and become even more of a problem — ah, I should say," he corrected quickly, noticing Meri's raised eyebrows, "I wanted you to be kept safe while I helped Meriwen. That's all."

Thistle glanced carefully sideways at Meri, who simply sipped at her tea. If there was anything she'd learned about being around creatures, it was that you had to let them be comfortable with you first, at their own pace.

Thistle paused a moment, as though waiting to see if Zanve would say anything further, before drooping its ears back and nuzzling into his chin as though to hide its face. It was a surprisingly human thing to do.

Zanve chuckled and scratched Thistle's feathery head. "Well, I should head out. Again, I'm sorry for the destruction I caused, and I hope you enjoy the basket. The jam is some of Wyn's best yet."

He smiled at her before he stood, heading toward her door.

Now! Do it now! You need him, despite your stubbornness to do things on your own, said the voice in her head.

"Wait," she called, her mouth moving faster than she could protest the thoughts in her head. She put down her mug and slid from the counter. She kept her face still, despite the bolt of lightning that shot through her leg, and looked up at the guard. "I do actually need the help, if you are offering. I... well, I won't be able to do it on my own for a while, and if you are offering... it could... be good."

It was like the sun broke out over Zanve's face. He brightened, eyes crinkling softly. "Okay. Great. I will be here tomorrow, then, to get started and to see what we need. If you have things to get done, I'll see how fast we can get the repairs done."

Meri opened her mouth to say yes, please start as soon as you can, but her leg throbbed painfully, reminding her that she probably wouldn't be able to walk tomorrow, let alone get out of bed.

"I'm... busy tomorrow," she said carefully, keeping her face still. "Come back in a couple of days, then I'll be ready for you."

Zanve nodded. "Can do. I look forward to it."

PART TWO

Dust and Journals

12

BADGERS, SQUIRRELS, AND RABBITS

Zanve

Zanve groaned as a knock sounded on his bedroom door, yanking him from sleep. He knew it was several hours too early for him to be awake.

"Zanve, darling, you have to get up or the day will be entirely gone. I've been knocking for ages."

Without opening his eyes, he turned toward the sound of his mother's voice. "Mum, please."

She opened his door and walked in.

Zanve groaned and threw his arm up over his eyes. "I had another night shift; you know I need sleep."

Captain Ludru had given him five night shifts in a row, padding each one with overtime as well, to make up for his absence to save Meri. They were catching up with him. Meanwhile, his mother was operating as though being asleep past seven in the morning was a crime.

All he wanted to do was sink back into the bliss of sleep. But of course, his brain had started to churn.

Skies, he should actually go and see Meri today. He had promised, after all, that he would come back in a few days to begin work on her greenhouse.

"Oh, shoot, that's right. Well, I just wanted to come in and say hello because I never actually see you anymore, even though I live with you, my sweet boy. Why don't I ever see you? You're always coming and going — you'll never believe—"

"*Mum.*"

Zanve peeled his eyes open, rubbing at his chest to try ridding it of the unease that was building. Whenever he went days like this, without deep, rejuvenating sleep, his body felt like it was constantly on edge, waiting for the battle that interrupted his rest.

His mother, Vena, ignored him, strode over to his window, and drew back his curtains with a flourish, before pushing open the shutters and letting in blinding sunlight.

"Come and see, the sky looks like it's *twinkling* today, Zanve."

He swallowed and pushed himself up on his elbows, squinting at her as his eyes adjusted. "What?"

"Come and *see*, you goose."

Pushing aside the idea of simply closing his eyes, rolling over, and getting a few more glorious hours of rest, he shook his head lightly and stood, before taking the few steps to come up behind Vena.

"What?"

She simply gestured outside.

Zanve frowned, looking outside and trying to see what she did. What on earth did a *twinkling sky* mean? Everything looked entirely normal, from the meagre bushes in his neighbor's garden to the dusty cobblestones outside that desperately needed some rainfall to wash them clean.

"I don't—"

"Mighty Savras, Zanve. I can't use your eyes for you. You're the one with magic in your veins, and yet I can see it?" His mother took his chin and tilted it up to look at the sky.

His eyes caught on the edge of a shimmer, and for a moment, Zanve wasn't entirely sure what he was seeing. It could've been just a glimmer of sunlight on an errant reflective surface, bouncing back — but no, the more he looked, the more wisps he could see. They slipped between the sunlight, dappling against the blue of the sky, shimmers here and there as though the world was now filled with whisper thin, delicate, shimmering filigree.

"Skies above," he hissed, narrowing his eyes at it. "What is that?"

"I haven't the faintest clue. I don't know if anyone has really seen it, properly, either — but I caught a glimpse of it when I got up this morning before I left for work. And there's this feeling in the air." Vena stopped, shaking her head.

"Feeling?"

"Go outside and see for yourself. Maybe you can make heads or tails of it. Your eyes don't see anything mine don't?"

"They never have, you know that."

"Still, there's never been anything like this." She cast one last look out the window before she turned, automatically moving to straighten his bed, erasing the last hope Zanve had that he could simply crawl back into the warm sheets when she left.

She fluffed his pillows into shape. "I'm going to go have a late lunch — or rather, an early dinner. There's coffee waiting for you out here, too, Zanve!" his mother called as she walked from the room and toward the front door. "Make sure you clean up after you eat."

Seeing as he was fully awake now, Zanve peeled off his shirt and trousers and padded into his bathroom to wash. After a refreshing wash and donning freshly laundered leathers and linens, he scraped his wet hair back and out of his face. He walked into the kitchen, pausing to grab a mug of coffee left out by his mother, and drank it down in a long pull of deliciousness.

Well, not worth putting it off any longer. He was oddly a little nervous about going back to the Witch's — to Meri's cottage. He couldn't really say why.

Zanve had told Meri he would be back in a few days, and he hated the fact he was making her wait longer than he intended. Life had simply slipped by.

The moment he was outside, he noticed the change. Vena was right; something was different. The air tingled along his skin and in his lungs when he breathed, carrying a particular freshness that didn't accompany salty sea air, no matter the season. He slowed, looking around him, noticing the flares in the sky once more. He had never seen anything like them.

Magic? It had to be.

He wasn't sure what kind of magic it was, though. There was something a touch otherworldly about them; as though he'd stepped into the fey realm or into dream. Granted, he didn't know much about magic at all, despite being able to shift into a panther at will. That was about where his knowledge ended, other than what he picked up from being friends with Wyn, Kaius, and Jay — each who had varying degrees of magic of their own.

(Though, Jay no longer used theirs. But that was another story.)

Someone knocked into his thighs, distracting him.

"Oh, apologies!" they said, half glancing at him and back up at the sky, patting his knee. "Do you see that glimmer, too?"

"Yes, yes I do," said Zanve slowly. The stranger shook their head.

"Strange times," they said, sounding oddly delighted. Zanve hesitated, peering at the person to get a better look at them. A tiny, brown-skinned gnome with a head full of tightly bouncing curls was laden with a number of supplies. A few paces away, a donkey pulled a cart, full of enough supplies to furnish a house. Though, Zanve wasn't entirely sure what household stocked glass vials the size of dwarves and books thicker than a man's torso, but to each their own.

The gnome continued, not noticing Zanve's polite bewilderment. "The air is positively *shimmering* with interest, dear man."

"Yes, it is — I'm sorry, I — do you need any help with this?" Zanve gestured to the cart. The gnome, who had been continuously staring straight up at the sky, simply smiled and shook their head.

"Not at all, good sir. I have a helper — oh, look there he is now! He was just making sure the other cart was coming in through the circle. He is all I need, I assure you."

The gnome — Zanve frowned at them, noticing their deep blue robes now, and the insignia of the crown stitched on the lapel that marked them as a scholar — waved at a harassed looking elf who was hurrying up the road, leading another cart.

"Alright," said Zanve, stepping out of the way as the scholar continued to gaze skyward. The elf, long brown hair cascading all over his shoulders and across his face as he hastened forward looking rather put out, also wore a set of dark blue robes, embroidered with the crown's insignia.

What are royals doing in Arrowmount? And what had the Scholar meant by *circle*?

The elf dusted off a shimmering substance from his hands and muttered under his breath as he passed Zanve, not once looking up. The cart that followed him moved without the aid of any beast; instead, the wheels simply rolled of their own volition.

Zanve simply shook his head and moved on toward the town gates, noting even more books and scrolls in the second cart, threatening to spill over the edges.

"Zanve!" Adrias waved from the front gate as Zanve approached, the dwarf standing alone on guard. "What on earth are you doing awake at this time?"

"Mum," he answered, yawning. "And I have an appointment with Meriwen today."

"An *appointment?* What in all the realms does that mean?" Adrias' eyebrows practically danced on his forehead. "How... proper."

"Oh, fuck off," said Zanve, shoving Adrias' shoulder as he crowed in laughter. "Did you see that Scholar come through?"

"See them? Zanve, they almost gave me a heart attack when they arrived right out of thin air. I thought I was seeing things, and suddenly the air was shining right out there, in the middle of the meadow, with these glyphs and symbols. Then, cool as you please, that Scholar came through the light, leading a donkey. And then the elf behind, with a cart that was—"

"Pulling itself," Zanve finished for him.

"Teleportation magic, I think," said Adrias, scratching his bearded chin thoughtfully. "I heard the Captain tell a story about it a while back, about the last time someone teleported into Arrowmount. It was *years* ago, before either of us was born. Decades. Before Lord Wymarc was Lord here, I think."

Zanve's eyebrows shot up. "The scholar was wearing the King's insignia. But I've never seen any royal travel like that before."

"Curious." Adrias shifted and sighed. "Well, I suppose the rumors will be swirling by the time dinner comes around, them having arrived like that."

"We'll find out sooner or later, I suppose."

Zanve almost asked about the shimmering sky, wondering if Adrias had noticed it as well, but as the dwarf glanced around, his eyes passed over the air without pause.

One weird thing is enough for the day, he thought, and continued on his way toward Meri's cottage.

As quickly as he could, Zanve traced the path up to Meri's cottage through the trees, following the same route he did a few nights before.

The small two-story building slowly became visible between the branches, a second-floor window catching the midday sun. As he stepped through onto her yard, his eyes tracked up to the sky as if drawn inexorably up. The gossamer threads were even more abundant here, occasionally catching thin rainbows in the sunshine.

And, this time as he walked out of the trees into Meri's garden, he noticed a subtle shift in the warmth of the place. Suddenly, he wasn't chilled beneath his jacket, and his breath no longer puffed out in a soft cloud around him.

He took in the garden, from the already growing plants poking out of the freshly watered soil to the birds dotted here and there amongst the trees, hopping around merrily, before spotting Meri standing in her doorway, as she had been the other night.

The feathered creature, Thistle, was nowhere to be seen; and the wyrmling wasn't curled around her feet or her neck. Instead, she stood alone, one hand gripping her staff and the other holding a mostly empty basket containing a few empty glass jars, as though she was preparing to step out.

"Zanve," she said as he approached, her voice smooth and melodic. "I was beginning to think I had scared you away."

"I am a man of my word," he answered, feeling warmth bloom in his cheeks. "But, I should have let you know, sent you word, that my shifts kept me from being any sort of productive during the day. My apologies."

She shrugged an elegant shoulder and stepped from her cottage door, barefoot, her feet gently settling on the ground. Something washed over her expression that Zanve couldn't quite place; a gentle straightening of her shoulders and a lifting of her chin accompanied it, as she met his gaze straight on.

He cleared his throat. "How are you feeling today?"

"A bit better," she answered, her voice impassive. But Zanve noticed how she grimaced gently when she took another step, leaning on her staff. "At least the headache has mostly vanished."

"Do you..." he held out a hand, motioning to the basket. "I could carry that for you, if you like?"

Meri shot him a sharp look as she moved past him. "I am not incapable of carrying an empty basket, Zanve."

"Oh, uh, that's not—" he grimaced, cheeks burning. Offending her was the last thing that he wanted to do. "I wasn't saying that, I was just—"

"Come on, we may as well get started on this mess."

He followed her after a beat, watching her walk away from him slowly, leaning heavily on her staff. Before he took three steps, though, there was a soft sound of anxiety from his right.

Zanve turned to see the wyrmling perched on the old chair, beneath the familiar worn coat. He hadn't seen the creature at all, the way it was balled up on the wooden seat, unmoving. Lock narrowed his eyes at Zanve and, though dragon-like snouts weren't really made to frown or scowl, he could have sworn the look Lock shot him was exactly that.

"Come, Lock. Leave him be," Meri called over her shoulder.

The wyrmling narrowed his eyes at Zanve before leaping off the chair and bounding around Meri's garden to follow her. Zanve was slightly surprised to see two wings extend from Lock's body, so thin the bottle-green skin was nearly transparent as it stretched between the finger-width bones that held them aloft. Lock used them to coast from garden bed to garden bed, but they didn't quite appear to be strong enough to actually help him fly.

As though the sound of Meri's voice calling across her garden was enough, the forest around stirred with activity. The little feathered creature, Thistle, tumbled out from a thicket of his namesake and toward her, frolicking about with what Zanve could only describe as childlike glee. Zanve blinked at it, wondering if it was just a trick of his own perception. It had only been a few days since Zanve had seen the creature appear in the clearing — was it possible it had grown already?

Zanve gazed around surreptitiously, trying to not reveal his pure awe of the garden as it came to life around them. Birds played between the branches around the property, twittering with glee. A number of rabbits and smaller creatures, whose names Zanve didn't know, peeked their heads out of the long grasses along the edges of the trees. He watched as a deer stepped into the garden around the side of the greenhouse, its coat a soft burnished brown, unbothered as Meri approached.

Even the trees themselves seemed to bend closer inward, their branches fluttering around with a breeze that Zanve couldn't feel.

Meri glanced up to the dancing leaves with a half-smile on her face, before she moved to open the greenhouse door. The light touched her as it rebounded between leaves, dappling her face and lighting the soft waves of her pale blond hair into an incandescent frame around her. For a moment, Zanve could only watch her, wondering at her softness and beauty.

Her skin was pale, enough to make the gentle purple circles beneath her eyes to stand out. Zanve wondered briefly if she was getting enough sleep, or if, like him, Meri was being kept up by something. Despite that, there was a gentle rose color along her cheeks as she gazed around at her garden, a small smile playing at her lips, her eyes alight with something akin to pleasure. Meri was dressed in simple, worn clothing; a dress that didn't quite hit her ankles, and an apron over top that had what looked like a handful of grass poking out of a pocket.

Zanve always knew that she was tall, too; but something about seeing her here, in her garden, gave her towering antlers an added level of... not intimidation, he thought, but pure ethereal beauty. The sharpness of her jawbone, the curve of her neck behind the cascading mess of near-white blonde hair that fell to her lower back—

He knew she was pretty, but why hadn't he realized how *beautiful* Meri was sooner?

She glanced back at him questioningly, as though she could feel him staring. He dropped his gaze to his feet, tucking both of his hands into his trouser pockets and following her.

The inside of the greenhouse was as they had left it, though with the bright daylight streaming in through the glass walls and ceiling, everything was thrown into even sharper relief. As Zanve ducked inside, he let out a long, arduous breath, and gazed around, slowly starting to take stock.

"First, we should probably clean some of this up," he said, casting a look around at the shattered plant bits as Meri, too, frowned around at the space. "Just so we can get a clear picture of what needs fixing."

"Right." With a soft breath, Meri whistled, taking another step inside. A soft skittering sounded across the glass roof of the greenhouse, pulling Zanve's attention up just in time to see a mass of mismatched feet pressing along the glass before a swarm of animals entered through the open door.

A number of birds, squirrels, rabbits, cats, a raccoon, and even one substantial badger lumbered in, heading directly toward Meri.

Zanve blinked, his mouth falling open, as Meri's face broke into a soft smile — one he hadn't seen on her before — gazing down at the assembled creatures. She hissed something under her breath that sounded much like the language she'd spoken the night before to light her staff, but nothing visibly changed in the space.

"I — we," she corrected, glancing up at Zanve with a quick look. Her voice was tinged with the softest echoing babble. The entire group of animals looked up, focusing on her. "We would appreciate your help in cleaning up the mess in here."

Zanve frowned. Was she *speaking* to these creatures?

As though in response to his thoughts, the animals launched into movement. The squirrels and rabbits as they started moving out larger bits of carnage as the birds flapped around expertly, breezing dirt and smaller bits out toward the open door.

Meri handed the badger a broom and nodded toward Zanve as she herself began to pick through some of the furniture bits that had fallen over or been torn asunder by Thistle.

The badger gave Zanve a snarling smile as it lumbered over, almost humanoid on its two hind legs, extending the broom toward him.

"Thank you," he said automatically. The badger nodded solemnly, as though expecting that response, and turned to help the squirrels and the rabbits clean.

What world had he dropped into, he wondered, as he started to sweep.

13

HANDSOME

Meriwen

Why it hadn't occurred to Meri sooner to ask her creatures to help was beyond her. She had been off the past few days; too in her own head, worried about the magic of Arrowmount, and in so much pain she couldn't walk much further than a few steps into her garden.

She'd had the spell to talk to animals for a number of years, found originally in one of her mother's old journals that she had stored on her second floor. Elestren kept a very extensive collection of journals, especially on the material realm. Meri had come across a journal of hers on druidic spells her mother had recorded after a brief stint in the Blackshell Forest. The speak to animals spell wasn't overly tricky, so she decided to try it out. It hadn't quite worked the way her mother had described it, but it was close enough.

Her mother was a Realmstrider — someone who could break through the barriers of the world, stepping from one realm to the other with ease — so, Elestren couldn't do spells outside of those in her purview. Despite that, though, she was a scholar first, and recorded whatever she learned, even druidic spells.

But Meri, with the pure power of the ley lines, could arguably do any spell that she tried. The easiest spells were tied to her brewing and crafting of tiny tinctures and remedies, and her rituals, of course. She hadn't ever needed to do anything more than that in all her years in this realm.

Meri had experimented with the druidic speak to animals spell. She tweaked it a little, to fit her natural magic better than what druids do, and it became simple. She tried first with the birds that fluttered across her kitchen counter, then with the deer that had decided to poke its head into her kitchen to check on her. After a while, she started having regular conversations with any creature that visited her garden. They always seemed happy to converse with her; perhaps they were reveling in the novelty of speaking to a humanoid person. The animals helping her today with her greenhouse seemed rather happy to help, too.

Today was the first day that she was able to walk this far into her garden, using the magic of the ley lines to help bolster her step enough to reach her greenhouse with Zanve.

"Is there anything you need replaced that we can get from town?" Zanve asked as he lifted the badger up high to hand off some softer, organic material to some birds who were collecting for their nests. "I'm going to take note of the furniture that need rebuilding, including the frame around the glass here."

He pointed to a cracked and chewed bit of wood along the bottom of some of the glass panes.

Meri's eyes traced the damage, a dull ache spreading through her chest. All this hard work, all of these years they had stood the test of time. Some windows were entirely shattered from whatever Thistle had done — so much so, the bottom row looked frosted over.

"I'll need to speak to the glass smiths to replace some of the glass," she said, wondering when she would be able to make it all the way down to the water's edge to the forge.

Zanve frowned. "What's wrong with them?"

"Those along the bottom are supposed to be clear."

His jaw went slack. "Oh."

"The glass was handcrafted by them, so it shouldn't be too much of a worry, I hope." She bit her lip. "I had them source sand from the beaches here to be melted down and mixed in."

Meri had thought it would be a nice touch, bringing some of the sea up to her that way. Not only for the symbolic nature, but also for the strength it would lend to her greenhouse magically, tying it to the town.

"That's possible?" Zanve blinked at her, his task forgotten.

"Sand is tiny particles of glass and other little broken things, in its essence, so, yes. If one was to sort out the bits that will melt correctly, and heat it hot enough..." she shrugged, taking a second to shift her weight off her leg and lean against the wall.

"Huh." Zanve looked off into the middle distance briefly. "Anything is possible, I suppose."

"*Almost* anything."

"True. I hadn't yet found a way to make Damian, my fellow guard, to stop talking out of his ass, so."

Meri sputtered out a laugh. "That part wouldn't be overly impossible, I don't think."

His eyes shone as he leaned a hand on a stool in front of him, leaning a little closer. "Good, I still have hope."

"Do you have much experience with magic?"

For some reason, the question slipped past her lips without hesitation.

Why she was so intrigued by this man, she wasn't sure.

"Not much, no," he said, glancing away for a moment. "I don't have any spell casting abilities myself. My friends have a bit more experience. Wyn, because she's an elf, and she naturally has magic in her. Jay, because they were trained as a sorcerer, but they don't use it any more. And Kaius because he's a fire elemental."

"Like the family that runs the forge?"

"His family runs it," said Zanve, nodding. "He will be more than happy to help with the repairs to your greenhouse, I'm positive."

The idea of bringing more people in to help her fix her greenhouse made her feel slightly ill. She didn't want even more people knowing the infamous Witch of the Woods was often immobilized by debilitating pain. She took care to never go into Arrowmount with her staff, only going into town when she didn't need it to move, so that they wouldn't suspect anything.

Why, she entirely wasn't sure. It wasn't as though she was embarrassed to have the disability, but... she liked the idea of appearing more stable and strong to those who spun rumors about her.

Plus, it would probably bring more intrusive questions, and she had spent enough of her life fielding those.

After a couple of hours filled with the scurrying of her animals and Zanve's idle commentary, Meri's greenhouse was looking much cleaner. Zanve, who turned out to be chattier than she had expected, entertained himself and the animals as they worked.

Zanve chuckled to himself as he reached out a hand to remove an errant leaf that was tangled in the badger's fur. The badger had taken to him *immediately*, which only resulted in the rest of her creatures eventually fawning over the man. It would be annoying if he wasn't so damned charming. Meri couldn't deny he was incredibly helpful, quick, and efficient in cleaning. And, his conversation was intriguing enough to take her mind off her own discomfort.

As they worked, Zanve told her stories about his life and his friends. She had a feeling that he talked mainly to fill the silence, which she had a little trouble getting used to, though it wasn't unpleasant. She was so used to working in the silence of her garden, listening to the trees and animals around her. The way that Zanve talked about those he loved made his entire body light up, not just his eyes; he was animated, gesturing to include not only Meri in the conversation but the animals, too. Though he didn't have any spell cast on him to make him able to talk with the animals, they listened, rapt.

"Can you believe that?" squeaked the squirrel next to her in a high-pitched voice. Meri was pulled from her thoughts, realizing that she'd been staring at the man while he continued on telling a story about his mother and his friend, Wyn. "I cannot believe those townspeople actually celebrate the moon! I mean, how ridiculous."

"It's tradition," she said back quietly, so as to not disturb Zanve's story. "After all, don't you hoard nuts all winter because of some mass ritualistic need to do so?"

"That's because of *the weather*," scoffed the squirrel. "Not because some deity tells us to. Or the moon. We simply need to stock up on food for the winter, and we know when it's coming better than you people do. Really, you should all learn from us." The squirrel shook their little furred head and climbed up to the rafters to help a robin to straighten out some of the tangled leaves on the hanging plants.

Meri leaned heavily against the wall, hoping Zanve would be too wrapped up in his story and the animals to notice her momentary lapse in movement. She'd only just been able to get out of bed yesterday, and being on her feet for any longer than a few minutes at a time had her entire body shaking with exhaustion. She should have planned better for this, brought in a chair or stool, or—

"Meri?"

She glanced up. Zanve had paused mid-story, looking at her. The entire greenhouse full of animal residents had their eyes on her. Meri immediately straightened and cleared her throat, her cheeks heating. "Yes?"

"I'll get you a chair."

He was out of the greenhouse before she could stop him. When they were cleaning, they'd removed the singular stool that usually sat in the greenhouse for exactly this purpose, but Zanve didn't return with that; rather, he returned with the old garden chair from outside her kitchen stoop.

"You didn't—" she sighed, feeling awkward and put out by how quickly he'd gone to help her. "I'm *fine*."

"Obviously you're fine, but it's got to be tiring to be on your feet this long already. Skies, *I'm* tired, and I'm used to being on my feet all day at the gates." He settled her old garden chair down, before he stopped and looked around at the greenhouse. "It actually looks like we're pretty much done, doesn't it?"

Meri could see a few more things she could clean, but for the most part, he was right. The animals — and okay, Zanve as well — had done an exceptional job.

"Yes, you could say that."

"Good. Let's get some fresh air and sunshine, shall we?" He offered her his arm, as though he was a lord and she a lady, holding her chair in his other hand. "I'll take your chair."

She bit her tongue and hesitated for only a moment.

"Shall we?" he repeated, his eyes shining in the sunshine pouring through the glass ceiling and walls of her greenhouse. Tendrils of his hair had escaped the low gathered bun he'd done when they started to work, framing his face and making Meri want to reach up and tuck them behind his ear, just to get them out of his way.

Gods, he was handsome.

The thought surprised her enough to let her hands act of their own accord, taking his offered arm. Which, of course, was quite muscly and strong.

She didn't usually have thoughts like this about others. Meri recognized attractiveness in others in a purely aesthetic way; nothing about their *prettiness* or *handsomeness* or the way their eyes shone in the light. She couldn't remember the last time she'd wanted to touch someone, let alone fix their hair.

Meri glanced surreptitiously at Zanve as he settled her chair for her, first reaching down to lift a little rabbit out of the way. The smile that broke across his face as he did so, as though the act brought him nothing but singular and perfect joy, made her heart ache.

He *was* handsome. In an entirely objective way. His face was incredibly symmetrical — anyone with eyes could see that. That didn't mean anything; plenty of people were handsome.

Meri settled into the garden chair and tried not to groan at the relief that spread through her the moment she was off her feet. Zanve pulled her stool from beside the greenhouse closer, his face breaking into an even wider grin.

Meri reached up to her face, wondering if she'd got anything on it without realizing. That happened a lot in her garden. "What?"

He sat on her stool, making it look *tiny* beneath him. "I never thought I'd be helping a rabbit hand off broken pots to birds. Or befriend a badger. Or see any of this happen. You live in a dream."

"It is simply my garden," she answered, not knowing what else to say.

"You're right about that. Your garden." He chuckled, then scratched his beard, his smile fading. "Did you find anything salvageable in your cleaning?"

"All that was salvageable I found earlier; everything else that remained in the debris was... just debris," she sighed. "It's going to take years to replenish all my stores."

"Gods," hissed Zanve, shaking his head. "I am so, so sorry."

"You've said that already."

"But I am. Truly."

Meri cast a look back at her greenhouse, at the animals still poking their way through the leftover bits of junk. The badger held up a particularly large chunk of a pot in appraisal.

"At least the broken bits will be used by those who need them. And most of the plants that were higher up are untouched." She found solace in that, at the very least.

"True," said Zanve, nodding as he followed her gaze.

They continued to talk for a little while, about nothing important. Meri could feel her focus shifting, her exhaustion pulling her down once again. She tried to remain as kind as she could, hosting this man in her garden — but the thought of going into her kitchen to make him more tea or grab something to eat was out of the question. Her leg was throbbing so hard she was beginning to question if she'd be able to walk inside at all.

"I should probably go," said Zanve after a minute of silence, his eyes tracing Meri's face. She hadn't noticed how quiet she'd gone, falling into her thoughts.

"Oh. Right." He probably had more to do at home, with his friends and family, and didn't want to be here in her garden talking to her anyway. He was just being kind, sticking around due to some sense of duty.

He stood, stretching, as he inspected the greenhouse once again. "I will be back in the next couple of days, once I get all the supplies I need, so if you think of anything specific that you want me to track down, I can definitely do that."

"Alright."

Zanve nodded and straightened his shirt, before he hesitated, opening his mouth a few times, visibly trying to decide if he was going to say something else. "I should ask, because I know Wyn is going to ask me. Did—"

"Her jam was delicious," she said, feeling a tiny smile break across her face. "You were quite right."

"Good. I'll let her know."

"Oh! Speaking of which—" Meri grabbed her staff, which was resting against the outside of her greenhouse, and pulled herself to standing. Root and ruin, she should have thought of this beforehand, but there was nothing more to it. She slowly started to make her way back to her cottage. Zanve fell into step with her, and held out his arm.

Annoyed with herself, she grabbed onto it.

"Apologies," she said slightly breathless. "I seem to have overestimated my energy today."

"Never worry about needing my help," he answered, pulling his arm in to help support her better. "I should have noticed how long we were out there — I should be the one apologizing."

Meri felt a little lost for words, walking alongside him through her garden.

The moment she reached her kitchen she left her staff at the door and relinquished his arm. She made her way around the perimeter of the room to her counter, where she'd left out the large magic book she'd been hunting through, and a small bundle wrapped in twine and brown paper that she'd prepared yesterday. Meri peeled a piece of paper free from a nearby notebook, one that hadn't yet been completely filled with her notes on her remedies or recipes, and started to write out a note to Marin Miirthgrove, the head glass smith.

Thistle came careening into the kitchen, before speeding off into Meri's bedroom, chasing a blue beetle that was flying at full speed away from the feathered creature.

"Take this, if you don't mind, to the glass smiths." She held it out to Zanve as Thistle chased the beetle out of the bedroom once more, sliding into her cabinets before back out into the garden.

"I'll make sure they get it," he answered, folding it carefully and putting it into the front pocket of his shirt.

"And this is for your friend, Wyn." Meri put the small wrapped bundle of herbs and tea she'd made for Wyn into the basket that had been previously full of jams and wonderful things. "A thank you, for her lovely basket."

"She's going to love this. Gifts are her preferred way of showing love."

"T-tell her also," said Meri, stammering slightly. She wasn't used to talking this much. "Tell her that if she ever needs any herbs for cooking or baking or tea or…" she trailed off, waving a hand. "She has free rein in my garden."

Zanve chuckled, taking the basket from her. "I think I'll leave out 'free rein,' she might take that literally and move into your lavender patch, just to have access to your glorious garden."

"If she wonders what's in there — there's a list on the back of the herbs, and instructions on how to brew the tea. It's one of my usual brews, a simple productivity tea, but I find it's quite one of my favorites."

Zanve blinked slowly. "A productivity tea?"

"Yes."

"Is that.... Just its name, or..."

"No, well. Yes and no."

Zanve blinked at her.

Meri looked away, cursing herself for not letting him go, having to keep her mouth open and *keep talking.* She wasn't good at interacting with other people.

"It's a blend with a touch of sage," she said quickly. "I find that sage can be an overpowering herb if treated wrong, just a pinch will get you headed in the right direction. Sage and lemon balm mixed in with my usual bits of chamomile and dried apple. When I dry the ingredients for the teas, I make sure to tweak them a touch to bring out their productive natures."

"You mean you're using magic?"

"Of course."

"Oh," Zanve said, brightening and taking a half step closer to her in her tiny kitchen. "You put magic in the tea?"

She was not expecting him to be so interested and backed up into her counter. "I learned to make mixes of different things through my mother and grandmother. Adding little things, like courage to a cup of coffee, or a bit of ease into an evening tea."

He looked at her wonderingly. "Could you infuse anything with a purpose like that? Like a broom to clean, for a pot to boil?"

"That isn't quite the same kind of magic as I use," she said, tilting her head, thinking. "With my infusions, they need a basis of herbs that already have properties to do such things. If I tried to infuse strength into a batch of cookies without first having ginger ground into the recipe, then the magic wouldn't have anything to tie itself to. I don't like baking, but that was just an example. Of course, it all depends on my intentions. And my emotions," she added, as an afterthought.

"It sounds quite complicated."

"It's rather simple, actually." She glanced down at the basket in his hands, unable to keep looking at his open, interested expression. "But with different magic, like a wizard's magic, perhaps those other things are wholly possible."

"They definitely would be," he said. "Just today, I saw a cart guiding itself into town."

"That's much more advanced than what I do."

Zanve scratched his chin and gazed around her property. "Does your Mum have a big garden too?"

Meri let out a started laugh. The idea was absolutely absurd, thinking of her mother Elestren tending to a garden. "No, gods no. She's a scholar, my mother. An explorer at heart." Meri shook her head. "You have things to do. I shouldn't keep you."

"I really like talking to you, Meri." He smiled at her, genuine pleasure crinkling his eyes. "I should've really learned more about magic before, come to think of it. It all seems advanced to me."

Meri's cheeks heated slightly. She had never had anyone tell her they enjoyed conversing with her, other than Caelynn, and that was simply because they enjoyed the same things.

There was a tiny beat of silence, before she remembered herself. "Thank you."

"Right, yes." Zanve patted the basket with a hand and took a step back, straightening. "I'll bring this to Wyn as soon as I can. And the letter for the Miirthgroves."

Meri shifted her weight and suddenly became fully aware of the pain ricocheting across her body once again. She tried to hold back a wince.

"I appreciate it, and all you did today. Helping me clean."

"It is the very least I could do. Plus, anytime I get to work alongside a badger and a racoon, you can absolutely count on me." He smiled, his face lighting up like the sun before he ducked his head and nodded to her. "I'll leave you to enjoy the rest of your evening. I'll see you in a few days?"

Meri nodded as he left, watching as he walked across her darkening garden. The day had passed so quickly, she was shocked to find it settling already into evening.

Zanve paused midway through her garden and patted a nearby rabbit on the head, before waving to the few remaining animals that were loitering around her greenhouse.

At the edge of her tree line, he turned back to her and lifted a hand in farewell. Meri found herself smiling as she raised her hand in return.

14

TEA AND TALK

Meriwen

Birdsong echoed through the early morning haze, and dew clung to the cottage's window sills and stone as the world woke up. Meri's head throbbed as she sat, slightly reclined, in her small living space. The weight of exhaustion pulled at her eyelids, every bone in her body begging to be able to fall asleep.

She'd been unable to get any proper rest, which was an unfortunately familiar experience throughout her life. Even with her sleep remedies, tinctures and teas she'd imbued with sleep agents, her mind refused to comply. The pain was simply too much.

Today, Meri had stopped trying to fall asleep long before the sun had made an appearance.

Lock was still snoozing in his nest he'd made out of one of her kitchen cabinets. Ever the guardian, he had chosen one that was angled exactly where he could watch both Meri's bedroom door and the entrance to the kitchen.

Thistle was also absent — she didn't really know what to do with him at night, but he seemed happiest to lay out in her garden, curled in a thicket of grass and growing wildflowers, instead of coming inside.

She leaned back as carefully as she could in her chair, pressing into the small cushion she'd placed at her lower back for extra support. The chair itself was plush and deep, meant to be curled up in. She had it specially made in Pralon and shipped out when she realized that her old wooden kitchen chairs simply weren't comfortable to sit on for long periods of time. Those, now, lived in storage on the second floor.

She should really be up already, going through her stores, she thought absently, making no move to rise. Instead, she pulled the blanket draped across the back of her chair over her shoulders and sipped at her tea, staring into nothingness.

She couldn't help but think of how Zanve had offered her his arm the day before, how if she just didn't have this injury, she would have been completely fine on her own. She would never have had to ask him for help, take him away from his everyday life, or lean on him like that.

If only...

Meri shook her head, trying to push those kinds of thoughts out, but they stayed all the same. If only she had never gotten on that creature in the Manid Empire, when offered a ride as a child; if only she had never been thrown from and trampled by it into the sand; if only the healer there had got to her faster; if only they were more capable...

By the time she had gained the courage to get up, the day was in full swing. She rose, lifting the blanket with her, and carefully made her way into the kitchen with her now empty mug.

Lock was perched atop the counter, staring hungrily at the birds hopping around the jars and such she had left out, including the remnants of her greenhouse's stores.

"Morning," breathed Meri, reaching out and touching the top of his scaled head momentarily. He murmured happily in response, the sound not really words; more of a grating rumble. "Any plans to terrorize the others today?"

Lock looked at her sideways before a small curl of smoke curled from his nostrils. Curiously, he simply looked up, as though seeing something on the ceiling that intrigued him, before shuffling his wings absently. "Mmmm."

Meri frowned at him before following his gaze upward. Upon her various beams studded with empty herb drying hooks, there was nothing except for an errant bit of long-dried greenery that she'd forgotten to take down. It was a sprig of holly that she'd brought in around the last holiday season, with a few shriveled dark red berries still clinging to the leaves.

She plucked it free and a few of the leaves turned to dust beneath her fingers, but the rest of the bundle remained intact. On one of the leaves, she noticed, was a tiny, five-pronged hole that looked, oddly, like a minuscule hand with thin and delicate fingers.

No creature of this realm has hands such as these, she thought to herself, looking back up at her ceiling. Not that she knew of, anyhow.

Though the berries were dried out, it was not quite enough to disguise the tiny bite marks through some of them. Meri plucked a sprig free and held it up to inspect, noticing the way the one bite mark was nearly perfect, and looked like human teeth — despite it being a fraction of the size.

"Hmm," she sighed, leaving the holly on her countertop. Whatever creature had made those marks could have made them a long time ago. It was probably long gone.

A couple of hours later, Meri had fortified herself with a large mug of productivity tea infused with a hearty addition of energy and pain relief, grabbed her staff, and had slowly made her way out to her greenhouse. Lock followed in behind, carrying her mug with him.

She stepped into her fey realm greenhouse with one of her notebooks in hand, ready to take proper stock of what she needed to replenish. It was the only part of her greenhouse that still had a solid surface to use for planting and repotting, the tables and shelving much less damaged than that of the main greenhouse.

Most of the plants that she had salvaged from the wreckage — the cracked roots and half living bits that she was hoping to coax back to life — were sitting in individual pots, having been assessed and repotted carefully. Meri had a distressingly small amount of her mortal realm plants; those had been nearly eviscerated, but in the fey realm section, there were still a number that had survived Thistle's attack.

After taking a quick broom to the rest of the wreckage — she hadn't shown Zanve this part, figuring that the main greenhouse was probably enough for the human to wrap his mind around — and sending a quick gust of fresh air through by opening up her windows, she brought in a stool.

Thistle padded his way into the greenhouse as she got to work. He carefully came over to her, stepping through the magical barrier and over the floorboards as though they were made of glass.

"You're welcome in here, Thistle," she said quietly. She reached up, adjusting one of the plants that was starting to inch its way toward her, the spiked bright blue plant inside leaning over the edge.

It felt nice to be back in her greenhouse, despite the damage and the destruction. Something about going through the motions of cataloguing, replanting and attending to the remaining plants was incredibly grounding and calming.

Meri wasn't entirely sure how long she worked, but when she heard someone faintly calling her name, she stirred to attention only to find Thistle fast asleep right at the entrance, curled up waiting for her.

"Sorry," she apologized quietly, taking a careful step over him.

"Meriwen?" came the voice again, closer this time. Meri frowned. It was incredibly rare for anyone to come calling — recently, it had just been Zanve, and he had a much deeper voice than this one. She ducked out of her greenhouse to find a very tall figure standing just to the side of her open kitchen door, gazing around at the garden.

"Oh! There you are," said Caelynn as Meri approached. "I swear, I peeked in there, but I didn't see you."

"It's good to see you, Caelynn." Meri smiled softly at the giantkin. "What brings you out to my garden?"

Caelynn chuckled and looked around once more, this time her eyes tracking up to the sky. "Well, Meriwen, there are some odd things happening, and I wanted to check in with you. And of course, I am actually taking you up on your offers to come visit for a mug of tea."

"I'm glad. I must apologize for the state of me—" she gestured down at her skirt, which was pressed with dirt and plant detritus and sighed. "It's been an interesting few days. It's the first time in a while I've been able to get back into my greenhouse."

Caelynn's gaze sharpened as she took Meri in. "Did something happen?"

"Oh it's—" Meri had just been about to say nothing, but then she heard the softest noise of interest from behind her, and Thistle tumbled out of the greenhouse.

A jolt of fear ran through Meri — what would Caelynn do, meeting this creature? She hadn't given it much thought to what would happen if anyone from town happened to see him, because no one really came out here to visit her. But now…

"Who's this?" Caelynn smiled warmly as Thistle crept closer, the little feathered thing keeping close to Meri's skirts. "My, I don't think I've ever seen a creature like him before. Where on earth did he come from?"

Meri chuckled dryly, feeling at a loss. "I suppose we have a lot to catch up on, don't we?"

Meri carted a secondary chair out from her house to join her old garden chair and started to prep the kettle for tea. All the while, Caelynn watched with interest as Meri worked and Thistle romped around in the long grass outside.

"Meriwen, love, did you notice the sky?"

Meri hesitated, holding one of her brewed teas imbued with fortitude — a dash of thyme and ginger to help pull it all together — as Caelynn sipped some meadowsweet tea.

"What about it?" Meri glanced up, seeing nothing more than a brilliantly blue sky that stretched beyond her trees.

"It was quite the event yesterday. Something I have never seen in all my long years here in Arrowmount. This is delicious by the way. Is that extra meadowsweet I can taste?"

"I hope you don't mind the bitterness," said Meri absently, eyeing the sky with growing unease spreading through her. "I can always grab some sugar or honey to soothe it."

"No, this is exactly right. I've never really had a taste for anything sweet in my drinks," answered Caelynn. "The sky yesterday had the strangest look to it — undulating bits of magic, as though they were ribbons strung along the wind.”

Meri frowned. How could she have missed that?

“I’m not accusing you of anything, of course, dear. I don’t quite know what it is you do out here, but I am aware of the magical movements of Arrowmount, and usually when you do... whatever it is you do around the seasonal shifts. This spring, nothing came about — but then we wake up yesterday, and the sky is positively glimmering!”

“I can’t imagine what it was,” lied Meri. Whatever the magic was doing, it was because she had missed the ritual.

Root and ruin, she thought. Here we go.

Meri wished that she had noticed the sky, so that she could have inspected the magic closer, and seen the extent to which it had materialized.

She waited, watching Caelynn’s expression as the older woman sipped at her tea, wondering if the giantkin would ask her more about what she did every season. It wasn’t as though Meri was supposed to keep her role as the Keeper secret; in the fey realm, it was usually better for a town or a place to know that the Keeper was there. But it was a bit unprecedented in the mortal realm. Explaining what Meri did would probably take a lot more than a simple, “I balance the magic.”

Meri started to order her thoughts, wondering how exactly she would have to explain to Caelynn, but the giantkin appeared to have moved on from the subject.

“This little creature,” the woman said, gesturing to Thistle who was curled up on Meri’s feet. She hadn’t felt him settle in. “Tell me about him! He’s absolutely adorable.”

“This is Thistle. He’s a rather recent addition to my garden. Do you remember when Cecily had that strange stone amongst her wares at her market stall?”

"Briefly, yes. It was quite out of place, with all of her more decorative bits."

"Well, he came from that."

Caelynn blinked at her, then at Thistle, sizing him up. "He came from that stone? How much has he grown?"

"I think that Cecily originally got that stone from Finnean, one of the bookstore owners, who had gotten it on one of his adventures at some point. I don't know why, but it found its way to me, and it sort of..." Meri hunted for the right words. "It opened up a doorway, and he tumbled out."

"What an extraordinary thing," mused Caelynn.

"Quite," said Meri, taking a slow sip of her mug, casting a wary glance up at the sky once more. "It was not the smoothest of introductions to the world, either. Do you know the town guard, Zanve?"

Meri recounted briefly the events of the other night, with Zanve arriving in her yard, Thistle, the resulting destruction of her greenhouse, and her renewed pain.

Caelynn leaned forward, concerned. "Are you alright?"

"It's a familiar pain," answered Meri simply.

The giantkin nodded knowingly, her long ears flopping gently against her shoulders. She eyed Meri's staff that was leaning nearby. "I thought there was something about you that knew pain. If you ever need anything, let me know — though you probably know a lot more about pain remedies than I do, if this tea is any indication."

Meri smiled at the mug in her hands. "I do, but the question of them working for me is always up in the air."

Caelynn's gaze travelled to Meri's greenhouse. "And what of your plants?"

Meri's chest clenched hard. "Some are okay, but... most were destroyed. Most of my stores, too. It's going to take months, if not years, to replenish all of it."

"You tell me exactly what you need from me, and I will make sure it gets to you. Plants, herbs, powders, spices, anything." Caelynn tapped Meri's hand, making her eyes feel hot.

Her chest squeezed. Caelynn's help would be so, so incredible to have; restocking at least a number of her mortal realm plants and her most commonly used ingredients would be a boon. As Meri got ready for the next change of seasons, making sure she had them ready as quickly as she could...

"That's... that would be so helpful," she said, the words almost getting stuck in her throat. "Though, a fair number of the plants in my greenhouse aren't things you can get in this realm."

"It's what friends do." Caelynn's eyes glittered with interest. "You've never mentioned these other-realm plants."

"Plants from my home realm, of course. I would show you, but my greenhouse is currently not fit for guests, being so empty."

"I will wait until you regrow and flourish again," agreed Caelynn. "I'm sure that it will be glorious. Just like your garden and menagerie out here!" The giantkin gestured out to the garden around them. "I should have come out and visited you much sooner."

Thistle nuzzled into Meri's legs, drawing her attention down. She leaned forward just enough that she could scratch him between his ears. He was truly only a little thing — lighter than most dogs would be at that size — and so gentle with the way he handled the plants, batting at them as though he was merely petting them.

How he had managed to do that much damage?

"Do you know what he is?"

Meri shook her head. "Not in the slightest. I haven't given it any thought. My mind's been rather occupied of late."

Caelynn *hmmed* pensively in the back of her throat. "He did come around at a rather auspicious time, it seems. Magic, you know, calls to magic."

"I think he's fey," said Meri softly, threading her fingers through Thistle's feathers, making him coo contentedly. "Like me."

"That would make sense. Creatures of all kinds tend to flock to you."

"But those are creatures of this realm," said Meri looking around at her garden, spotting the birds and rabbits playing at the periphery of her garden. The one stoic deer that was often in her garden was grazing near Thistle, seemingly unbothered. "Even Lock is from this realm, despite being magical. I've never come across any other fey creatures in my garden."

"Perhaps it was simply a matter of time." Caelynn patted her hand affectionately. "He seems to like it here. I wonder, if you found out more about him, maybe you'd be able to discover where he came from, and what exactly he's capable of. Because as you and I both know, most living things have much more hidden beneath their skin than they may show."

Meri nodded, furrowing her brow. She'd been so preoccupied in the past few days with her stores and her pain that she'd barely given a second thought to the little creature, except to make sure that he was safe and happy. She barely knew what he ate, other than the occasional flower, and even then it looked as though Thistle was just testing their taste, not seeking sustenance.

"So tell me about this Zanve," said Caelynn, shooting a glance toward Meri. "From my impression and what I've heard around town, he's been here quite a lot."

Meri snorted. They were making it sound like he was haunting her doorstep.

"Only twice. He's offered to help fix up my greenhouse," said Meri. "I think he feels terrible, so he's just being kind. Truthfully, without him offering, I don't know when I would be able to have my greenhouse back up and running."

"Mhmm. It is quite nice he offered." The giantkin's eyes sparkled with humor. "And you can never go wrong with having a handsome man around. He's the tall one, with long hair?"

"With the blue eyes," added Meri.

"Hmm, I always thought they were grey," said Caelynn as though she was commenting on the wind. "Maybe I simply haven't looked hard enough. Or had reason to be gazing into his eyes as such."

Meri blinked slowly, feeling as though the giantkin was alluding to something that escaped her. "I didn't have any reason to be, I simply noticed."

"Naturally." Caelynn conceded, although Meri still felt like she was missing something.

The conversation devolved into other topics, Caelynn filling Meri in on the many goings on around Arrowmount. After a while, Meri rose and made more tea for the both of them, deciding against any magical add-ins, while Caelynn wandered around her garden beds.

From her dwindling kitchen stores, Meri wrapped a bundle of pain relief tea for Caelynn to take with her when she left, before joining her out by the lavender.

Caelynn left a little while later, equipped with the bundle of tea and a few choice clippings from the fresh growing plants around them. She waved and promised to return, giving Thistle a little pat on his head as she ambled back toward the tree line.

Meri sighed and rubbed at her chest, feeling slightly overwhelmed. Her eyes turned skyward, wondering about the glittering strands of magic, about her missing her ritual. What was it that was going to mean for the people of Arrowmount like Caelynn?

15

CHERRY WINE

Zanve

Zanve left his coat at home as he set off into Arrowmount for the first time that season, feeling a warmth in the air that he had missed. He smiled at the folks around him, seeing life returning to the town once more as people started to shake off the dust and cobwebs of winter.

Something about the warmth and the sunshine reminded him of Meri as he walked through town, stopping first at A Second Story to pick up the next installment of his favorite book series to read when on shift, then continued on toward the Old'n Narrow. Perhaps it had something to do with how he kept turning their last conversation over and over in his head, keeping her top of mind. He wanted nothing more than to go back to her cottage and pick her brain about magic, listen to her talk about the way hers worked and how she made her teas, for hours on end.

Zanve opened the door to the Old'n Narrow and was immediately surrounded by the intoxicating scent of Corwek's cooking. It smelled as though Corwek had made something rich and hearty, layered with spices and something that wafted the place in the nutty spiciness of roasted turnips.

"Zanve!"

Wyn waved him over to a spot just off to the side, where she, Kaius, and Jay were seated. The two of them leaned in toward her as they conversed, like she was their center of gravity.

"You made it," said Jay as Zanve pulled out a chair and joined them. "I thought you would still be in bed, after all the night shifts."

Zanve glanced up, catching the barmaid, Briar's, eye. He winked at her and she lifted a tankard in reply.

"Captain's got me back on morning shifts for the moment," he said to the table. "Thankfully. Much livelier than the night shift."

"Your ale," said a warm, familiar voice from over Zanve's shoulder. He looked up to see Aeric, the incredibly attractive waiter, as the elf passed over the fresh tankard. "Handsome as ever, Zanve."

"You look well," said Zanve, his smile warming. Aeric simply shifted a shoulder up, his face practically glowing with happiness as he shifted away, his long black hair swaying across his back.

When they were young, Zanve and Aeric had a dalliance; but it was definitely a bad match. Though attracted to one another, Zanve couldn't handle the elf's dramatic tendencies and overt flirtatiousness; whereas Aeric found Zanve relatively boring — and regularly told him so. Thankfully now, though, it had been so many years, the two of them had evened out into amiable friends.

It helped that Aeric had fallen in love with the blacksmith's youngest son.

How could love change someone so much? He found his eyes traveling after Aeric around the bar once again, noticing that he was wearing an oversized knitted jumper with paint on both of the elbows. Zanve smiled, pleased to see Aeric in something other than all black.

"Did you hear?" Wyn nudged him back into their conversation. Kaius was still frowning at Zanve, as though puzzling something out. "Aeric and Morgam are to be married this fall."

"No, really?" He grinned, looking at the elf anew as he glided around the bar. He paid almost no one any attention and simply drifted along with a soft, dreamy look on his face. "Good for them."

Kaius swallowed a bite of his food. It looked incredibly tasty; a rich stew with a fresh knob of bread to accompany it. "Any word on if Kir is coming back for it?"

Kirandir Dulra, Aeric's best friend and the sister to Aeric's betrothed, Morgam, was traveling with her girlfriend, Lottie, and following a dream of bardic greatness. After their departure, there had been rumors that Lottie Luck was not just vacationing in Arrowmount to see her sister, Cecily, that she was actually a thief on the run, but Zanve didn't believe a word of it.

Their town didn't attract that kind of attention, let alone from renowned thieves.

"I'm sure she will," said Jay, nodding. "If she brings her girlfriend with her, I'm sure there will be a line out the door just to ask her questions."

"Lottie better come prepared then," chuckled Zanve.

"Something's different about you," said Wyn suddenly, leaning forward to peer closely at Zanve.

Used to Wyn's antics, Zanve simply shrugged.

"No, really. Something I can't put my finger on." Wyn frowned.

"Well, while you think about it, I'm going to go order food." Zanve pushed himself to standing and made his way to the bar.

"Afternoon. Can I get you anything to eat?" Briar beamed at him; her thick mess of brown hair tangled atop her head in a rather lovely bun. With it up, Zanve could see her round cheeks and soft crinkles at the corners of her eyes.

"Whatever is making that delicious smell," he answered.

Briar nodded. "Coming right up."

He turned to find Wyn right behind him, hands on her hips, that half frown on her face as she watched him. "Hello, Wyn."

"It's Meriwen, isn't it?" Wyn's face relaxed. "Oh, that makes so much sense."

Zanve, who was entirely lost, blinked at her. "What about Meri?"

"Oh, nothing," she said loftily, a soft smile on her face as she turned away. "You'll see."

"What?" He followed her back to their table. "Wyn? What do you mean?"

"Just that I can see something has changed. And that's all I will say." She smiled triumphantly as she slid back into her chair.

Zanve, about to question her more, found himself looking at a new figure who had joined their table, having taken his chair.

"Hello! Oh, you're that lovely man who offered your help on the road yesterday," the person said, turning toward Zanve, a genuine grin spreading across their face. "It is a pleasure to see you again."

"You as well," Zanve answered, sliding into a different chair and pulling his ale toward him to make room for the Scholar. "Zanve Einar."

"A pleasure, a pleasure!" The Scholar was decked head-to-toe in the same kind of robes they were in yesterday; however, this one was a deep ruby red and had a variation of the Pralon crown crest embroidered on their lapel: two interlocking swords with an open book above them. The Scholar also had a book beneath their elbow and a set of thin, shining spectacles shoved up into their curly hair, glinting in the bar light.

Zanve cleared his throat. "To what do we owe this pleasure today, Scholar...?"

The scholar shivered slightly in their seat. "I am Scholar Sarrai Daruka, but please, no need for formality. You can call me Sarrai. I'm not sure what drew me out of the Lord Wymarc's library in the middle of the day, but something about the sun shining outside told me I should explore your lovely town."

"Something in the air?" asked Wyn airily. Zanve shot her an annoyed look as she kicked him under the table.

"Yes, quite that." The Scholar looked up in slight shock as Aeric appeared behind them and deposited a tiny glass of cherry wine on the table. "Oh, young man, how did you know?"

"You seemed the type," said Aeric dreamily, winking at the scholar, before gliding off again.

"What interesting waitstaff," commented Sarrai happily before taking a small sip of their wine.

Kaius rubbed at his chin, the lava churning under his rocky skin breaking through momentarily before solidifying once more. "What are you here studying, if I may ask?"

"Have you heard of the recent rumors circulating in the academic community about recent fey activity?"

The table gazed back at the Scholar blankly.

Zanve shifted in his seat, leaning back. "Fey?"

"Yes, *fey*." Sarrai said the word as though every ounce of their slight body quivered with anticipation. "It is my life's work, to chase the odd, the new, and the totally undiscovered. I have been a scholar devoted to unravelling many mysteries of the fey realm, which is why I am here in Arrowmount."

"I had no idea that our little seaside town would be so interesting to a

Fey Scholar," said Wyn, leaning forward.

"Despite the wonderful people and the glorious beaches I've heard talked about at length from folks back home who have had the opportunity to vacation here? Many, many things my dear..."

"Wyn," she introduced herself with a soft smile.

"Wyn. Pleasure." The Scholar took a sip of their cherry wine and smacked their lips happily.

"So, Sarrai," prompted Zanve. "What is it about Arrowmount that draws a fey scholar to us? Does it have anything to do with the weird shimmering things in the air yesterday?"

This morning, the first thing he did was look outside to see if the sky was still shining as it had been. But, to his slight disappointment, the world outside his window was as normal as ever.

"Well, that was actually a fun little surprise to find when I arrived. For, you see, I came for an entirely different magical event, and when I stepped through the transportation circle, I was greeted with an entirely different oddity I cannot explain! Isn't it wonderful?"

Zanve chuckled. "I suppose you could say that."

"But oh, I haven't even been here a full twenty-four hours and yet I could already keep you pinned to your chairs until dawn with the stories I've learned about your lovely little town." Sarrai sighed happily.

"Oh?" Jay tucked a long strand of hair behind their ear and leaned in, sliding their fingers into Kaius'. "Do share."

"What I can tell you is this: the rumors of heightened fey activity have originated here, of all places. I was expecting something to happen for the past few weeks. We've been monitoring the levels of magic back at my university, and were waiting to see if something would come of our hypotheses and the like. An event, we assumed, would probably occur near somewhere like Feycross!"

"Why Feycross?" asked Zanve.

"Feycross, my good sir, is a doorway," explained the Scholar. "A doorway direct to the fey realm. There are only a few permanent doorways to the fey realm around the entirety of Ravar, so it is quite rare. And usually, if something — or rather, more properly said, some*one* — were to come through with enough power, the scholarly and magical world would feel it. Have any of you any experience with magic? You of course, must, my dear fellow," said Sarrai to Kaius, who was most obviously the most magical being at their table, seeing as he was a fire elemental.

Jay held up a single finger, and Wyn nodded, scratching at one of her elongated ears.

"Then you may or may not have noticed it, but the event that happened just a few days ago, give or take a week, caused a shift in the magic. Momentarily. Like a door being opened."

Zanve had a flash of a memory then, the scene of looking over Meri in the clearing, surrounded by a white light, before a tiny creature launched itself into the world, as though it had walked through a door.

"That is why I am here. I am studying what occurred, what we can learn from it, and what that event caused. All of the juiciest of field research. Perhaps it is nothing, but we shall see!"

"If you need anything, feel free to let any of us know," said Zanve. "You can always get a hold of me through the guard barracks, or Wyn is at the market during the day."

"And I'm at the glass forge down by the water," said Kaius, nodding to the scholar.

"Why thank you. You know, I didn't quite believe other folks when they mentioned that I would find the kindest of people here — but they weren't wrong!" They sipped happily at their cherry wine.

The table fell into soft conversation about the town, Sarrai eagerly asking questions about their little town. At one point, Jay and the Scholar got into a rather boring conversation about gardening and the proper care of a specific kind of long grass native to this side of the continent that went completely over Zanve's head.

Eventually, though, the Scholar had finished their wine, the rest of them their lunches, and everyone had to be off to finish their days around town.

"I will send my assistant Argyle to offer an afternoon of tea for you all once we are settled in," said Sarrai, hopping down from their chair.

"That would be wonderful," answered Zanve sincerely. "It's been a pleasure."

Wyn waved the Scholar off as they all paid. Then, just as they were about to leave, her hand wrapped itself around Zanve's arm and she pulled him back.

"I think you know the event the Scholar mentioned," she whispered. "Something about a bright light and a creature appearing in the forest?"

Zanve, whose suspicions had been rising since Sarrai's description of such an event, frowned. "Perhaps. I don't really know how a little thing like that could have caused such an intense magical event, though."

Wyn shrugged. "Something to ask Meriwen, then."

Zanve tucked the information away for later.

16

FLUORESCENT PINK

Zanve

Zanve approached Meri's cottage the following morning, smiling at the creatures he could see in the trees dotted around the garden. They were happy in the morning sunshine, birds chirping loudly as they danced around the branches.

He had just dropped a bundle of timber and tools by the greenhouse, preparing to start fixing things up. He wasn't entirely sure what he was going to do with the timber — or if he'd brought any of the right tools — but he was ready to figure things out.

A bundle of feathers caught his attention as it shifted in the growing long grasses along the periphery, two beetle-black eyes shining out at him.

"Hello, Thistle," he said softly, watching the creature's face light up. Thistle rolled out of the grass and tumbled his way, all limbs and baby clumsiness; if Zanve wasn't mistaken, he had grown already, and was more akin to a medium-sized dog now. Regardless, when Zanve bent down to scoop him up, his body still felt light as air. "Are you enjoying the morning air?"

The creature cooed in his arms before he snuffled his wide, flat snout into Zanve's neck and chest, sniffing him all over. Zanve scratched along Thistle's chin, eliciting a happy purr from the creature as he melted into Zanve's hand.

He knocked on the door of Meri's cottage, gently rapping, before putting the little creature back onto the grass.

"Hello?" Meri called from inside, before Zanve heard her start to move around.

"Meri, good morning!" he called back. "I hope I'm not too early, I wanted to get a good start on your greenhouse, and since I have today off, I—"

Zanve stopped mid-sentence as Meri opened up her kitchen door. She was a touch disheveled, as though she'd just rolled out of bed. He couldn't help the soft smile that broke across his face as he took in her slightly fuzzy hair, bound in a long messy braid down her shoulders, and the softly wrinkled clothes, as though she had slept in them.

Thistle sat on Zanve's feet, almost wiggling with happiness as he looked up at the two of them.

"Good morning," said Zanve slowly. "I didn't catch you sleeping, did I?"

"No, no, you're just on time," she answered, casting a look down at herself, before running a hand quickly over her hips. "Care to come in for a cup of tea, first?"

Zanve couldn't think of a better offer. "Absolutely, if you don't mind."

Meri took a small step back and let him inside, before guiding him to the counter. Thistle tottered into the kitchen, rubbing against Meri's leg and jostling her skirts. Zanve wondered at the thing; he was sure he wasn't seeing things this time — the creature had indeed grown. Where Thistle had been small enough to hide under Meri's skirts before, he was now tall enough to graze her knees.

Zanve stationed himself on the one lone slightly rickety kitchen stool and Thistle situated himself right by his feet.

"What can I interest you in this morning?" asked Meri as she ran a finger across gathered glass jars scattered about on her counter, disturbing a lone bird that hopped out of her way with a chirp.

"What kind do you have? I'm open to trying anything."

Meri considered him. "Perhaps, energy? Strength?"

"Either sound good. I do have a fair bit of both, though, seeing as I drank coffee this morning and am... well." He shrugged with his arms, trying to demonstrate that he was quite strong, before rethinking the movement and dropping his hands. Zanve could feel the heat rising in his cheeks. He didn't quite know how to act around her.

Meri's eyes skated over him, a tiny smile playing at the edges of her lips. "Resilience, then? Something to last you the day."

He nodded, not really knowing what that would do. "That sounds perfect."

Meri uncorked a small jar, tapping about a tablespoon of whatever was inside out into the pestle in front of her, before she turned away and began to hunt through tiny vials behind her.

Lock *hmmed,* irritated, from behind them somewhere, shuffling around a few times, making as much noise as he could. He stuck his long, green face out and glared at them both.

"Morning, Hemlock," said Meri, shooting the wyrmling a look.

"Mmmmmmm."

"Mmmm to you, too," said Zanve, deeply amused. "I apologize for waking you this early."

Lock leapt up onto the counter next to Meri and watched her fish around in her stores as the water boiled behind them, before he stuck a clawed hand into the nearby bowl of fruits and extracted one of the last apples from the bottom. Keeping one eye on Zanve, Lock sat up on his hind legs and began to nibble his way through the apple.

"Here we are," said Meri after turning her attention back to her jars. Zanve leaned across the counter a little closer to her, crossing his arms and looking at it with interest.

"What is that?"

"This is a curious little herb from my home," she answered. "One that my mother liked to call the wren herb, though its true name is one that most have a hard time pronouncing."

"Try me."

Meri's mouth quirked into an almost smile. "Scumbrlwrengigelu," she said, watching him.

He silently mouthed the word — or what he thought he had heard — a few times before trying. "Scumber... Stumble... Scumberlenwrengig-gles — no that's not right."

Meri shook her head, her smile breaking fully across her face as she tipped tiny, dried blood red blossoms of the herb into her pestle, before taking a pinch of something Zanve couldn't name along with it. After a moment of consideration, she added a touch of dried apple and citrus crumbs into the mix — those Zanve could name because of how they smelled — and began to blend them with her mortar.

Zanve watched in fascination as Meri focused on the mortar in front of her, her movements rhythmic and perfectly even.

He couldn't deny it, though; he was wondering if anything flashy would happen with her magic.

Meri stopped before transferring it to a mug and pouring boiling water over it, and slid it across the counter to him.

"Do you take sugar or honey? Or milk?"

"I would love a touch of honey and milk, if you have it."

After passing him the additions, she turned to begin work on her own tea. Zanve watched her all the same, noting a few differences in what she added. What did they all mean?

He itched to ask her hundreds of questions, but he wasn't quite sure where to start.

"You mentioned your home — from the way you said it, I could tell you didn't mean here. Where did you mean?"

"The fey realm," she answered, tipping tiny balls of what looked like shriveled orange grapes into her mortar. "I grew up there until my mother decided I was old enough to handle travelling, and then off we went. Some of my herbs are from the fey realm — specific parts and regions, of course."

"The fey realm," he repeated, his voice soft. "Do you remember much about growing up there? What was it like?"

"Wonderful and terrifying, off and on." Meri turned the mortar a number of times around, grinding the herbs together. "There was this brilliantly pink and yellow tree that grew fruits the size of my pinky nail that had enough juice to rival an apple from this realm. It tasted like if you bit into a mango while smelling cooking meat. The way the sky turned inky black before it lightened to navy at night, rather than the gradual descent the skies here do. And the feeling of the air, it was almost tropical, heady and full of secrets."

Meri smiled in a vaguely reminiscent way as she poured her tea mixture into another mug, swirling water over it.

"I would love to experience that one day," said Zanve, testing the side of his mug with a careful touch, making sure it wasn't too hot. "Excuse

me for this question, as I haven't met any fey folk other than yourself —
but, are you as unique as you seem?"

She hesitated. "No. Well, yes and no. I'm sure there are many others
who look a little like me, but I am not fully fey, as you can probably tell."
She gestured at herself. "I assume my father is either human or elf, seeing
as I look mostly humanoid."

"Except for the antlers."

"Except for my antlers." Meri reached up and touched one gently.
"Why?"

"I..." Zanve chuckled and looked down to his hands before shooting
a glance at Lock, who was still seated up on his hind legs, now nibbling
at the core of the apple as he usually did, making his way through the
entirety of the fruit bit by bit. "I have been told that sometimes I can get
too friendly, too curious, so I apologize if any of my questions come off
the wrong way."

"Not at all."

"I think you're rather wonderful, Meriwen, and I want to get to know
people who I think are wonderful. Especially those who are still incredible kind despite me having a hand in destroying their greenhouse."

"I appreciate that. You can ask me whatever questions you like, as I sort
through some of my stores. Actually, I..." she frowned, looking out her
open kitchen door. "I have something to show you, if you don't mind. I
would like your opinion on something."

"Alright." Zanve stood, holding his mug in hand, steam wafting in
soft curls out of the top in an entirely unnatural way. Normal steam did
not look like this: perfect, playful wafts came up and caressed his face,
bathing him in a soft lemony scent. He grinned at it, before he reached
over and handed Meri her staff from where it was resting by her kitchen
door.

The wyrmling left the stem of his apple on the counter and leapt down before extending his clawed hands up toward Meri, offering to carry her mug. Zanve marveled as Lock carefully began to totter out of Meri's kitchen on two legs, holding the mug steady.

Meri led them out to her greenhouse once again, Thistle following behind.

"I haven't shown anyone this section of my greenhouse, except for those who built it," Meri said, opening the door to her greenhouse.

Zanve frowned, looking around. There was nothing out of the ordinary with her greenhouse that he could see — it was the large, one room. What could she mean by sections?

"It's not visible to just anyone," she explained, moving over to the corner. She extended her hand, drawing it along the panes of glass there.

"What is?"

"Come here."

He approached her without hesitation and took her outstretched hand. Meri stepped forward, as though she was about to walk directly into the glass, but then her form shifted from view, as though Zanve was looking at her through water.

Zanve sucked in a breath, trying to keep his fingers steady as she pulled him forward. He blinked once, and could hardly believe his eyes.

"This part of the greenhouse is usually much more... well, not destroyed," Meri said, sighing. "As you can see, Thistle got to this part, too."

"Wow." Zanve shook his head and let out a low whistle, eyes tracking over the plants. He had no idea what any of them were — gods, that one near the back was bright fluorescent pink and looked as though it had mouths for petals. He placed his tea mug on a nearby surface that had miraculously escaped the Thistle damage, taking in the rest.

It wasn't quite so bad as the other room, but it had still been affected.

Zanve bent, still holding onto Meri's hand, and scratched behind one of Thistle's long, floppy ears. "What in all the realms are you, little guy? How could you do this much damage?"

"He's fey, that much I know," said Meri quietly.

"You think?"

"He somehow got into this part of my greenhouse without me here to bring him through — and I'm beginning to suspect he was drawn here," said Meri as though choosing her words carefully. "I want to try and figure out more about him, see why he's come to Arrowmount. To my garden."

"It makes sense, seeing as you draw creatures to you."

Meri blinked in surprise. "I... Yes, I do."

"It doesn't surprise me that you'd eventually draw something more magical than our good friend Lock to your doors," said Zanve. "What surprises me more is that you haven't drawn something more magical sooner."

The wyrmling made a softly irritated sound from beyond the fey realm greenhouse. He hadn't followed them in; instead, he was just visible outside the portal, a slightly blurry figure, still holding Meri's tea.

Zanve laughed. "Not that you aren't extremely magical, Lock."

"Careful, you may just puff up his ego too much," murmured Meri to Zanve, ducking her head close to his ear so Lock wouldn't hear her.

Zanve snorted in laughter before he sipped at his tea, appraising the space once more. "You're going to need some work done in here too, then. I'll grab some more timber when I go back to town later — oh, I didn't mention, but I was thinking of having my friend Kaius come along with me in a few days to assess the greenhouse glass, if that's alright with you."

Meri didn't respond as Zanve took a few steps around her greenhouse, eyeing everything, sipping tea all the while.

He couldn't quite pinpoint what he was feeling, exactly, but he felt inexplicably warm from head to toe, and like his muscles were perfectly warmed, ready for anything. The tea itself was delicious, too, singing on his tongue with a zest that went beyond any kind of lemon he had experienced before.

"This is incredible by the way," he said, gesturing to the mug. "It's like I can taste the magic on my tongue."

"You weren't disappointed that the magic of it wasn't some large show of sparkles and light?"

"Aha, no, not at all," Zanve said, chuckling. "I figured it would be something more subtle anyways. I can feel..." he hesitated and shifted, trying to find the right words, before shrugging. "It's working, and that's magical enough for me."

17

SPARKLES AND LIGHT

Meriwen

M eri left Zanve to his work in her greenhouse — he mentioned something about "assessing" the damage — and ventured back out into her garden. Thistle followed her, ambling out happily, before taking off after a shining blue beetle.

She watched him for a moment. "What are you, little one?"

She was quite sure he was fey, but what kind of fey? And where had he come from? Had he come right out of that stone, or had the stone just been a conduit for him to enter this realm?

Had someone been on the other end, sending him through? Or had he simply... done this entirely on his own?

And why?

Meri's mind swam with questions as she stood there, watching the little creature. He rolled, all four limbs splaying out as he did. When he got up again, he had a bunch of dirt and grass stuck in his feathers all around his wide snout and eyes.

Her pain had kept her within the boundary of her garden and house, and so she hadn't been able to go back to the clearing where she had brought Thistle through to this realm to clean up her ritual supplies.

That's right, she thought, the memory sliding into place. She brought him through, with his help. He — or, perhaps someone else? she couldn't imagine this little creature being able to communicate across realms like that — had guided Meri through a ritual. Like they knew what kind of magic that she was capable of.

A soft shiver of unease threaded over Meri's spine. She also hadn't really stopped and thought about the bond that the creature and her had, assuming the bond came from their shared proximity from her taking the stone home with her. Something had pulled the two of them together from across the realms long before Thistle had come through that door.

Meri had an inkling that the answers to the creature were in the stone that he had come from.

She started walking before her mind had fully decided to, gripping her staff and slowly making her way to the clearing. Lock uncoiled himself from the garden chair and scooted up alongside her. Thistle remained a little way behind, the blue beetle forgotten, as he tracked Meri with his eyes.

Mmm...Mmm...Meri?

She froze, every bone in her body stiffening as the word slid into her mind. It was a soft, sonorous voice, and entirely familiar.

"Thistle?" She looked back at the little creature as his eyes shone as he gazed up at her. Pride and excitement emanated from him in waves. Meri could feel it across the bond, the spot below her ribs heating with the sensation. "You can talk?"

Meri.

"Yes, I'm Meri. And you're Thistle."

Meri.

Well, he could talk a little bit. One word would most likely lead to more. She looked down at Lock and extended her arm, needing some kind of familiarity to steady herself as she watched the little fey being. Thistle's voice unsettled her a little, unexpectedly deep and entirely not what she expected from a baby animal that chirped like a bird and purred like a cat.

It was the voice of something much more ancient and knowing.

Lock let out a low croon of anxiety, his hackles raised. He glanced between Meri and Thistle, frowning heavily. "Mmmmm, Meri?"

"It's alright, Lock."

"Mmmmm. Thistle not talking?"

"Right. I must have imagined it." Meri gave herself a little shake before she turned back on her path, bare feet crossing from the warmer soil of her garden to the cooler, harder soil surrounding Arrowmount. Here, winter was still hanging on by the skin of its teeth. Though, today, the sun was warm, the birds around her were singing.

Spent candles dotted her way, long since doused and partially melted in the grass, leading toward the clearing where she had first met Thistle. The ingredients from her ritual were still there, in the vague shape of an arch; a couple had been upended and shifted around in the time since she was last here.

Meri crossed right to the center, where she had stood that night, and cast her eyes around for the shards of stone that should still be there. Lock slid down off her shoulders and mirrored her stance, staying close to her skirts, kneading his little hands together.

Thistle, curiously enough, stayed at the edge of the clearing, about where Meri would estimate the soil started to get colder. He sat, watching her, waiting.

"Lock, can you find me bits of that stone?" Meri said, turning so that she could survey the entire clearing. The wyrmling started to hunt around, diligent as ever.

She ran through her memories of that night, trying to remember every detail. That night flashed through her mind, appearing in fragments. Meri remembered lacing protection spells through whatever larger latticework of a ritual she had been doing — and she remembered speaking in an ancient fey tongue.

It was familiar, whatever she had done. Not quite something that she recognized doing herself, but something that she recognized in her bones, as though she had witnessed it at some point in time, or like it was some kind of magic that her soul knew it should remember.

She remembered the gateway. The pattern of the candles, the light illuminating in the shape of a doorway, and Thistle coming through.

Only those like her mother, Realmstriders, could make doors and gateways through the realms; Meri had no such magic. The ritual she had performed was much more complex than the magic her mother could do; Elestren's magic was nothing more than a gesture, a yearning to step through the folds of the realm that carried her through. What kind of magic had Meri done — and was she capable of doing it again? She thought about the ritual, but any memories of the words she had said felt as though she was listening through a waterfall; without help, she probably wouldn't be able to.

"Meri," crooned Lock, breaking through her thoughts. He held up two sizeable chunks of the stone. The insides were completely solid, the odd, shifting color running through the whole piece. There was no space within to house a twig, let alone a creature.

Thistle didn't *hatch*, then, she thought as she took them from Lock. The stone really was a conduit for the ritual that opened a doorway.

Meri ran her thumb along the grooves and pits on the surface of the stone, wondering. This kind of magic was entirely unfamiliar to her, whatever it was. She had never heard of a creature needing a conduit to pass through realms like this.

Lock picked up the rest of the stone for her, and they returned to her garden, leaving the candles where they were. She would send out some of the smaller animals to collect them for her later.

Meri slowly lowered herself to the ground in the middle of her garden, right where the nexus of ley lines converged, and the magic was strongest. She breathed in, holding the bits of stone in her lap, channeling the power coursing through the earth and sky through her. She kept the intake gentle, light; she simply needed their constant flow of power to focus.

Gently, Meri let her head fall back until her face was pointed up to the sky. She closed her eyes, fingers brushing over the surface of the shards of stone.

She felt Thistle carefully settle in by her knee. His little head nestled in on the edge of her leg, facing her. She wasn't entirely sure if he was looking at her or the stone that had brought him into the world. One way or another, his presence grounded her, his head feeling like a soft hand on her knee, keeping her steady.

The magic that was once in the stone started to sing into her skin, confirming her guess. Wherever this stone had come from, whatever it may be now; it had been a key to opening the door. The stone itself was practically bathed in power that Meri could only describe as something that was akin to her mother's magic, but older. More... creature-based, animalistic.

Despite the solstice being in a few months, she herself couldn't go to the fey realm; the only door she knew of was in Feycross, which would take a few weeks of travel on a good leg. Then the fey realm itself; it was constantly fussing with time, pulling at the fabric of reality between realms. If she was there for what felt like a day, it could be anything from a month to a year in the mortal realm.

Who knew what would happen, with the ley lines unbalanced here in Arrowmount for that long. Shimmering skies, though she'd missed them, were only the start — she was sure of it.

Her eyes opened and she let out a soft sigh, thinking of the countless journals in her attic, filled with knowledge that her mother had gathered over the years.

A plan started to form in her mind. Meri had no way of contacting her grandmother or mother — something that they were definitely going to have to address, how it hadn't come up in all these years was beyond her — but those journals could have something that would help. If all else failed, Meri was going to have to go talk to someone in town to see if they knew of anyone who could help get her in contact with her family.

18

A LOVELY DAY

Zanve kept getting distracted. He had been utterly astonished to find out about Meri's secret greenhouse, though he tried not to show it; he couldn't put it together in his mind that there was a whole extra room just existing in space, invisible from the outside or the inside unless you knew where to look. It simply folded in between the existing glass of the greenhouse effortlessly.

But, he kept reminding himself, there really wasn't that much of a reason to be surprised. He lived in a world where magic existed around every corner, and the tea he drank imbued his entire being with resilience.

Once he stepped free of the secret room, it vanished from sight. He was going to have to ask Meri how he would be able to get back in there without needing her help every time, but for now, he had to focus on figuring out what he needed to do in the regular greenhouse for repairs.

He should've brought something to take notes with, he thought, running a hand along the front door frame. The frame itself would need to be rebuilt, along with a number of shelving and tables. The majority of the wooden tabletops could be salvaged; the legs were what Thistle had wreaked most havoc on.

He wandered back over to where the secret room was hidden — or rather, where he remembered it to be, as he could no longer see it — and put his hands on his hips, surveying the whole greenhouse from his perspective. Three large, long tables could be restored, the doorframe needed redoing, and of course the massive shelving unit that had been nearly obliterated. That would need particularly good carpentry skills that Zanve did not possess. Plus, the framing of the entire glass structure looked as though it had been compromised, so it would need to be entirely reinforced.

Kaius will probably be open to helping, and Jay. They were good with building things, and Kaius would be here anyway for the glass. Though, Zanve didn't know how good he would be with wood, since he was made out of magma.

The list kept growing in his mind.

He took a breath, frowning at it all. He was definitely going to need help.

The thought crossed his mind for the third time in the last ten minutes. Zanve didn't particularly want to bring more people onto this project, though. Not that it would hurt his pride — skies, he would ask them in a heartbeat if it was a project just for himself. But, Meri was already skittish with him there, if he brought more strangers tramping into her yard...

Alright — *and* he didn't want to look bad in front of Meri, if he was incapable of doing the work he promised himself. Maybe it would hurt his pride a little. *Maybe.*

Zanve breathed in heavily, and was immediately assaulted with the scent of the greenhouse. It felt as though there was something else laced within the heady scent of growing things and dirt; as though he was passing through a memory he couldn't quite place. It had a lingering scent, floral and fresh. Perhaps it was because he was so close to the magic concealing the secret room, or that he was surrounded by the kind of greenery and growing things he wasn't entirely used to; whatever it was, made him want to slip into his panther form and get a proper sniff.

He wondered what Meri was doing briefly, eyes hunting for her through the dappled glass walls of the greenhouse. Making more magic with her ingredients? Gardening? Simply sitting and reading? He wondered whether she liked to read, and what kind of books she was interested in.

Zanve suppressed the urge to poke his head out of the greenhouse and search, just to ask her that very question. He wanted to know her favorite book, what stories she liked best. Skies, what he wouldn't do to be able to share *his* favorite books with her.

Come on Zanve, he scolded himself and tried to focus once again on the greenhouse.

Zanve dragged his hand through his hair, only to get his fingers caught in the neat leather tie he had bound it back in earlier that day. He tried to subtly extricate his fingers, only to swear under his breath as the whole thing came apart, the bit of leather falling to the floor and the full length of his hair tumbling unbound around his shoulders.

He tried to scrape it back into something less unruly, holding the tie between his teeth. Meri walked out of the forest then, her wyrmling walking next to her and Thistle bounding in behind, like a puppy following his owner.

Zanve didn't know enough about other creatures aside from himself and the occasional cat and dog he saw in town, so he couldn't say whether or not Thistle was fey or from their realm. If he had to guess, though, he would believe Meri above anything else; she had a knack for gathering her creatures close, no matter how strange they were. Out here in her garden that seemed to be warmer than anywhere else, gentler than anywhere else.

Through the greenhouse's windows, sunlight caught on Meri's hair, lighting her curls in a halo. He broke under the pressure and poked his head out of the greenhouse, watching her silently.

With one hand on her staff, her hair unbound and unruly around her, tendrils being teased out around her by the wind, and a half smile on her face as she idly scratched the wyrmling's head—

He was nearly sent to his knees.

Ah, skies, he was staring. He ducked inside the greenhouse and rubbed the back of his arm against his forehead, trying to get his mind back on task. He was here to fix his mistakes, not ogle the poor woman and make her even more uncomfortable than she already was.

It was time to get to work. Repairing a few tables and shelves would be quick, rather easy work, right?

That was a no.

About an hour later, Zanve came to the realization that he was definitely *not* cut out for this whole fix-things-up business. He was not handy in the slightest. He hadn't realized how difficult it would be to do.

A bead of sweat rolled down his nose, dripping onto the grass. He could also feel his shirt sticking to his back unpleasantly as he tried, for the fifth time, to cut a board of timber straight. He propped one end up against the chair, settled his saw, and started to cut through the board with such ferocity that his teeth rattled.

Frowning, he stopped when the board fell in two, picking up both pieces to examine them closely.

Once again, they were a mess. He'd even cracked one of the pieces in his vigor.

"Fuck," he swore quietly, standing up and wiping his arm over his forehead. He figured that maybe a bit more speed would've helped keep things straight, but... well. The graveyard of timber pieces was proof that he truly had no idea what he was doing. He was alright with putting up the occasional pre-cut shelf for his mother, or cutting firewood to keep the barracks warm in the dead of winter — but when it came to using a saw, building, measuring; he did not have a clue what he was doing.

Meri had spent most of the morning passing back and forth between her kitchen and her fey greenhouse. Each time, he would glance up and wave at her as though nothing was going wrong. And every time she passed him by, she would smile softly at him as though surprised he was still there, and exchange a few pleasantries.

It kept him working on the failed project much longer than he cared to admit. But, right then, he was about ready to fling all of his tools in the sea, reparations be damned.

To cap it all off, he had a splinter.

He swore colorfully under his breath and tossed the wood onto the ground and started to suck on his thumb, annoyed at himself. He was definitely going to have to find someone who actually knew what they were doing to help him.

"Had enough for the day?" Meri's voice drifted across her garden as she walked out of her kitchen, carrying something in both hands. She walked slowly, tenderly, as though every step was like walking on glass.

He immediately closed the distance, taking the wares from her hands so she didn't have to come any further.

"I have found myself utterly incapable of cutting a board straight, if you would believe," he admitted.

"Ah, that's unfortunate," said Meri, an expression flickering across her face that took Zanve a moment to recognize.

"You've noticed I'm absolute dragonshit at this, haven't you?" He chuckled despite himself, abashed. It's not like he was hiding his incompetency; half of the timber he brought was lying in uneven pieces around the entrance to the greenhouse, and nothing was yet fixed.

She laughed as well, her cheeks turning slightly pink. The mood he was in vanished at the sound. "I may have noticed that you were having a bit of trouble. I did think you would figure it out, though. I didn't want to completely undo all your confidence and bravado—" she waved a hand in the direction of the mess as Zanve shook his head and looked away, playfully trying to hide his shame.

"I can't believe that I made all these promises to you and can't even follow through on them on the first day," he laughed, shrugging. "I think I've used up every bit of extra resilience you gave me this morning."

Meri straightened slightly and lifted her chin, eyes still sparkling. She cleared her throat and extended a small, neatly wrapped brown paper package. "I thought you might want some tea and things to take home."

Zanve took it with a warm smile. "I appreciate that, thank you. I know my mother will love it."

Meri nodded in response. The two of them fell into a slightly awkward companionable silence, the garden around them twittering with life.

Zanve's stomach growled, reminding him of the time. She probably was just waiting for him to leave, to get off her property, rather than stick around with his failed attempts at carpentry. "I am going to have to find help for the woodworking," he confessed. "I thought I could manage, but, as you saw, I don't really know what I'm going, and I want you to have a beautiful greenhouse that won't fall apart with you inside."

"I... appreciate that." Meri's eyebrows twitched slightly as she looked at him. Zanve caught a soft look of bafflement cross her face before it smoothed out once again.

Zanve ran a hand over his hair, noticing how much of it had tumbled free of the knot he'd tied at the back of his head. Gods, he must look a mess. "I should be off, then. Have a good night, Meri."

"You as well."

As he left, moving back toward the greenhouse to gather the bits of lumber that he'd absolutely destroyed and piling the untouched ones close to the structure so they wouldn't be in the way, he felt her eyes on him. Not malevolently, but interested. When he turned to look at her over his shoulder, he caught Meri's look again as she watched him leave. Perhaps it wasn't bafflement, but annoyance; he couldn't quite tell.

Either way; she looked completely and utterly ethereal, standing in the sunshine. Lock was stationed up on her shoulder, with Thistle at Meri's feet.

His mind wanted to make up a hundred different reasons he could stay longer, talk to her more, but without the ability to actually do what he promised he would do with his own two hands, he didn't have a reason. He couldn't even fake one.

But gods, did he want to. He wanted to get to know her, see that smile, hear her laugh again. Zanve was beginning to get the feeling that he was in trouble.

19

DUST AND JOURNALS

Meriwen

Meri cursed as she pushed harder on the box in front of her that was refusing to budge. "Root and ruin, just a smidge more—"

Lock's concerned *hmmm* sounded from below her as he tried to lend a hand, pushing as hard as he could, but even together, they couldn't move the large, wooden storage box. It was full of her mother's journals from the few months she'd spent in the Nerian Empire, stuffed so full that Meri was sure dust couldn't even touch the pages inside.

Meri swore again and slumped against it, defeated.

"We'll have to simply work around it," said Meri, wiping sweat off her brow and peering past the box into the rest of the room. It was hazy with dust up here on her second floor, which made her frown. She really should make a point of coming up more often.

After waking from a restful sleep to find that the lavender in her sleepy tea had left her with zero of its usual side effects and that the pain in her leg had finally started to lessen, Meri decided to make a trip up to her second floor, which was really more of an attic than anything. She cast

166

her eye around at the space full of boxes and overflowing shelves.

She had her house built to accommodate her needs, with a bedroom on the main floor so she would never have to climb stairs during a flare-up. In doing so, she had quickly realized that she didn't actually use the second floor, and reverted to using it for storage.

Meri's mother, Elestren, had made a life as a scholar and traveler; she had written in enough journals to fill a small library. And of course, since Elestren was never in one place for very long, she needed somewhere to put all those books.

That somewhere had turned into Meri's attic when Elestren first heard of Meri's decision to settle on the outskirts of Arrowmount.

Meri wanted to check her mother's journals to see if she had any clues to what kind of a creature Thistle was, and if she had ever recorded what happened when a Keeper missed a ritual. Meri wasn't overly expectant to find much from the fey realm in the journals, but it didn't hurt to try and look. With her well rested mind, she wanted to comb through what she could.

Meri knew better than anyone that her mother preferred to be anywhere but the fey realm. Even when Meri was growing up at her grandmother's house, Elestren barely recorded anything of their time there.

As a child, Meri had been pulled along on many different adventures across realms and the vast places across Ravar itself, following no pattern but the whim of her mother's choices. Elestren only stayed in the fey realm when Meri needed to be with her grandmother, learning about being a Keeper, and after Meri's injury that kept her bed ridden for many months. Meri believed that Elestren simply liked the shiny and new, and exploring other realms other than the one she had spent so much time in as a young fey was how she fulfilled that.

"Alright," breathed Meri, sliding carefully across the top of the immovable wooden box and staring at the stacks around her. She crossed the space, with much maneuvering of various shelves and boxes, until she reached the back window, and threw the panes open to let in fresh air. Dust motes danced in the breeze that came in, glittering like bits of fairy dust from children's books.

She turned to look back at Lock, who was now perched on the box with his head slightly cocked, waiting. "Let's find those journals."

It took her a solid hour of searching amidst the tomes and dust before she tracked down the oldest, rattiest journals in the entire collection. Frowning, Meri held up the lot of books and counted only a fraction of the ones that her mother had for the Manid Empire alone.

"Well, isn't this a mess," came a strange voice from the stairwell that Meri didn't recognize, making her jump. Lock, who had been curled up on a pile of twenty tomes about the Nerian Empire's dragons, bolted upright with a squeak and tumbled out of sight.

"Oh! Apologies, little guy," said the voice again.

Meri moved into sight in time to see a woman with long, pointed ears slide over the unmovable box and peer behind the stack where Lock had fallen, returning him swiftly back to his perch. The wyrmling looked distinctly uneasy and sneezed, dust and smoke blasting from his nose.

"Are you alright?" said the woman to Lock, peering into his face. Lock, always the most chatty and personable creature, curled away from her and let out a low murmur of anxiety, before he sprang off the books and hurtled himself at Meri.

"Forgive him," said Meri carefully, brushing a layer of dust off of Lock's snout as she stood from her spot with a wince. Her right leg had gone slightly numb from her sitting position. "He doesn't take well to new people."

"The complete opposite to this beautiful fella," said the woman, brushing aside a long curtain of startling red hair and looking down at her feet. Meri was slightly surprised to see Thistle there, shining his dark glittering eyes up at the newcomer. "You tottered right over to me without even the slightest fuss, didn't you? You are the neatest little creature. What exactly are you?" At this, she looked at Meri expectantly.

"I'm not exactly sure. I was — I'm sorry, but who are you?"

The red-haired woman took up so much space — not in her curvaceous body and bright hair, but with her presence. Something about her seemed to shine, demanding to be experienced.

"I am so sorry," answered the woman, putting up both hands in apology. "Where are my manners — I'm Wyn, Zanve's friend. I thought I'd drop by and thank you for your delectable tea in person, since I felt odd just sending Zanve back with my word. After all, someone had to take things into their own hands since he has been here so often and hasn't even taken the time to introduce us to you."

"Us?" Meri felt slightly ill at the notion that she would have to meet even more people today, Wyn's energy already more than Meri was prepared for. She knew that Zanve himself was coming with Kaius tomorrow to look into the glass of her greenhouse, but she hadn't been expecting anyone today.

"Oh, no, I didn't bring anyone but myself this morning," said Wyn with a soft laugh. "I, for one, hate when people impose on my hospitality, so I didn't want to do that to you."

Meri had only a moment to nod in understanding before Wyn continued.

"I wanted to stop by and give you a sample of some of my newest wares and since your kitchen door was open and you had the most delightful little family of birds hopping around your kitchen counter, did you know some of them are bright pink? — and well, now that I'm here, what is it exactly that you're doing?"

Meri cleared her throat, feeling as though the dust up here had coated it. "I was hunting through some of my mother's things, trying to find any information I could on Thistle."

"Thistle!" exclaimed Wyn delightedly, looking down at the fey creature. "That is an exactly perfect name for him. I know Zanve mentioned meeting him after he found you in the woods, but didn't tell me he had a name. How are you doing, by the way? I hope it wasn't too serious of a fall."

Meri took a second to blink, feeling unmoored at the speed with which Wyn talked. Perhaps the lavender in her tea last night had affected her more than she thought. "It could have been worse, I suppose. But I am feeling a fair bit better than before."

"Good, I'm glad. Let me help." Wyn moved before Meri could answer, reaching for the stack of journals that Meri had amassed to bring out into the open and begin rifling through. Meri took an involuntary step back, watching Wyn warily. Immediately, the woman stopped, realization crossing her features. "Right, sorry. I remember Zanve telling me once that I was a bit too forward with, well, everything. I... I probably should have just knocked and waited at your kitchen door instead of coming upstairs, shouldn't I?"

"Perhaps," said Meri with a soft sigh. A small voice in the back of her mind that sounded a lot like her mother's said, *if Zanve likes her — in fact, has called her one of his best friends — shouldn't you be a little bit more kind?*

Wyn's expression was pinched and worried, looking like a small child caught in a wrongdoing. She seemed genuinely abashed, and while overly energetic, Meri could tell she meant well.

"No, it's alright," said Meri after a pause. "I wasn't expecting anyone.

I've been told that I can come off rather prickly."

"Not at all," answered Wyn, a warm smile sweeping across her face. "Who told you that?"

"My mother, in fact." Meri gestured half-heartedly to the collection of tomes around them. "She is the reason for this mess."

"Oh, excellent. A scholar and a well written one," said Wyn, looking around. "It is a bit dusty up here, though. What say we move this operation down to your kitchen? I could even get that table, there, and bring it down with us. I'm surprised you don't have a table in your kitchen anyways, they're the best to have around for when you're hosting friends."

"I don't often host other people," said Meri absentmindedly, bending to grab another journal and adding it to her growing pile. Carefully, she started to extricate herself from her spot behind the stacks. "In fact, it's only recently that I've even needed a second chair."

Wyn frowned. "What do you do when friends come over?"

"Friends?" Meri chuckled, looking at the little wyrmling who was wrapped around her shoulders, his clawed hands digging into her skin. "Most of my friends don't talk back. Only this one does."

Wyn's mouth opened slightly as though she was going to say more, a look of confusion flashing across her face, before she seemed to think better of it. "Well, if you have found yourself hosting more than before, then what's the harm in bringing it down? Besides, you might like it down there. Extra workspace."

"I'm..." Meri took a breath and bit her lip, looking at the table tucked away in a corner, mostly hidden by stacks of journals and a few of the matching kitchen chairs that had gone with it. It had been so long since she'd had her table out; the very table that she had taken from her childhood home in the fey realm and had been with her her entire life.

She'd put it up here with her mother's journals and research books a long time ago, mostly because she had very little use of it once she had built a table inside her greenhouse. Plus, it took up so much of her kitchen.

"It's quite heavy," she said after a beat, Wyn looking at her expectantly. "I don't think I can bring it down myself."

"Did you get it up here?"

"Yes, but—"

"Then, with the two of us, it shouldn't be a problem." The woman moved toward the corner, starting to move things out of her way with relative ease. Meri grimaced behind her back. She really didn't want to be a bother.

"I... I'm not in the same health that I was when I brought it up here," said Meri slowly, watching Wyn for any kind of reaction. The woman looked over her shoulder at Meri curiously. "I wasn't entirely injured anew when Thistle first arrived. He caused a particularly bad flare up in my leg, which regularly pains me, and well..."

"Ah," Wyn nodded sagely, as though she completely understood. "My father has pain like that in his shoulder. A really old injury from when he was a boy — I think he got it from an arrow, but he won't tell the same story about it twice, so I'm not entirely sure if it's that or if he got it from a wild boar when hunting up in Alieweth, which is where he's from. Either way, he's often pained by it so terribly that he can do very little except sit around in a sort of daze from this medicine that the local clerics gave him."

Meri's curiosity instantly piqued. She hadn't ever had experience with any clerics or healers — no matter where in the realm she had been — where they actually were able to help her and her pain. "He went to the clerics, and they helped?"

"Well, he kind of, um, made them help him." Wyn winced. "I never got the full story, but it was something to do with a lot of yelling and blackmail, since they were resistant to him for a long time. He's a bit of a forceful man. And they made it work, though I know he hates the medicine. Says it does something to cloud his mind. Have you been to see any clerics?"

"I did, once," Meri nodded slowly. "I think they gave me something much like what your father takes. I couldn't stomach it."

Wyn nodded. "I believe it. I hated seeing him so… foggy and not himself. But we each do what we can to survive, don't we? Anyways, about the table. I am stronger than I look, so I don't think I'll have much issue with this."

"No, I—"

"What's the harm in trying? I — OH!" Wyn had dislodged one of Meri's old kitchen chairs to reach the table and startled back. "Uh, M-Meriwen, did you know you have a nest of some kind back here? Well, at least I think it's a nest."

"A what?" Meri moved closer and peered over Wyn's shoulder. There was a bundle of old material gathered together, hiding a small hole in the wall. Immediately, as though waiting for her appearance, a small, bright green face with long pointed features that looked vaguely like a hummingbird's poked its head out of the hole and looked up at her.

Wyn squeaked, holding her hands over her mouth, eyes almost comically wide.

Meri simply sighed.

Pixies.

She'd only experienced them once personally, coming across a nest of particularly bothersome ones deep in the Nerian Empire Royal Library — her mother was once allowed to explore the library for an afternoon when Meri discovered the nest behind an old history shelf — but Meri honestly didn't love the idea of coming across them again. They were persnickety and very particular about their way of life, and often wiggled themselves into some of the biggest, best archives and libraries in any realm.

In the tiniest voice that was reminiscent of twinkling bells, the creature spoke. "Ah, you've found us, have you?" The little green faced being sighed, looking distinctly put out. "It's just me here at the moment, I'm afraid. Do you mind if we chat about this, uh, predicament a little later?"

"I — I suppose not, no," said Meri haltingly. "Do you mind me asking, how long have you been living up here?"

"A fair while," answered the pixie airily. "Longer than you'd care to know, I think."

"Right. Well. Okay." Meri's brain felt as though it was wading through mud, trying to compartmentalize all the new information thrown her way recently. Zanve, Thistle, Wyn, and now pixies. "Tomorrow, then?"

"Tomorrow." The pixie ducked its head back into the hole and disappeared.

"Pixies," said Meri under her breath, shaking her head. "Just what I need."

"Pixies?" Wyn looked both nervous and as though she wanted to ask a million questions. "I had no idea they were so verbose. Or existed outside of the fey realm."

"I suppose any creature of the fey realm can exist wherever it likes to, if it has the means," said Meri with a shrug. "For now, though, I'd like to find out more about *that* fey creature," she pointed at Thistle, who was waiting patiently atop a box, "rather than trying to spend time figuring out how those found their way here."

"Right, of course. One thing at a time. First, table."

It took Wyn surprisingly little strength to move the table from its spot, carting the dusty chairs out of the way before she managed to shift the unmovable box at the top of the stairs to the side. Then, as though the table was built of a light alder wood, rather than some of the heaviest, most durable fey realm trees, Wyn hefted it in her arms and carted it out of sight down the stairs.

"Well come on then Meriwen," said Wyn, her smile bright and full of determination as she reappeared and grabbed the stack of chairs. "Let's bring this down to your kitchen and start sorting through these journals. Two heads always work better than one. Plus, I brought some freshly baked bread from Gable's, so we are ready to settle in for a bit of research."

"You can call me Meri."

Wyn quirked an eyebrow at her.

Meri's lips started to quirk up into a smile. "You did just uncover a pixie nest and carry my kitchen table down the stairs for me. And Meriwen can be a mouthful."

20

THE STORM

Zanve

The sun warmed Zanve as he walked through town, despite the chilly breeze that flirted around the stone and wood buildings. The cobblestones under his boots clacked pleasantly as birds chirped above, swooping down between the multicolored flags that stretched above the path. Smaller, twittering forest birds that lingered during the beginning of spring and into summer hopped around the feet of passers-by and up around the eaves of shops around him.

Spring was fully here, now.

The townsfolk of Arrowmount were out in full force today, selling wares, shopping, or simply meandering about in the gloriously beautiful spring day. Zanve breathed in deep, raising his head as the sun hit him, closing his eyes momentarily. He always forgot how much he missed the warmth of the sun throughout the autumn and winter months.

He walked through the town center, bypassing the collection of market stalls bustling with people and instead, he headed through town on

176

a slightly winding route, stopping to purchase the tools that Kaius and Jay had specified the night previous. Both of them, though they didn't spend their days as craftsmen or woodworkers, knew more than enough to make up for Zanve's lack.

Jay, ever the sensible one, had outlined the multitude of uses for a level and a measuring stick, and a proper table or bench for cutting lumber on, assuring this would lead to a much better result than free handing the cuts in the air like Zanve had. Zanve was loathe to admit they had a point.

Jay and Kaius had agreed help complete the project; Jay had a few jobs they had to finish up around town first, but Kaius had agreed to come out today to scope out the greenhouse glass. Zanve could have always asked the Alderidge twins, of course, since they were the best wood workers in town — but, he didn't want to overwhelm Meri with more new people. There was also a little voice in the back of his mind that made him want to keep Meri to himself.

As he walked back through the town center, Zanve noticed how a few heads started to turn his way. He smiled at a few of the townsfolk, nodding hello, before he noticed the way they were looking at him. He caught the eye of Della, one of the pair of elderly gnomes that often frequented the market, as she tapped the shoulder of her wife, bringing Neema's attention to Zanve.

He hesitated, almost walking into a passing birdfolk who ruffled their feathers haughtily at his apology.

Zanve frowned, casting a look around the market, seeing more than a few eyes on him now. Was there something on his face?

He continued on, dropping off his supplies at home, before he headed toward the Old'n Narrow. By the time he got there, low cloud cover had rolled in, lacing the air with a heavy stillness that usually only came with summer storms. He squinted up at the sky. It was far too early in the year for this.

"The weather can't seem to make up its mind, eh?" said a gruff voice from beside Zanve, startling him from his thoughts. He hadn't realized he'd stopped right in front of the bar, looking up at the sky.

"Ah, Chervil, apologies. Coming or going?" Zanve stood aside for the imposing elderly fiendling with incredibly large, heavy blue horns that curled down the back of his head.

"Coming. I've been watching the sea from the top of the lighthouse this morning — do not tell Sage, she'll have a cow if she finds out I've been up there alone, but what else is an old lighthouse keeper to do? Not like she can just pop over from the Caspasian Isles at a moment's notice to help her old granddad." Chervil extended one gnarled, aged dark blue hand and pushed the door open as he talked. "Anyhow. This storm? It's not natural."

Chervil shook his head, horns swaying side to side. They walked into the bar together, Chervil immediately heading to the counter where Briar was, serving a couple patrons.

Zanve stepped up to him, holding up a hand. "Wait — what do you mean by not natural?"

"You felt it too, didn't you? The way the sky is heavy, like a late summer storm. Something's not right about it. In all my years as lighthouse keeper, I have never seen something like this roll in at this time of year." Chervil pointed his finger at the ceiling. "Unnatural."

Zanve leaned into the bar, a little lost for any coherent thoughts. For a moment, his mind went blank.

Unnatural storm... like a late summer storm... *unnatural*...

Did that mean Chervil thought it was *magical*? The gravity of that hit Zanve square in the stomach. He had only read of magical storms in history books, from long ago when the last storms of such ilk had hit the shores of Arrowmount. There wasn't much left of Arrowmount after that.

"We've got to let people know, Chervil. If this storm is unnatural, then—"

"Why do you think I'm here, boy?" The old fiendling eyed him sharply. "Aren't you a town guard?"

Zanve nodded, his shoulders straightening. It was part of his job to protect the town, in any sense of the word. People needed to get inside, seek secure shelter; until the storm passed.

He turned to Briar, who was standing behind the bar, serving customers. "Briar, spread the news. The storm that's coming in is out of season," said Zanve, keeping the word unnatural from the statement. He didn't want to overly panic anyone. "Out of season, something that could be quite dangerous."

Briar's eyebrows rose. "A storm that's out of season?"

"Chervil's never been wrong before," said Zanve, tilting his head to the fiendling.

"Tell everyone you see," said Chervil, turning to walk out. "I should go keep my post. Something's coming."

"Alright," said Briar, looking back at Zanve. "Go find a runner, start telling people outside, I'll cover everyone in here. Folks must have noticed something already; they'll be quick to listen to you."

"Maybe." Living in a seaside town often gave folks a measure of storms, but one could never be too careful.

"Zanve," said Briar, stopping Zanve as he turned from the counter, "you may want to go tell your girl about this." Despite the serious set to her eyebrows, she smiled.

"My... girl?" An image of Meri sprang to mind, but there was no way that Briar could know about her already. Not that Meri was *his* girl, Zanve corrected his errant thoughts. She was just someone he owned a debt to.

Briar was already walking away, so he tucked that thought away to think on later. Skies. He was *really* enjoying being around Meri. Maybe he did want her to be *his girl*.

Zanve stepped back out of the inn, stopping the first few people he saw and passing on the news. He made sure to stress that it was Chervil, the lighthouse keeper, who had brought this news. That made folks straighten and hasten home, waving thanks.

He found a small boy peering into A Second Story, the bookshop, hands in his pockets as though he wasn't entirely sure whether he wanted to go in or stay out on the cobblestones.

"Can you do something for me?" Zanve said, reaching into his pocket and pulling out a silver. The boy's eyes widened, and he nodded fervently. "You look like you have a good set of lungs on you."

"Best in Arrowmount, sir!" answered the boy, projecting his voice so loud that a few folks turning onto the street a number of buildings down looked up in alarm.

"Good. Run to the market and tell everyone you can there's a storm coming. Big, unpredictable — and say that Chervil brings the news."

"Got it." The boy nodded once before he looked back at the bookshop with yearning in his eyes.

"You do know there is a library in the back, for children like you to take books home to read. Words on a promise you'll return them, of course."

The boy's face lit up. "Really, sir?"

"I'm sure Arileas, that's him there with the white hair, will help you out with anything you like. But first, deliver the message."

"Right!" The boy took off running, yelling about the storm.

"You said something about a storm?"

Zanve turned to see the white-haired elf, Arileas Damaris, standing in the doorway to the bookstore. "Yes, Chervil just brought news. Something unnatural about this one. Unseasonable. Make sure to close the shop up tight."

Arileas let out a long sigh of unease and looked up at the sky. "Good to know. Finn?"

"Yes?" came a voice from the far back of the shop.

"Close up, make sure Sophie is safe inside — oh, you already have her, perfect. I'm going to go down to the lighthouse to see if there is anything I can do."

An attractive man appeared between the shelves, carting a tiny brown tabby cat. "What's going on?"

"I'll bring May, she may be able to help with the storm too."

Zanve frowned. "Help with the storm? What are you planning to do?"

"It's not natural, you said? Something about this..." Arileas looked up at the sky and started to pat around his belt. "Skies. Hold on."

The elf reached up and made a quick motion in the air, and a few seconds later a tiny cloth bag came zipping toward him through the shop.

"You think it's magical?" Finnean asked, putting a hand on his partner's shoulder. A thin gold band glinted on his third finger. "Truly?"

"Can't you feel it in the air?"

The moment Arileas said it, Zanve's back erupted in shivers. On instinct, he pulled himself further into the shop as the rain started, all at once like someone had opened up a river in the sky.

"Ah." Finnean hugged the cat tighter to his chest. "Now I do. Be safe, my love."

"Always, darling. Make sure to put up those boards behind the windows, just in case." Arileas kissed his husband before patting the cat between the ears. "Zanve, you can stay here if you like, but if you are going to try and spread the word—"

"I'll come with you." Zanve's mind filled with Meri, wondering if she was experiencing the same onslaught of rain they were. He ducked into the street as the elf conjured a thin stream of magic that fanned out above the two of them, acting as a barrier against the rain. He probably wouldn't be able to get to her in time, and if he was there, what could he possibly do to help?

Arileas' eyes twinkled a little as he looked at Zanve. "You're thinking about that woman I've heard you're with, aren't you? The Witch?"

"I... I am, yes." Zanve shook his head, a little in disbelief, as they walked toward May's Cafe a little way down.

"This town has a way with rumors." Arileas appraised the sky. "You don't think you may want to get to her to help her prepare before the storm hits? I can feel something off about it. Go spread the word — I'll do what I can."

"But—"

The elf looked at him shrewdly. "Is there anything you can do against storms? Magically?"

Zanve glanced away, annoyed. "No, of course not. I'm better off going to help others. Alright, go — go, see what you can do. And good luck."

"You as well." Arileas grasped Zanve's arm before speeding off toward May's.

Zanve took off through the streets, noticing most folks had hidden inside shops and businesses, all of them looking up at the sky with the same unease that was spreading through Zanve's stomach.

It took a second, but now that he was currently being drenched by the rain, he could feel a tiny bit of what he assumed Arileas was talking about when it came to this storm.

It felt much like the air had the other day when the strange, shimmering sky had shone above Arrowmount. There was tension in the air, like something was waiting and watching from somewhere, leaving all the hairs on Zanve's arms standing on end.

He stopped a few times as he ran through the town, ducking his head inside shops to make sure folks knew about the potential severity of the incoming storm. Thankfully, the boy he had recruited had done a fairly good job in spreading the word before the rain had hit.

The sky twisted on itself as Zanve launched through the empty front gate, abandoned by whoever was on watch to find drier ground. The storm picked up speed, turning the sky into an ominous blur of purples and reds. A deep rumbling echoed from somewhere far above. It was unlike anything Zanve had ever seen grace the skies above Arrowmount.

As he ran, Zanve's fingers worked at his shirt and peeled it off over his head before he stopped just a heartbeat to practically jump out of his sodden trousers before he shifted. He grabbed the sopping wet bundle of clothes in his jaws before he sped off into the trees. It was the fastest way to get anywhere; his human form could run quite fast, but nothing could compare to being on four legs.

He crashed through the trees before coming to the edge of Meri's garden. Her cottage blurred through the rain as he shifted back and tried to struggle back into his soaking wet clothes. He only managed to get his pants on before Meri appeared in her doorway and caught sight of him in the trees.

"Zanve?"

He ran to her, ignoring the fact he had his shirt in hand, and pulled her back inside her place. "Stay inside! The storm—"

"I know," she answered, shivering head to toe as though something cold had run down her spine. "And I think I can help."

"You can?" said a familiar voice that Zanve was not expecting to hear. "Why helllll-ooo, Zanve Einar. What are you doing here, rushing in like a knight in shining — or rather, soaking — armor?"

Wyn stood in the middle of Meri's kitchen, her eyes alight with amusement. She quirked an eyebrow and looked Zanve up and down with purpose, before looking at Meri.

"Zanve, you must be freezing," was Meri's only answer, before she hurried off into the depths of her house, skirting around a table that had materialized in the middle of her kitchen, and coming back with a knobbly knitted blanket. She draped it over his shoulders and wrapped it around his chest.

Zanve couldn't speak for a moment, completely caught up in how close she suddenly was to him. This close, he could see the scattering of freckles across her nose and the way her eyelashes dusted down over her cheeks as she fussed at the bits of the blanket around him.

"I'm f-fine," he stammered, trying not to look at Wyn who was probably doing some little suggestive dance or something equally ridiculous in the corner. Keeping his eyes on Meri, trying to not become too captivated by the way her eyebrows were crinkling in concern, he asked, "Wyn, what are you doing here?"

"I'll explain everything in a moment," Meri said for her before she turned to the table and the positively enormous stack of journals atop it. "First, the storm."

"Do you really think you can help whatever this is?" said Wyn. She moved up close to Zanve, peering outside. "Fucking hells, that's... what is going on out there?"

"Chervil and Arileas seem to think the storm is magical. When I told Arileas, he set off with May hoping to stop it. I had no idea wizards could do something like that; but maybe druids can? I don't know much about what May can do."

Meri let out a soft gasp and turned toward the piles of tomes on the table, flipping ferociously.

"May's not that magical, though," said Wyn, biting her lip, eyeing Meri. "I wish I was more attuned to the magic in my veins to help, but I'm at a loss."

"Wish we had an arch mage or something nearby." Arch mages were incredibly skilled magic users that tended to have incredibly strong magical abilities, hence their title. They were rather rare, seeing as it usually took close to centuries to achieve said title. Zanve had only ever read about them in books.

"Huh, yeah, wouldn't that be helpful."

Meri bustled past, tearing Zanve's mind away, her hands furiously working through the book in her hands, hunting for something. "I swear it was in — oh, here!"

Zanve and Wyn stared, nonplussed, as Meri ran her finger along the page, mouthing something under her breath. She looked up, eyes unfocused, as her mouth worked over and over, mouthing the same shape again and again.

He glanced sideways at Wyn. "What—"

Before Wyn could reply, Meri handed the journal to Zanve and stepped out into the storm once again.

"Meri, wait—"

"Let her," said Wyn, pulling him back. "She seems to know what she's doing."

Zanve couldn't help but think of the fact that it was pouring sheets of icy rain, and that Meri was currently barefoot walking across the mud-drenched garden, her hair already plastered to her head, her dress soaked through in an instant. He watched, half in awe and half in panic, as the rain started to swirl outside, mimicking the swirling clouds. Lightning flashed, an unnatural blue. Wyn shuddered beside him.

"What is this storm?" she asked in a whisper, rubbing at her arms hugging herself close.

"I haven't the faintest idea," answered Zanve. "Magic like this... this doesn't feel right."

"It's like something from another world."

They watched Meri stand out in the storm, her hands out at her sides, as she continued to get drenched by the rain. The sky darkened further, casting Meri's garden in an eerie nighttime-like glow. More lightning sparked across the sky, starting up a roiling, constantly churning light show, as the thunder crashed around them.

Between flashes, Meri's arms reached to the sky — and for a moment, Zanve couldn't comprehend what he was seeing.

Meri lifted off the ground as though pulled by puppet strings. The air around her began to glow gold.

Zanve threw off his blanket and flew back out into the storm, toward Meri, despite Wyn's protests. The closer he got, the louder Meri's voice became. Her eyes were closed, and she was chanting something unintelligible over and over, shouting it into the sky. The glow around her increased. Thin tendrils of pure golden light began to twist themselves around Meri's arms, threading themselves around and around until they wove into each other. Zanve circled a garden box, pacing like an anxious cat. He watched in a mixture of fear and awe as the continuously weaving tendrils started to rise off of Meri, heading toward the churning storm.

Then—

Time stretched as though it was something tangible.

Meri's eyes snapped open, staring into nothingness, that same bright golden light shining from them. The golden tendrils combined above her and shot skyward, piercing the clouds. Everything exploded in light, and for a moment, Zanve couldn't help but shield his eyes against the brilliance.

With a soft gasp, Meri crumpled gracefully down to the ground as the world turned dark once more. Zanve caught her as she fell, wrapping his arms around her. Her eyes blinked rapidly, still bright pools of gold. It felt as though she was buzzing under his touch, as though whatever power she had channeled was still there, churning under her skin. Her hands grasped onto his arms like she was trying to ensure that he was actually there.

Her eyes blinked a few times, each time the light in them dimming back to her usual soft brown.

"Oh," she said softly, then, realizing he was holding her. Her eyes traced his face before they looked beyond him, up to the roiling sky above. "Well, hopefully that helped."

Zanve glanced up, too, as he brought her back to standing, making sure she was steady on her feet. From here, he couldn't see the town or any kind of tumult by the lighthouse; he couldn't even begin to picture what was happening down there, with Arileas and the others trying to quell the storm.

Here, in Meri's garden, the storm began to break. Where the golden magic pierced the sky above, the churning clouds had started to pull back, leaving the sun shining behind them.

"That was..." Zanve shook his head, gazing back at Meri, who was still clutching his arms. He found her already looking at him, as though she was studying his every feature. "That was unlike anything I have ever witnessed, Meri."

"I guess we have my grandmother to thank for that one." She shook her head slowly. "I—"

Wyn chose that moment to yell, "would you two please come out of the rain so you don't *freeze* and catch your *death?* You're both soaked! And Zanve, for all the pantheon's sake, you're not even wearing a *shirt.*"

21

BORROWED TROUSERS

Meriwen

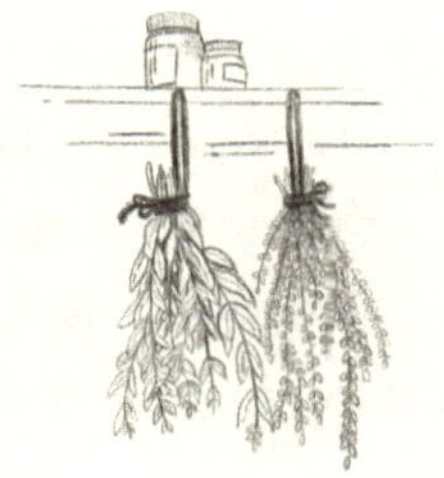

Meri wrung rainwater out of her hair onto her front stoop once the rain fully stopped. "Zanve, put your clothes out on the floor in my bedroom, I will get them dried in a moment."

After Meri's spell had pierced the churning storm, the clouds had retreated across the sky, leaving a brilliantly sunny day behind. As though nothing had happened at all.

"And what in all of Ravar are you going to wear instead?" hissed Wyn from her spot next to a Meri's mother's journals, quiet enough that Meri figured she thought only Zanve could hear her. "Meri's old garden jacket?"

"That is unfortunately soaked through," said Meri, handing Zanve the blanket he'd dropped on a nearby chair. Zanve's cheeks were pink. "There's this, but I'll hunt for some trousers that may be big enough for you."

Meri produced a pair of handmade trousers that were cinched in at the

189

ankle from the bottom of her clothes cupboard. It was an old pair that she had made about a decade ago in an attempt to 'try something new,' but never fell to liking the style very much. They fit Zanve for the most part; but they were rather tight in the thighs and behind. She hoped he wasn't uncomfortable — they were all she had.

She quickly changed into one of her favorite yellow dresses and ran out to her laundry line with both her and Zanve's clothing, hoping that the sun would at least dry them slightly.

She brushed her hands along her arms as she returned to her kitchen. Her skin was still tingling, as though the magic that had coursed through her from the ley lines was still skating across the surface. The hairs along her arms stood up and she shivered involuntarily as she sank into one of her kitchen chairs.

Zanve gestured to the table full of journals, blanket still wrapped around his chest. "What is all this?"

Meri laid her hand protectively atop the nearest one. "My mother's journals."

"You should see the whole collection, Zanve," said Wyn emphatically. "The entirety of Meri's second floor is filled with them. They're all full of research and her experiences — exploring everything from our realm to the shadow realm to the fey realm and others I can't even name!"

Zanve blinked in surprise. "How old is your mother? How has she had the time to travel that much?"

"That's a good question, actually." Meri frowned, wondering. From what she understood, hundreds of years — at least. "I'm not exactly sure. But, us fey have a rather longer life expectancy than regular mortals. Rivalling those of elven descent, I think."

"I've heard arch fey can live much longer than even the oldest elf, so you'd probably be right," nodded Wyn.

"Your mother..." said Zanve, gazing at the journals around him before flipping open the nearest one. "She really wrote all of these?"

"Yes," said Meri simply.

"And why—"

"Meri was looking for information on Thistle," said Wyn, motioning to the creature, who was bundled in the corner, snoozing comfortably now that the storm was over.

"I thought, also, I could maybe understand a bit more about..." Meri bit her lip, looking between Zanve and Wyn for a moment, then decided to change tactics. "I was looking through the spells in here. They're technically my grandmother's spells — but my mother Elestren wrote them — okay."

At Zanve and Wyn's twin expressions of blankness, Meri sighed and put both hands on the table in front of her.

"My grandmother is something special in the fey realm, someone we call a Keeper. She knows a lot about spell work, rituals, the crafting of magic and manipulation of power. My mother, Elestren, is called a Realmstrider, someone who can create doorways to pass through to other realms and planes of existence. I knew that my grandmother had once sat my mother down to teach her a variety of spells. Or at least, to *try* to teach her. My mother doesn't have a knack for spell work unless it is directly related to her realm travel.

"But, Elestren recorded everything, even what my grandmother tried to teach her, even if she was unable to do the spells. And so..." Meri gestured to the journal pile in front of her. "She wrote them down. These spells go far beyond what my grandmother taught me."

Zanve nodded in understanding. "Is your grandmother the one that taught you magic, too?"

"Of course," Meri answered. "She taught me all I know."

Wyn tapped a finger along the journal that still lay open to the spell that Meri had used to quell the storm outside. "So spells like this one—"

"That one's not anything like I know." Meri drew the book closer to her, running a finger along the tight lettering and shook her head. "I didn't even know this kind of magic was possible."

"And you just decided to try it out?" Zanve raised his eyebrows and let out a low whistle.

"I saw it when I was flipping through to look for anything related to my mother's doorway spells, and it stuck in my mind," she answered with a shrug. Her eyes caught on Zanve's, but she kept quiet.

"It was fucking glorious, if I don't say so myself," said Wyn with a laugh. "Like the veritable Maigsir came back to Ravar. You should really test out more of the magic in these journals. See what else you can do."

"Wyn," said Zanve softly.

"What? If your grandmother taught your mother, what's the harm?"

Meri simply chuckled. "Let's see if we can make any headway on the Thistle issue first. You can help me look through some of these as we wait for our clothes to dry."

"I should really get back, I should have made at least two batches of jam by this point," said Wyn as she made her way out of Meri's front door a couple of hours later, laden with a bundle of tea and fresh herbs.

Thistle followed her out, playfully chasing her feet as Wyn jumped back and forth, laughing all the while. She waved back at the cottage. "See you! Let me know if you find *anything*."

Zanve moved to stand, preparing to leave as well. Meri's mind churned. Maybe he could help her puzzle out a few things.

"Zanve, before you go, I wanted to talk through my theory about Thistle."

He settled back into his kitchen chair and leaned forward, eyes focused entirely on her.

"You saw Thistle come through the doorway, right?'

"I did, partially," he answered. "I didn't get a good look at the rock, though. The thing that exploded."

"It was weirdly pitted and lighter than a stone that size should have been — and too small to be a housing egg of sorts for Thistle." Meri held up her hands to demonstrate the size, which was much smaller than Thistle was when he came through. "I went back to the clearing to collect the pieces, the day you were trying to start rebuilding my greenhouse."

"Trying is a word for it, but I'd go with *failing*."

She chuckled and turned, pulling a small plant pot from her shelf that rattled when she lifted it. Carefully, she withdrew chunks of Thistle's stone. "These pieces have residual magic very similar to my mother's."

"The Realmstrider magic?"

"It's not quite the same, but it has the same... flavor of fey magic that I recognize from my mother's spells. That is why I went hunting through her journals for some kind of explanation, and to see if she had any information about creatures from the fey realm."

"Did you find anything?"

"The spells, I have to do more research on; but my theory is that this stone acted as a gateway, somehow. When I was in the clearing, it was as though Thistle was speaking to me already, from wherever he was. He — or rather, someone? I don't know if Thistle is intelligent enough to have done this — guided me through this incredibly complex ritual that brought him through."

Zanve hesitated, frowning. "He spoke to you?"

"Something like it. There's... it's fine," she said, shaking her head and brushing the topic aside. Her face heated as she realized how much she'd been talking. She shouldn't have asked him to stay back; she could figure this out on her own. She didn't want to waste his time.

"I would like to know, if you want to tell me."

Meri stopped. She sat back in her chair and held her breath before letting it out in one long sigh. Did he really mean that? Did he truly care that much about her and Thistle, who had been practical strangers to him only a few weeks ago? Or was this just him being polite? His face was, as always, open and interested, his kind eyes locked onto her own. They were a rich blue, almost the color of the sea in a storm.

"Thistle spoke to you," he prompted, leaning closer to her.

Meri hesitated only a moment before she launched into an explanation of how the night of the ritual had gone before Zanve had shown up; everything from the way the stone had pulled on her as though through an invisible tether, before taking over and walking her bodily through the ritual.

"The outline of a door that appeared along the ground before Thistle came through and I was knocked unconscious." Meri traced it in the air with her fingers. "Like an arch, a gateway."

Zanve held the shard up. "I bet this was a conduit to help Thistle cross over. But why, though?"

"That is the question, isn't it?"

The two of them glanced at the creature, who was sitting in the kitchen doorway, looking out across the garden a king overlooking his kingdom.

"I think the answers will come with understanding what he is," said Meri softly.

"Would your mother have any insight on that?"

Meri sighed, shaking her head. "My mother was incredibly thorough and expertly recorded many things — especially when it came to realms other than our own. But there is very little about the fey realm itself in any of her journals."

"Sometimes we think the most highly of what is elsewhere, rather than where we're from," said Zanve. "We don't often think our homes need to be studied like that. It's a comfort, mostly, no?"

"I never thought of it that way," said Meri, turning the idea around in her mind. "I always thought she hated being there, always wanting to go off to another realm, studying, discovering, and meeting new people."

Meri looked up to find Zanve studying her face. The way he looked at her made her stomach clench. She had no idea what to do with the softness in his eyes, or the interested focus he had placed on her. No one had ever really paid attention to her or what she had to say like this, not even her grandmother. Seraph was one to teach, never one to truly listen unless she chose to.

Zanve cleared his throat and turned his attention down to the journal in front of him. For a moment, the two of them sat in silence, flipping through Elestren's journals together.

"I may know another place where you can get information about fey creatures," he said slowly, breaking the amiable silence. Meri blinked up at him from the journal she had been skimming through.

"A Second Story? I thought of visiting the bookstore to see if they had anything of notice, but haven't had the energy to walk all the way down into town yet."

"There, yes, but — I should have mentioned before, but I met a Scholar the other day. One from Pralon; they brought an assistant and everything."

"Oh?"

"They said they were studying an event that happened here, something that felt as though something had come through a portal, if I remember correctly. Something that came through from the fey realm."

Meri's eyes went wide. There was no doubt in her mind that it was Thistle's arrival that had alerted the Royal Scholars. Root and ruin— "Zanve, why didn't you tell me this before?"

"It completely slipped my mind!" Zanve held up his hands in defense. "I apologize, I completely forgot to bring it up."

"It's alright," said Meri, distracted. A Scholar? In Arrowmount? If Thistle coming through was big enough to trigger Scholars all the way from Pralon feeling it... what in all the realms was he?

Meri glanced at Thistle, fear trickling through her. If he was that powerful, not only to cause damage to her greenhouse but to be able to walk between realms... "If anyone from town finds out about Thistle, what will they do?"

Zanve shook his head slowly. "I honestly don't know. Perhaps take him; lock him away from you."

Meri shuddered at the thought of the creature being taken from her, perhaps all the way to Pralon to be studied. She didn't want to even entertain the idea. "But if they are a Fey Scholar, perhaps they know more than the average fey realm person," she murmured, thinking ahead to what the scholar could answer for her.

"They won't *hurt* Thistle, I can say that for sure," said Zanve. "Scholar Sarrai Daruka is quite kind, from what I gather. And has a penchant for cherry wine."

"It's not the Scholar I'm worried about," Meri said after a moment. "It's the rest of the town. What if they find out about him and don't want him here? What if they think he's dangerous?"

"What could they do, anyway, come out in a mob?" Zanve chuckled, gesturing to Thistle, who was back in the corner, sleeping. "Besides, they can't be scared of him. Look at how small he is — completely harmless!"

"Harmless." Meri chewed her lip. "I don't know if my greenhouse would agree with that. And he's already three times his size he was before. How much bigger will he grow?"

"True. How about this—" Zanve took one of Meri's hands in his, leaning across the table. She looked at it, wondering briefly how a human's hands could be so warm. "Let's figure out what Thistle is first, and then we can worry about what all that comes with. We'll know more about what to expect when we know more about him."

Meri slowly started to nod. "Yes. You're right. Would… would you be open to meeting with the scholar first? To see if they would be a good source of information on this?" She held her breath, knowing she was asking him for a lot.

"Absolutely," said Zanve without hesitation.

A little while later, Meri couldn't control the yawns any more. She tried to swallow them, but the exhaustion was pulling her down again. Zanve made his excuses, and once Meri retrieved his shirt and trousers from the line — finding they were still damp, but he didn't complain — he donned them and left.

Thistle followed Zanve across the garden as he had Wyn, the little creature gamboling about in the late afternoon sunshine. Zanve bent and played with him for a few moments, laughing.

Zanve turned back to the small cottage halfway through her garden.

"What about the other thing you mentioned that you were looking for? In your mother's journals?"

"It's… nothing." Meir leaned against her doorframe, easing weight off of her right leg. She wasn't entirely sure if she wanted to tell him that *she* was the reason the magic was unbalanced in Arrowmount. What if he started to believe that she was something evil? Something that lived up to the moniker of The Witch? Worse, what if he looked at her with disappointment or hatred?

She knew somewhere deep down that these were baseless anxieties, but she couldn't help but wonder — but *what if?*

"Alright," said Zanve. "Let me know if you do find whatever you're looking for. And what it's about. Or, if you need help puzzling it out. But if it really is nothing." He shrugged playfully.

She couldn't help but smile. A small part of her hoped — perhaps *knew* — he would never believe those things about her. Zanve had already shown that he was incredibly kind, and didn't seem the type to judge without hearing her side of things. If she told him, he would probably sit in her kitchen all season, helping her figure out how to fix the magic once more, how to get her stores back in order, or how to get a hold of her grandmother or mother.

Meri would tell him, she decided. But not quite yet.

As Zanve walked from her garden and vanished into the trees, Meri looked up at the now cloudless sky.

What a day it had been.

PART THREE

Spring

22

THINK OF FLOWERS

Zanve

The following day, Zanve walked through Arrowmount on his way to Kaius' family forge, eyeing the buildings to make sure nothing had suffered any damage from the storm. Thankfully, from the looks of it, and from the talk that swirled through the town, whatever Arileas, May, and a few others had managed to do magically had protected the buildings along the coastline from any terrible damage. No one in town had known how to calm the storm itself, though; everyone believed that it had simply gone away on its own.

No one seemed to have noticed the giant beam of light coming from the forest, north east of the stables.

Zanve waved down a runner and handed them a missive to send off to Sarrai at Lord Wymarc's manor, asking to meet for tea in a few days.

He kept walking until the crowds of people thinned into a small trickle and eventually died, leaving him the only one remaining on the cobblestone streets as he approached the Miirthgrove glass factory. The lone structure billowed steam into the air from a number of vents, a column of white against a cloudless blue sky. It was set away from other buildings, as it used to be rather a dangerous place to be around, before Kaius' grandparents had installed a cooling system within the walls and floors, making the entire production facility much safer in all aspects. It also helped in the making of the glass; those who worked here were able to cool the glass inside the facility.

A large water wheel was built outside, turning relentlessly with sea water. It acted as both the energy to fuel the glass forge inside and brought water into cooling pipes that ran throughout the facility inside.

Zanve had been let inside the factory a few times when he was younger, but he never really liked it; the intense heat that clouded every inch of the place was too much, despite the cooling system. Even simply looking at the factory, a haze lingered across its surface, warping the facade slightly. Zanve stayed across the street from it, where the sea breeze chilled his skin.

The ocean beyond rushed quietly, waves low and calm, the sound instantly causing Zanve's shoulders to relax.

"Zanve!"

He held up a hand in greeting as a figure stepped out of a side door of the Miirthgrove glass factory. Kaius' large rock frame lumbered out toward him. Thick molten cracks ran all through Kaius' body, a deep shining orange-white light emanating from deep within him. He wore only a pair of rather burnt and crusted-over trousers, and carried a thick canvas bag over one shoulder.

"Give me just a mo'," called Kaius, motioning to the side. Zanve walked at an angle to meet him, and watched, amazed as always, as Kaius' body changed in front of his eyes. The glowing fissures along Kaius' chest and arms closed, cooling and hardening over, until Kaius was mostly midnight-black stone with only the occasional thread-thin fissure breaking through. Kaius began to rummage through his canvas bag, unearthing one of his nicer button-down shirts, and a proper pair of trousers.

"Busy day?"

"Eh, the forge is working as normal despite the storm," said Kaius with a shrug, sliding off his trousers after a quick glance around the deserted area, stepping deftly into the unmarred ones. "Though there was a problem with the eastern pipes, again."

"Gramps hasn't figured out a way to unclog that yet?"

"No," sighed Kaius, sliding the button-down on, speedily running his fingers through the buttons. "For some reason, that one pipe just acts strange, whether it's because of the water or the way the sea rises. I have no idea how to fix it, but I'm starting to think we're going to have to hire a mage to help magic a solution. It ended up backing up so bad at midnight that we had to clear out the factory, it was too hot to keep working, even for us."

Zanve whistled low. He couldn't imagine how hot that would have been.

"Anyways." Kaius slung the canvas bag back over his shoulder, standing up straight and giving Zanve a smile. The bag clanked mutedly, something heavy and metal inside shifting. "Off to the Witch's, eh?"

"To see Meriwen, yes," Zanve corrected as the two set off. "I think you'll be surprised at how much damage there is."

Kaius snorted. "You told me it was a small creature. How bad could it really be?"

"Well." Zanve lifted his eyebrows and shook his head. "You'll see what I mean. Thistle is something else."

Kaius mouthed the word Thistle, looking sideways at Zanve. After a moment, he stopped Zanve with a hand.

"What?" Zanve ran a hand over his shirt, wondering if something was out of place or he forgot to do up a button.

"Your eyes." Kaius narrowed his own to peer closer at Zanve. "I've never seen them this color before."

Zanve blinked and looked to the side, as though he could see his own eyes. "What do you mean?"

"They look purple, almost. Sort of blue, sort of not. Like they don't really know what color to be."

Huh. Zanve shrugged. "I couldn't tell you why, I feel normal."

Kaius smiled, a soft chuckle escaping his chest. "Whatever it means, I guess we'll find out, eh? Let's go see this W— sorry, Meriwen."

"So, are you going to tell me anything more about Meriwen, or are you just going to stare off into the distance and walk so fast that I'm basically running to keep up with you?"

Zanve's attention snapped back to Kaius, remembering where he was. Kaius laughed, slapping Zanve across the back with a large hand as Zanve consciously slowed down.

"There isn't really much to tell."

Kaius's eyes flickered with amusement. "You were moving so fast I'm not sure you weren't trying to leave me behind."

Zanve laughed, shoving Kaius with his shoulder.

"Should I be worried? Is she going to go and steal our beloved Zanve Einar out from under us? Bury him in the backyard so he can be eaten by worms and such?"

"All I've been doing is going to help fix parts of her greenhouse," Zanve said, though he knew that something inside of him wanted to be at Meri's cottage for more than simply fixing her greenhouse. He kept finding himself daydreaming about having tea with her. "Besides, if she steals me away, Wyn will probably come rampaging out there just to bring me home."

Kaius smiled fondly. "Yeah, she would."

"She was at Meri's yesterday, when the storm hit," said Zanve. "I think she went over just to try to befriend Meri, but ended up staying and getting pulled into a new mystery."

"That's my Wyn," chuckled Kaius.

"Ey, Einar!"

Zanve's skin crawled, immediately knowing who was calling his name as the two of them approached the front gates.

"I've heard some pretty interesting news about our favorite wonder boy," said Damian as he leaned against the stone gate, crossing his arms and looking all too smug. He looked over his shoulder at Quinlan, who was accompanying him on guard. Quinlan shot Zanve a look and rolled his eyes.

Zanve sighed.

"There's a little rumor floating around that you're practically falling over yourself for the Witch of the Woods," sneered Damian, missing Quinlan's look. "You're going up there every day at this point, no? What, does she have you under some kind of spell? You can't have that many things to do at her place, unless..." he looked suggestively at Zanve, wiggling his eyebrows, before his attention caught on Kaius. "She must be absolutely *on fire* in the sheets, if you catch my meaning."

"Fuck off," Kaius grumbled, his body starting to smoke.

"This makes sense though," said Damian, gesturing between the two of them, "bringing him along, Einar. I wasn't entirely sure if you swung that way, but seeing as you're always with Wyn, makes sense. Just bringing more weirdos into your little nest, eh, Miirthgrove?"

Kaius took a menacing step forward, but Zanve put up a hand.

"You're just mad that Zanve is getting more action than you are," piped up Quinlan.

Damian's sneer flickered as he turned his ire on Quinlan and Kaius. "At least I'm *loyal*. I only need one partner to satisfy me."

Zanve's fury boiled in his chest. "You're purposely being dense. You know very well that that's not how polyamory works."

"He's just jealous that he can't even find one partner to love him," grumbled Kaius, a cruel smile on his face. His body started to crack open, his shirt and trousers threatening to burn off him. Zanve's hands began to smart where he was holding Kaius back, but he didn't let go. "Back off, rat boy."

"So you're not bringing rock boy to the Witch to...? Oh, okay, sure," said Damian, scoffing as though he didn't believe it.

"Meri," Zanve corrected, his voice nothing more than a growl now.

"*Meerrrri*. Is that what you call her? You don't call her baby, or Meri dear? Dearest darling? Apple of my eye?" Damian laughed, the sound awful and forced. "I know what I would call her if I got in her in my bed."

Without realizing that he had let go of Kaius, Zanve lunged. A surge of animalistic anger roared out of him as the pale man laughed, Damian's face contorting in a grotesque smile. The panther in Zanve's blood threatened to bubble up and out, straining at his skin.

"Enough," Zanve said, his voice coming out half growl. He grabbed the man by the front of his guard uniform and slammed him into the stone wall behind them. Damian's face flickered with shock as he took in Zanve's face. Briefly, Zanve could see the man's fear, but then, as though finding himself dangling in the air by his throat was an everyday occurrence, he started to sneer.

"Zanve," said Kaius, his hand closing on Zanve's shoulder. "He's not worth it."

"Easy, boy," Damian crooned. "What kind of beast do you make yourself out to be? Some big bad wolf out here, protecting your damsel in distress?"

Blood pounded behind Zanve's ears, the panther crawling at his throat. He could feel his teeth elongating as he snarled at the man. "ENOUGH."

"Or what? What exactly would you do if I happened to go visit the Witch? You said it yourself — you're only there to fix her greenhouse. Perhaps she'd like a visit from a real man, eh? Not some... *mutt*."

"Zanve," Kaius said, squeezing his shoulder.

Zanve blinked slowly before he shoved Damian bodily away from him, not caring how hard it was. Quinlan muttered a curse from behind them, but Zanve barely heard it. Instead, he simply breathed in long and slow, knowing very well that his eyes were probably a burning, simmering crimson, and he didn't really care.

"I'm going to kill him," he said softly as Kaius steered him away from the gate and toward the forest. He looked down at his hands, curled into such tight fists that it took him a moment to realize they had partially transformed into paws, his razor-sharp claws threatening to break through the skin of his palms.

"Yes, well, I'd rather you not do it at the gates to town," said Kaius. "And please do something about your eyes, they're fucking terrifying. Think about flowers or something."

He had half a mind to make a snappy comment, but Zanve breathed through his nose and out his mouth, thinking of flowers. Flowers that grew in wild patches along the edge of a lovely, cultivated garden, lavender and beautiful marigolds and roses and daisies and many more he couldn't name, all tended by a gentle hand.

Meri.

"Now that's even more terrifying," breathed Kaius, looking at him sideways, the two of them coming to a halt in the middle of the road. "Your eyes have never changed that fast."

"What?"

"They were glowing coals of fire like, a second ago. Now? Back to that purple blue. What did you do?"

Zanve shrugged, shaking his head, looking down at his hands, which were no longer clawed. Zanve ran his tongue over his teeth, feeling them recede back to their normal size. "I thought of flowers, like you said."

Kaius sighed, letting go of Zanve's arm and settling a hand on his shoulder. "Listen. I know Damian is an ass, but he's harmless. The man can't do anything except get under your skin."

"He's particularly good at that."

"Apparently. I've never seen you break like that around him." Kaius eyed him carefully. "I know you've heard it a million times, and not just from me. But try not to let him get to you, okay? He's a flea."

"Right. Yeah. You're right. Gods, sorry, Kai." Zanve ran his hand over his face, trying to wipe away the simmering unease still sitting under his skin.

Kaius chuckled and stepped back. "It was a damn treat to see him get thrown on his ass like that, the smarmy bastard. But I'd rather not see him maimed, alright?"

"Right."

"Keep thinking of those flowers."

23

FIRST, TEA

Meriwen

Meri leafed through yet another of her mother's journals, hoping with each page that the spell she was looking for would appear. But, no matter how many storm-quelling spells or snow-conjuring ones she came across, there wasn't a mention of any cross-realm communication anywhere. Granted, she did have a couple of other journals to go through, but her hopes were low.

She laid the journal down on her kitchen table with a sigh, deciding to head out into her garden to clear her head.

Thistle bristled at her side, his attention catching at something that Meri couldn't see or hear. Meri hesitated as her fingers reached toward the patch of lavender, about to begin assessing the plants.

"What is it?" she said, glancing around her garden. Lock was snoozing on her garden chair, as usual; wisps of steam curled out from his nostrils contentedly. Birds flitted between the trees, a few of the regular deer and rabbits hovered along the tree line; but nothing out of the ordinary.

Thistle stood a touch straighter, eyes locked on a part of the forest that

209

Meri usually took to get to the main road into town. She withdrew her hands, watching Thistle and listening for any noise.

It took a few moments, but distantly, she could hear a set of feet walking toward her garden through the trees. The footfalls were incredibly heavy, as though the being coming through the trees was vast and large, like a giant only seen in the depths of the tundra or desert.

"Hello?" Meri called, a thread of fear coursing through her. Thistle was still visible; his entire back was flared out with his feathers, everything puffed up to make himself look bigger than he usually was. Then, as though he was locked in on some new sound, his body hesitated, then completely relaxed before he bounded forward on the path.

What in all the realms—

A voice called through the trees, ahead of the footsteps. "Meri!"

Zanve.

Meri couldn't help the small smile spread across her face, despite her confusion at the weight and heaviness of the footfall. That wasn't the same as Zanve's usual gait; she listened harder, finally picking out his much lighter tread.

Zanve stepped through the forest with a bright smile on his face. He swiped his hair back from his face, his cheeks a soft pink.

His companion emerged through the branches behind him, at first looking like an enormous, heavy shadow; then it peeled away, revealing a second person made entirely of stone.

Meri waved to them, feeling slightly foolish at how scared she'd felt. There would never be any giants here, that was for sure.

"Meri," said Zanve again, before gesturing to the second person. "This is Kaius Miirthgrove. Kai, this is Meriwen."

"Pleasure," said Kaius, his voice rumbling and low, like stones colliding. As he extended his hand to shake, Meri noticed the cracks in his skin, a hue of molten orange leaking out .

"Welcome to my garden," she answered, shaking his hand without hesitation. His hand was warm, but the stone was as cool to the touch as any skin would be. Kaius looked slightly impressed, as though that wasn't usually the reaction folks had when grabbing his hand.

"Hello," said Zanve, bending to scratch Thistle behind his head. "Kaius, this is—"

"Thistle," said Kaius, interrupting with a knowing smile. He bent at the knee and held out a hand toward Thistle. "I promise I come with no harm intended to your home, little guard."

The little fey creature narrowed his eyes as he studied Kaius, but approached all the same. He gently sniffed at Kaius' fingers, before his whole body relaxed, feathers dropping back into place. Thistle sat, then, looking at Kaius curiously.

"You haven't seen many people that are as rocky as me, hey?" Kaius chuckled, reaching forward and rustling Thistle's feathers. "Doesn't mean I can't still be gentle."

Thistle melted under his touch.

"He likes you," said Meri, feeling, through their bond, how the fey creature warmed with pleasure.

"Not many people dislike Kaius after meeting him properly," said Zanve, slapping his friend on the back. "We're here to take a look at those greenhouse windows that need replacing."

"Of course."

Meri gestured toward the building, where Kaius immediately headed. She showed him around the exterior of the greenhouse first, motioning to the panes that needed to be replaced. The fire elemental whistled low, shaking his head at the destruction as he lowered himself to examine the panes closer.

"I have never seen anything like this happen to our glass. Even when hit with magic, it can crack; but this is…"

"Something else entirely," said Meri low, looking at the little fey creature who was laying in the long grass once again, eyes tracking the progress of a beetle flying near him. "I don't truly know what he is, but if my suspicions are correct, he's fey, like me."

"Do you know much about fey creatures?" asked Kaius as he turned his head to look at her, remaining crouched by the greenhouse.

"Not really, no." Meri glanced at Zanve. "We were trying to discover what he was, possibly using some old research of my mothers, but there wasn't… there isn't anything about fey creatures."

"I was going to ask that Scholar, you remember Kai—"

"The one from the Narrow?"

"Yes, them. I sent a note over this morning to the Lord's manor, hoping that Scholar Daruka would be interested in having tea."

Kaius turned back to the glass for a moment, frowning, before reaching forward. The tips of his fingers started to glow a scalding red before he gently ran them across the outside of the pane, the glass melting beneath his touch. With ease, he popped it out into his hands, as his skin settled back to solid rock.

"I think it would be incredibly beneficial to have that Scholar on your side," he said. "But I also think, whatever this is and whatever's going on; all of it — the Scholar turning up, Thistle, the strange magic about town. It's all connected."

Meri breathed in and slowly nodded. *Too right you are,* she thought, trying to control the anxiety that rose again, knowing that the magic and the storm were entirely her fault.

If she hadn't missed the ritual…

Zanve, she noticed, was watching her with a quiet intensity, as though he knew she wasn't saying everything on her mind. She could almost feel his eyes tracking her, and to her surprise, it sent a soft thrill down into her stomach.

She looked away, her cheeks warming, and turned her attention to the pane of glass in Kaius' hands. It was holding together, but close up and with the afternoon light hitting it at this angle, Meri could see the thousands of striations that were embedded in the very make up of the glass — as though whatever Thistle had done had not simply shattered the glass; it had taken the glass apart so thoroughly all over the pane it was obliterated. There was also no singular place of impact; it had completely shattered all over.

"How is that holding itself together?" she breathed, running a single finger over the pane. She could feel the irregularities along the surface as she did so, skating against her skin like a cat's tongue.

"Pressure, I would think." Kaius gestured to the thick bead of glass that was nearly cooled along the entire edge. "Glass is my specialty, after all. If you don't mind, I'm going to take this pane back with me to the forge; I think that my family would be incredibly interested to see what happened here."

"I..." Meri glanced worriedly toward Thistle. "I don't know if others should know about him. The more who do, the more widely known he is — we don't even know *what* he is — the more likely they will find out how destructive he was. I think that he would be seen with fear."

"I will make sure to keep Thistle out of the conversation," said Kaius, eyeing the pane. "I think most of my family will be more interested in looking at the structural aspects of the actual pane than wondering how it happened. If anything, it is far more believable that an errant forest animal got in and wrecked the place."

"Thank you," said Meri, breathing a sigh of relief.

He smiled then, the stiff peaks of his face cracking and shifting into an incredibly pleasant expression, but his eyes were no longer on her; they passed over to Zanve.

Meri let Kaius take stock of what else needed fixing in her greenhouse, measuring and noting each and every pane that needed replacing. He took a moment to marvel at the mechanism that Meri had installed in her greenhouse that allowed her to lower the topmost windows at an angle, letting in fresh air.

After a few minutes, Meri retreated to her kitchen with the design to make them all a drink. She was still rather new to this hosting thing, and having both Wyn visit yesterday and Kaius today — she wasn't entirely sure if she could keep this up, chatting with new people all the time. Root and ruin, even Caelynn had come to visit recently. If it hadn't been for Zanve—

And then there was Zanve. He was an entirely different entity, one that was making her feel rather... unsettled? No, that wasn't the right word, because it was a pleasant sort of unsettled. Unmoored. As though the ground beneath her bare feet was starting to swell and shift whenever he looked at her. He always seemed to be looking at her lately, with this soft expression on his face — and he wanted to know things, constantly asking her questions and eager to hear her thoughts. It felt as though he could actually see *her*, not just what people wanted to see when they glanced her way.

It *was* quite unsettling to be seen.

"Meri," Zanve said, ducking into her kitchen, jarring her from her thoughts. "Are you alright?"

"Y-yes, I just came in... to make some tea," she said, motioning to the three mugs now set before her. When had she taken those out? "Any requests?"

"Whatever you recommend."

She swallowed and busied herself with making lemongrass tea as he settled against her counter, his eyes tracking her movements.

Meri didn't have enough experience with other people to tell. All her life, she'd either been a shadow of her mother as they traveled the realms or a small addition to her grandmother's garden as the elder Keeper taught her all she knew. Even here in Arrowmount, she only needed to talk to her animals and the occasional townsperson — she didn't know, really, how to spend time with someone.

Was that something you learned, or were you born with the ability to easily converse with others? To be able to tell what someone's intentions were?

Why don't you just ask him?

The water had reached boiling point behind her by the time she turned to fully look at him. The fact that he was already looking at her made her hesitate for only a moment. A soft fluttering echoed at the base of her throat, an entirely new sensation.

Could she just ask?

"You have something on your mind," he said, eyes tracing her face. "I'm always here to listen, if you wish to tell me."

"Do you truly like hearing about the things going on in my mind, or are you just being nice?"

The words had escaped her before she could stop them. She froze, wondering if she had overstepped.

Zanve rose and came behind the counter, taking one of Meri's hands — the one that wasn't currently holding her pestle aloft — gently. "Meri, I sincerely want to know everything that you think about. I would sit and talk with you for days, weeks, forever if I could. I find it all fascinating."

"Fascinating?" she repeated.

"You, what you do here. Your life. Your creatures. Your teas. Every little bit of it." His eyes were shimmering in the sunshine streaming in from her kitchen windows and had turned almost the exact same shade as the lavender that was growing outside. "Especially you, though."

"Your eyes are purple," she said, the only thing she could think to say as her stomach flipped around on itself.

"It's a recent development. I don't really know why they're doing that," he answered, his voice soft.

Before she could get any more flustered, she looked down at his hand still holding hers. His thumb was running along the back of her knuckles, sending shivers up her spine.

"I have a theory — no, not a theory," Meri breathed in, acutely aware of how warm his hand was, and steadied herself. "I *know* why the magic in Arrowmount has gone all... odd."

Zanve hesitated. His eyes sharpened on her face. "You do?"

Nothing for it now.

"I'm the reason. It's all tied with Thistle, though not purposefully on his account." She glanced outside, noticing Kaius' form exiting her greenhouse and starting toward the house. She'd forgotten he was here. "I'll tell you more, later. Let's... let's have some tea, first."

24

BALANCE

Meriwen

After Kaius had gone back to Arrowmount with all he needed to start fixing her greenhouse windows, Meri brewed more tea just for something to do with her hands. It was time that she told Zanve everything about what she had done — disrupting the magical balance — and what she did as a Keeper.

Meri handed Zanve his mug and took a steadying breath. "Have I ever told you why I moved to Arrowmount?"

I don't believe you have, no," Zanve answered, taking a sip of the tea. They were surrounded by her mother's journals, sitting at Meri's kitchen table once again. "I don't really even remember when you moved here, you were always here."

"I haven't *always* been here. I was born in the fey realm and lived with my grandmother and mother; and when I was old enough, I started to travel with my mother around the realms."

"Right, I remember you said as much."

217

"We traveled the realms for many years, but after my accident, I wanted to stop for a little while. We came to the shores south of Arrowmount, and something kept calling me up here."

"Interesting. Most folks in Arrowmount joke about there being some kind of magic that calls people to these shores, so maybe it was that."

Meri simply nodded, which caused a little crease to form in between his eyebrows. "They're not entirely wrong, actually. People simply don't know what it is, calling them here, but there definitely is something. Do you know anything about ley lines?"

"Fey lines?"

She shook her head. "*Ley* lines. They are pure pathways of magic that run through the core of this mortal realm and many of the realms that mirror it. The fey realm is particularly dense with them, which is why time acts strange there. But here in the material realm, the lines ferry magic and energy through the very earth beneath our feet and through the air around us."

Zanve gazed around her kitchen, as though he could see the lines if he looked hard enough. "Like, physical things?"

"Yes and no," she said, tilting her head this way and that. "It's rather more intricate than that. And they're not usually visible, unless you have the right... *abilities* to see them. And happen to be looking for them at the right time.

"I knew the moment I stepped foot here in Arrowmount that I was meant to stay," she continued. "My mother didn't have the same reaction, but here in Arrowmount, we could tell something was different. She and I stayed here for a few weeks together, studying what we were feeling; then, when the solstice happened, everything became even more clear. That was the night I chose where my cottage was going to be built."

She swallowed, trying to find the right direction to go next. Her eyes landed on her mother's journal, the one with her grandmother's spells written inside. "You remember the storm — when I stopped it?"

"When you erupted with light and magic."

"Yes. I tapped into the power of the ley lines for that." Meri nodded to the journal. "My grandmother's spells, every single one in that book, are to be used by pulling on the ley line magic."

"So you moved here to access that power."

"No, not to access it — *balance it.*"

Zanve shifted slightly in the chair. "Can you see them? The ley lines?"

"During the seasonal shifts, like the solstice, yes, I can see them." Meri smiled slightly, recalling the way the ley lines had lit up beneath a perfect sunset during the winter seasonal shift. "They're quite beautiful, actually. Like gossamer threads of purest light and color, barely there, connecting across the world like a web. Since then, I've been tending to the lines, as I said. Balancing them. Reinforcing them."

He leaned forward, threading his fingers together. "What exactly do you mean?"

"I'm what we call a Keeper in the fey realm, like my grandmother was. Every seasonal shift, every equinox and solstice, I perform a ritual to keep everything in balance, as she does at her nexus in the fey realm, and every other Keeper does as well. I bind the magic here, strengthening the ties, keeping the course of the ley lines clear and strong as they path through Arrowmount, because this little town is special. It not only has the knot of ley lines here at my cottage, but it has another smaller one, directly in the heart of the town."

"Two spots? Is that rare?"

"Quite," she said. "Even in the fey realm, where there are a multitude more ley lines flowing about, it is particularly rare for multiple crossings to happen in such close proximity. Especially as strong as the ones in Arrowmount are. Feeling that kind of power, I knew without even having to ask any locals that this was a place, despite it being rather small and quaint, where great things have happened. Take Eldar's Wall, for example."

Zanve frowned. "The ruins outside of town?

"More particularly the event. How exactly do you think a tiny seaside town was able to hold off an entire force of enemies with nothing but a wall and a particularly hearty group of locals? Something about this place had power, and whatever that power was, protected its own. Without that, Arrowmount would have fallen, and the enemies would have had full access to the ports here, and who knows what would have happened to the town, let alone the empire as a whole with that power shift.

"Wherever ley lines run through in greater numbers, or cross, is where people often build their lives. That's one of the many reasons towns and cities often pop up in specific places. Whether they know it or not, everyone is drawn to their power."

"So that's how you get people saying the town has a magic of its own," said Zanve wonderingly.

"Exactly."

"So you perform rituals to keep everything running smoothly." Zanve peered at the journals around him, nodding. "What did the magic do before you got here?"

"It would have still flowed, though with much more fluctuation and the potential for attracting danger, upheaval," she answered. "With me here, I offer the town consistency and protection. Keeping the farmers' fields bountiful, those in town happy, and never at danger for any ranging beasts or folks with evil in their hearts. It's not a failsafe, but it's worked fairly well for as long as I've been here."

Zanve hesitated for a moment, one of his fingers trailing along the edge of a journal absently. His mouth was open just so, as though he was pulling together what he wanted to say.

"You do all of this, and the town doesn't know?"

"How would they know?" she answered. "No one has ever asked, and out here, not many folks have made a point in getting to know me or what I do. I'm just the Witch of the Woods."

"You are so much more than that," he said, slightly breathlessly. She studied his face, her cheeks heating despite herself. Meri had never been looked at quite as intensely as he was looking at her right then; as though he could see through her, right to her core.

Zanve leaned forward, shifting on his chair. "Alright, so. Rituals. You would have done one more than a month ago, right? Right around..." he frowned, calculating.

"I was supposed to, but Thistle happened," she said, wincing. "All of my preparations for the equinox, which was the following day, were in my greenhouse."

Zanve's face fell. "Oh. Oh, no."

"And I couldn't make up for it, with all my wares destroyed. I didn't have the chance to even attempt the ritual the next day, and so the season changed and the magic unbalanced."

"Even your fey realm plants — oh, fucking skies above, Meri I am so sorry."

"It is not your fault," she said, squeezing his hand, realizing that she had long forgiven him. Root and ruin, she didn't even think she blamed him at all in the first place; all that had been there was pain and anger at herself. "The universe simply works in ways like this sometimes."

Still, he grimaced apologetically. "What does that mean, exactly — the magic unbalanced?"

"I'm not sure what the magic will do — but what I do know is that when you miss a ritual, after years and years of constant balance, the magic of the ley lines can go awry. What Arrowmount has been experiencing since then is a result of that imbalance."

"The weird shimmering sky, the storm..." Zanve blew out air from his mouth, shaking his head. "What could that mean we have yet to experience? Will it get worse?"

"Probably, yes. But, I will fix it, if I can. At the next seasonal turn — the summer solstice — I must be ready. But, of course, I don't have all my plants anymore, and am woefully out of supplies." Meri's voice pitched up at the end, feeling very suddenly overwhelmed.

"Is there anyone we can talk to about getting the right herbs from the fey realm? Your mother, perhaps?"

"I would," said Meri slowly, running her teeth over her lower lip. "But my mother is not really... reachable, if she's in other realms. If she's in the material realm, then maybe. But last I heard, she was doing a venture into the shadow realm."

"Your grandmother?"

Meri shook her head. "I have no way of contacting either of them. I'm realizing now how inconvenient that. I should really remedy that."

"Is there anyone else we know who can travel to the fey realm for you? Could I take you to the fey realm? I know next to nothing about other realms, so please correct me if I'm wrong."

Meri nodded, a slightly hopeless laugh escaping her. She'd thought all of this through already, over and over again. "We could, but the closest access to the fey realm is in Feycross. That would take at least two weeks of travel to get to, if not more, depending on my pain and whether or not we would be able to find horses and transportation in time. And then another couple of weeks to get back — that's already a month, gone. We only have two more. Plus, we're talking about diving into the fey realm, and time gets really soupy there. It's one of the effects of having so many ley lines — we could be in the fey realm for what feels like a day, and come out again and it's three months later in this realm."

"So, that wouldn't work, it wouldn't be fast enough."

"Possibly not, no. And I don't want to risk that," she said with a sigh, running a hand across her face. "This is the first time in all these years I wasn't able to do a ritual, all because of a creature. Everything feels wrong this time."

Zanve tapped a finger absently on the kitchen table, the two of them falling quiet.

"You mentioned before that you swapped out a normal herb for one from the fey realm, to make your brews more powerful."

Meri looked at him, curious. "When did I say that?"

"When you first made me tea," he answered. "Is it possible to do the opposite? Find something that would match what you need the fey realm one to do?"

Meri sighed. It wouldn't be a terribly bad thing — and honestly, she hadn't thought of it as an option until now — but... "It would be a partial fix. Not as strong, and it wouldn't completely function the right way. But it is an idea, if all else fails."

"I wish I knew more about this so I could help you more," he said.

"Do you truly mean that?"

"Yes, Meri." He chuckled lightly. "Yes. I absolutely do. I would learn anything you could teach me, if you were open to it. I find everything about you and your life fascinating. Like a mystery book I haven't yet figured out how to solve, but not... really that mysterious? Something in between? I—"

She quirked an eyebrow at him. "I'm a riddle to be solved?"

"No — gods I'm messing this up." Zanve shook his head with a laugh before he reached for both her hands, holding them tight. Her heart stuttered at the contact, his hands warm and strong. "I mean, Meriwen, Witch of the Woods. You are a very enchanting person. I really enjoy being around you, and I would like to keep being around you — I would like to learn all about you, if you'll let me."

"Why?"

It was nothing more than a whisper. In all the years in this realm, she had never come across someone in all her years that actually wanted to converse with her, to learn from her. She was used to her solitude, her creatures, and this man had waltzed right into the middle of it.

"Why? Skies, Meri. Because I *like* you. I like you rather a lot, when I think about it for longer than a second. I am always trying to count down to when I can come and visit you, at any point in the day."

"But y-you have other friends," she said, knowing full well that was not what he meant at all. This man's feelings were written plainly across his face, his affection for her, his want beneath that all. How hadn't she seen it before? It hurt down to her bones knowing she may never be able to give him that back. "Why do you want me in your life?"

Zanve reached up and traced her cheek with a soft finger, leaving behind a thread of heat as he tucked her hair behind her ear. "Meri, don't you see how wonderful you are?"

She held his hand to her face, closing her eyes. There were too many emotions running rampant in her right then to even parse through what he was saying fully. "You're the wonderful one. I've never been... I'm not used to people," she said lamely, laughing.

He took a half step toward her, and she felt her body drift closer, unbidden. She kept her eyes closed, terrified what she would see if she opened them.

"I think you're doing perfectly fine," he said, his voice barely above a rumble, before he kissed her gently on the forehead. His lips lingered, sparking along her skin, and for a moment, all she wanted to do was draw him down to her. She wondered if he would taste like her tea. Then she wanted to sit down and talk for hours more, until the sun came up. Something in the pit of her heart clenched at the thought of him leaving her, walking back toward town and going home. She already was beginning to miss him.

Meri frowned, completely at a loss where that feeling had come from. Her eyes snapped open and she gazed at him, unable to fully draw breath. She didn't know she *could* feel that way toward another.

"Are you alright?" Zanve's other hand came up to cradle her jaw gently. She grabbed hold of both his wrists, keeping him there.

"Yes," she said simply, unable to stop the pure, true smile breaking across her face. "Yes, I am. I have one more thing to show you."

25

MERIWEN OF THE GARDEN

Meriwen

eri led Zanve into her garden. "It's going to be less surprising, since you saw me use the ley line magic to quell that storm. But I thought I'd show you properly what the ley lines can do, outside of the shifting of seasons."

Meri stepped forward until she was in the middle of her garden. She breathed in, letting the feel and the energy of the earth seep up into her bones, filling her up from below. She smiled at Zanve's expression as bits of her hair started to float around her, unbidden by any breeze.

"The ley lines are the most pure form of magic," she explained. "Outside of it ferrying natural power throughout the realm, the energy in the ley lines, in the soil and in the air, all around us, is constantly helping things grow. Forests, rivers, what have you. It all uses just a touch of that power. Magic, when magic users put it to use, is a concentrated effect of

226

that energy flowing around us. Come here."

Zanve stepped forward carefully, completely in awe. He extended his hand and laced it with hers gently, warm and steady. She slowly let the energy building inside of her out, acting like a conduit for it as it poured out of her in streams. The moment it transferred from her hand to his, his whole expression changed from wonder to pure glee.

A laugh ricocheted up from his chest, filling the space around them as he looked down at his hands. "I half expect to see myself glowing, this feels incredible."

"Your hair is loving it," she said, laughing. His hair was escaping the tie he had secured it back in, floating around him, held aloft in an intangible breeze.

Zanve pulled her to him with a completely carefree laugh, wrapping her in his arms in such a quick movement that all the air inside of her burst out in a shocked squeak. He spun her around, lifting her up off the ground, laughing all the while. For a moment, just a lingering moment, the magic drew up from the ground with her, following her weightlessly into the sky — filling the two of them with a soft buzzing power.

When he finally put her down, he did so gently, carefully — but he didn't let her go. He wrapped his strong arm around her waist, keeping her close enough that she had to fully tilt her chin to look up at him. It was a rare experience, looking up at another being, being as tall as she was.

Being this close to him, she could see every line and crease the brilliant smile made across his face, the slight chip in his tooth that made it look like a sharp canine, and every speck and rich tone of purple in his eyes.

They were much more vivid now, the blue entirely swallowed.

"Your eyes are completely purple," she breathed, looking at them in wonder. Carefully, she reached up and touched the smile lines by his eyes.

He smiled even bigger, the creases deepening. "They weren't that color when I met you."

"I should probably tell you a secret I've been keeping. Not on purpose; it's just not something I tell most people, even though we live in a world of magical beings from all walks of life. Sometimes it's nice when they think you're nothing more than human."

Meri frowned, wondering what he could mean. "And that means you're not human?"

"I am," he chuckled. "But I also am more. I don't know if you remember the night I — well, the night Thistle came around, as you said. Did you notice any other creatures around that night?"

"I thought I saw..." she hesitated.

"You saw a panther, didn't you? A very large cat?"

"I—" Meri stopped, the pieces clicking together slowly. *Panther.* She'd heard that term before when she was travelling with her mother in the Manid Empire. It was an incredibly powerful creature that was part of the cat family, but much, much larger than a normal tabby cat. "You?"

"I'm a shifter." He smiled and his shoulders softened. "I would love to show you, if I can."

"Yes," she breathed, faster than she intended. "I haven't met many shifters in my life. Each one was quite unique."

Zanve's purple eyes sharpened with interest. "You've met others?"

"A couple, when I was quite young. There was one who lived by us in the fey realm — he was fawn, so it was rather interesting to occasionally see a fawn slip into a snake and slither through the underbrush, but I never thought much of it until I met a bear shifter in the Nerian Empire. It only then occurred to me how rare it is."

"I have never met another," he said carefully. "I would love to one day. But for now, it's just me."

He took a step back from her, trailing his hands across her back as though he didn't want to let go, leaving a shiver of goosebumps behind.

"I am going to have to ask you to look away, though. If you don't want to be met with..." he gestured at himself, before his fingers started to work at the buttons of his shirt. "I've ruined enough clothing in my life shifting to learn my lesson."

"Right." She turned away, facing her greenhouse instead. "So is that why you were wearing my old garden jacket that night? Because you were naked?"

Zanve let out a shocked laugh. "I didn't realize you remembered that as well."

"Some sights do stick in your mind fairly well, I'm afraid. And the sight of a beautiful man's thighs showing in a shorter jacket, well—"

Ah, root and ruin, she had probably said too much.

There was a beat of silence, then, sounding amused, Zanve said, "a beautiful man's thighs. I'm going to remember you said that."

Then, his hand touched her shoulder, and as she turned, he dropped down into a large, silky black-furred creature. It was almost an effortless transition of space and time; if she had blinked, she would have completely missed it.

"How rare you are, Zanve," she whispered, looking at his sleek panther body. The panther, though very much an animal and something that shouldn't have been able to have humanoid expressions cross his face, seemed to appear bashful as he started to move around her, as though showing off his whole body. She extended a hand, but before she touched him, she caught his eye, waiting for permission.

He let out a chuff that sounded almost like a laugh and nuzzled into her hand.

Meri ran her hand across his smooth body, reveling in the perfectly thick, soft fur he had. If he could talk, he would probably joke about how she was petting his shoulder, she thought, a soft burst of a laugh escaping her nose. Zanve turned to look at her, his purple eyes shining brilliantly against his dark, black fur.

"Thank you for showing me this," she said, carefully running her hand over his head, dropping to her knees so she was level with him. She smiled as he bared his teeth playfully, then watched in slight fascination as he transformed back, remaining crouched in front of her, now very naked. And incredibly close to her.

He laughed at her expression and shook his head, as though trying to clear it.

"This place smells so fiercely of flowers and earth," he said, his voice lower than usual. "It's hard to communicate I'm changing back when I'm like that, so I apologize for how... untoward this is."

"It's not like I've not seen a naked man before," she said blithely. There weren't many instances, and if she was being honest, it was only brief glances at a public bath or in some of the farther reaches of secluded villages. Then her tongue kept going on its own accord. "Though, you're probably the most beautiful one. That I have seen."

He touched her face, carefully. It sent a fire down into the pit of her stomach, so intense and sudden that she sucked in a breath and pulled back, despite wanting nothing more than to lean into him.

Meri stood slowly, pulling herself up with the nearest garden bed, and tore her gaze away from his incredibly beautiful face, his burning purple eyes, and the shape of his large shoulders and the hair on his chest — ignoring the way her stomach clenched with something more than anxiety. She grabbed his clothes and held them out to him, averting her eyes as he pulled them back on.

"That's the second time you've called me beautiful, and I haven't even managed to tell you how beautiful you are once," said Zanve. "That's unfair. I need to catch up."

She waited until he touched her shoulder again to turn around, only to find him standing closer to her than she anticipated. Once again she looked up at him, breathless, as he smiled softly.

"You, Meriwen of the Garden, are beautiful."

"Not Witch of the Woods?"

"No, because that would be unwise to name a being so beautiful and ethereal out here, in her own garden, as her hair flies in the soft wind, anything but her true name."

Meri reached up to her hair floating around her, noticing that she was channeling the magic of the ley lines unconsciously.

She breathed out, letting the magic go, and tried to figure out what on earth was making her stomach do flips as it was right then.

Zanve left as the sun sank in the sky, leaving the night to bathe the world in soft purples and blues. As he left, he waved and kept glancing back at her the entire way to the tree line.

The old boughs of leaves shook in a light breeze as he vanished, and Meri could have sworn that she could feel their attention turn to her.

"I know," she breathed, looking at them briefly. Meri gazed after Zanve long after he vanished from view, filled with a sense of wonder so acute she couldn't take in a proper breath. "I don't know what's happening either."

For a moment, as he had spun her in her garden, she'd felt as though she had wings.

26

EPHEMERA

Zanve

Zanve wandered through his house the following day, finding himself smiling at objects for no particular reason. His mother, Vena, had already left for the day; leaving a half-drank mug of coffee next to a freshly sliced loaf of bread, crumbs spreading out toward her regular chair, in her wake. He could almost picture her sitting there, cutting a slice of bread before rising, still eating it, trailing crumbs across the surface.

He chuckled, thinking about what Meri would make of his mom. What his mom would make of Meri.

He snatched a chunk of cheese from the cold block as he started toward the door. He had a couple of things to do in town before he was to meet up with the Scholar Sarrai at Lord Wymarc's manor for tea — he also had to go pick up his plate armor from the barracks, now that he thought of it.

He was already cringing at the thought of wearing it, but he figured it would be necessary for going to the Lord's manor. He should look his best, after all.

The regular stash of paper and notebooks that his mother had jammed into one of the small book cases near the front door caught his attention. His mother loved collecting journals of all kinds; but unlike Meri's mother, Elestren, who seemed to keep a vast, immaculately organized collection of journals that chronicled adventures she took, Zanve's mother preferred to simply collect the pretty stationary. A few of them contained jotted down thoughts for lists that ended after a few pages; though, most remained blank.

Zanve hesitated, considering the multitude of untouched tomes. There was a smaller one on the end, about the width of his palm, that would be perfect to slip inside of a pocket.

It wouldn't be a bad idea to start his own notebook, like Meri had, he thought as he took the two strides to the shelf and slid the short journal into his hands. There was a soft layer of dust coating the top, which he quickly swept away, before he cracked it open. It creaked slightly, the spine unbent and pages untouched. The cover was soft, muted brown cloth that was pasted over hard boards to protect the pages and to provide a solid writing surface.

He pocketed it, along with a stylus and a bit of charcoal to write with as he walked around Meri's garden, learning from her. It definitely wouldn't be as pretty as the notebooks he saw at Meri's, her notes filling the pages with a pretty and neat script, but it was something.

The town bustled with a fresh energy today; the chilled spring air was invigorating and clean.

When he arrived at the town center, it was bustling with mid-morning activity, folks going about their morning shopping. Aeric from the Old'n Narrow was skirting around the stalls, a basket in his arms that looked as though it was already laden with goods. Della and Neema, the elderly gnomes that lived on Fetterly Place and ran many of the events around town, where arm-in-arm with one another, chatting as they wound around the vegetable stall.

Birds trilled above, hopping along the lines of multicolored flags that ran above the streets of Arrowmount. Zanve often forgot about that staple decoration, his eyes slipping past them on a day to day basis — but today, the birds called his eyes up, and the sight of the dancing flags made him smile. As a boy, he'd often gazed up at those flags, pinned along twine and strung across the cobblestone streets. He was often mesmerized by them, and ended up helping the volunteers regularly taken them down to be replaced once the elements had discolored them or they had become torn.

"The birds have been really having a heyday this spring," said a voice near his elbow. He looked down to find Cecily Little crouched a few feet from him, gathering bits into a box.

"I haven't noticed until now, but there definitely has been an uptick in them." Zanve smiled and bent to help her finish the last of her packing.

"Maybe it's something to do with that bizarre magic floating around," said Cecily with a chuckle, as though she didn't quite believe it. She swung her long bright green hair over her shoulder, exposing the side that was shorn close to her skull. She smiled back at him, her cheeks rounding along the whorls of bark on her skin. "What brings you to the town center today?"

"I had half a mind to run some errands ahead of a meeting I have a bit later, but I got a bit distracted," he answered.

"When the gods want, they'll take you anywhere, hey?" She gestured with her chin to her table, where Zanve deposited the box on a chair behind her table for her.

He could feel her eyes on him after a moment of him perusing the selection, but not in the usual way she did when someone was scouting her wares.

Zanve looked up, catching her eye. He lifted a single eyebrow in question.

"Sorry, I just have to ask."

"About?"

"Gable and I were at the Old'n Narrow last night and overheard some of the other guards — specifically Damian and his ilk—" she said, rolling her eyes, "bragging up and down the bar to whoever would listen that he was going to pay a visit to the Witch in the Woods, like it was some grand adventure."

Zanve froze, every nerve standing on end. "He said that?"

"Of course, he's just trying to play with the rumors that are swirling about you and her," said Cecily placatingly. "You know that man doesn't have a spine in his body to truly work up the courage to go and see Meriwen. He'd be too scared she'd turn him into a rabbit for the rest of his days."

"True, true. Though Meri would never do that. I don't even think she even *could*, mind you. Did you know she channels her magic through the ground and air for the most part? And puts it in teas and the like." An idea sprang to mind as he looked at Cecily, remembering who he was talking to. "Is that anything like your druidic magic?"

She snorted in response. "No, no. It's not quite what she does. I think... I remember reading something about fey magic. Of course, like us here on the mortal realm, there is magic of all kinds in the fey realm. Druidic magic does often find itself mentioned among the fey magics — but she explained a bit of it to me, once, in passing. It feels like hers is more centered on the energy around us; and mine is pulled from in me."

As though to demonstrate, she gestured fluidly in the air and from the tips of her fingers a bundle of tiny, beautiful little wildflowers sparkled into being.

"It's just me, my magic. Hers is deeper than that."

"Gods, I wish I had learned more about magic growing up. Even though I'm—" he looked at her meaningfully, "—you know. I never really considered paying attention to anyone else's magic in the world."

"It's never too late."

After a few more minutes of chatting, Zanve went to leave, planning on finally starting his few planned errands. Perhaps he would start with picking up some baked goods from Gable, Cecily's partner.

"Have you heard anything from your sister lately?" Zanve asked Cecily, turning a half step back to her stall.

"Yes, I have." A small smile grew on her face, a bit of pleased colour blooming on her cheeks. "Her and Kir are currently in the Kingdom of Zidien, if you can believe it. Apparently, Kir has created quite the loyal following through one of the bars there, so much so that the Crown-guard asked them to find a bigger venue. They simply couldn't all fit inside."

"That's fantastic," said Zanve, remembering how Kirandir, one of Arrowmount's favoured town bards, had finished out the Moon Festival the previous fall season. She truly had a knack for performing. "I remember listening to her occasionally at the Old'n Narrow when she played, she was absolutely fantastic. I can only imagine what it's like when she gets a whole city bar behind her."

Cecily laughed. "I think this summer Gable and I are going to take a trip out to Zidien to visit them."

"I'm sure she'd love that. You think they'll still be there by then?"

"I hope so," she answered. "Of course, with Lottie's choice of employment, one doesn't really know. But... she did let on that she had a contact in Zidien that was helping her procure proper, steady employment at the university, so hopefully she's turned that around a little bit. She was pretty cagey in her letter about that, but I can tell she's excited about something."

"Oh, and — I wanted to ask, before you head out." Cecily held up a hand to stop him. "I haven't seen Meriwen for a number of weeks, and I meant to ask the next time I saw her how that stone of hers is doing."

"Stone?"

"She bought this unusual stone from me," explained Cecily. "It was oddly light, and shone like nothing I've ever seen, and had all these pits on the surface, kind of like granite. But it definitely was not granite. You haven't seen it around?"

Oh, he'd seen that stone before.

"I think so," he said slowly, trying to keep his face impassive. "Where did you get it from?"

Cecily chuckled. "Finnean, of course. I think he got it on one of his last jobs in a treasure trove before he and Arileas decided to settle down here."

Zanve snorted in disbelief. "Odd, that he would have grabbed a stone. Was there no gold around?"

"It was a fey beast hoard, so who's to say what treasures were around. Anyhow, let me know if you do see it. I was quite a bit intrigued by it."

If only Cecily knew, he thought.

"I will," he lied.

"Say hello to Gable on your way out, they baked some fresh cinnamon buns this morning. If they have any left."

After bidding Cecily farewell, Zanve headed directly to Gable's stall, following the scent of sugar and butter through the winding market.

A lot of the stalls had canopies that varied slightly in height and color, creating a practical medley of color and fabric around him.

Gable waved as he approached, two gloved hands immediately moving toward the last two cinnamon buns at their stall.

"You're a savior," sighed Zanve, taking the buns from them. "I'll also take a couple of those twists there, they look incredible — and a loaf of your tastiest bread."

"Coming right up."

Armed with his goods, Zanve weaved his way back through the town center and down a side street, biting into one of the doughy twists. The pastry was flaky and buttery, swirled with chocolate to absolute perfection.

His eyes fell on the outside of the apothecary shop as he rounded the corner.

He'd heard of it from Meri, of course, and his mother over the years; but had never stepped inside himself. He popped the rest of a twist in his mouth and tucked the rest of the baked goods inside his jacket, hoping he wouldn't squash them too much.

When he entered the small shop, he had to blink a few times, wondering if he had stepped through a portal into a Meri's own greenhouse, before his vision adjusted. This place wasn't quite like her greenhouse — for one, it lacked any proper windows, aside from one large one at the front that was mostly covered by a large shelving unit housing hundreds of tiny sections. It looked like the wall at the postal office on a miniature scale, except this one was filled to the brim with so many varieties of plants that he couldn't even begin to name them.

Then, there were the rest of the shelves filling the shop marking out narrow aisles between which Zanve could barely fit. Each standing shelf in the middle of the shop was slightly mismatched, heights ranging from hip height to just a touch shorter than Zanve, sporting everything from lush potted plants to curling vines that didn't seem to be tied to any visible roots or soil systems. There were bits and bobs for planting and plant care, and a myriad of herbs and spices, each one labeled carefully in tight, looping writing, explaining what each ware was, and in even smaller writing, what it could be used for.

He didn't notice the giantkin standing behind the counter as he took in the space until she shifted, nodding to him in greeting.

She smiled at Zanve as he poked at the shelves of dried herbs. For a moment, she just watched him, saying nothing. His face heated as he chewed his bottom lip, trying to look as though he knew what he was doing, but it was probably obvious that he hadn't ever been inside this place before, and he was woefully out of his depth.

"Can I help you, dear?" she said finally. "You seem to be on the hunt for something specific."

Zanve straightened, immediately knocking his head on the low hanging drying plants. Some crumbled on impact with a soft crunch, plant dust and detritus coating his hair and his shoulders. "Oh gods, sorry, I—"

"Don't worry about it, I do that exact same thing multiple times a day. You'd think, after having been here for years, that I would know better — but no, I always forget how dried thyme can absolutely cascade down one's back at the slightest provocation." The giantkin stood, proving her point almost immediately as the top of her soft furry head brushed the bottom of some flowers that were drying above the counter. "I'm Caelynn, by the way. I don't believe we've met in person, but I have heard a fair bit about you recently, Zanve Einar."

"Ah, have you?" He smiled, trying to hide his cringe at the thought of others talking about him.

"Rumors," said the giantkin with a soft lift of her shoulder. "I have a delivery that Meriwen placed with me a couple of weeks ago — she sent an emergency list of what she needed, for whatever it is she does up there every year. Most of the plants I was missing for it just arrived. Good timing, too, because that means you can take them to her."

Zanve blinked at her. The giantkins' eyes twinkled knowingly.

"Well, I don't know exactly what she does, but it's quite difficult to do something to *that* magical level without someone noticing something. Especially me, as familiar with magic as I am, with my plants and such. Oh, you don't need to look so worried — I'm sure that I'm the only one who knows Meri and put two and two together with the seasonal shifts." Caelynn chuckled slightly as she touched one of the potted plants nearby lovingly, the leaf bouncing back to her. "If it's not Meriwen doing something every season, then I'll eat this plant. Pot and all.

"Ah, right." Zanve scratched his head. "I wanted to help refill her greenhouse, actually. I know she lost a lot of plants, not just the ones she needs for her magic. I was hoping you would be able to help me?"

"I would be happy to!" Caelynn clapped her hands together. "Do you know what she had in her greenhouse specifically?"

Zanve grimaced. "No, I only saw the state of it after the... well. I never saw what she had."

"Ah, yes, alright." Caelynn tapped her lips, thinking as her eyes traced the outline of her shop. "Well, you see if you can find out exactly what she is missing — knowing her, she kept a very meticulous record of her collection somewhere. When you find out, you can bring that to me, and we can start patching the holes. But for now, let me see what plants I have that one can never have too much of, and that everyone needs. Other than what she ordered, of course."

Caelynn led him past her counter and out into a spacious greenhouse absolutely brimming with life. It took Zanve a moment to adjust to the slightly different climate and to tamp down his immediately over-whelmed panther senses that wanted to run headlong from the place.

He sniffed hard, rubbing at his nose, trying to hide the way his eyes watered.

"Oh my apologies, it is probably quite strong in here for you," Cae-lynn said, turning to look over her shoulder. When he froze, looking at her, she simply smiled. "My dear, you think you can hide that you're a shifter, but your eyes have changed color twice since we've been in my shop alone."

"That is a bit presumptuous of you isn't it?" he said, raising his eye-brows at her. "Shifters are quite rare. What makes you think that I'm one?"

"Certainly, they are rare," she answered nodding. "But I know a little bit about you. Did you know your mother used to come here regularly when you were a boy to grab pain relieving herbs? Or did you used to think those poultices and sweet cakes she made you were simply that good at helping you heal?"

Zanve gaped at her. As a boy, his transformations had been immensely painful to endure, keeping him up at night. His mother was always by his side, soothing him. His mother would always be there, when he changed back, ready with something to help him; whether it be wounds, stomach, or soul. As he'd grown, the transformations became less painful, and he hadn't given those poultices or sweet cakes or teas that his mother had made him as a boy a second thought.

"You knew?"

"Aha," laughed Caelynn, her laugh sounding like an old braying hound. "I know things about this town, boy, that you never will. Feel free to hold your sleeve over your nose, if it helps. My old senses are so used to the burn and shift of life here — I can't imagine what it's like to have a heightened nose."

He did so, feeling slightly sheepish, falling into step beside her as she moved to the back of the greenhouse. "I must thank you, then, for taking part in so much of my healing, even though I didn't know it."

"Nothing to worry about," she said, taking his hand and patting it amiably. "I am happy to help everyone I can. And that includes our Meriwen!"

The giantkin turned and clapped her hands together, casting a learned gaze around the space.

Before long, Zanve's arms were full of clippings, tiny pots, and plants of all kinds. He followed Caelynn's form back through to the front of her shop, where he deposited it all down on the counter as she tallied it up.

He quietly plucked the notebook from his pocket, and the bit of charcoal, and started to write down the names of the plants as Caelynn muttered under her breath, leaving a bit of space to write what they could do or what they were for when he learned from Meri. He frowned at his handwriting as it sped across the page, messy and rather loopy, and nearly illegible.

"As long as you can read it, that's all that matters," said Caelynn, eyeing him over a rather tall and spindly plant. He held the book close to his chest, slightly embarrassed to have been found out. "Are you keeping track of anything in particular in that little book of yours?"

"I..." Zanve nodded slowly. "I was hoping to keep a bit of a record of what Meri teaches me. She's already taught me a bit — I have to go back and write it in, but, for now... It's sort of silly, but I just thought..."

"It is never silly, young man, to take interest in things," said Caelynn, her eyes sparkling. She held up a rather thick leather volume, held together with thick twine. The pages within it were bulging with ephemera, from extra pages slid in for safe keeping, to dried plant clippings and who knew what else. "I have been doing it for years. Keeps my old brain from losing my way too quickly."

Zanve smiled, feeling unexpectedly shy.

"Meriwen's teaching you, is she?" Caelynn continued to tally up the remainder of the plants and extraneous bits that she had gathered. At his nod, she narrowed her eyes slightly at him, as though calculating something. "Good. I think that's good."

He wasn't quite sure what that meant.

She held up the hand written receipt and handed it to him. "There's your list with all the proper spellings. If you wish to simply stick that bit into your journal, that would work as well."

He glanced down at the receipt, noticing there was no price tallied up at the bottom — it was simply a list of names and quantities.

"What do I owe you?"

"Nothing," she answered. When he tried to fight, pulling out his coin purse, she added, "for our Meri, and for whatever she does for this town, this will be my gift. To help her greenhouse get back on its feet. Now, get on with you. I hope to see you back here again, Zanve. It's been a pleasure."

"I expect I will be," he answered with a smile, scooping the plants into his arms after tucking the receipt into his journal and the journal back into his pocket.

27

ROOT AND RUIN

Meriwen

Meri did her rounds through her garden, trying to quell the anxiety rising in her. It felt as though she had a ticking clock over her head, despite having more than a month left to figure out what she was going to do about the missing plants and herbs. She had made an order with Caelynn for the material realm plants that she needed, but when it came to the fey realm plants, she had no idea if or how she was going to get her hands on them.

While reading through Elestren's journals, Meri had come across a message sending spell — but it was only viable if both parties were within the same realm. She would need something, or someone, much more powerful to contact her family.

Meri was going to have to go into Arrowmount and ask around. She hadn't been able to walk much further than the length of her garden since her flare up, and so the thought of going to town hadn't been on her mind. If she was going to make that walk...

Perhaps tomorrow, she thought, kneading her leg, gauging her pain. She didn't want to hurt herself more, cause another bad flare by walking too far too soon.

She rubbed her chest as she moved onto her next garden bed, trying to ease the anxiety.

It didn't help that the hair on the back of her neck kept prickling like someone was watching her.

"Mmm, Meri," croaked Lock from beside her, startling her enough to flinch back. "Okay?"

"I'm alright, just... lost in thought," she answered, letting the wyrmling slide up onto her shoulders and settle there. He was warm and comforting there, settling her racing heart ever so slightly. "Lock, do you think I've failed the town?"

"Mmm?"

"With the ritual. There's nothing I can do — I can't open a doorway to Fey, let alone travel to Feycross where there is a door that I can use in time to get the ingredients and plants I need. Everything is muddled."

Lock remained silent for a beat, before he shifted slightly. Meri could immediately tell he was looking off in the direction of Thistle, who was snoozing happily in the long grasses at the edge of her garden.

"No, Lock. It's not his fault."

"Mmm. But."

"But nothing, it's not Thistle's fault that things have been muddled. Sure, he might be a reason why, but he didn't ask to be brought into existence here."

Meri, thoughts starting to spin again, picked up her half empty basket and returned to her cottage, ignoring the other duties she needed to do for the day. Her mother's journals were still stacked neatly on the table that Wyn had unearthed from upstairs, waiting to be returned to their shelves. All except for one, which she had left sitting open to a page detailing odd creatures that her mother, Elestren, had come across while observing her grandmother's garden.

Oftentimes I wonder what it is about Mother's garden that attracts beasts of all kinds to its perimeter — but I have yet to really find the answer. Mother says it's the nexus, because all living things are drawn close to nexuses and ley lines that cross wherever they may be; but I am starting to believe that it's more about her than the magic here. Because why would they be attracted to the ley lines, only for them to follow her around like they are all her children?

Meri gazed down at the journal, the first words on the page standing out as though her mother had traced over the letters a number of times with the same pen, her mother thinking things through. It was the only one out of twenty-three — Meri had counted — of her mother's fey realm journals that had contained information about various fey creatures. There were mentions in others, fleeting sentences of observations about plant life, Elestren's internal musings about life in the fey realm and how much better life beyond that realm would be, but nothing of import. It was odd, seeing her mother's handwriting run across countless pages, intermingled with hand drawn illustrations to accompany the passages. These were from so long ago that her mother would have been near the age she was now, already an explorer at heart.

Lock shuddered around her neck, distracting her. He growled low in the base of his chest, a sound that Meri had only ever heard when he was deeply uncomfortable, before he slid off and hid himself inside her kitchen.

"Hello?"

Meri blinked at the unfamiliar voice rising from her garden, confused. Who on earth could be visiting her now? Hadn't she met enough people in the past few weeks?

She stepped out of her kitchen door to almost run headlong into the black-haired guard she recognized from the few times she'd seen him at the front gates of Arrowmount. Meri was fairly certain that whatever uniform this young man usually wore wasn't as neat as this one — because he looked supremely upright standing on her stoop, as though he was consciously trying to keep the uniform from wrinkling.

"Hello," she said, uncertainly. As his eyes fell on her, an expression crossed his face that she immediately recoiled from. She wasn't sure whether it was the slight sharpening of his gaze that gave off an air of someone trying to be discreetly predatory, or the subtle curl of a smile that lingered at the edges of his mouth that appeared sinister.

A sense of danger rose in the back of her mind, so she began to gently pull a thread of power from the ground, keeping it curled around her fingers, just in case. What was he here for? Was Zanve alright — had the guards sent this man out here to tell her something had happened to him?

Thistle stirred at the edge of her consciousness. Meri's heart leapt into her throat; he was still asleep, hidden in the long grasses, but if this man, this stranger found out about him—

"Ah, you are home! I was beginning to suspect that you had left your wondrous garden all alone, unprotected from vandals and thieves."

"I can assure you, I never do," she said, frowning. "Can I help you?"

"Perhaps," drawled the man, smiling at her in a way that she supposed he thought was charming. It honestly looked as though he was having a difficult time passing gas. "I must confess, I have heard wonderful things about you, Witch of the Woods. But, I haven't had the confidence to come up here and meet you myself until recently."

"Oh?" Meri very much did not like where this was going. She kept her magical awareness locked on Thistle's twitching form. He felt as though he was about to wake.

"Yes," he said, chuckling self-deprecatingly. "At least, it was until my dear friend Zanve convinced me that I should simply try... to reach out to you, and see... well, see if you were open to a conversation, at least."

She narrowed her eyes minutely, setting her jaw. If she had to bet, Zanve had never spoken to this man about her in this way. "Is that so."

"Which is why I am here," he continued on, unperturbed by her cold tone. "I simply had to try."

"Try?"

"Try and connect with you. I... I am almost too embarrassed to say." The man ran a hand over this hair as though it wasn't plastered into shape by some kind of adhesive. "I have immense feelings for you."

"You? Have feelings for me?" Meri couldn't help but laugh, absolutely astonished. "I hate to disappoint you, sir, but we've never spoken to each other a day in our lives."

His charming smile slipped right off his face and was replaced by a very ugly, angry expression that pinched his lips.

Meri suppressed the urge to roll her eyes. "What is your name, sir?"

"Damian," he answered, sounding slightly disappointed that she didn't know it automatically. "Damian Briggs."

"Well, Mr. Briggs. I appreciate you coming here to try and woo me, or whatever it was you thought you were going to be able to do." She folded her arms over her chest. "You don't even know my name, do you?"

Damian's mouth opened and he froze. Then, as though mimicking her, he crossed his arms just as she had, and stood slightly to one side, which made her even more irritated.

"If you don't have the common sense to begin a conversation with 'Hello, my name is Damian, what's yours?' then I'm afraid we have nothing much to say to each other." Her heart rate picked up as she felt Thistle wake properly, turning his attention to her.

No no, she tried to send along their connection, *please don't move, it's not safe for you to come out*! Though he sent back a burst of irritation, he stayed crouched in the tall grass, hidden.

"Well," said Damien, bitterly, "I'll have you know, Witch, I should have known how rude you would be. You're always floating through Arrowmount as though you're better than everyone else; what even is it you do out here all day, except playing in the soil? Plotting the demise of the town? Try and cook up new ways to be mysterious and — and—" Damian wiggled his hands in front of his face in a mocking imitation of magic.

A soft burst of angry sputtering came from behind her, startling both her and Damian. She half expected Thistle to have burst out of hiding, but instead it was Lock, puffing himself up and practically spitting at this stranger, stalking out of his hiding spot in the kitchen.

"Oh, root and ruin," she breathed, bending down faster than she should have, scooping the wyrmling into her arms. Her leg twinged in unhappy protest at her motion. Lock growled low at the man.

"What in all the hells is that?" said Damian, his eyes wide with fear and disgust. "Control your beast!"

"It is a wyrmling," she said, her voice brittle with irritation. "Cousin to the dragon. They're incredibly common in the Blackshell Forest and up north in the mountains around the Nerian Empire. Now if you please, you're scaring him, and I must ask you to leave."

"I — I'm *scaring him?*" The man sputtered in shock before pointing at her in a way that she suspected he thought was menacing. "You're out here harboring creatures that should be put down. You really are a witch, you know that? Watch your back."

"He's just—" she put up a hand, trying to placate the man.

"Prove it then. What is this creature good for?" Damian took a menacing step forward, closing the space between him and Meri in an instant, and grabbed her wrist. "I don't need you casting any curses on me. I—"

"Let go of me," Meri snapped, trying to keep her voice firm. His grip was surprisingly strong, and almost painful. If he tried to push her or steer her somewhere, she was going to run the risk of stepping wrong and hurting her leg more. She couldn't chance that.

"Don't interrupt me, Witch."

His grip tightened threateningly. She started to draw energy from the ground, even though she didn't know if she even had the capability to defend herself. She had never needed to before.

Lock solved her dilemma by lunging at him, his jaws clamping around the man's forearm. Damian let out an almost inhuman shriek, tearing his arm back, leaving long gouges along the skin that immediately started to bleed.

Thistle, through their bond, began to shake with the restraint he was using to stay hidden.

Stay, please. He would only make it worse.

"Control that beast!" The man yelled, backing away, back toward the path leading from her garden. "Control it, or I will have to—"

Lock growled at him, narrowing his eyes. Honestly, Lock was nothing more than the weight of a cat all told, but for the first time, Meri could see something more feral in him that startled her.

Damien stalked out of her garden without another word.

"Root and *ruin,*" Meri swore. "That's not going to go over well, is it?"

Lock, of course, simply hummed in her arms, winding his way up around her neck once more, a soft trail of steam coming from his nostrils as though he had done absolutely nothing wrong.

A tiny laugh sounded from above Meri, crinkling like tiny crystals of broken glass. She stepped out of her cottage and looked up toward the second floor.

"That was something," said that laughing voice, and for a moment, Meri just blinked up at the spindly creature currently sitting on a stone that jutted out from the wall.

The pixie started to swing its legs as it looked down at her.

"Hello," said Meri carefully, eyeing the pixie's mischievous expression.

"You know, it would have been far more entertaining if you loosed that creature of yours on that man," said the pixie. "That's what he wanted, at least."

"Who, Thistle?" Meri asked, gesturing to the feathered fey creature glaring at her accusing from the long grass.

"Yes."

Meri frowned at the pixie. "I don't understand. What do you mean, it's what he wanted?"

The pixie shrugged. "Should've let him at that man. He would have handled the human easily. Terrible man, by the way. He's not a friend of yours, right? What was he doing here?"

"Skies only know," sighed Meri. She rubbed at her chest, feeling her heart rate finally slow now that Damien was gone. Looking up at the pixie, she remembered the nest hidden up in her attic. "It's been a bit of a trying time. I apologize for forgetting about our meeting."

"Well, since you didn't thoroughly boot us from your wonderful home, I wanted to extend our gratitude, on behalf of our entire nest, for letting us stay here."

Seeing as Meri had forgotten the pixies' existence almost entirely —

she had so much going on at the moment — she hadn't even thought to care, although she wisely kept that comment to herself.

"You've kept yourself hidden for so long — why decide to talk now?"

"I may have overheard your little conversation with that man while I was in your kitchen," said the pixie, looking slightly sheepish.

"You were in my kitchen?"

"I was hiding with the birds," it explained. "You caught me unawares, I thought you were going to be out in your garden long enough for me to grab a leaf or two of your meriwen plant. But when he arrived, I couldn't help myself but sit back and watch. Mortals can be so entertaining."

Meri frowned. "I don't have any meriwen plant left. All my stores are gone."

The pixies' movement halted. "*Gone*? Oh, don't tell me, it was also part of the 'destruction' you were talking about with that other man? Root and ruin, that is dreadful news."

"If I had some, I would willingly share," she said with a heavy sigh. "But unfortunately, a lot of my fey realm herbs and plants were destroyed."

"By him," said the pixie, pointing down at Thistle, who had come out from the grasses finally and planted himself in front of Meri. He puffed himself up, trying to make himself look bigger. The pixie held up a single, long and fragile looking finger. "I mean no harm. I am simply stating the obvious. Your master is missing incredibly vital herbs. Not only to her, me and my nest need those herbs as well, I'll have you know, fluffy-feathery beast. All because of you."

Thistle deflated at that, but he still kept his eyes on the pixie.

"Vital? To you?" Meri narrowed her eyes. "What do you mean?"

"Well, if you High Fey paid attention to anything the other species did, then maybe you would know that meriwen is a very important herb to us pixies, as it helps us keep our own magic flowing. So, if you could get some again, that would be grand. Your supply of meriwen kept us going for years, and we really aren't looking forward to having to move."

"I'm hoping to find more, soon," sighed Meri. "If you know of anyone who can get to the fey realm or contact the fey realm, please let me know."

"Noted," said the pixie slowly.

"If you need anything else, please let me know. I actually don't mind having a gaggle of you all up in my attic — you're taking better care of those journals than I ever could. How long have you been taking up residence in my cottage?"

"It's been our pleasure for the past five years," the pixie answered, tilting its head, considering her. "The author of those journals knows a fair amount of interesting things. You, also, are a very interesting person, with all you have going on here. It's only getting more interesting, with all these new arrivals recently. The mortal realm, though simple, is quite *interesting*."

Meri had nothing to say to that statement, so she simply nodded. As the pixie started to climb back up toward Meri's second story window, a thought hit her: where had the pixies come from before they found her home? If they had journeyed from the fey realm, perhaps they knew of a way to get back.

"Without the meriwen," she said, interrupting the pixie's ascent, "what will you do?"

The pixie paused, looking down at her.

"We will have to go someplace else to find more. Perhaps back to the fey realm, though I'm sure most of us would be loath to leave your cottage." The pixie seemed to deflate at the thought. "You are sure you have a way to get more, yes?"

"I—" Meri grimaced. "Maybe. My grandmother lives in the fey realm.

She's also a Keeper, like me."

"Oh, good. You can just talk to her then, and she can send some. It would save all of us having to go back to that dratted realm with its weird time and odd creatures that insist on trying to eat us."

Meri held back a groan of frustration. "I don't have any way to contact her, or anyone in the fey realm, for that matter. I can't get there and back in time for the next ritual, let alone quick enough to replenish the plant for you."

"Ah. That is an issue." The pixie scratched its nose, looking away from Meri. "Well, if you do find a way…" It had been curious and open mere seconds ago; the shift to this rather cagey expression made Meri immediately suspicious.

"Wait — can *you* go to the fey realm?"

The pixie's eyes skittered away from her. "No?" it replied, although it came out sounding more like a question. Meri narrowed her eyes at it.

"You don't have a way to go or you don't want to?"

"We don't want to."

Meri blinked. "You *can* go to the realm, though."

"Ye-e-e-es…" the pixie seemed more and more reluctant to keep the conversation going, inching back up the wall.

"How?" If there was another doorway nearby, closer than Feycross, make she could find her family in time to help. But the pixie was already shaking its head.

"We just go."

Meri blinked at it, perplexed. "What? Without a door?"

"Yes."

"I don't understand. Do you have some kind of magic that lets you?" She furrowed her brow, trying to remember if her grandmother or mother had ever mentioned creatures with similar powers to Realmstriders. Thistle's stone came to mind; perhaps there was some connection?

The pixie tossed its thin hands up in the air in exasperation. "Like this."

"Like what?"

The air around the pixie shifted ever so slightly, and then it disappeared and reappeared a half foot to the left. "Like that. Please don't ask me to do that again, it is horrendous, even for a moment."

"You can... you can go to the fey realm," she said slowly. "That easily?" Meri was stunned.

"Yes." said the pixie desperately. "But no, before you ask—"

"Does it hurt you?"

"Well, no, but we find it unpleasant, having to—"

Meri's mind was already running ahead of her. "Since you are living in my house, and I've been so generously hosting you for so long, it would be the least you could do for me," she interrupted, raising her eyebrows. She started to pat down her many pocketed dress, hunting for a journal. "I need you to — hold on—"

She ran back into her cottage and quickly started to scrawl a quick note to her grandmother with a list of plants cuttings she needed. Her grandmother would know instantly why she wanted them. Meri didn't have time to explain everything, but she added a post script at the end:

And also, grandmother, we must come up with a way to contact one another over the realms. It has been far too long.

Meri tore the page from the journal and hurried back out to the pixie, who had now been joined by a couple of others.

"Please take this to Keeper Seraph, and she will know what else to do. I appreciate it greatly." The pixie and its companions looked greatly put out.

"I never agreed to go!" said the first pixie, obstinately.

"If you want to keep staying at my cottage, you and your whole family," said Meri sternly, holding the note toward the pixie, "you will do this for me."

They stared at one another for a long moment, Meri and the pixies.

"I'm sure that Keeper Seraph will also have some kind of lemon cake for you," said Meri, coaxing, knowing that a lot of the fey creatures that lived around her grandmother's cottage loved her baking and sweets. "She loves to share, especially with those who are incredibly helpful."

"Oh, lemon cake!" Piped up another voice. A fourth pixie poked its head out of the gap in the bricks, looking down at them. "I love lemon cake. Let's do it. It really won't take that long."

The first pixie groaned. "Fine. Fine! A trip back to the fey realm to request herbs and plant help from Keeper Seraph. In exchange for being able to live here longer, without being bothered."

"Thank you," said Meri breathlessly as relief flooded her. "As quickly as you can."

The two pixies drifted down to Meri, taking the note.

"It'll be good to go home," said the fourth pixie, who was grinning. "Feel time on our skin again. And taste lemon cake!"

The first pixie grumbled in response, before they vanished into thin air. Meri waited, hesitating, wondering if they would simply turn around and come back in a flash.

But of course, she knew how time worked in the fey realm. It would never be that easy.

Meri sighed as a tight knot of tension throbbed in her chest. She'd been so worried that she wouldn't be able to find a way to get her plants and herbs, but if this actually worked? She could fix the magic in Arrowmount. She could make everything better again.

28

A Treasure Trove

Zanve

Zanve safely brought the plants for Meri to his place after leaving Caelynn's, choosing to bring them to the cottage after his meeting with the Scholar Daruka. He then went to the barracks, outfitting himself in the shiny, ceremonial plate armor stored there for him, and headed off toward Lord Wymarc's manor.

Upon his arrival, Zanve followed a woman dressed all in purple through the halls of the manor, trying to keep his eyes from straying around the place too much. It wasn't overly grand, which was unexpected, having only seen the structure from the outside. It was an incredibly large manor house situated on a sizeable property, spanning a number of side buildings and such, but Zanve had expected the place to be much more lavish. Wasn't that how all lords lived?

Then again, he supposed that Lord Wymarc wasn't much like a pompous royal or noble-born. In the past, whenever Zanve had come into contact with him, he'd been rather subdued and personable. Zanve had read in books that nobles dripped in gold and opulence; but Wymarc tended toward simpler, well made and fine but more modest styles.

The inside of his manor was much the same. While everything was wide and spacious, the dressings weren't gilded in gold and rubies.

A few other servants passed by them, nodding to Zanve politely. He touched his armor, feeling out of place. He didn't wear any part of the metal on duty; none of the town guards did. There hadn't been a need for that level of bodily protection for decades, if not centuries; yet, the Arrowmount guards still had sets made, just in case. Most of the time, partial plate armor was used during events or to put on a fancier face if royals ever decided to come visit.

Thankfully it wasn't the *full* plate set — in addition to the cuirass, pauldrons, faulds, and vambraces he was wearing — or else he'd be rattling like a cart full of glassware. He already was making a lot of noise as it was.

As he walked down the wide halls of the Wymarc manor, the metal shone in the sunshine that was pouring through the vast skylights above. Zanve adjusted his shoulders and flicked his head as a curl escaped the leather tie he'd tried to control his hair with this morning.

The armor made him feel rather like a child playing dress up with his father's clothing, if he was being honest. It wasn't as if he had ever or would ever see battle in it.

Plus it was *so* shiny; as though it had been polished last night. Zanve felt like he was a beacon drawing every eye his way.

The thoughts of his obnoxious armor vanished as Zanve was led into the library. Now *this* room was one that aligned almost perfectly with what he assumed kings had at their disposal. Three stories of books practically rose around him, a new level built below and above, with rows of thousands upon thousands of books adorning rich, cherry wood shelving. He stepped around the central opening to the lower level, leaning briefly over the railing of shining, smooth wood that matched the shelves, before continuing on to the left, after the woman in purple who was bustling through the stacks.

Who needed gold and rubies when you had rich wooden bookshelves practically bursting with stories and information to be read? If he could spend a few hours browsing these shelves, he'd be the happiest man in Ravar.

As they walked, they passed alcoves and rooms full of books. Every so often Zanve's eye caught on golden name plates, flashing under the warm arcane lights that lit the space. He yearned to explore this room.

"Just over here, sir," said the woman, her purple robes brushing along behind her inn a soft susurration of material. "And please don't mind the mess. I believe Scholar Daruka requested *everything* on otherworldly magics; which, as you can imagine, was a lot of texts."

Zanve made a noncommittal noise in the back of his throat as the woman led him into a back part of the library, which opened up into a secondary, round room. It had a number of tables and desks surrounded by curving bookshelves, hugging the walls. The ceiling gave way to a perfectly circular opening to the second floor, shelves extending up around that section as well, with a beautiful glass-wrought dome letting in natural light capping it off. It was an absolute masterwork of glass. Briefly, as they approached a table where Scholar Daruka was working, Zanve wondered if the Miirthgroves had a hand in it, or if it was magic wrought.

"Scholar Daruka, may I present Zanve Einar, town guard."

Zanve bent at the waist, feeling rather silly.

"Ah! Zanve," Sarrai said, immediately standing and bustling over to him. The Scholar was in the same regalia as the first time that Zanve had seen them in, though this time their hands were covered in ink, and their sleeves pulled back to leave their hands free. "It almost slipped my mind that you were due for tea. And my, you look rather nicely done up today. I hope I am not the reason!"

The Scholar chuckled happily as they sorted a few of their books to the side, making room for Zanve at their table.

"I hope I have not arrived at a bad time?"

"Not at all, not at all my good man! Come and sit, let us chat. Elsie, if you don't mind getting us some tea? Perhaps some biscuits?"

The woman nodded, briefly looking at the state of the tables around Sarrai with a distinct look of displeasure before she swept off.

"I have been having a grand time here," said the Scholar. "Though Lord Wymarc's servants have their hands full with myself and Argyle."

That's right, there was an assistant, nodded Zanve, remembering. He glanced quickly around the space, noting the distinct lack of said elf, Argyle, today. "I'm sure they appreciate the company."

Sarrai chuckled. "Company and a great number of scholarly and academic messes to pick up after. I regret to say that when my mind takes me off on a course of thought, I regularly forget the piles I create around me."

"Perhaps it'll do them good, having to actually clean up after you," said Zanve, lowering his voice conspiratorially. "It is just Lord Wymarc in these halls. No rowdy children or anything."

"I've heard that his niece may come and join him at some point, due to some... unwanted noise and rumors back in Pralon, but for now, you are correct." The Scholar's eyes twinkled. "How have you been, dear man? How did you weather that unbelievable storm?"

"Fairly alright," said Zanve, settling into his seat as best he could with his armor in the way. "The whole town is uneasy, though."

"I am sure they are," said the Scholar, nodding. "Even in these halls, the rumors are boundless! Everyone has their own theory as to why there was such a magical storm. It is all very fascinating, and with what I'm here to study, I cannot help but be intrigued. If I'm going to put my own two copper pieces into the pot for a theory, I would hazard a guess that whatever broke through the boundary between realms is causing it."

Zanve shifted in his seat, trying to school his face into a politely interested expression. He wasn't entirely sure how much Meri wanted him to divulge to the Scholar about the magic of Arrowmount's imbalance, if anything at all. He was here specifically to see if Sarrai knew much about creatures of the fey realm; and if they could help identify Thistle.

Zanve leaned forward, eyeing the open books around them. "Have you had any breakthroughs with what you're here to research?"

"Oh, not as of yet — but I have definitely found a treasure trove of things within these books here, and I'm only just beginning to dig through it all." Sarrai hesitated and leaned back as Zanve heard the tinkling of a tea set and tray behind them, Elsie reappearing with an array of food in hand. The tea pot steamed merrily as Sarrai started to pour them cups of tea, mixing in a touch of sugar and cream in their own before sitting back with the cup in hand. "So, my dear man. I get the sense that you are visiting me in my scholarly trove here for a specific reason."

Zanve mixed his own tea — a heap of sugar, and a splash of milk — before he looked back up at the Scholar. "I was wondering if I could pick your brain about magical creatures."

The Scholar looked momentarily contemplative, nodding their head. "In what capacity? Dragons are more of my colleagues' specialty — as are their tiny cousins, the wyrmlings."

"More along the lines of your studies, actually. Fey creatures."

"Oh! Then I may be of help. They aren't my entire focus, I'm more interested in the phenomena and magics of the fey realm, but I do have an extensive background in studying as many branches of the fey realm as I could. Geography, flora, fauna, you name it." Sarrai chuckled and sipped their tea. "I happened to be the only academic in my graduation ceremony that had three simultaneous degrees, all in the same blanketing subject: the fey realm. One for magics, of which I am now pursuing in my work; one in beings, and one in creatures!"

Zanve raised his eyebrows, impressed. "I've never actually met anyone who studied at an academic level like that."

"It was my biggest dream as a young child to pursue a higher education, and now I get to do so every day. But that's beside the point — what exactly can I help you with? I can't imagine there are many fey creatures out here, running amok." The Scholar laughed again, but Zanve found it hard to follow. He sipped at his tea before he settled it on a tiny square of space on the table between them.

"That's the thing," said Zanve slowly, lowering his voice and leaning forward so that, even though they seemed to be alone, if there were any servants lingering amidst the stacks of Lord Wymarc's library, they wouldn't hear. "I think I may know what caused the event that brought you here, and I think you can help us with figuring out more about him."

The Scholar looked positively perplexed. They leaned forward and whispered, "Excuse me, my dear man? Him? Us? What is the meaning of all this?"

"It would probably be best if I let my — my friend tell you more about this," said Zanve. "I wanted to see if you would be willing to help us, and also if you would be willing to keep it a bit of a secret. At least until we figure out what really happened and what he really is."

Sarrai hesitated, looking intently at Zanve. There was a moment, briefly, where Zanve thought he had read the Scholar entirely wrong; but then their eyes widened with delight and practically began to sparkle as they smiled. "My dear Zanve. Secrets are my third favorite thing, after my scholarly pursuits and cherry wine. I stash them like jewels in the recesses of my mind — I quite possibly couldn't be more honored to keep them!"

Zanve left a few moments later with a missive from Sarrai to Meri. It asked to meet that afternoon to chat, wherever she liked. Zanve hurried home to free himself from the confines of his plate armor, unbuckling the pieces and dropped them unceremoniously onto his bed. He collected the various plants and supplies he had picked up from Caelynn's and hastened out of town.

Adrias chuckled as he saw Zanve approaching the front gate, his head shaking. "Out to see her again, are we? Oh, the start of a romance is so delicious — the will they won't they, the sneaky touches, the longing glances. I remember what it was like when I first laid eyes on my Tala..."

Zanve snorted. "You've been with Tala since we were boys, and let me just say, your touches still aren't as sneaky as you think they are."

"I'll have you know that Tala and I keep our romance alive and well on the daily." Adrias chuckled. "However we can."

"Oh we all know that," added Nisri, who was hidden by shadow as they leaned against the Arrowmount wall.

"Besides, this isn't that," said Zanve dismissively. Meri and he hadn't spoken of anything close to romance; despite what he felt for her, he didn't want to assume that she felt the same. Although, the moment they had shared in her garden... he didn't want to get his hopes up too much, but he thought there might be something there.

"Sure, sure." Adrias nodded to the plants. "Did she send you to pick those up, or are you buying her presents already?" He must've seen something change on Zanve's face, because he fell into raucous, knowing laughter.

"Ah, love," said Nisri blissfully.

Zanve took a few steps away from them, shaking his head, before he remembered what Cecily had said about Damian and turned back. "Did either of you see Damian today?"

Adrias grunted. "No, thankfully. Why?"

Zanve gestured toward Meri's. "I heard tell that he was going to visit her."

"Oh that rumor? Bah, I can't believe it."

"It's true," said Nisri, gliding out of the shadows. They looked entirely too entertained by this tidbit of information they were about to share.

Zanve's heartrate picked up. "True? What did you hear?"

"I didn't really *hear* anything," they said slowly, "but I did see him. He was trying to be all subtle about it, but—"

"I don't think I will ever believe he tried to be *subtle*," interrupted Adrias with a grunt.

Nisri continued on as though they hadn't heard him. "—he headed up the road toward her cottage. He had his hair greased back *and* his uniform was so starched you could've hit it with a cart, and it wouldn't have wrinkled."

"When was this?" asked Zanve softly, his stomach roiling with unease.

"Eh, about an hour ago," said Nisri, looking as if they were positively bursting with anticipation. Zanve recognized this emotion well in them; this is exactly how they looked right as they were about to share the juiciest part of the gossip.

"Where was I?" asked Adrias, baffled. "I didn't see anything."

"He came back not even ten minutes later, all disheveled and looking like he saw a ghost!" continued Nisri. "He was muttering under his breath about some *beast*. I think he was even bleeding! Something got him good in those trees."

Adrias snorted. "He probably saw the Witch — sorry, *Meriwen* — crouched down doing some gardening, caught sight of her antlers, and thought she was a demon or something."

"Whatever it was, bird or rabbit or bear, it spooked him good," chuckled Nisri. "I don't think you have to worry at all, Zanve."

That's not what he was afraid of. He was afraid of Damian's intentions — what he was going out there to do, originally, and what he would do now. Also, what had he seen that frightened him so badly?

"Thanks," said Zanve to the two guards, leaving them snickering as he picked up his pace, heading toward Meri's cottage.

29

DUST AND RED EYES

Zanve

Z anve tried not to break into a run in his haste. The moment he was hidden in the trees, though, he picked up his pace, jogging the last stretch, heart in his throat.

"Meri?" he called, casting a quick glance around as he strode into the garden. Everything looked fairly in place; there were birds flitting about the trees, a few cats dotted about beneath the garden beds poking about, and the green wyrmling was curled up on the garden chair out front. Thistle burst out of the long grass and hurried over to him, long ears flopping.

Zanve bent and pet the feathered creature, and a delighted Thistle turned onto his back for belly scratches.

"Hello?" a voice called from the depths of the little cottage, drawing him inside.

"It's me," he answered, pausing at the counter to unload all of the bits he'd bought, including the slightly squashed package of baked goods

266

from inside his jacket.

"I'm upstairs."

Zanve followed Meri's voice, weaving around her house before finding the stairs to the second floor tucked behind a shelving unit that had been shoved out of the way.

His eyes tracked the space, watching the brilliant sunlight coursing down the stairs that revealed puffs of dust that hung almost like glitter in the air. When he crested the last stair, he found himself momentarily wondering if he had walked back into Lord Wymarc's library. It took him a moment to realize that these were Meri's mother's journals. The sheer number of tomes around him was astonishing.

He whistled low. "Now, when you said she had a lot of journals, I assumed maybe a hundred. Not a veritable *library* of them."

"She once told me that to call a collection of books a library, you'd have to have a thousand books," said Meri's voice, preceding the woman herself as she ducked out from a side room that was also full of journals. A thin strand of cobweb had tangled in her antlers. "I once tried to count the journals my mother decided to store in my cottage, and was very unsurprised to have passed two thousand before I had to concede. She's unstoppable."

"Amazing." Zanve reached and untangled the bit of cobweb from her antlers gently, causing her to freeze, her eyes tracking his movement. "You're covered in dust."

"Agh." She grimaced and wiped furiously at her nose. "I am well aware. I will be —" she sneezed furiously three times in a row, "sneezing for years at this point."

"What were you doing up here?"

"Giving the pixies some more material for their reading," she answered, gesturing off toward the opposite wall, where a fairly large hole was scoured out, replaced by swaths of brilliant fabrics.

Zanve froze. "Pixies?"

Meri looked at him, bemused. "Did I not say? Wyn ended up un-earthing a nest of them up here when she helped me bring down my kitchen table. They're completely harmless, though, so you don't have to worry about them."

He nodded slowly, absorbing this information. Then he asked the next obvious question: "Pixies can read?"

Meri flinched, holding up a finger, as a small, very irritated voice sounded from the nest of fabric.

"Of COURSE we can read, you illiterate degenerate!" A small brilliant blue creature that looked like a collection of sticks appeared from the shelf of books right next to him, frowning. "We know the value of a library when we see one. And this one? Unlike any other library in the entire realm, you dolt."

"I—" Zanve blinked at the tiny creature, completely baffled at the vocabulary coming from it. "My mistake, I have not had the honor of meeting a pixie before."

"Well, now you have," it said, looking quite put out. "Meriwen — did you happen to find the tomes from your mother's sojourn in the shadow realm?"

"Yes, they're all through there, behind the sky realm ones," Meri answered, pointing toward the room that she had come from. "Feel free to read as you wish. Zanve, come, let's go downstairs."

"I... Okay," he said slowly, feeling quite out of his depth. The pixie drifted off in the direction Meri had indicated.

"Sorry about that," said Meri, dropping her voice as they descended back to the first floor. "I didn't realize how precious pixies could be about their reading material until today."

"You're letting them stay?"

Meri shrugged. "I'm not using the upstairs space, and it's nice having them around, for the sheer fact they will use my mother's journals more than I ever would."

"You're not worried they'll ruin them, are you?"

"Not in the slightest. Most of the realm's best libraries have pixie nests within them — they are some of the best custodians, too. They are quite precious about their books, let me tell you." Meri shook her head. "And I made a deal with them. A few have gone back to the fey realm for me to gather some of my missing herbs, and in exchange, they can basically take over my attic."

"Fantastic!" Zanve exclaimed before he hesitated. "Wait, they can go back to the fey realm? How? I thought the only door was in Feycross, and that was weeks away."

"Yes, well. Turns out pixies have a number of powers that I'm sure scholars would love to know about, including the ability to cross realms at their will."

"So they can just..." he snapped his finger.

"From what I understand, yes. Hopefully that means they'll be able to come back rather quickly." She smiled softly at him, relief written all over her face. "But I've been really going on. What brings you here today?"

"I have a present for you," he said, sweeping his arm out in front of him as the two of them turned the corner and into her kitchen. When she saw the plethora of greenery and baked goods on the counter, her mouth dropped open. Lock had made his way inside after Zanve and was sitting on the counter glaring at a few birds who were trying to peck their way toward the baked goods.

"Zanve," Meri breathed, reaching out and touching a few of the plants. "This is too much."

"Courtesy of Caelynn," he said. "If you need more plants, let me know exactly what, and I will get that information down to Caelynn. This is for the rest of your greenhouse. I thought—"

Her arms wrapped around his chest, stopping him mid-sentence. She hugged him fiercely, tilting her head slightly so her antlers didn't knock him in the face. Zanve wrapped his arms around her and held her tight, breathing in her scent. She smelled of freshly turned soil and that unknown floral scent, which he nonetheless found quite lovely.

"Thank you," she said, letting him go. "Thank you, thank you."

"It was nothing," he said, a sudden urge to reach forward and grab her back to him. Instead, he tucked a loose strand of hair behind his ear. "I also thought I'd bring you some baked goods. I managed to grab the last two cinnamon buns before Gable ran out."

"Oh, excellent. I haven't eaten anything since this morning."

"And..." Zanve hesitated as Meri began to move around her kitchen, unearthing the package of baked goods from beneath the greenery. She cast him a look from beneath her eyelashes, curious. "I heard about Damian."

Meri sighed and shook her head. "What an irritating man."

"So he really did come out here?" Something inside him that had held on to a small hope that Nisri had been mistaken deflated. He tried to remain aloof, as though this didn't bother him at all. "What uh, what did he want?"

Meri rolled her eyes. "He came claiming he was interested in starting a relationship with me," she said, rolling her eyes. "I don't know what put it in his mind to do such a thing."

"Oh?"

"Truly. He doesn't even know my name." Meri pulled a large plate from one of her cabinets and placed both cinnamon buns atop it. "I think he was rather put out when I told him he must have been fooling himself if he thought telling me he had immense feelings for me was going to lead to anything."

Zanve chuckled, feeling much lighter all of a sudden. "He didn't like that much, did he? He should know your name, by the way. I mentioned it just the other day. It's just like him to not remember. Is that why he ran off?"

Meri grimaced. "No, though I really do think he was about to leave—" Meri's hesitation made Zanve worry. He knew what things men were capable of, especially angry, humiliated men like Damian. "—but then Lock decided to bite him, and he took off running."

Zanve burst out laughing. The wyrmling had since migrated inside, and was curled up in the middle of the kitchen table, surrounded by journals. "Hemlock, you are my hero."

Lock looked distinctly smug as smoke started to curl out of his nose.

"I do hope it didn't do him *much* harm," sighed Meri. "I never expected Lock to do something like that."

"Mmmm. Protecting," grumbled the wyrmling.

"I know, Lock." Meri shook her head at Zanve. "Hopefully that's the last I see of him. I don't know what he was thinking."

"He was probably doing it because he thought it would upset me," Zanve said, unable to completely keep the growl out of his voice. Damian was truly the worst kind of man alive. Going after those Zanve held close — throwing jibes at Kaius for his polyamory, coming out here to accost Meri with false claims — was too far.

"Why would he do that?" Meri settled her hip against her counter, taking a bite of cinnamon bun, looking at him curiously. "He did mention he was a friend of yours, but I've never heard you talk about him."

"He is the furthest thing from a friend," answered Zanve with more bite than he anticipated. He held up a hand at her raised eyebrows, waving away her astonishment. "Apologies. There is just something about him that gets under my skin. He and I have never seen eye to eye — he is constantly trying to bother me, set me off. I don't know why, I have never done anything to him, from what I remember."

"Well, hopefully now that Lock has had his say, Damian won't come back."

Zanve smiled at the wyrmling, thinking about the way Damian must have looked when Lock sank his teeth into the man's arm. Then he remembered Thistle, and the letter currently sitting in his pocket. "Oh, I nearly forgot — Sarrai told me to give this to you. I met with them this morning."

Meri's eyes went wide and she immediately tore open the missive and began to read. "They want to meet today! Well, alright, I suppose I could... yes, why not."

"They seem incredibly knowledgeable — apparently, they are an expert not only in magics and phenomena, but also in the people and creatures of the fey realm. I think they're our best bet at getting more information on what Thistle could be."

Meri's eyes unfocused for a moment, staring into the middle distance. Her hands clenched and unclenched, then, as though coming to a decision, she nodded. "Alright, then. Let's go."

"Go?"

Meri grabbed a bag, slinging it over her shoulder, before grabbing her beautifully wrought wooden staff. "To town. Let's meet with this scholar, and finally get answers. And—"

She turned to him, biting her lip.

"What is it?" He joined her at her side. An errant hair had slipped down over her cheek; he resisted the urge to tuck it behind her ear.

"Damian. I should let you know, he did grab me. Just in case he tries to hold that over you." She flicked her sleeve back, revealing a few very faint bruises. Instantly, Zanve felt as though he was on fire. He touched her. He left *bruises* on her. He would not breathe for another day. HE—

"Not that he hurt me, I just wanted you to know. Are — Zanve, your eyes are red." Meri reached out, stopping him with a gentle touch on his chest and looked at him worriedly.

He blinked furiously, as though that would do anything, and breathed out long and slow. "The thought of him doing anything to harm you—"

Meri reached up and touched his face gently, silencing him. Softly, she traced her thumb on his cheek, just above his beard, leaving behind a line of what felt like sparks. "I can promise you that he did not harm me, and I would never let him get that far. Not in the way he was insinuating when he approached me, not any way at all. I can handle myself. I just didn't have the opportunity before Lock got his teeth into him."

"Right. Right. Sorry." Zanve closed his eyes, momentarily leaning into her touch, breathing in the scent of Meri and her garden beyond the kitchen door.

"My cottage sits on a power source," she added when he finally opened his eyes again. "I'd like to see him try. Then I'd show him exactly what the Witch of the Woods is capable of."

Zanve laughed.

30

FEY BEAST LAIRS

Meriwen

Meri's heart kept skipping beats as she walked alongside Zanve through the meadow toward Arrowmount, one hand on her staff for support. Zanve walked on her right, next to her free hand. They were close enough that their knuckles kept brushing. It didn't always happen, but so far, she counted about five times that her and Zanve would gently drift toward one another.

Every single time, it left her skin tingling.

"Where would you like to meet the Scholar?" asked Zanve softly as they approached the town gates.

"Somewhere where we won't be overheard, I think — not at the Lord's manor." Meri readjusted her grip on her staff as they walked up to the gate. "Perhaps A Second Story? They have that room in the back with tables we could sit at."

"I'm sure that Arileas will be willing to clear out the space for you if need be. That would be smart, not going to the Lord's place — for one, there are always servants loitering about. And I don't particularly wish for the Lord of Arrowmount to hear about you."

Meri frowned at him. "Why don't you want him knowing about me?"

"Oh," Zanve answered, "because you said you were worried about the rest of town finding out about... our little friend." He glanced around them to make sure they weren't being overheard. A gentle blush spread across his cheeks. He then lowered his voice slightly, leaning in closer, their knuckles brushing once more. "And I don't know really what Wymarc would do, tying you to Sarrai and their research. Maybe he'd poke around you more with questions, and I know how quiet you like things. Plus, questions could bring people, and then..."

"They may find out about Thistle," she breathed, feeling a new bout of concern flood through her as they approached the town gates. "I didn't think of that."

Zanve nodded before waved to the guards stationed at the gates. "Adrias, Nisri. This is Meriwen. Meri, these are two of my more tolerable colleagues."

One of the guards, an incredibly handsome dwarf, was looking at her with unadulterated astonishment. The other was leaning against the wall half hidden in shadow.

"A pleasure," she said, giving the dwarf a soft smile as he walked up to her, clasping his extended hand. Adrias eyed her and Zanve, a grin breaking across his face.

"Adrias Waylan, and the pleasure is all mine," he said. "What business do the two of you have in town today?"

"We're headed to the bookshop," answered Zanve.

"Ah, you know Zanve and his reading," said Adrias with a chuckle. He clapped Zanve on the forearm amiably. "Make sure he doesn't get too lost in all those books — Nisri, come off that wall, you look like an overgrown bat. And close your mouth, flies will get in."

The other figure jolted into movement, hurriedly brushing back their hair. "A-apologies. I was simply taken aback at how beautiful you are, Meriwen."

Both Zanve and Adrias groaned audibly before Meri could formulate a response. It *was* rather forward.

"Meri, ignore them," said Zanve. "They like to think they're an expert with women, but, they get more nervous than Lock when he sees danger if a woman ever approaches them."

She laughed, amused. "I don't mind."

Adrias snorted at the expression of fear and admiration that crossed Nisri's angular face.

"In fact, it seems almost unfair that two such handsome people as you are guarding the town," she said, gesturing between Adrias and Nisri. "There must be something in the water you guards consume."

"If there was, then Damian wouldn't be such a sniveling rat," said Adrias happily. Nisri seemed to have succumbed to that numb, unmoving shock once again. "Carry on you two, enjoy your day. Say hello to Arileas and Finnean for us."

They passed through the gates, Meri taking a moment to accustom herself to the cobbles — or at least to the best of her abilities — before she frowned up at Zanve. "You read?"

Zanve simply chuckled. "Of course I do."

"What do you read?"

"Mostly adventure novels," he answered, casting a look at a passerby over Meri's shoulder. "I do love a good pirate novel, too. There's something about the swashbuckling and swords that I adore."

"When do you have time to read?"

Zanve raised his eyebrows at her as they turned down a street to the right, taking Fetterly Place down to the bookstore. "Do you know how dull my work is? I'm a town guard in a town that hasn't seen any kind of conflict in decades, possibly more. I don't know if you know this, but it's thanks to a certain witch who lives at the edge of the forest." He added the last bit in a lowered tone, his eyes and expression teasing.

"Oh, you don't say. I'll have to pay her a visit, see if she can cure this awful bother of mine."

"What's that?"

"This man keeps showing up at my door, offering plants and baked goods. I simply don't know what to do with him!"

Zanve chuckled as they reached the shop. A few townsfolk were staring at them, open-mouthed. Meri had barely noticed them as they walked into Arrowmount, but now glancing around, she noticed that almost every eye was on the two of them.

She was used to having eyes on her, but not like this. It was as though everyone was staring *through* them, not just *at* them. The intensity and the whispers were all too much.

She hesitated, momentarily stumbling on one of the cobbles. Zanve was there in an instant, his hand around her waist to steady her. Without even pausing in their conversation, he threaded his fingers through hers. Her heart stuttered.

"Well, if she gives you a remedy, please do not use it," said Zanve, opening one of the gorgeously wrought double wooden doors leading to the brightly yellow painted shop that had somehow appeared in front of them. Meri honestly couldn't tell how. "I rather enjoy bringing you baked goods and plants."

He then leaned down nearer to her as he held the door open, and whispered, "Ignore them, Meri. I have you."

"Thank you," she said, squeezing his hand. That touch alone grounded her, steadied her, more than her staff ever had. "Not just for that — but for everything."

"Even locking Thistle in your greenhouse and putting you into this mess?" His eyes glittered, their faces rather close together.

"Without it, I wouldn't have you," she answered plainly, walking into the store, pulling him with her. Zanve fell into step close enough to her that she could feel his warmth radiating from him and had to actively stop herself from leaning back into him. She turned, their hands still linked, and found herself almost encircled by his arms.

"Are you... going to go fetch the Scholar?" she said, her voice quieter now that they were inside the store, enveloped in the warmth of the rich green walls and books.

His lips formed a soft 'o.' "Right. Yes. I will. First I wanted to... make sure that you got in here alright."

She chuckled. "And here I am, safe and sound, delivered by my faithful knight in shining... linen and leather."

His eyes burned into hers, a grin breaking wider across his face. "I knew I should have left my plate armor on. It's perfectly shiny and clean, unlike any decent armor should be, but at least then I'd be able to take a sword for you. In theory."

"Hello!" called a voice from further into the shop. Meri stepped slightly away from Zanve, but not enough to let go of his hand, as Zanve kept her fingers twined in his, bringing their joined hands to his side. "Ah, Zanve! Back again, I see."

A rather handsome man with long, curling brown hair, and an incredibly charming smile came into view.

"Finnean," said Zanve, nodding in greeting.

"What are you in for today? You didn't bring another storm with you, did you?" The man winked rather attractively before he gestured with his head toward somewhere deeper in the store. "I can grab Ari, if you need him to help you find anything specific. Another one of your adventure novels?"

"I'm not staying long," said Zanve, before looking back to Meri, as though his eyes couldn't help but lock on hers. "I was just..."

"He was simply walking me to the shop before heading back out. Zanve has graciously organized a meeting here for me," said Meri quickly. "And now that I'm here, I may as well look for a few books. It's been a long while since I've been in the store."

Finnean grinned at her. "Pleasure, pleasure, of course. Well, if that's the case, I know nothing about books, so I will get my partner. Zanve — are you really running off so soon? Just leaving this lovely woman behind?"

"I am just going to do another quick stop, and then will be right back."

"We'll hold down the shop until you come back." Finnean winked at him, briefly looking down at their entwined hands. Zanve's fingers slipped from hers before he exited the shop, casting one last glance at her.

"I actually wanted to talk to you, too." Meri said to Finnean as he moved to head back through the shop. He stopped, surprised. "A while ago, I acquired a stone from Cecily, and she told me that you were the one who gave it to her? The weirdly pitted one?"

"Ah yes!" His eyes lit up. He held up a finger and took a few steps away from her, heading toward the winding stairs leading up to a second-floor. "Give me just a moment, and I'll regale you with that story."

A small brown cat appeared, daintily stepping down the stairs to join them. The cat meowed up at the two of them, the sound almost a squeak, before Finnean bent and scooped her up.

"Ah, Sophie, where have you been hiding all morning? You silly tabby, you missed Calian coming in. You know how they love to pet you."

The cat *mmmrped* in response.

Finnean turned and directed his voice upward. "Ari, love! Customers!"

Moments later, a set of shining, well-loved boots appeared at the top of the stairs, preceding a tall, white-haired elf, who hurried down the steps. He was wearing a rather fine knitted blue sweater that looked supremely cozy.

"Hello!" he said, smiling kindly at Meri. "Welcome back to the shop, it's been a while."

"She's come looking for something in particular," said Finnean, "and also asking about the stone I got from the fey beast's lair!"

Arileas shot a look at his partner, rolling his eyes. "Ah, yes, of course. Your last heroic adventure."

Meri was intrigued. "You found the stone in a lair, yes? Cecily told me a little bit about it when I picked it up."

"We fought this beast, myself and a group of rather younger adventurers," said Finnean, grinning at the memory, gesturing animatedly with the hand not holding the cat. "It was an incredible fight. The beast itself was huge, and nearly tore me in two!"

"He was just fine, from what I hear," said Arileas dryly.

Finnean scoffed, rolling his eyes playfully at his partner. "*Just* fine. Just fine? I—"

"The stone, darling."

"Right. When we were raiding the beast's hoard afterward, finding more treasure than I had ever come across in my lifetime, I came across that rather odd stone. Something about it felt special, even though I could tell well enough it was not a gemstone or anything like that, and I figured, why not bring it home? When I did, though, I didn't know what to do with it. Even Ari didn't know what it could be. Then one day, the idea just came to me — why not give it to Cecily? She would have a better time with it, she knows more about magical objects than I do."

"Stolen items from fey beast lairs are not really my forte," said Arileas. "Plus, I don't really know much about magical artifacts at all."

"So, we handed it off to Cecily. And you're the one who got it! I'm happy it found its rightful place."

"It has," said Meri, thinking of Thistle snoozing amidst the long grass around her garden. "I was hoping you'd know a bit more about it, since it has proven to be a rather interesting artifact to have. It's intriguing."

"You've never seen anything like it?" asked Arileas, eyeing her interestedly. "I thought, perhaps, with you being fey..."

"No, unfortunately, I know very little about rocks and creatures and such from my home. That's actually why I'm here." She gestured to the shop. "You wouldn't happen to have any books on fey creatures, would you?"

"Oh, we have a few!" Ari started off immediately toward the back of the shop, to a wall of books tucked in a corner. Finnean drifted behind a beautifully wrought wooden counter, the cat in his arms. "What in particular would you like to know? General information? Large beasts? Night beasts?"

"Rare beasts," she answered. "If you have anything of the sort."

"Let me see." Arileas eyed the shelves, fingering a few of the tomes and pulling them out, stacking them in his arms. "I am curious as to why you are interested in the fey realm and its denizens."

Meri took a large tome from him, looking down at the cover. It was an extensive bestiary of the fey realm, and claimed to be a nearly exhaustive list. *Nearly.* Hopefully Thistle was included. "My mother is a scholarly adventurer, and though she keeps many, many journals of her findings, her work on the fey realm is woefully lacking. I find myself wanting to know more. I think perhaps that, uh, stone prompted me."

"Ah, she's one of those 'magic shines brighter in other realms' people is she?"

"You could definitely say that."

Meri flipped open the tome in her hands and eyed the first few pages, wondering at the sheer amount of information offered up right at the beginning. There seemed to be a veritable menagerie of fey creatures gathered in these pages.

"These could start you off," said Arileas, holding up three more books. "We have a little room off to the side, if you want to leaf through them and see if you can find what you're looking for."

Meri nodded. "I would love that, thank you. Finnean didn't mention — but Zanve is bringing back another person for a little meeting."

"Oh, the Scholar?"

"Yes," said Meri, surprised. "How did you...?"

"News about that particular Scholar has spread through town rather quickly," said Ari, chuckling. "I am happy to let you use the space. Let's get you set up."

31

THE SCHOLAR

Meriwen

Once she had settled in a chair, leaning her staff against the nearby wall, Meri settled in to start flipping through the Bestiary, passing by innumerable detailed descriptions of so many varied creatures that her eyes swam. If Thistle wasn't in this tome, she wouldn't know where else to look.

After a half hour, though, she still hadn't found him. Page after page of familiar and unfamiliar creatures that populated the fey realm, and yet none of them spoke of any that could pass through doorways or portals. There were some more powerful beasts that could open them, but none that spoke of reaching out to you through your mind, guiding you through rituals to open the pathway on their behalf.

No feathered creatures that appeared, using a magical stone to cross realms.

A little way away, the shop door opened, softly brushing against the floor and barely breaking through Meri's focus as she read. But then she

283

recognized a set of footsteps and instantly looked up.

Zanve appeared in the doorway, two figures following close behind. Arileas gestured them inside before walking back to the front of the shop.

"Meri, please meet Scholar Daruka." Zanve motioned to the tiny figure. "Sarrai, this is Meriwen."

"Meriwen of the Fey," breathed the Scholar. The gnome wrapped both their hands around Meri's one as she proffered it and shook warmly. "It is an absolute pleasure to meet you, and to get to talk to you. I have met only a few fey in my life, but each time, it is an even greater pleasure."

"I'm surprised to hear you've met more fey, seeing as not many of us venture into the material realm regularly. Where did you happen to meet them?"

"Other than the many that I've met during my ventures into the fey realm itself, I've only had the pleasure of meeting one in this realm, and that was due to her coming to the university when I was a student there. Oh, the conversations we had!" Sarrai grinned at the memory.

Meri shifted on her chair, wondering. It sounded a lot like what her mother did, often seeking out places of study to discuss with scholarly people. She was a scholar of a sort herself, though not in title. "That wasn't by chance someone by the name of Elestren, was it?"

"Yes! We had tea together, something that she made herself — it was such a delicious tea — and we ended up chatting for hours about her home and her adventures around the material realm."

"She didn't bore you with stories about the material realm?"

"No, on the contrary," the Scholar beamed. "Hearing about one's own realm and life from someone who has lived a very differently is always an interesting conversation. And Elestren was one of the best conversationalists I've had the opportunity to meet — even among my fellow Scholars."

Meri glanced sideways at Zanve. "Well, if I ever see my mother again, I'll let her know you think so highly of her."

Sarrai's eyes bulged. "Your mother? Your mother is Elestren Fair?"

"Yes, yes she is." Meri smiled at the addition of her mother's expanded, human name. Naming practices in the fey realm were different from the majority of what was normal in the material realm. If a fey decided to take on an extra name other than their given one, it was to tie them to the court they belonged to, or the lord they served under. Her mother had taken a second name, "Fair," because she'd heard some people call the fey Fair Folk, which she thought was quite funny. Most of the fey realm, in her mother's words, were "the furthest thing from fair."

Sarrai sat down across from Meri with a happy little shudder, their eyes glowing. "My oh my, what a treat. Alright, dearest Meriwen Fair, what an honor it is to meet you. How may I be of service? Zanve here has alluded that you may have some of the answers to some rather interesting aspects of my research."

She glanced at Zanve, suddenly awash with an entirely trepidatious feeling, wondering if this person, this Scholar from a Kingdom that she herself had spent barely a week in, was worth her trust. Zanve, though, raised an eyebrow, the trust already there in his eyes.

If he trusted Scholar Daruka, then that was enough.

"Zanve told me a little bit of why you are here," she started, settling back into her chair. "Studying a magical event that was felt all the way in Pralon."

"Oh yes," said Sarrai, clasping their hands together. Meri noticed immediately the soft ink stains along the tips of their fingers, splatters from their craft, much like the dirt under her own nails. "I believe I told your lovely guard here that something happened in Arrowmount a number of weeks ago. An event that should not have happened unless there was a door or some kind of connection with the fey realm. Something akin to an incredibly powerful arch fey walking through the doorway in Feycross, if you will."

Meri leaned forward, intrigued. "So, when such a being does cross like that, you — meaning Scholars like you — feel it?"

"Yes, well. Has to be a very powerful person, mind. When beings of that kind of power come into the material realm, the magic here gets very agitated. We can feel it — well, perhaps 'feel' isn't the right term. We can sense it, magically. If you are a powerful magic user attuned to power at that very moment, you would sense something as well."

"And you believe something happened here, in Arrowmount, yes?"

"That is why I am here. When we felt those intense movements of magic, my colleagues and I decided that it was probably prudent to investigate the phenomenon. It was peculiar and so exciting to see such activity coming from the south east of the kingdom."

Zanve, who had been listening attentively, tapped a finger on one of the books that Meri had brought into the room with her. "These beings when they come into our realm. Do they need to be High Fey? I mean, do they need to be a person? Or could it be a creature?"

The Scholar *hmmed* softly, their eyes getting a slightly far off look as they mulled the question over. "Theoretically, it could be either. But you must understand, the doorway at Feycross is something that only people, High Fey or otherwise, can use. It requires a choice and a conscious opening of said door. A creature cannot just lumber through, if that is what you're asking. There are wards against that, because what would happen if the material realm was suddenly overrun with creatures we don't even know the names of?" The Scholar chuckled amiably.

"But, there *have* been instances of creatures crossing over," said Meri softly. Sarrai hesitated, eyeing her. "For one, one of the purveyors of this very bookstore fought and killed a large fey beast that was terrorizing part of Feycross last summer. And mistakes happen — people are people, of course. We cannot be infallible, no matter the race, or the level of power. In fact, the more power some have, the more fallible they tend to be, I've found."

Sarrai pursed their lips. "Hmm. You're not wrong, though it is incredibly rare. We did not know of such a beast crossing the Feycross doorway. So, when it did, its magic did not disturb us in Pralon. To find a creature *that* powerful? I don't believe they really..." The Scholar frowned, looking slightly annoyed at themself. "Well, that's not exactly right, now. I have studied creatures that may have immense power, but they are so rare, that... bah, what am I saying? This event mimicked that feeling, as though a powerful being passed through the door at Feycross, but here in Arrowmount. Where, from my knowledge, there is no door."

Meri nodded slowly. "I believe I know what caused that event."

"Zanve indicated as much this morning." The Scholar sat up straighter, eyes sparkling. "Do tell, my dear. You're keeping me on the edge of my seat!"

"A little while ago," said Meri slowly. "I purchased a stone from a seller here in Arrowmount, who got it from Finnean, here at the bookshop." She pointed out toward where the booksellers had disappeared to. "It was an odd stone, lighter than it should have been for its size, and shone like an oil slick. It was pitted all over, and was of a geological variety I had never seen before. But that wasn't what called me to it. It was like something in my chest connected with it, and drew me to the booth, and to pick up the stone in my hands.

"I kept the stone in my garden for a while, moving it every so often, because it just didn't feel quite right wherever I placed it. Then, as spring started to creep closer and my lavender began to grow, I nestled it there.

It finally felt almost right.

"And then that night, something... happened." Meri paused, eyes moving between Zanve and the Scholar. They were both watching her intently.

"What?" breathed Sarrai, entirely rapt.

"Something slipped into my mind and started to guide me though a ritual, making me take the stone out to a clearing by my cottage. And then... well, Zanve probably knows this next bit a bit better than I do."

"I was on guard that night," he said, the Scholar turning to look at him, their eyes bright as though they were a child listening to a ghost story. "I saw a bright light in the forest, once, twice; I had to go investigate. When I arrived at Meri's cottage, I saw something break the stone apart and appear."

Meri nodded. "What I remember is the stone pulsing suddenly, as though it had waited for that very moment — and my ritual had drawn the distinct pattern of a door or an archway — and then—"

"The stone exploded as a creature appeared. It injured Meri and we were thrown into chaos." Zanve shook his head with a soft laugh. "I locked it in her greenhouse, which I will forever be sorry for."

"I am not sorry for it," said Meri softly, laying a hand atop Zanve's, feeling slightly brave. His eyes practically glowed purple at her. She looked back to the Scholar. "Now I have this mysterious fey creature in my cottage, who has an odd connection to me, and I'm not even sure what he is.

"That's why I wanted to talk to you, Scholar," Meri continued. "I have never seen a creature like Thistle. And I'm not entirely sure what he can do, or why he's here. Why he chose me, my garden, that night, to come here. If his appearance is the moment you noticed and came here to research, you're saying that it let off enough magic to be felt all the way in Pralon. We must find out what he is."

Sarrai looked as though they were about to burst. "Oh, I — I this — all of this, is so much. I did not expect to find my answers so quickly." They paused, biting at a fingernail, momentarily lost in thought. Then they leaned forward eagerly. "Would it be possible for me to meet the creature? That would help me identify it, of course, and to really see if he — Thistle, you said? What a name — to see if Thistle is the reason I am here. How big of a creature is he?"

"He was once about of the size of my wyrmling," said Meri as explanation. "And now his head stands as tall as my thighs. He is covered in feathers like a bird, but looks more like a cat and a dog merged together with a bear, with a wide face. After he arrived, after he injured me accidentally, he was cautious around me, as though he knew he had done something wrong, and since then, he's been incredibly perceptive. I wish I knew what magic he could do. I haven't witnessed him do anything, just the aftermath."

"What did he do exactly?"

Zanve sniffed hard and shifted on his chair. "When I locked him in the greenhouse, he... destroyed it. Decimated it."

"Which, at first I didn't think was out of the ordinary. It was perfectly reasonable to imagine an anxious beast had rampaged through my greenhouse," said Meri. "But I should've noticed how odd it really was. The panes of glass in my greenhouse along the bottom were shattered, and much of my stores and my plants were cast about with such violence — he was so small, and so light, there was no way he could've done that physically."

"You're suggesting he has powers in him, enough that just moments after his birth, he was dangerously destructive?"

"Not necessarily dangerous," said Zanve. "I think he was just acting as any creature would when they are put in a place alone, anxious, and not knowing why."

Sarrai chuckled. "I understand, I understand. A creature backed into a corner will react as instinct wants it to. I do agree, we are dealing with a rather rare creature."

"Do you know what he could be?" asked Meri earnestly.

"Oh I have no idea. But I am greatly excited at the prospect of finding out!" Sarrai leaned forward and took both of Meri's hands. "I will help you solve this mystery, in return for you helping me solve mine. And if you will allow me to study this creature, perhaps we shall learn things that will aid the scholarly community as a whole. Oh the possibilities!"

PART FOUR

Unrest

32
HALOED IN GOLD

Meriwen

A few weeks passed, and spring fully languished in itself beyond Meri's door. In her garden, all of her plant beds were in full bloom, practically overflowing with life.

Meri stuck her head out of her front door, wondering where Zanve was. She was fairly certain he wasn't on guard duty — his next shift was starting much later tonight. It was the first day in many that she hadn't seen him, and for the life of her, she couldn't shake how much she missed him.

She turned from the door and settled back at her table, pulling one of her mother's journals toward her. The surface of the table was absolutely covered in journals and notes that she, Wyn, and Zanve had made as they perused the work. Wyn had begun visiting Meri's cottage nearly as much as Zanve did, bringing Kaius or Jay along to help Zanve with the greenhouse while she sat with Meri to pore over the journals.

They had also had another magical storm rip through Arrowmount, surprising residents in the middle of the night with brilliantly purple clouds and rumbling, continuous thunder; everything lit up with lightning that skated across the churning skies. Meri used the same spell she had before, struggling for a little longer to try and make an impact, but eventually, she quelled the storm once again. It had definitely been stronger than the previous one, which made her vaguely nervous for another, if it rolled through. Would she be able to stop it?

Absently, Meri began to massage her leg with one hand and started to leaf through the journal in front of her with the other. Upon waking today, she'd found her leg stiff and shooting with pain as though she had lightning trapped in her scar. After a few mugs of tea to shore up her strength, she tried to go about her usual morning, but found herself unable to walk very far.

The weather was perfect for gardening too, which made it all the worse. She had been stuck in a terrible mood, unable to move and enjoy the day.

Thankfully, Sarrai was sending her updates nearly daily on their research, breakthroughs or not. The updates arrived regularly, brought by increasingly curious children; Meri knew that they were the runners that were often around the streets of Arrowmount to send messages. It was oddly a welcome sight.

The first couple children that had arrived in her garden were very nervous. They were practically trembling as Meri came out of her kitchen to see what they wanted. But, each time as she sent them away with a soft smile after they got to see Lock or whatever animal that decided to make an appearance, the children seemed to relax.

The last few that had come around seemed eager to be there, handing over the notes from Sarrai with grins on their faces, drinking in her garden with bright eyes as though expecting it to reveal hidden secrets they could then bring back to their friends.

Thankfully, each time the children came only Lock was visible — Thistle remained hidden in the long grasses around her garden when they approached, despite him desperately wanting to say hello. Meri could feel annoyance and worry through their connection every time a new set of footsteps could be heard on her garden path. Each time, though, he remained hidden as she had asked.

Thistle had grown so much in the last couple weeks that the grass was only *just* hiding him now; it reached up to Meri's thighs in the shadow of the tree line surrounding her property, which was where he preferred to lurk, watching the garden. Thistle had taken to poking his nose into Meri's side when he was standing with her in the garden, making sure she knew he was there. His long, flopping ears had started to grow a soft down of feathers, and whenever Meri pet him, his bones were starting to feel substantial.

The last thing that she wanted was for a few children to start spreading rumors about Thistle around town. No one needed to know about him until absolutely necessary; and for now, it was easier to keep him hidden.

Besides, the children found enough joy in her anxious wyrmling. Lock was rather charming when he wanted to be, and was surprisingly good with the young guests. He was certainly far less irritable than he was when adults came around.

Meri blinked, eyes turning back to the journal in front of her, realizing that she'd been staring out the window for a solid few minutes. She was still on the hunt for anything helpful in her mother's journals, whether for communicating cross realms, or perhaps any hint about what Thistle could be. She had begun to read beyond the fey realm journals, though a couple of those still remained on the table. Meri had found a number of spells she wanted to try, though hadn't had an opportunity to yet.

After a long while of reading through her mother's thoughts on the weather in the sky realm — honestly, multiple chapters on the matter was a little ridiculous, but Meri was hoping to find a tidbit more about any storm quelling magic within the pages — she sat back, stretching out her legs in front of her.

Thistle's wide face popped up above Meri's half-open door. He immediately brightened when he saw Meri inside, seated at her kitchen table. His feathers were covered in a light dusting of pollen and plant detritus, haloing him in gold.

Over the past week, Thistle had begun expanding his vocabulary more; occasionally surprising Meri with one- or two-word exclamations through their bond as she was gardening. He seemed rather proud of himself for picking up the ability as quick as he could.

Zanve.

"He's not here, Thistle," she said to him out loud, reaching over from her spot on a kitchen chair and opening the door fully. "I don't know when he's—"

Thistle stepped over the threshold with only one foot, looking at her expectantly. *Zanve. Comes.*

Moments later, she heard Zanve's familiar footsteps coming through the trees. She smiled, then caught herself, before shifting impatiently on her chair. Root and ruin, what was with her?

"Zanve," she said as he walked up to her open door, his fist half raised to knock on the wooden frame. "To what do I owe the honor of you being here today?"

"I caught one of those runners with a missive from Sarrai for you — figured, since I was thinking of coming out this way, that having a reason would probably be better than just showing up." He smiled widely at her, his purple eyes shining in the mid-day sunshine. "Though, that child definitely looked put out that I was stopping them from coming out here. Did you know that you're so popular with the youngest members of our town?"

Meri took the rolled-up scroll from him with a soft laugh. "Zanve, you can come by any time. Besides, Thistle was missing you."

"Thistle was missing me? What a treat." He winked at her before scratching the fey creature between his ears. He hesitated, before running his hand carefully over the crown of the creature's head. "I think you have some little horns coming in, Thistle."

"Really?" Meri leaned forward carefully and slid her hand across Thistle's head. Thistle, to his credit, was very pleased to have two people petting him at once, and nearly melted into Zanve's knee, eyes closing.

Above his ears, two hard lumps that could easily have been mistaken for his skull bones were apparent. They most definitely hadn't been there the week before.

"Horns," breathed Meri. "I wonder what you will look like when you're fully grown."

"Probably fearsome and handsome," said Zanve, scruffing the top of Thistle's head. The creature rolled away from him onto his belly. "How has the research been coming?"

Meri unfurled the scroll from the Scholar and quickly glanced over it. "They've been having a grand time perusing the Lord's library — there have been a few creatures that Sarrai has found that could be Thistle, but of course, they want to come out and meet him before solidifying their answer. It says here — they wish to come out tomorrow evening to meet Thistle properly."

"Fantastic," said Zanve. "Finally, too. It's been weeks."

Meri scratched Thistle under his chin, eliciting a happy grumble from the creature. "We'll know what you are soon."

"Speaking of weeks," said Zanve as he settled against her counter, giving her that soft, crinkling smile that she had come to absolutely adore, "have you had any pixie activity?"

"Not a drop," she sighed. "I have no idea when they're going to come back. But hopefully soon."

"I'm sure they will," he said.

Meri stood slowly, testing her weight on her leg. Pain spidered through her muscles, but she held onto the chair's back and gritted her teeth. Through a half smile, she gestured to her tea things. "Would you like some tea?"

Zanve's eyes narrowed, focusing on her intently. "Are you alright?"

"Bad pain day," she answered, gesturing to her leg as she slowly made her way behind her counter. "What kind would you like?"

"You really don't have to," he said.

"I want to," she said, shooting him a warning look.

"Alright. Surprise me." Zanve removed a couple things from his pocket, rifling through them. "Do you mind if I take a look at Elestren's journals?"

"Not at all."

Meri began to make tea, choosing to make Zanve a sweetened lemon blend with a few of the fresh herbs that he had brought from Caelynn's shop. She ground them with her mortar and pestle, the fresh scent rising around her pleasantly.

"I wish I knew more about this," said Zanve, his finger trailing along a page of one of Elestren's journals as he glanced up at her.

"About?"

"Magic in general. Spells." He shook his head with a sigh. "Gods, I wish I knew about your teas and what you do with them. It's so odd to think that we live in a world so full of so many different kinds of magic but most of us have no idea how it works."

"What do you mean?"

"Just that—" Zanve gestured animatedly. "Take Wyn, for example. She's an elf, right? And elves are supposed to be magical beings, and have the ability to become really powerful. Look at Arileas, he's got the talent and skill, and worked for it. But since Wyn never really wanted to pursue her magic, she doesn't really know the limits of what she can do. She didn't go to school, didn't find a master or whatever it is she would need to do — she just is. And so her magic is small, minute."

"Everyday magic that can be quite big, though," said Meri. She hadn't really given the magic of individuals much thought; her focus had always been to keep the ley lines balanced. Up until now, she hadn't really even thought much about what people could do with their magic. "It is the magic that keeps life moving forward."

"That's a nice way to think about it," said Zanve, furrowing his brow. "You were taught your magic, though, right?

"I probably wouldn't have figured it out on my own if I wasn't raised by my mother and grandmother, that's true. But we can go on forever about the what-ifs and how's. I think if it's out there and you have the ability to, you can learn more about anything at all. So, why not learn? Most of what I do now is experimentation based off of those skills my grandmother taught me."

Zanve tilted his head, nodding slowly, clearly thinking something through. "Would you teach me?"

Meri hesitated, eyeing him. He was mostly human, despite the shifter abilities — and most of the magic she did with her teas was from inside her, her innate feyness, drawing only a touch from the world around her. He would need a well of his own.

"Not to *do* magic," Zanve quickly added. "I know I wouldn't be able to achieve the same things that you do, but I'd love to learn about what you do. The magic with the tea and the tinctures and your herbs. How it works. I would like to know."

"Okay then." It could be fun to teach him what she did, she thought; she had never had that opportunity before, to teach someone what she knew. "As long as you promise not to go spreading my secrets around town."

"I would never." Zanve tapped something on the counter with his finger. "This is my own journal. I figured... since you keep a journal, and your mother keeps many, it seemed like a good way to remember what you teach me. I've been carrying it with me for a bit."

Meri nodded in understanding. "I always find it helpful to be able to refer back to my notes."

Meri used the motion of making herself some more tea to detail to Zanve specific ingredients and what they did in her usual meadowsweet brew. As she mixed, she considered how she should best go about teaching him.

What would she start with? Simple was best — she looked over at Zanve as he flipped through her mother's journal on the fey realm, the one where she had found the storm quelling spell, with a soft crease between his eyebrows. Something at that level was difficult for her to grasp occasionally, even at this level.

She should start with the basics, she decided. Plants, their properties, and how to combine them into simple tinctures and teas.

Once they had finished their tea, Meri tested her leg once more. She could probably get through a little bit of a lesson today, with a new pull of magic into her limbs. Meri grabbed her basket that had been left beside the counter.

"If you want to learn, then we start with the basics. You can help me replenish some of my fresh stores, and prep things for drying."

"Great." Zanve followed her from her kitchen, handing her her staff. She grabbed it, leaning on it gratefully.

Strangely, tiny butterflies had taken flight in her stomach the longer that Zanve had sat with her, talking about how much he wanted to learn about what she did, what she loved. Before, when she had travelled with her mother, she was always just her mother's daughter, someone to take notice of only in half measures, never someone that actually was interesting enough to take the time out of their day to talk to. Even when she moved here, she was just an odd, reclusive Witch of the Woods, in her garden away from the world.

But with Zanve, she felt more herself than she had before. Or, perhaps she was simply more aware of herself in a way that she hadn't been.

"So, plants." Zanve put his hands on his hips and looked quizzically at her raised garden beds. Like her, they reached his thighs; the perfect height to garden without having to bend overmuch. "It is usual for gardens to be this abundant, this early in the year?"

"Not at all," she answered. "But, most of these are just sprouts. I planted those," she gestured to the nearest bed, which was full of tiny shoots of green, promising a wonderfully full bed in a few weeks' time. "Just a fortnight before Thistle came to me. They should be ready to for pruning and harvesting later this season, and into summer."

"What about these others?" Zanve gestured toward the thickly growing plants along the back of her garden. "They look like they've been out of winter for ages. If I know anything, it is that our Arrowmount winter is not kind to plant life."

"No, it is not," she agreed. "Most of my plants along the back are heartier, and ones that happen to like winter. But, the majority of what I grow pulls from the earth for a quicker abundance." She grimaced. "I don't really know how right it is, pulling some of the ley lines' power directly to grow my own plants. But, it's such a small amount, I don't believe anything is affected by it. The ley lines seem to be rather happy to be so helpful with my plants."

"Right, I had forgotten you mentioned they help with the growth. That's fascinating."

"It helps that the nexus of the lines is right around here." Meri gestured to the middle of her garden, where she had shown Zanve the power of the ley lines before.

Meri guided Zanve through her garden, showing him the different kinds of flowers she had grown along the middle beds; from the lavender where Thistle's stone used to lay to the growing alliums, brilliant red and orange daisies, marigolds, and the spots where yarrow would soon grow, too. Then she showed him the rosemary, oleander, and salvia that had been growing most of the winter, but was now nearing its end of season as spring sank into the world around them.

"Do these not feel the elements?" He ran a hand over the heads of some rosemary, releasing its woody, almost minty scent into the air. "It can get rather severe with the snow and cold."

"It does," agreed Meri. "I do have ways to protect my plants, of course. They love a bit of added mulch before the frosts, and to blanket all the beds in heavy snowfalls, I have covers that go over them."

"Brilliant little plants," Zanve whispered, bending to look at them all closer, again running a gentle hand over their leaves. "How is it that you are all so resilient, to survive such a terrible thing as cold?"

Meri continued on, starting to point out other herbs that she had nestled within the beds, most of them growing low to the soil. Zanve simply soaked it all in, asking occasional questions, running a careful hand along many of their leaves as Meri talked over their various properties and how to identify different plants in the wild.

Finally, she had him take clippings of some of the herbs and flowers, teaching him the right way to do so. "When you wish to cut some, find a node — a spot where a leaf is going to grow — a few inches down, and cut just below that. Good, that's exactly right. And you want to make sure never to take more than you need — you always want to leave more to keep growing."

They ended up spending a few hours together, in her garden, and then finally in her greenhouse as she taught him the proper way to prepare some flowers and herbs for drying, letting him hang his choices from the hooks installed on the rafters, joining a sad looking dried dandelion bundle that had been left out. Turns out, dandelions are not the best to dry. It had been an experiment of hers from the previous summer, long forgotten.

As she worked, the pain in Meri's leg crept back. She kept pushing the ache away, begging it silently to let her enjoy this day; but it was a shadow in the back of her mind the entire time. Meri had to stop many times in the middle of her explanations to focus, pulling more magic up through the ley lines, bolstering her.

Zanve paused their lessons to bring her a chair after the second time he noticed her breaks in conversation.

As the sun began to sink lower in the horizon, casting the world in soft blues and purples and pinks, Zanve walked from her garden with a soft look of genuine pleasure on his face.

He had rolled up his sleeves partway through the tour, his skin now peppered with dirt and earth up his wrists and under his nails, even after washing in her kitchen sink.

"Did you enjoy today?" she called, causing him to turn and look back before he reached the tree line.

Zanve beamed back at her. "More than you know. I hope you don't mind how much I'm going to be bothering you now, as you teach me more of this. Because we didn't even get to the magic part. Or the fey realm plant part."

"I don't mind." She bit her lip. "I don't think I could ever mind," she said softly to herself.

"Goodnight, Meriwen of the Garden."

"Goodnight, Zanve of the..." she frowned, not knowing exactly what to call him. He laughed and shook his head, before lifting a hand in farewell.

"You will figure that out in time, I'm sure."

"I will."

33

ALL IT TAKES

Zanve

Zanve rolled over, eyes barely open in the weak morning sunshine spilling in from around his window. He blinked a few times, focusing on the form of his mother in his doorway. He hadn't even heard her knock.

"Mum? Is everything okay?"

"Oh, everything is perfectly fine, love. I just received word from a runner that you're wanted at the Lord's manor." She stepped into his room and handed him a thin scroll. "Something about a Scholar...?"

"Right." Zanve rubbed his eyes furiously, sitting up and unfurling the tiny message. "There's a Scholar staying at the Lord's manor, I don't know if you've heard?"

"I've heard rumors. They're here for some kind of research, but no one really knows what exactly. Some folks are speculating they're here because elf the strange happenings we have going on." Vena shrugged, glancing out the window. "Thankfully we haven't had anything else happen in the past little while. I wonder if it was just a singular happenstance? Perhaps the gods are up to something."

Zanve snorted. "Mum, the gods haven't been seen on Ravar in centuries. They're not going to randomly start playing with the magic in a small seaside town." Besides, he knew exactly what had caused the magic to ripple and change and unbalance.

"What's got you smiling like that?" His mother sat next to him, her eyes sharp as a hawk. "I haven't seen you this busy and preoccupied in weeks — oh, I didn't put any stock in the rumors floating around Arrowmount, but it has to be! You've found someone, haven't you?"

"Mum, please," Zanve said as she reached out to turn his chin to look at her.

"Your eyes are purple," she breathed, an astonished smile breaking across her face.

"It's new, apparently," he said, running his thumb over the parchment in his hand. "And well... yes, alright. The rumors are true, to an extent. I have met someone. Whom I find incredibly special, and have been spending a lot of time with because I'm fixing her greenhouse."

Vena blinked at him slowly before smacking his knee. "Why haven't you told me any of this? How long has this been going on? I can't believe I've had to listen to *town gossip* to hear about my own son's life, and I *live with you*."

"Mum," Zanve groaned, though he immediately felt guilty. Before this, he usually made sure to carve out time to spend with his mother, seeing as their opposing schedules meant they could often go weeks without seeing each other. "I know, I've been busy. Let me make some coffee and I'll tell you about her."

"*Her*." A mischievous smile broke across his mother's gently lined face. He couldn't help but smile back at her, and laughed.

"Yes, *her*. Meriwen."

After making both him and his mother coffee and setting out a fresh loaf of Gable's bread and some of Wyn's latest jam (an orange lemon that made Zanve's mouth water just thinking about it), he told his mother about Meri.

He tried to omit Thistle from his tale, but it proved difficult, as that feathered fey creature was the reason that the two of them had come together. He made it sound more as though Thistle was a pesky dog, and leaned mostly on the fact he was helping Meri with her greenhouse. Through that, they had become much closer to her than he anticipated.

He also left out anything to do with the magic, ley lines, and much everything of importance that they were currently dealing with. His mother knew and regularly talked to many folks in Arrowmount; though he loved her dearly, Vena's mouth often ran off on its own accord. More often than not, as a boy, he'd receive unprompted advice from random neighbors and street vendors on his own personal squabbles.

Though, he supposed, she did keep the important things quiet when she wanted to. Like his shifting. That was up to him to share; she never once divulged that information to people unless she absolutely had to.

But when it came to her son meeting someone? There was no way that any information he gave her wouldn't be immediately parroted around Arrowmount for all to hear.

"Not that there is anything to talk about, yet," he said, wrapping up his story. "I simply like her. And I believe she likes me, but we haven't talked about anything like that yet. I just..."

"Like being around her so much that you go off to her cottage practically every day?" Vena grinned happily over her half-finished coffee. "I can't believe I didn't notice sooner. Zanve, my darling, you are in love with the woman. You can't fool me even though you think you can fool yourself. Look at your eyes — they are proof of it."

"Proof?"

"Your eyes have never been this color before," she said, tapping his hand. "This is love."

"I've loved others," he said, thinking back to a few of the relationships he has had in his life. But even though he thought he loved those he was with, and did believed he did love them in a way, the feeling he had now for Meri completely and utterly outshone them.

"Yes, you may have, but..." Vena shrugged, "something is different about this woman. Not only when you are around her but when you think about her — you, my love, are different."

Zanve couldn't stop the smile on his face. "We'll see if anything comes of it."

"Oh," Vena made a noise that sounded like *pshaw*, "of course it will. You let me know when you want to marry that woman. I'll get out my grandmother's ring for her."

Zanve choked on his coffee as his mother stood, tapping him on the shoulder. *Marry her?* "Skies, mum. We've known each other for a few weeks, that's all. Slow down."

"Sometimes that's all it takes to know. Even less, really." Vena leaned her hip against a nearby counter much like Zanve himself did. "Now, isn't this Scholar waiting for you?"

"Yes, yes they probably are." Zanve stood, downing the last of his coffee in one large gulp. "And please try not to spread too much of this around? There are enough rumors about Meri and I as it is."

"Of course. But do I have permission to be a little excited?"

"Sure, fine."

"Good." Vena tapped him lovingly on the cheek before he hurried back into his room.

Zanve walked quickly through Arrowmount, scraping his hair back into a leather tie as he did, the strands still wet from his quick morning wash. Most of the town was up and about, but it was still rather early; the morning light fought to shine through the monotonous cloud cover that stretched over Arrowmount.

The servants lead him into the main entrance hall and asked him to wait as they fetched the scholar, leaving him to peer around the grand entrance. He caught sight of a new portrait along the stairway, one with a rather pretty young elven woman between two dour elves. It was alongside one of Lord Wymarc himself, standing alone. The tiny smile on his face was nothing compared to the beaming girl, but it was still nice to see amidst the entire wall of stone-faced lords and ladies that adorned the walls around them.

Zanve had never posed for a painting, but he supposed it would be rather difficult to keep a genuine smile on your face for so long. Though, perhaps the painters themselves decided to add in the expression, for some variation. Or as a reflection of the personality of the person being painted.

"Ah, Zanve! Good morning, my dear sir," said that familiarly warm voice as the Scholar Daruka entered the entrance hall from a side door. They were followed by the elf that Zanve had seen on the day of their arrival, and he supposed this must be Sarrai's assistant.

The assistant — Zanve remembered Sarrai mentioning his name was Argyle — looked rather harried, and carried about six tomes in their arms. "Shall I continue—"

"Yes please Argyle, I will return later with *much* to discuss."

"You still won't let me know what this is about?" Argyle asked, looking at Zanve with an exasperated expression before gesturing — as much as one could with a stack of books in their arms — at the Scholar. "What is this town guard doing here? What has he got to do with this? Will *you* tell me what's going on?" Argyle directed this last question to Zanve.

Zanve glanced at Sarrai, who looked rather amused at their assistant's blathering. "I will leave that up to Scholar Daruka once they return. Shall we?"

"Absolutely, my dear sir. Onward! Argyle, if you don't mind, please set up again in the library and see that my previous research is ready for me when I get back. We have an adventure at hand! A possibility of much to discover!"

They left Argyle looking positively crestfallen at the prospect of being left out and left behind while his superior went on an adventure.

However small that adventure would be.

"Where are we headed?" The Scholar asked as they stepped out onto the cobblestone streets.

"Out to Meri's cottage, which is on the outskirts of the forest around Arrowmount," explained Zanve. "She is expecting us."

"I am all a flutter," Sarrai said, beaming. "I have been pouring over countless books, and I think I may have narrowed down the search to our correct area of study, but I must see Thistle before I make any conclusions and bring it all together. My colleagues often were quite annoyed with me and my style of information gathering — but alas, it is how I keep a little flare in my life."

He led Sarrai out of Arrowmount, passing Nisri and Cadoc on duty with a wave, before they approached Meri's cottage. The tiny Scholar skipped along beside Zanve, who slowed his usual long stride to ensure that Sarrai didn't fall behind. The entire way, the Scholar kept up a stream of conversation about the town and how beautiful everything was; the way the birds sang, the growth of the meadow and wildflowers around them that would — no doubt — be the most beautiful flourishing flowers in the heat of summer.

Finally, they broke through the tree line into Meri's garden, finding it already filled with a number of creatures. Meri herself wasn't visible, but Zanve could see the badger that had helped sweep up the greenhouse poking around the base of the lavender bed. A number of birds hopped around above it, pecking at a pile of freshly deposited seeds. There was also a beautiful deer visible at the edge of Meri's garden, grazing on the grass, not to mention the countless squirrels that bounced from tree to tree around them. And of course, Lock was on the garden chair, steam curling from his nose as he raised his head in their direction.

But, the moment they entered the garden, the animals and creatures all snapped to attention and scattered.

That's a bit odd, thought Zanve, frowning at them all as the garden was vacated by everyone but the two of them and Lock, still on his chair.

"That wyrmling is named Hemlock," said Zanve with a low voice to Sarrai. "He's a bit particular, but he's rather harmless."

Harmless, unless you're Damian, he thought with a stifled chuckle. Zanve had luckily not been scheduled with the man since the incident, but he had crossed paths and shifts with him a number of times. Each time, Damian had remained quiet and stoic, pretending as though Zanve was not there. Plus, though their uniform had long sleeves, Zanve was certain that one of Damian's arms looked tighter in the sleeves than the other, as though padded with a thick bandage.

It was an immeasurable improvement to Zanve's interactions with him. But, Zanve did still wonder what Damian's ultimate goal was; or if, by some miracle, that the man had simply backed off, never to darken their proverbial doorsteps again.

There was a rustle between the long grass as Thistle came bounding toward them, a delighted expression on his wide face. But the moment that Thistle noticed that Zanve wasn't alone, he hesitated, looking warily at the Scholar.

"Is this... Thistle?" breathed Sarrai, their eyes practically bursting with wonder. Thistle stood almost at a height with the Scholar.

"Thistle, everything is okay," said Zanve, extending his hand to the creature. Thistle tilted his head as he listened to Zanve, his eyes pinned to the tiny scholar, before he almost seemed to nod and walk over. He was far more cautious than Zanve had ever seen him, but the creature came up to them all the same.

"Meri?" Zanve called, casting his voice toward the house.

"Coming!" her voice returned, immediately filling him with warmth. Meri appeared in the doorway in a swirl of skirts that were dotted with tiny yellow flowers, her hair beautifully curling down her back in thick waves. They were, Zanve noticed, much more tamed than they usually were; not that Zanve minded at all. He loved her hair in whatever state he saw her in.

"Good morning, Meriwen!" chirped Sarrai. "Thank you for inviting me to your lovely home — this place is a practical *wonderland* of beauty."

Meri's cheeks tinged pink as she smiled. "I appreciate that, thank you. It's simply my home. Would you like some tea before — well, I see you've already met him. Thistle, this is Scholar Daruka. They are here to help us figure out who you are."

The fey creature looked at Meri with an expression that Zanve could've sworn said *I already know about me, what's the point of this* before Thistle made his way to Meri's side and sat dutifully, eyes on alert.

Sarrai cleared their throat and gave a tiny bow to Thistle. "It is a pleasure to meet you Thistle, I can assure you."

Thistle, whose gaze never left the Scholar as they spoke, blinked slowly, before he dipped his head in a definite imitation of a bow. Zanve caught Meri's eye as the Scholar stepped forward before kneeling before Thistle, chattering away to the creature.

Meri was already looking at him, a soft look in her eyes.

His chest squeezed and his stomach did a somersault. His mother's words came back to him. *"Sometimes that's all it takes to know. Even less, really."*

Meri peered around the garden, frowning. "Apologies for the animals around my garden, they are a bit spooked."

"Why's that?" asked Zanve, glancing around. It was incredibly odd to be standing in the sunshine of her garden without the usual chatter of animals.

"I was out in the clearing where Thistle came through last night," said Meri, "and when I came back, they were all in an uproar. They seem to think a stranger was in the garden, but I couldn't find any evidence of it."

"Thistle didn't see anyone?"

Meri hesitated. "He did sense someone, yes. But by the time I came back to the garden, they were gone."

34

A Creature of Immense Power

Meriwen

Meri watched Zanve's face still, his eyes darting around the garden as though hunting for an intruder. She lifted an eyebrow subtly, and he nodded, looking back toward Sarrai. She didn't want to worry the Scholar.

"Ah, someone probably interested in seeing what a beautiful place you have here!" Sarrai smiled at the two of them, seemingly unbothered. "Let us start, shall we?"

Zanve touched Meri's elbow lightly as he passed, eyes questioning. *Are you alright?* He seemed to ask.

She felt her face soften; the tight tension she was holding melted away as she nodded. Yes, of course, she was alright. There weren't any intruders; she would have known if there were. The creatures of her garden were probably just paranoid.

Meri rested her hand on Thistle's head, running a thumb over one of his smooth feathers, as the Scholar began to ask questions. Zanve brought out a couple of Meri's kitchen chairs to allow them all to sit in the garden with more space to relax, accompanied by tea that Meri had prepared.

Thistle sat next to Meri, his attentive, shining black eyes pinned on the scholar. Meri could practically feel the tie between her and the creature as they sat there, together, touching.

"If you don't mind, I'm going to try and ask questions directly of our feathered friend," said the Scholar, looking absolutely delighted at the prospect of this study, "I believe you, Meri, mentioned that you had a connection with Thistle, so if it is at all possible, you could translate what he says for me?"

"I think we could make that work," she said with a tilt of her head. "Thistle doesn't have immense vocabulary in words, but I can generally get a feeling for what he means."

Sarrai nodded, then took out a tiny notebook from the folds of their robes. "Let us begin!"

Thistle made a low sound in his throat like an exaggerated purr, lifting his chin in assent.

Sarrai tapped their chin a couple times with a stylus, looking in the middle distance for a moment. "Do you remember where you were before you came here?"

Thistle shifted on his feet before Meri got a distinct *elsewhere* answer over their bond.

"He says elsewhere, but... that could mean anything."

"Does the answer come with any specific feelings? Images? Emotions?" The scholar scribbled on their notepad.

Meri threaded her fingers through Thistle's feathers as they talked.

She poked at the feeling that Thistle had sent her. "It's something... both familiar and distinctly other. I can't quite place it, it's as though he's remembering something warm to him, but not altogether known. I don't think he knew where he was, only that it was where he always was before coming here. A sort of home."

"Hmm." Sarrai nodded, tilting their head to the side, pondering. "And you, Meri, when you performed the ritual that the disembodied voice put you through, did you get a sense of who that voice belonged to?"

Meri blinked. "I never really thought about it. I thought it was Thistle, but that voice was eloquent, speaking to me in full sentences. Thistle can't do that quite yet, and... I don't think he would have been able to from across a realm, if he can't from sitting right next to me."

"Interesting, interesting. So someone else pushed him through the doorway. I wonder who? Or what? And for what reason?"

The questioning continued on as such, the Scholar seemingly poking at random at little feelings or moments from the night that Thistle had arrived in the forest, and what Thistle himself knew. Every so often, Sarrai would direct a question to Meri to clarify a detail about her experience, all the while scribbling away in their notebook.

"This is definitely very helpful," said the Scholar a while later, once all three of their teas had long been drained and the sky around them had begun to darken. "There are just a few things that I wish to know, finally, that I think will help me pin down what exactly you are. Why are you here?"

The question was so simple that for a moment it floored Meri. *Why was he here?* Perhaps that was the key to answering what he was.

Thistle didn't hesitate in answering through Meri. He also finally took his eyes off of the Scholar and turned them on her, sending a shiver right through her.

I protect Meri. Garden. Keeper.

It was the first full sentence he had transferred over their bond.

"He said... he said he's here to protect me," she said, her voice shaky. Feelings of protection washed over her, images of Thistle keeping the garden happy and safe as he lived here, Meri thriving, the ley lines remaining strong. "He's here for protection. For the garden. For... for me, as a Keeper."

"Ah," said Sarrai, drawing out the sound with a soft happy finality. "Now, that may be our ticket."

"Do you know what he is?" Zanve asked the Scholar. He cleared his throat, the sound of his voice slightly croaky from disuse. He had been sitting quietly, observing the conversation between the three of them. A gentle, chill wind spun between the three of them, sending goosebumps up Meri's arms.

"I think this last bit of information will help me truly pin it down," said Sarrai, sounding incredibly satisfied as they tapped their notes with a finger. "But I do need to double check a few things with my research. I won't say anything without confirming it — for now, I will take this back and deliberate with Argyle. I think it's time I finally clued him in," they winked at Zanve, who chuckled. "I should have your answer and all the information I can give you on the morrow."

A smile burst across Meri's face as she reached forward and grasped the Scholar's hands. "Thank you, thank you so much."

"Thank you, my dear! Without you and Thistle, I wouldn't have been able to uncover what was the true source of our magical event. Because, I'll tell you this," Sarrai leaned in conspiratorially to Meri and Zanve with a gleam in their eye, "whatever he is, this creature you have here is something absolutely incredible. A creature of immense power, truly. We are all lucky to behold such a being."

Meri threaded her fingers through Zanve's and squeezed, needing something to hold on to. They were getting answers — *finally*. With answers, she could make sure that Thistle was safe, that no one could ever try and take him from her, if they ever found out about him.

Sarrai patted Thistle on the head amiably. "And just a baby one, at that!"

They settled into their chairs for a little while longer, conversing about Arrowmount and Sarrai's research in other aspects of the fey realm. Meri rather enjoyed chatting with Sarrai; she could definitely understand why her mother had spent so much time conversing with them.

As the sun started to sink behind the tree line, Sarrai rose to leave. The wind picked up around them, tossing Meri's hair back from her face. Meri and Zanve glanced skyward, Meri's skin starting to crawl uneasily. The air changed, tightening, with one gust of wind to the next.

"A storm is coming," she breathed quietly. "We should head inside. "

"Meri!" A voice called out, followed by the quick, crashing footsteps through the trees toward Meri's cottage. "Zanve!"

The three of them turned toward the noise and Thistle stood on alert, eyes locking on the pathway as Wyn and another figure came bustling through. Meri didn't recognize the person; their skin warm as the summer sun glistening off the rich dark sand of the Manid Empire, but she figured the only other person Wyn would bring to her cottage would be her other partner, Jay.

"Wyn, Jay, what's wrong? What's happened?" Zanve immediately caught up to them, taking Wyn by the hands. "Is everything alright?"

"Captain Ludru wants you," said Wyn quickly, looking at Zanve. "Urgently. There's unrest in the town that's about to boil over — if it hasn't already — and Chervil came in, saying another storm is on the way."

"Another..." Meri figured she already knew the answer to her unsaid question, but let her eyes flit between Wyn and the others.

Jay nodded, dismay filling their eyes. "It's another magical one. Feels stronger than the last one, he said. I don't know why, but everyone's practically losing their minds in town — before they even heard about the storm. Zanve, you have to go to them. Something... something's not right."

Meri breathed in deep, trying to calm her heart rate. Thistle leaned into her side, steadying her.

"But, the storm..." Zanve looked at Meri, uncertain.

"I will be fine," Meri said, trying to put a reassuring smile on her face. "I've quelled two storms, what's one more? Besides, I have Thistle with me. And Lock. They'll take care of me."

"And us," said Wyn, gesturing to Jay beside her, "We'll stay with you, make sure you're safe. I don't have much magic, but what I have will be able to help if something goes wrong."

"I will stay too," said the Scholar, looking all too excited at this turn of events. They tossed back their sleeves with two flourishes of their wrists and rubbed their hands together. "I do have one or two tricks up my sleeves."

Meri watched as the Scholar twinkled their fingers, tiny sparks alighting at the tips. It was fire, but Meri thought she recognized something distinctly fey about it. "You're a fey mage?"

"Of course I am. When one studies the fey realm, one should take the chance to learn all they can about the magic of the place. How it works, what it does, and how one uses it." Sarrai winked. "My magic is not akin to a true fey's; it is simply a wizard's recreation of it. But, my one trip to the realm did help me gather the power I needed. I would love to be of help to you, Meriwen."

Meri reached for Zanve unconsciously as a wave of crackling thunder roared across the sky, deafening them all for a moment. The clouds began to swirl menacingly once again, the sky darkening unnaturally. She could only imagine what kind of view those by the seaside had.

Zanve pulled her toward him, eyes fierce as he wrapped his arms around her. "Stay safe, alright?"

"I will," she breathed, caressing his face. "You too."

"I will," he echoed, before dipping his head. There was a beat, one moment where she thought he was about to kiss her lips, but instead he kissed her forehead, and momentarily crushed her in an embrace before letting go and taking off into the trees.

"Well," sighed Wyn, her arms wrapped around herself. She lifted an eyebrow at Meri, the side of her mouth quirking just so. Meri's cheeks went hot.

Before Wyn could say anything further, Jay leaned into her, looking up at the sky worriedly. "Let's get inside until it comes, shall we?"

"It's the best we can do." Meri nodded and gestured for them to follow her into her cottage as the rain started to fall.

Wyn's hand slid around Meri's upper arm as they entered. Meri tipped her head toward Wyn's as her voice snuck into her ear.

"I know it's not really the time, but we should talk about that kiss. About you and Zanve."

Meri's face instantly heated and her stomach clenched. *Did I do something wrong?* "We should?"

Wyn winked at her. "We should. Because I'm your friend, and I think you should talk about the people you love with your friends."

The people you love.

"Alright," breathed Meri, nerves tumbling around in her gut. "But first, tea. And we must deal with this storm."

Meri brewed a quick pot of tea for them all, choosing to make a calming brew. In the meantime, Wyn unearthed a journal from the stacks on the table and started to rifle through it at top speed.

"Here," she said, handing it off to Meri and picking up her mug. Wyn breathed in deep, letting the steam of the tea wrap around her. "That's the spell, right?"

Meri ran her hand down the page, noting the storm quelling spell, and nodded. "I'll see what I can do with this."

35

UNREST

Zanve

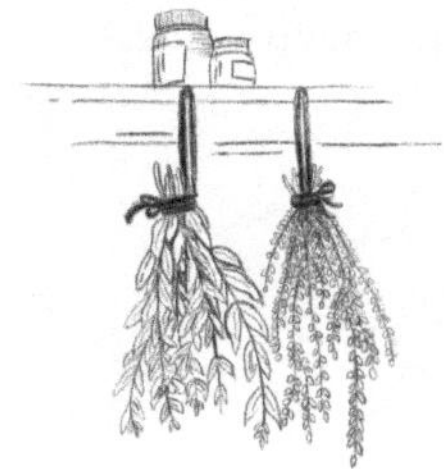

Rain pelted down, soaking Zanve in minutes as he ran through the woods toward Arrowmount. He didn't stop to shift, knowing there probably wouldn't be enough time to change in and out of his clothes on both ends.

Unrest in Arrowmount. What could that even mean? He hadn't, in all his years as town guard — gods, in any of the years he had been *alive* — ever seen unrest or anything close to it in Arrowmount. Of course, there were disagreements between folks, but that can't be avoided in a town. Take him and Damian. But *unrest?*

That was only something that he had heard of in big cities, in his adventure novels, not in a sleepy seaside town like Arrowmount. Unrest happened in times of great upheaval, in large cities.

He approached the front gates at a full sprint, noting the lack of guards standing at their posts, and continued on into town. Buildings and the occasional person passed him by in a blur; most folks were

322

already inside, closing shutters, and hiding from the rain. The multicolored flags draped across the edges of the Arrowmount streets whipped around, colors indistinguishable from one another as the rain soaked them through.

A small boy darted out in front of him, a piece of discarded trash above his head to try keep himself dry.

"Hey!" Zanve snatched the back of his shirt, and the boy yowled like a caught cat.

"Mister, I've got books in my shirt! I can't get them wet!"

"Sorry—" Zanve said apologetically as the boy glared, "do you know where Captain Ludru is?"

He didn't even have to clarify. The boy's eyes went wide. "Town center."

The boy took off again, finding shelter under an eave before disappearing into a nearby storefront for his and his books' safety.

Zanve took the most direct path through town, following the cobblestones, and only started to slow when he noticed the crowd of people still lingering outside as the market stalls came into view.

Then, he heard the noise. It started to warble alongside the sound of the rain and the roiling thunder, but the closer he got, the louder the people became. For a moment, Zanve couldn't quite pinpoint what he was seeing. The town center was as full as it ever was, which was odd in itself, seeing as there was a storm rolling in. But what was stranger was the fact that the market goers, stall owners, and even some shop owners were all standing and yelling at one another from two sides of the market.

The sky was purpling now, the first shivers of lightning starting to appear between the growing clouds.

"Captain!" Zanve called as he approached, spotting the man standing between two people, trying to keep them apart. Nisri, Adrias, Cadoc, and a few other guards were peppered throughout the crowd, trying to be heard or restraining people of their own. Amalin, Captain Ludru's second in command, was nowhere to be seen, which Zanve thought was very odd.

"Einar, thank gods — maybe you can talk some sense into these people." Captain Ludru gestured him over with a slightly frantic jerk of his head. A crack lit up the sky above, before fresh waves of rain started to pummel the ground, market stalls, and every single person there.

Yet, no one seemed to even notice. If anything, they started to yell louder. Even standing right next to someone, Zanve couldn't quite make heads or tails of what the argument even was.

"What's going on?" he yelled to Ludru as he stepped closer, hauling one of the people — an elven man with a scar that decorated one half of his face who was practically screaming at the other person, a catfolk who was currently snarling and snapping at the air in front of them — back a couple inches.

"Some fight broke out over one stall owner taking another's spot," shouted Ludru, momentarily ducking out of the way of the catfolk person's wildly jabbing elbow. "Amalin tried to quash it, but everything got out of hand, and she sent for help. We thought we had it under control, but... then everything started to spiral with everyone taking sides, and now I don't even think half the people here know what they're fighting about. Amalin neither."

Zanve looked to where Lou pointed, just off to the side, where Amalin was currently arguing rather heatedly with the grocer, both of them red in the face. Something shimmered in the air around their heads, catching in Zanve's periphery. Realization slammed into Zanve.

The magic.

"It's all their fault!" shouted the elf in Zanve's grip, snapping his attention back to the fight in front of him. He struggled hard, trying to break free, but Zanve held firm.

"What is?" asked Zanve. "Maybe if we just talk this out—"

"There is no more time for talking," interrupted the catfolk, their voice half yowl. "I have had enough of this idiot's antics, always in my way, always stealing my things — I know it was you who took the gems, don't even try to deny it! It was either you or your stupid little child who doesn't know how to wipe their own nose!"

The elf in Zanve's arms gave a surprisingly strong yank. "I did NOT! You insult me and my family!"

"This is all over a stall space? I thought those were decided and set at the beginning of every season?" Zanve tried to flick some of his hair off his forehead, the rain plastering it down into his eyes.

"They are," snarled the catfolk. "And I did NOTHING wrong. I am in my rightful spot; this idiot is overstepping their bounds!"

"No! It is their useless wares that are always falling over on my stall."

Zanve tried not to roll his eyes, but really, all this? Over a tiny little misunderstanding?

"Listen, we need to get everyone under cover and to safety," Zanve yelled to Ludru, ignoring the struggling pair between them. The crowd around them tipped and roiled as another roll of thunder cracked through the sky, shaking Zanve's bones.

Ludru shook his head, casting a glance around the crowd. "Oi! Briggs! Where in all the nine hells have you been?"

"Sorry boss," said Damian, who was skirting through the crowd with a slightly annoyed look on his face, as though coming here was the highest inconvenience. He glanced at Zanve and didn't say anything as he came to stand next to him, not bothering to step in or help in any way. He looked around at the crowd, and for a moment, Zanve thought that his lips quirked into a smile.

Instantly, Zanve's blood started to boil. This man, this slime of a man who had nothing better to do than to go bother the woman Zanve was beginning to care very much for, should be allowed to even stand in front of him. Let alone standing there as though nothing was the matter around him, all calm. He should be taken down a peg. He should be cut down.

Woah there, a little voice in Zanve's head. Zanve shook himself, sending water into his eyes. He accidentally let go of the struggling elf as he tried to wipe his vision clear. The anger currently coursing through him was not the regular level of animosity he felt toward Damian. This was unnaturally high.

"Einar?" Ludru's voice was far away, as though being heard distantly through a wall. "Briggs — get—"

His fists clenched and unclenched at his sides as he tried to bring himself back under control. Sharp pain stabbed at his palms as his entire body began to itch.

That wasn't something he'd felt for years. Decades, practically — that was an itch that only appeared when he lost control.

He looked down at his hands, trying to see clearly between the sheets of rain pouring down. They were half transformed and bleeding, claws extending out of his fingers as they stuck somewhere in a paw shape, but didn't quite fully get there.

He had to calm down.

Stay in control of yourself. If Meri saw him now...

He closed his eyes for a breath, thinking of her garden, the sunshine, and Meri's beautiful face. Her smile.

Between one breath and the next, his anger subsided just enough for him return to his right mind. Damian was now holding onto the struggling elf and looking as though he was having a much harder time keeping him under wraps. That alone made Zanve a little bit happier, which helped.

The crowd heaved around him. Everyone just needed to calm down a little bit, sit down and come back to themselves. It would be fantastic if there was magic that could do that.

Then he got an idea. "Sir, I think I have a solution. Give me five minutes."

"Whatever it is, hurry. We have to get the people out of the rain before the worst of it hits."

Zanve took off through Arrowmount once again, lightning crashing above him as he careened over the cobblestones. He threw himself down Fetterly Place and to the bookstore, practically ripping the doors off their hinges to get inside.

"Arileas!"

"My gods man, you scared the living daylights out of me," the white-haired elf blurted as Zanve burst in, bringing half the ocean with him. "Please, stay away from the books, if you don't mind."

"We need your help. There's something happening to the townsfolk —the storm — their emotions—"

"Emotions?" Arileas frowned, but stepped toward him all the same. "I haven't had a chance to look outside, is this storm as bad as the last—" he ducked and looked out one of their windows, cutting himself off. "Ah. Yes. Well. We have to deal with that, too, then."

"Meri's got the storm handled," Zanve said, hoping to all the gods that he was right. "Do you know how to calm emotions?"

"With magic? Depending, it can be a fairly easy spell."

"For approximately thirty townsfolk who are currently at each other's throats?"

"Ah." Arileas blinked slowly. "Less easy. Are they magically affected?"

"As best as I can tell, yes. There's something shimmering in the sky around their heads — the storm is making it worse, whatever this magic is."

"Let me get my stash of dragon scale, and I will see what I can do. In the meantime, go see if Calian is at May's. The two of them may be able to help with the storm, in case Meriwen runs into trouble."

Zanve nodded and sped down the street to May's, where there were only a few people inside — a couple that were soaked to the bone being served hot drinks by Andrew — and May sitting in her usual spot with Calian, the giantkin, the both of them staring out at the growing rain.

"Hello," said Calian as Zanve burst in. Everyone turned to look at Zanve as he did so — he couldn't imagine what a state he was in. "Do we need to come help, once again?"

"It's bad," panted Zanve. "I don't know how bad, but something's different with this one."

Calian nodded before they took one more slow drink of their coffee, standing as they did. May stood as well, the two of them immediately moving to the door as Zanve turned around. Calian and May headed off toward the lighthouse.

Outside, he met Arileas, who hadn't bothered with the magical umbrella this time and instead was just letting the rain hit him. His usually lovely white hair was plastered to his head, limp tendrils stuck to his cheeks. Arileas was holding something in his fist, too small for Zanve to make out.

The rain was coming on all sides now, pouring down the cobblestone street like a river. The wind was whipping around, lifting bits of trash and plants and whatever else it came across.

Zanve and Arileas took off toward the town center as the storm heightened, worsening with every step. Zanve sharpened his eyesight, letting the panther peak through so he could see. Arileas grabbed onto his arm as they battled the elements together.

"This way!" shouted Zanve, leaning close so that Arileas could hear him.

They approached the town center, seeing the battle still raging there. Zanve caught sight of Gable, the baker, who was usually the most calm, lovely person to deal with, standing off to the side in a full yelling match with the grocer. Their entire face was contorted into something positively terrifying.

Arileas stepped forward confidently. He lifted his fist still clutching something and released it above him and toward the crowd, a burst of white glittering powder before his hands moved in patterns too quick for Zanve to recognize. The powder, instead of disappearing like it should have in the onslaught of water currently attempting to drown them all, transformed into thin wisps of light that scattered out over the crowd.

One by one, the wisps found purchase on the brows of those part of the crowd, the magic glittering against their skin.

As though there was one giant intake of breath that rolled through the crowd, the fighting stopped. People blinked at one another, their expressions freezing in masks of anger before they all flickered into uncertainty, then total disbelief as they took in the storm around them.

Zanve stepped forward, gesturing them along. "To the Narrow! Get out of the storm!"

The crowd of people all set into a run after him, hands pulling shirts and jackets up over their heads as though that would do anything to stop them from being absolutely soaked through.

Zanve burst through the doors of the bar, bringing with him the crowd of shopkeepers, market stall owners, and whoever had been caught up in the strange magic in the town center, shocking Briar who was behind the bar. Corwek, the cook, materialized from the back room wiping his large hands with a towel, ducking low to avoid hitting his head on the low ceiling of the Old'n Narrow.

"What in all the…" Briar looked at them all before raising a questioning eyebrow at Zanve and Arileas who were leading them.

"Just a… small misunderstanding," muttered the catfolk from before, somehow materializing next to Zanve's elbow. They didn't seem to be focused on anything in particular, their eyes glazed over.

"If you don't mind," Zanve said, his voice sounding rather loud in the space now that he wasn't in the middle of a raging storm, "could you serve all these people something warm? It's been an odd few minutes."

"Absolutely," said Briar, pointing to Corwek, who nodded and ducked back into the kitchen.

Captain Ludru appeared beside Zanve and put a hand on his shoulder. The rest of the guards all came after, looking distinctly worn out and soaked to the bone. Arileas nodded to Ludru as the Captain looked to him.

"I don't know what exactly you did, but I appreciate it greatly," said Ludru, shaking Arileas' hand. "Without that bit of magic, I don't know how we would have stopped that."

"Whatever it was, it seemed to be getting worse by the minute. I mean, they were fighting — actually fighting, look at those two," added Adrias, who gestured off toward two store owners who were bleeding and appeared distinctly unwell, being helped into chairs, "over things like someone's ware being in the wrong spot or their prices being a couple of copper pieces off from what they were used to. I mean, that's not something to lose an eye over!"

"Literally," muttered Nisri, cringing as they looked over at the bleeding pair. "And those two aren't the only casualties, either."

"I'll send for Healer Bryndis," said Arileas, "they will be able to help patch these folks up." He ducked aside, pulling a small pinch of the sparkling powder up as he started to draw patterns in the air, before speaking low into the symbols.

They dissipated as Arileas turned back to them. "Have either of you ever seen or heard of anything like this happening in Arrowmount? What could it have been?"

"Whatever this mood is has to be tied to this godsforsaken storm," said Ludru, rubbing his chin. "But I have never heard of anything of the like even remotely close in Arrowmount. Perhaps something down south of the Manid Empire or in the Caspasian Isles, but even then. Magical storms? That's not common."

Zanve's heart rate was returning to normal as he had a moment to collect himself. The storm outside raged, thunder cracking overhead. It had been a while since he'd left Meri's; her and the others should have gotten the storm under control by now.

Unease flooded his stomach.

Zanve simply shook his head. "I should get back to Meri."

"Absolutely not," said Arileas, putting up his hand. "Have you seen what it's like out there? It is not safe."

Zanve shook his head as a rumble of thunder shook the Old'n Narrow. "I have to make sure she's okay."

Arileas frowned, looking ready to argue, but Captain Ludru sighed. "Go on. It's on your head, Einar. When this storm is done, we are going to need all hands to help fix whatever mess we find we find when it's done, so don't hurt yourself out there or you'll have me to contend with."

"Yes, sir."

Zanve nodded to Quinlan, Adrias, and Nisri who were standing next to a waterlogged and confused looking Amalin. They waved him off. Zanve stepped back out of the bar, Briar and Corwek already beginning to serve the sopping townsfolk.

The storm above him raged on. As Zanve ran back out of town, shingles flew off homes, plants crashed into windows, and bits of wood were torn fro frames as the wind tore its teeth through Arrowmount. It was so dark now that the only light he could see by was an odd red tinge to the sky and the now almost constant lightning crashing between the churning mass of clouds in the sky.

If there was ever any doubt, there was no denying now that whatever was causing this storm was magic. And this one? This was much worse now than the last time. If Meri hadn't done her spell by now, something must have gone terribly wrong.

36

A FAVORED FEY

Meriwen

Meri was fighting with the sky.

It was the only way she could really describe what she was doing. She had done the spell to quell the storm exactly as before, with all the gold light and lifting off the ground — but this time, the sky was fighting back.

The magic was *adapting*.

That thought frightened Meri more than the storm itself. Magic was a force in the world, something that grew, fueled, and powered many other things, but she had never once thought of magic as *sentient*. People wielded magic to their bidding; the magic never wielded itself.

Yet here it was, fighting back. It felt full of vengeance; of anger and misplaced rage.

"Come on," she groaned, her back arcing as she pulled more magic from the ley lines around her, her hands contorted in an upwards battle as the gold light emitting from her continued to dull. The sky twisted around, then a thin, spiraling storm cloud funnel branched down toward her magic and swallowed it whole, bit by bit.

Without warning, her magic failed.

Meri let out a shriek as whatever force that her spell had been emitting vanished entirely with a snap; dropping her flat on the ground in a crumpled heap.

"MERI!" yelled Wyn as something barreled into her, throwing her to the side. She gasped, looking up between swaths of her own soaking wet hair now covered in dirt, watching as that funnel of cloud touched down in her garden, right where she had been standing.

Thistle stood over her, all his feathers on end, baring his teeth at the clouds.

"I need help," Meri breathed, barely audible to even herself. But there came Sarrai and Wyn, and even Jay after a moment's hesitation, into her garden.

"Are you okay?"

Meri nodded at Wyn as the woman helped her to her feet. "I need something more to ground me. Whatever this is — it's fighting back."

"Here," said Sarrai, holding out their hand. "I read about this once — it's not often done, but apparently magic can be channeled through others, and if we can channel through you, Meriwen, then perhaps we can steady and anchor you enough to help you?"

"It's worth a try," said Wyn, holding out her hand to Jay questioningly. "I know you don't use your magic anymore, love, but..."

Jay looked down at her hand silently, before glancing once at Meri, then the sky. Then they laced their fingers with Wyn's. "For Arrowmount, I'd do anything."

Wyn gave them a soft, reassuring smile, before holding her hand out to Meri. "How do we channel our magic to Meri?"

"Focus entirely on your magic, whatever your source is, and imagine it's a river travelling down into your hand and through it to the next person. Jay, you try now with Wyn, to see if we can get this started." Sarrai shook out their hands with a flourish.

Jay nodded, then furrowed their brow slightly, staring at their entwined hands. Nothing happened for a moment, then—

"Oh," Wyn gasped, her eyes lighting up. "I had no idea your magic felt like *that*."

"First time for everything, I suppose," said Jay through gritted teeth, as though they were fighting through immense pain. "Let's finish this."

Meri gathered her thoughts as the churning funnel in front of them continued to rotate impossibly fast, hovering above the ground, as though it was waiting. Her plants were struggling to stay within their little homes, their leaves being whipped this way and that by the wind. Meri sent out her heart to them, hoping beyond anything that they stayed unharmed.

Sarrai grasped Meri's right hand, and Wyn her left. Thistle, then, stood up and knocked the Scholar's free hand with his head, looking at them all with an intensity that made Meri shiver slightly.

She didn't have time to think this through. As soon as she turned her attention to the sky and started to recite the spell, the funnel hit the ground with a vengeance.

Soil, grass, and bits of plant debris exploded outward as it moved toward her. It carved a path as she chanted, faster and faster, pulling as much power as she could from the earth around her.

She began to rise, floating with the power coursing through her, but her friends' hands kept her anchored to the ground.

Her spell took effect; gold light shot out from her once again, but instead of arcing up toward the sky, it shot straight at the funnel's core. Magic completely unfamiliar to her began to pour in through both her hands, hot and warm from Wyn and something spidery and comfortingly otherworldly from Sarrai. She used everything she had, pushing the magic at the storm.

There was a thundering, shattering scream as the magic began to tear the storm apart. The sky around them contracted in a single breath; then slammed outward in a concussive blast of rain and magic, toppling Meri's raised garden beds, plants and dirt littering her garden. Her kitchen door crashed open; the windows of her house exploding inward. A number of shingles on her roof ripped clean off.

The four of them stood strong, Meri angling her head into the storm to keep herself there, forcing the magic back.

For a moment, just a heartbeat, Meri could have sworn she saw something corporeal standing in the middle of the explosion, as though the storm had come down to stand on two legs in front of her. She felt its eyes on her, crackling and completely inhuman, as though made from lightning itself.

She blinked. As though it had never started, the funnel cloud was gone, and the gold beam of magic from Meri shot straight into the sky, piercing the storm clouds cleanly in two.

She felt the magic pull out of her, and, drained of everything she had, she crumpled once more to the ground. This time, though, she pulled the other four figures with her, all of them collapsing amidst the wreckage of her garden.

The rain continued to fall, but in a softer downpour, the sound dulling from a continuous roar to the gentle patter of raindrops.

"Fuck," groaned Jay, curling in on themself before sitting up slowly, cradling their hand. "Please tell me it's over."

"It's over," breathed Meri. Thistle was there, then, burrowing his whole body into hers, sending warmth and worry through the bond between them. "I'm okay, Thistle. I'm okay. We're all okay."

"Mostly," said Sarrai, looking at Jay. "What exactly is going on with your hand?"

Jay groaned, trying to stretch their fingers out but being completely unable to. Their fingers were stuck in a rictus of pain, contorted inward as though still holding onto Wyn's hand.

"Skies," breathed Wyn, gently laying her hand on Jay's thigh. "Jay, you—"

"Don't tell me I shouldn't have," they grumbled. "It'll pass in a few days."

Jay extended their hand for Meri and Sarrai to see. Etched as though with pale bone, a pattern of scale had erupted all along Jay's skin, starting along the skin of their fingers and extending up the wrist.

"Cursed by a dragon sorcerer," they said before Sarrai could ask — the Scholar's mouth was already open, half forming the question — and withdrew their hand. "I have the power granted to me by these scales, but whenever I use the magic, it turns back on me. The scales grow fresh every time."

Wyn's eyes were pained as she looked at her lover, gently touching their shoulder.

"You still wanted to help?" Meri asked, feeling slightly overwhelmed.

"As I said, anything for Arrowmount." Jay locked eyes with her for a moment before turning away, bringing their hand to their chest as Wyn wrapped them in a hug. "I'll be alright. Haven't done anything that powerful in a really, really long time."

"MERI!"

She turned to the voice as Thistle stood, his whole body tense for just a moment before the sounds of familiar footsteps crashed through the forest toward them. Zanve broke through the trees at a full sprint, soaked down to the bone, his hair plastered to his head.

"Is everything all right?" Meri let Wyn help her up to standing and took a step toward Zanve before he crashed into her, wrapping her up in a hug so fierce she lost the ability to breathe for a moment. He then stood back, holding her away from him so he could inspect her, making sure she was all right.

"Yes, we figured out how to calm the townsfolk — are you — oh, Meri, your garden." His face fell, his mouth opening in shock as he tore his eyes from her and took in the surroundings. "What in all the hells happened?"

"We fought a storm spirit," said Wyn matter-of-fact. "I think that's what it was."

"That storm had *teeth*," said Jay, shivering. Thistle rubbed up against Zanve's thigh, pushing him and Meri further together. Zanve chuckled and petted the creature between the ears.

"Come inside, let us all get dry," said Sarrai, ushering them all toward Meri's shattered house. Meri threaded her arm through Zanve's, leaning on him.

Meri brewed them all tea as they filled Zanve in on what happened in her garden. Instead of sitting in her kitchen, though, they moved into the back of her cottage and squeezed into her cozy sitting room. Jay ended up on the floor with Thistle draped across their lap. Meri found herself sitting on the edge of her armchair where Zanve was seated, while Sarrai and Wyn took Meri's small, squishy couch.

Lock was perched awkwardly by the long unused fireplace, standing up on his hind legs looking at them all as though wondering what on earth they were doing back there.

"That was really something," said Sarrai, sounding tired, though their eyes still sparkled with interest. "I think everything I've seen today has justified and confirmed a few of my suspicions about our Thistle here, and well. About you too, Meriwen."

"What's that?" Zanve asked before Meri could, his fingers squeezing hers reassuringly.

The Scholar took a dainty sip of their tea and let out a soft, happy sigh. "Well, I did say earlier that I wanted to take a look at my research before making a full decision on Thistle, which still stands. But as for Meriwen, my dear," Sarrai leaned over and tapped her knee, "I can fully say with all my confidence that you are truly special. I cannot believe the lengths that you have gone to for Arrowmount — and I believe that I'm only beginning to learn. With everything you told me about Keepers, and what I've seen you do today alone, I cannot fathom why you aren't applauded more in town. Half the people — no, ninety percent! — don't even know your name."

"It's... really nothing," said Meri, feeling a little awkward as everyone's attention turned to her. "I simply do my job as Keeper."

"It's not just a job for you, though, is it?"

Meri hesitated, her mouth open to say of course it was just a job, this was what she did, and there was nothing special about it; but she stopped herself. It wasn't *just* a job, being a Keeper. And it hadn't been for a long, long time. Now, with people she could call friends around her, it most definitely wasn't just what she *had* to do.

"It's my way of life," she said quietly. "To protect those in the town I live in, but also those I... those I love."

Wyn's eyes sparkled with soft tears she didn't let fall.

"You're a phenomenon," said Sarrai simply. "A truly favored fey, if you allow me the alliterative phrase."

Meri didn't quite know what to say to that.

"I would like to hear more about what you do as Keeper," said Jay. "I haven't really been privy to all those conversations."

"Of course," chuckled Meri. Zanve wrapped his arm around her, placing his hand on her upper leg, right where her skin had been twisted into untreatable pain decades before. Slowly, carefully, she slid off the armchair and into his lap, leaning into him. He resettled his arms around her, fitting her into him perfectly. She didn't have the energy to feel embarrassed about it, either; she caught Wyn's smirk out of the corner of her eye. "I'm open to any and all questions."

They chatted for what felt like minutes, but by the time their conversation wrapped back around to what had happened today, the light outside was darkening as dusk fell upon them.

"Can you do the ritual early?" asked Wyn, grasping her now empty tea mug. Jay leaned into her, lending her their weight and warmth. "Fix all of this?"

Meri sighed and shook her head. "Even if I could — the magic wouldn't do anything without that crucial turn of the seasons. Additionally, I don't have my fey realm herbs yet. I'm still waiting for them."

Zanve *hmmed* under his breath, the feeling vibrating into Meri's back. "Is there anything you can do in the meantime, perhaps to protect Arrowmount? Protection spells, warding spells?"

That was something that Meri had never thought of before. She had done smaller protection spells on an individual scale; brewed into teas, placed into baked goods and the like.

"I don't even know if there is a protection spell big enough," she said, but all the same, she got up and headed toward her kitchen slowly. She picked up a few of her mother's journals from the stacks on her kitchen table, momentarily brushing off bits of glass and debris, and brought them back to the others with her. "But that wouldn't be a bad idea."

"Back to the hunt then?" Wyn winked at her, pulling a journal close as Meri placed them on a small footstool in the middle of the room. Zanve's warm arms enveloped her again. "Have you seen anything of the like in the journals you've looked through already?"

Meri furrowed her brow and tried to think; all the different entries from her mother were blurred together in her mind, spells for forgetting, for remembering, for enhancement, for helping your lettuce grow sweeter, and hundreds more spiraling through her.

"There has to be something," she breathed, running her hand over the journal with the storm spell inside. "I have to *do* something. Because there are..." Meri let out a long, slow breath, counting in her head, "only two weeks left before the solstice, and if this storm was any indication, it's not going to be the last."

Sarrai, Jay, Wyn, and Zanve's faces all cringed at the thought.

"We'll find something," said Zanve, running his thumb over the back of her forearm. Since he had come back, racing through the trees to find the four of them in a heap around a mound of upturned earth and multiple of her garden beds on their sides, carnage of plants and debris strewn everywhere, he couldn't seem to keep his hands off of her.

Of course, with her seated in his lap, she found that she didn't want to stop touching him either. She *ached* for it, for him. She leaned into him, wanting his warmth, his heat, his sureness and steadiness in this moment.

Meri turned her head to look at Zanve. His brilliantly purple eyes settled on hers with a soft expression.

Right then, she knew beyond a doubt as his thumb traced absently along her skin that she was completely, utterly, in love with him.

She would do a lot to protect this town, that was for certain. But to protect those she loved?

Meri would do anything.

37

THISTLE'S PURPOSE

Meriwen

The following day, Meri couldn't focus. Her chronic pain made it impossible for her to walk, and so she had gnawed through each of her fingernails instead of pacing back and forth. From all the action yesterday, the pain in her leg was back with a vengeance. Instead of going to start cleaning her yard of the debris, all she could do was sit in her kitchen doorway and watch as the animals tried their best to help.

The crater that had been carved by the funnel cloud had torn up most of her garden, creating an uneven, dangerous path that she knew she shouldn't even attempt to cross.

Meri had called to the creatures and animals around her once again, much like she'd done with Zanve when they cleaned out her greenhouse. They had helped her clean up the majority of her kitchen so she wouldn't be in danger of cutting her feet on shards of broken glass from her poor windows, but the garden had to wait.

Despite Zanve and Wyn wanting to stay and help her clean the evening before, she sent them home with special brews of teas to strengthen them over the next while. Arrowmount was hurting, she knew; she hadn't seen it with her own eyes, but if this is what the state of her garden was, she couldn't imagine what the town looked like being right next to the ocean. This morning, Zanve had sent a runner to let her know that he couldn't visit today, as he was needed to help organize the clean-up and repair of the town.

But none of that — not the lack of her friends, not the pain, not the destruction, nor watching her wonderful animal helpers tidy as best they could — was why she couldn't focus.

She'd received a second missive from that runner detailing how Sarrai was going to come this afternoon with news on Thistle. Meri tried not to read too closely into it; but her mind lingered on the way that Sarrai had signed the simple note:

BRINGING NEWS AND BAKED GOODS THIS AFTERNOON.

- SARRAI

The waiting was sending her out of her mind. She yearned to be able to do something, anything, to occupy the time; but instead, she was pinned to her chair in an increasingly irritated mood.

As she watched as a badger, deer, and Lock all fought to right one of the garden beds and fail, her heart pained. Maybe her mother had some kind of spell written somewhere?

Meri started to leaf through the pile of journals once more, wondering if one of the gardening spells that Elestren had copied from Seraph, Meri's grandmother, would be useful to help the creatures in her garden.

She lost herself in flipping the pages, reading through her mother's tight, neat script that recounted memories, thoughts, and spells, before something caught her eye.

MOVE EARTH, her mother wrote, underlining it.

SOMETHING THAT SOUNDS BOTH SIMPLISTIC AND GARGANTUAN AT ONCE; HOW DOES ONE MOVE EARTH? I'VE SEEN MOTHER DO THIS SPELL MANY TIMES AND NEVER KNEW WHAT IT WAS, WHAT SHE WAS ACTUALLY DOING. LIKE SHE CALLED THE POWER OF THE LEY LINES EVERY TURN OF THE SEASON, SHE CALLED TO THE MAGIC ROOTED IN THE EARTH TO ASK IT TO DO WHAT SHE WISHED. I TRIED, BUT OF COURSE, MY MAGIC DOES NOT WORK THE WAY A KEEPER'S DOES. MOTHER SAYS THAT YOU NEED A STRONG WILL, AND A WANT; AND THE MORE YOU WISH IT TO DO, OF COURSE, THE HEAVIER IT WILL BE AND MORE ENERGY IT WILL EXPEND.

The entry ended there. Meri sat back, thinking hard. Was it some kind of other magic that her grandmother was tapping into? Elestren made it sound as though the earth had a magic of its own. But that didn't quite make sense.

The power of the ley lines ran through *everything*; up into the sky and down deep into the earth, through every living thing that grew from the ground. When her grandmother moved the earth, she was using the ley line magic in it; just like Meri was when she pulled strength from the ground to help ease her pain on days her body failed her.

Meri reached out with her good leg, stretching it beyond the threshold of her door, her bare foot settling into the grass. Slowly, she let herself reach down into the earth and pulled up with a breath, filling herself with the magic there.

Delicately, Meri raised her hand with the magic coursing through her. She imagined a bit of the dirt and mud around her foot pushing out, much like she would do with a shovel to dig a hole for a new plant.

The dirt responded in kind. It was messy and definitely not quite as neat as Meri had imagined, but it very much looked like an imaginary shovel was digging dirt out of the ground.

The more she played with the magic at her grasp recently — with the storms, and now with this — she was beginning to wonder if she hadn't been letting herself get by too simply before.

Footsteps sounded along her path, sending a renewed sense of urgency into Meri's throat. She felt Thistle's interest pique before familiarity settled into both of them, recognizing the quick, happy step of the Scholar.

Meri relaxed her fingers, releasing the magic. She would have to experiment with that later.

Her bad mood evaporated in an instant as the small form of Sarrai appeared between the trees.

"Good afternoon!" Sarrai came bustling through the trees, carefully stepping around the perimeter of Meri's garden to avoid most of the damage. As they had promised, they were indeed carting a bag that looked like it was from Gable's.

Meri stood very carefully, pushing up with her good leg entirely, before using her low shelving to move her way into her kitchen. "How has your day been so far?"

"Oh, absolutely splendid. I spent most of the evening last night regaling Argyle on our adventure and all my findings and thoughts. This morning, though we both got very little sleep, we pored over everything from the past few days and weeks here in Arrowmount. Shall I get plates?"

"They're just up there, by the tea cupboard. Lock can get them — Lock?" she called out, and the wyrmling detached himself from the other creatures currently working in her garden and scurried inside. He first rinsed his claws, cleaning off the dirt accumulated there, before he snaked up to the higher cabinets and handed two plates down to Sarrai, who chuckled happily.

"My, oh, my, your garden really is just a place of splendor," said the

Scholar as they watched the animals moving about the dirt through one of the broken windows. They placed a plate in front of Meri before withdrawing a sugary pastry from inside the bag. It was nearly the size of Meri's head, banded with buttery flakey crust, and looked as though the inside was filled with some kind of chocolate. "Even with the wreckage from yesterday. I wish I could spend days here, sitting and listening to the birds."

"They always have a lot to say," said Meri. She started to pick apart the pastry, too nervous to eat.

Sarrai took a healthy bite of their matching pastry. "My, the baker Gable truly has a talent. I was worried, seeing as most of the town center was wrecked from the altercation and then the storm, but thankfully Gable's kitchen was unharmed. What would we do without baked goods!"

Sarrai chuckled amiably and took another bite. Meri itched, wishing that she could force the words out of the Scholar. But instead, she remained quiet as they munched happily.

"But! Of course, that is not why I am here, my dear Meri, I have news!"

Meri immediately leaned forward. "You know what he is?"

"Absolutely, without a doubt, I am sure I do."

Relief flooded through Meri.

She wished Zanve were here, her fingers flexing on their own accord as though seeking his hand. Instead, she simply sat up a touch taller, and breathed out. As though sensing her sudden excitement, Thistle himself stepped into the doorway, sniffing at them.

"Come in, Thistle, this concerns you just as much as Meri," said the Scholar, gesturing the creature inside. "As always, it is an honor."

Thistle tilted his head slightly, almost in a bow of recognition, coming to sit by the Scholar's side. Sarrai scratched him on the head, threading their fingers through Thistle's feathers. It was an odd sight, seeing the Scholar and Thistle sit side by side, exactly of a height with one another.

"Have you noticed his horns?'

"Yes, he's got two growing," said Meri, motioning to her own antlers in demonstration.

"I think there might end up being four, not just two, at some point," said Sarrai, looking at Thistle with a keen eye. "There's the two larger bumps, but just behind them, there are two more little bumps that I suspect will grow to a fairly impressive size."

Lock settled around Meri's shoulders, deciding to join them instead of heading back outside to help with the clean-up. He wrapped his tail around her upper arm, familiar and welcome.

"Yesterday, when we were all joined in fighting back that magical storm together, I felt Thistle's magic well and true. The power of it — that wasn't really ever in true contention, of course, because we know that he broke through the realms to be here. But, what was up for debate was the creation of that door; the voice in your head, guiding you along. That, I think, boils down to Thistle's species as a whole."

"Species?"

"He is of a family of fey creatures that very, very few Fey Scholars have studied. One particular Scholar, millennia ago, when the world was a much different place and gods walked among us, made it their prerogative to learn about the rarest of creatures across all realms. They fell in love with the fey realm, thankfully, for us Fey Scholars of today! They were elven, I believe; and lived for a very long time. They devoted their entire life to the study of the realm. Much of their research remains, though not many have perused their earliest recordings and studies as I now have."

Meri nodded, slightly surprised at the idea of a being so old. Sure, her mother and grandmother were both high fey, and were centuries old themselves, and she knew that arch fey could be hundreds if not thousands of years old when they reached that title, but *millennia*... that was unheard of.

"They studied what were originally called the Rare Ones for about two hundred years. The Rare Ones, specifically, in our language; but in the fey realm, I do believe they are referred to as the Thnathi. Thistle, specifically, is a branch of Thnathi called a Kefithnath."

Kefithnath. Of the Thnathi family. Meri had never heard of those kinds of creatures. "What does that mean, exactly?"

"The word kefi, specifically, according to another one of my colleagues who specializes in languages from the fey realm, refers to something with... positivity," explained Sarrai, gesturing with their hands to en-compass everything. "Joy, in some instances; in others, a positive force. There are many argued points about the direct translations of language, of course, but that generally gets the sense across. Most of this, of course, was something very tricky to uncover for that Scholar. Because, as that original Fey Scholar studied the Thnathi, it took them centuries to garner what little information we have about these rare beings."

"Why is that?" Meri interrupted.

Sarrai chuckled. "Thnathi are drawn to very specific places and people. They are rumored to seek out places of great power and people of purest heart. And well, there are many kinds of Thnathi, and even in the branch of Kefithanth, I assume there are many kinds of creatures. But..." Sarrai hesitated, hunting in their mind. "Thistle, I gather, is here because of you. Because you are a Keeper, yes, but also because you are who you are. Your energy, kindness, and life drew him here through the realms."

"I simply picked up a stone from a market seller," breathed Meri.

"Fate and the universe will make things so, if they wish it to be," said

Sarrai with a shrug. "Or the gods. Whatever powers at play one believes in. The world is vast and full of incredible findings, so we all must keep searching."

"It passed first from a fey beast's lair, then to Finnean the ex-adventurer and now bookseller, then to Cecily, then to me."

"Until Thistle knew he had found where he was headed." Sarrai winked at the fey creature, who was sitting beside the Scholar with a bemused expression on his feathery face.

"I also believe that the destructive power Thistle demonstrated when he first arrived here, having been locked in the greenhouse, was simply his attempt to get back to you, to make sure you were alright." Sarrai scratched Thistle under the chin. "He is here to protect, of course. Like a guard dog. I believe that they appear to Keepers in the fey realm — rarely — but what summons them, no one really knows. Nonetheless, what that Scholar surmised long ago was that the Kefithnaths are able to bolster a Keeper's magic and the ley lines' magic; that, and of course, protect the Keeper from any danger they may encounter. They are beings full of power, full of possibility, and I think they lend that possibility to the place they choose to stay."

Meri was overwhelmed. A fey creature, breaking through the realms, simply to be with her?

"Where did he come from?" She knew he had crossed over from the fey realm, but where exactly, and how—

"Where does any fey creature come from?" answered Sarrai cryptically. "The Scholar never found out, and no one ever has since. I choose to believe that whatever voice guided you along was some kind of magic at play, or perhaps some greater being in charge of the Thnathi and where they go. It's yet another mystery of the fey realm that I would love to discover!"

Perhaps it had been Thistle's soul speaking to her from the other side, or some other force that Meri couldn't fathom.

"It is fascinating and truly an honor to have met a Thnathi in the flesh. And one so young! I cannot wait to know what he is like when he grows to his full size."

Meri blanched. "Full size? He isn't going to get much bigger, is he?"

"Oho," chuckled Sarrai, popping another bit of pastry into their mouth and speaking around it, "I think that Thistle is going to be a rather large creature. The few recorded Thnathi were gargantuan — larger than buildings — however, most of the Kefithnathi that the Scholar described seem to be much smaller than that when full grown. Still substantial creatures, though. Who's to say, truly. Perhaps Thistle will be the size of a small horse, or too large to fit through your door."

"The fey realm can produce rather startling and beautiful things," said Meri softly, gently overwhelmed. Would she one day look at Thistle eye to eye? "I... I can't thank you enough, Sarrai. For everything. Not just Thistle — but the magic last night, being here to help. Helping a town you don't even belong to, people you just met."

Sarrai's cheeks turned slightly darker in complexion. "It is simply the right thing to do, is it not? Help those who are kind to you?"

Much later, after Sarrai and she had finished their pastries, after the scholar had left, and the animals outside had finished their work, Meri stood tentatively on the threshold of her cottage once more, leaning heavily on her good leg.

"You came for me?" she breathed, looking down at Thistle, who was seated calmly by her side, surveying the garden. The creatures had done a surprisingly good job, having saved some of her plants, and taken whatever couldn't be salvaged to build their dens and nests. "Why me?"

Thistle, the Kefithanth, looked at her with an expression that spoke of some deeper understanding than Meri could fathom. A feeling of deep protectiveness shuddered below her ribs, through their connection.

You. Keeper. I protect Keeper, Keeper protect Arrowmount.

Meri let out an unsteady breath, feeling entirely overwhelmed. She felt undeserving of such loyalty.

Thistle nudged her thigh gently, and she started to pet him, feeling the horn nubs under his feathers. He sent her images, flashes of emotions, a jumble of impressions she somehow understood; something that felt deeply good. His presence wasn't only a protection for her specifically — he was here, as she was here, for the town. Thistle presence meant more bountiful goodness for Arrowmount.

Abundance. He brings abundance to those he protects, she thought, the thought brushing into her mind almost unbidden.

"My Kefithnath," she said, laying her had atop his feathery head. "My protector."

38

TIME, SUNSHINE, AND RAIN

Meriwen

The days folded into a week as spring continued to unfurl in the world around them. Zanve walked out so regularly to Meri's cottage that Meri was sure he could do the trip in his sleep. The world was shifting into the warmer season, ever closer to summer, which Meri could nearly smell on the breeze now.

Zanve, Kaius, and Jay had steadily worked through repairing Meri's greenhouse and were officially installing the final glass panes in a few days. The Mirrthgroves were extremely meticulous with crafting each individual pane, and so, progress had been slow. Plus, with the storms, her project had been pushed back to allow for the emergency repair efforts in Arrowmount to take precedence.

In between the installations of Meri's greenhouse windows, Kaius would help Zanve with the actual construction and repair of the inside of the greenhouse. They had rebuilt Meri's herb tables and shelving, adding in extra elements that she wished to have, like a part of the table tops that could shift up or down depending on how Meri was working with her plants that day, seated or standing.

Thistle had grown taller, stronger, and his horns were showing above his feathers now. The more that Meri spent time with him, the more that Thistle seemed to drink in the world. It was fascinating to see him grow, and Meri couldn't wait to see what he would become in the coming years.

A few days out from the solstice, though, Meri felt the stirrings of panic once more. Though her greenhouse was back in order, and the material realm plants nearly back and flourishing inside — thanks to Caelynn and Zanve — her fey realm greenhouse was woefully empty.

The pixies hadn't come back from the fey realm yet. Meri was starting to believe that she was going to either miss this ritual, or have to try a half-baked solution by swapping out fey realm herbs with ones from this plane. After the magic being sent so off balance, though, she was not willing to risk that kind of experimentation. This imbalance needed a big correction; the true, proper fix would only be to use the fey realm herbs as she had been taught to do.

And if Meri was being honest, she should do the ritual in both spots in Arrowmount — the nexus by her cottage and the one in the middle of town — to ensure the magic of the ley lines was truly back to normal. But she was only one person; there was no way she could be in two places at once. Except for her, no one had the ability to channel the ley lines, either; so, she couldn't even teach one of her friends to do it.

Lock settled in around her shoulders once more, bringing her wandering mind back into her body. He grumbled low; the sound full of anxiety.

"What's the matter, Lock?" Meri tickled under his chin absently, peering around to see if anything was amiss.

Over the past few days, Meri had been playing with her new-found abilities, slowly re-sculpting her garden. It was incredibly arduous work; the energy needed to pull and smooth the large scratches and craters that the storm had made was immense. It drained her every time she tried to shape bigger parts of the earth, and felt as though she was actually doing manual labor with a shovel at first. But the more she flexed the muscle of magic, the easier it seemed to get.

Lock made the sound again. "Intruder."

Meri's spine straightened. "Again? Where."

"Mmm. Before." He shifted on her shoulders. "Nervous."

Meri had noticed. The creatures that usually frequented her garden had mostly vanished; both with the storm and the intruder from before, the creatures ventured rarely into her garden. If they did, they walked warily through it, poking at the plants and bits that were carved up, before fleeing back into the safety of the forest.

"I know, Lock." She sighed, turning on her heel, taking in her whole garden. The back of her house was still pockmarked with broken windows and mud splatters that had caked on to the stone walls; but for the most part, things were back to the way they used to be. She hadn't sent any word to town for help on her windows yet; she wanted to make sure that the townsfolk were taken care of before her. She could manage with a few broken windows.

Her eyes drifted up to the tiny crack in the second floor where the pixies had made their home and wondered for the tenth time that day — hundredth that week — when they were going to make their return. When it came to time in the fey realm, nothing was linear; they could appear at literally any second, or weeks from now.

Neither of which was good for her nerves.

She needed to be doing things, keeping her hands and mind busy. So once again, she set to work fixing her yard, slowly dragging out the magic from the earthen ley lines and pulling it up, reshaping her home to how it should be.

"Meri?"

Meri turned to the voice as Wyn appeared at the edge of her garden, bearing a basket on one arm, and dragging a cart full of wood with the other.

"Hello," said Meri, her face splitting into a warm smile. "I wasn't expecting you today, what a lovely surprise."

"I come with treats and help." Wyn walked up inspecting Meri's garden. Her jaw dropped, seeing it almost back to normal. "Though, from the looks of it, you've got most things handled here. Your garden looks practically untouched! Besides the fact that it's all mud and dirt now, and not the lovely swaths of grass it was before."

"Grass takes time to grow again," said Meri with a small shrug. "It'll come back in time."

"We could always get some of the druids in town to help. May or Cecily would be happy to."

Meri smiled softly. "No, that's alright. Though magic is a quick fix, sometimes things need to be left natural. Besides, all it needs is time, sunshine, and a bit of rain. By the end of summer, it will be like nothing ever happened."

"Alright. Well, how about your house then? I'm here to get your windows measured up, so that my partner can fix things properly for you. He's nearly done the last couple panes for your greenhouse; adding on the few windows that were broken at the back of the house won't be any trouble at all."

Meri felt her face heat. "But the rest of the town—"

"Is getting the help it needs. You, however, are out here all alone. So we're helping you."

"I didn't ask—"

"I know." Wyn winked at her. "Sometimes people just need to be helped, whether they ask for it or not. Sometimes."

Meri sighed, letting the matter drop. "Alright."

There was a soft *mmrrow!* from the inside of Wyn's basket, which made Meri jump. Lock's tail tightened on her arm, his little clawed hands digging into her shoulder.

"What's that?"

"Oh, that's Tiny," Wyn said, gesturing to the basket. "Every few hundred years he insists on being brought everywhere with me."

"Few hundred... oh, you're joking." Meri caught the sparkle in Wyn's eye. Wyn pulled back the cloth covering the basket to reveal both an absolutely ginormous cat that looked to be both a thousand years old and a baby all at once. He was nestled in with an array of jam jars and a neatly packed loaf of bread, protected from the cat with brown paper.

Though, brown paper certainly wasn't the be-all fix-all to protecting bread from cats; Meri caught the hungry glean in Tiny's eye when Wyn revealed his flat, feline face, though it quickly turned into a stoic disinterest as he looked out at the world.

"Percival, this is Meriwen. Meri, this is Tiny, whose given name is far too proper for him. We have no idea how old he actually is, only that he is probably going to outlive us."

"Cats are all immortal beings in disguise anyway," said Meri, stretching out her fingers so that Tiny could sniff them. He carefully inspected them before he leaned his chin, letting her pet him.

"He won't be much trouble, will he?" asked Wyn.

"Not at all," laughed Meri. "There are usually several of cats around here, but recently they've decided to give my place a bit of a wide berth."

Wyn raised her eyebrows. "Why's that?"

"There was apparently someone lurking around my garden a few days ago, and it's set all the animals on edge." Meri smiled and shook her head at Wyn's nervous glance around. "Don't worry; I have yet to see any evidence of wrongdoing. It was probably someone from town exploring on a walk. Come on in, let's crack into that bread. All the magic I've been doing has made me absolutely ravenous."

The two of them split most of the bread before Wyn helped Meri clean and repair more of her place. Wyn was surprisingly handy with a hammer and nail; Meri secretly wondered why Zanve hadn't asked her to help when he started to fix up her greenhouse, but she wasn't going to comment.

Wyn climbed all over the outside of Meri's garden, inspecting each of the windows, noting down their dimensions and repairing bits of broken frame work here and there. She even waved at a few of the remaining pixies, stopping to have a chat with them.

Through most of the afternoon, Wyn told Meri about herself, and constantly peppered her with questions. It shocked Meri, to say the least, to learn how easily the two of them conversed. She also hadn't realized that the two of them were rather close in age. Both elves and fey had a very, very long lifespan.

While Wyn worked on the windows, Meri fixed up the last few divots in her yard, smoothing everything over with a gentle gesture of her hand. Tiny decided to make Meri's garden his playground, leaping up on a few of her garden beds and nosing along the scarred bits of land as he explored, before he decided to lay down in a sunbeam to nap.

"Wow," said Wyn after a bit, coming down off a ladder and wiping her forehead with the back of her arm. "This looks phenomenal. You really are just a constant surprise, you know that?'

"I could say the same about you," said Meri. "I can't get your honey jam out of my mind. What do you put in it?"

"I work with the beekeepers on the other side of Arrowmount," she said, smiling. "My secret ingredient will remain secret, I'll thank you. But those little industrious little ladies are the real workers."

Thistle, who had spent the time they were working inspecting the garden keeping his eyes on things, stiffened in Meri's periphery. For a moment, Meri couldn't hear anything; she wondered if perhaps Thistle could hear footsteps that she couldn't, but then she felt it.

The slightest shift in the magic around them. Like the pressure of a door opening.

Wyn frowned at both Meri and Thistle. "Okay, what's happening? Both of you froze, as though—"

Something shifted along the line of the trees, slightly off to the left of the path out of her garden. All Meri could think at the moment was *intruder.* Had the lurker come back, this time for something more? She couldn't help thinking of that awful man Damian coming back with a vengeance.

But instead, a familiar waft of magic poured over Meri. A woman stepped through the trees, accompanied by a number of birds and tiny, branch-like creatures.

The pixies had finally returned — and they weren't alone.

A second, older woman stepped in behind. They were both wearing long, flowing dresses, their features mirrors of one another, except for their hair; the older one wore hers as a brilliantly white-haired bun, and the other's was a mess of curls just like Meri's with dots of grey starting to arc through the faded brown. They both turned their warm eyes and twin smiles to Meri, who had to hold back an unbidden sob that was climbing up her throat.

Her grandmother never left her own garden in the fey realm. She hadn't in millennia. Now, she was here, having crossed through realms, and was standing in Meri's garden.

"Mother?" Meri said, barely above a whisper. "Grandmother?"

"Meriwen," answered her grandmother Seraph, holding her arms out as they crossed Meri's garden. She folded Meri into a hug. "My darling."

Her mother wrapped her arms eagerly around Meri next. Though Meri stood tall with her antlers crowning her, Elestren stood as tall without. Meri knew most people found her narrow-eyed focus intimidating and a touch otherworldly, but to her, those eyes were home.

There was something to both her grandmother and mother that was a home that Meri hadn't realized she was missing until they were standing there in front of her.

The little birds around the two fey settled in the trees and along Meri's garden beds, twittering merrily. The pixies that had accompanied her family waved to Meri, most of them carrying bundles in their hands — which they immediately carried inside to deposit on Meri's kitchen table.

Behind them, through the trees, came another group of creatures. They ferried the largest amount of goods in a number of crates, carefully tottering over the ground. For a moment, Meri thought her freshly smoothed garden was being torn up anew; but the closer they came, Meri recognized the little creatures as the lumpen, rock fey that often were found around her grandmother's garden.

"My Meriwen," said her mother, drawing her chin up with graceful fingers to focus on her. "My love, my darling, it has been so long."

"I didn't expect you," said Meri, taking them both in.

"Why not?" chirped one of the pixies, the one who had spoken to her previously. They settled on the same bit of stone that jutted out of Meri's cottage, as though they had never left. "You told us to bring the letter to Keeper Seraph, and we did. So, we brought her with us to answer it back. Along with everything you asked for. Simple enough."

"But, your garden." Meri reached for her grandmother's hand.

"It will survive without me for the time being. I have made friends with a new Keeper who lost her home. She's staying at my place for a little while, and promised to take care of the ritual there when the time comes. It will not miss a turn of the season." Seraph tapped Meri's hand lovingly. "My dear, you don't think I would let my garden go unguarded? Besides, I wasn't going to miss this. A missed ritual at the same time that a Kefithnath decided to come to this realm. Incredibly intriguing."

Meri let out a soft gasp. "You know—?"

"Darling, of course I know." Her grandmother chuckled. "Now. Before we fall into more chatter to catch up, for it has been some time and I miss your wonderful teas, I think you have some introductions to do."

"Right." Meri gestured to Wyn, who had been standing rather uncharacteristically gobsmacked just behind her. "Mother, Grandmother, this is my friend Wyn. Wyn, I am pleased to introduce you to my mother, Elestren, and my Grandmother, Seraph, both high fey of the fey realm. The cat in the sunbeam is called Tiny."

"His official name is Percival," said Wyn in a small voice. "But we call him Tiny to keep his hubris in check."

Seraph held out a hand to Wyn. "A friend of my granddaughter's is a friend of mine. It is an absolute pleasure to hear that she has made a friend, after all these years. It is far too quiet up here in this little cottage all alone. Oh, don't give me that look, Meriwen — I know why you chose this place, and I know it's full of your wonderful creatures much as my garden is. But there is nothing quite like the company of friends."

"And you're Elestren, I've absolutely adored reading your journals," Wyn blurted, shaking Meri's mother's hand. Elestren's face split into a delighted smile.

"You've been reading my journals? My daughter has finally taken down those old tomes and is using them for something other than pixie food?" She ignored the shouts of indignation from the pixies that were opening the carefully wrapped herbs in the kitchen. "I feel like we have quite the story to catch up on."

"We do," said Meri softly. "And this is Hemlock," she gestured to Lock draped over her shoulders before she motioned toward the feathered creature at her side, "and that is Thistle, the Kefithnath."

Elestren looked curiously at Thistle. "What exactly is a Kefithnath? Mother, I don't believe I have ever heard you speak of one before."

"That is because I never have, dear." Seraph tapped her daughter's cheek lovingly. "Well met, wyrmling, and well met, young Thistle. Now. Tea?"

The two lumpy fey creatures settled their bundle of goodies down near the door to Meri's cottage. Meri beamed at them, nodding her thanks, as they sat in the sunshine near Tiny, waiting for Meri's mother and grandmother.

Meri gestured to her cottage. "Tea it is."

39

THE EVERYDAY

Meriwen

Elestren stirred her tea absently as she looked around at the kitchen, taking in the shattered windows that were open to the garden outside. "What on earth happened to your lovely cottage?"

"We've been having a bit of trouble with the magic in Arrowmount," said Meri. "Thanks to Thistle and me."

"Missing the ritual," said Seraph, her voice stern. "You know I raised you better than that."

"Grandmother, I know," Meri sighed. "But there are only so many things one can do when one is unconscious, their entire stores of ritual prep destroyed, with nothing to fix the problem."

"I could have helped."

"Yes, well. We don't exactly have a way to talk to one another, do we?"

That made both Elestren and Seraph go quiet.

"I can't believe we didn't think of that," said Elestren. "In case we needed to get a hold of each other urgently."

"Well, that's something we can fix." Meri sipped her tea. "What's done is done. Thank you for bringing the plants."

"Tell me everything that happened," said Keeper Seraph, slipping into a teaching register that Meri recognized very well from her childhood.

And so, Meri did exactly that. She left nothing out — telling them everything from the moment that she picked up the stone, to Zanve saving her, to befriending Wyn and her partners. She told them of the unbalanced magic, the storms, and to the Scholar who helped them figure out what Thistle really was.

By the end, Meri's voice was hoarse, despite the half-finished tea in front of her. Wyn was sitting next to Elestren, Tiny now snoozing in her arms, looking rather surprised at having heard the whole story.

"You really used some of my journals to help?" Elestren was gently rubbing the corner of one of the tomes that was still on Meri's kitchen table, a wistful expression on her face.

"Yes," said Meri, reaching and flipping toward a now well-read page. "Especially this one. This is what I used to help stop the storms."

Seraph looked it over as Elestren ran her finger down the page. "Ah yes, I remember telling you about that, Elestren. You never had a knack for this kind of magic, but I didn't realize you had written it all down."

"It was something for me to do whilst you were teaching Meri," shrugged Elestren. "I knew it would never work for me, but thought, perhaps one day it would be useful to make note of it all."

Seraph nodded, skimming the spell. "I can show you a way to help strengthen this without the need of your friends channeling their magic into you. Though that was quite quick thinking, I'll give you that."

"That was Sarrai's idea."

"I would love to meet that Scholar again," smiled Elestren. "They had such wonderful stories. And loved their cherry wine!"

"I'm more than sure they would love to see you again, too," said Meri.

"And this Zanve," said Seraph, looking suddenly up at Meri with a sharp expression. "You must invite him to dinner so we can properly meet him."

Meri's cheeks warmed at the thought of Zanve meeting her family. "Alright, that would be nice. If you are staying until the solstice, I'm sure he can find the time. With all the clean-up and repair of the town, though…"

"He will make time," said Wyn. "I'll make sure of it."

Elestren stood and gestured to Wyn. Wyn's eyes went slightly wide, but stood all the same. "I like you, Wyn. Let's go into the garden. I have a feeling you're full of stories, and I'd love to pick them out of your brain."

They stepped out Meri's kitchen door, Wyn looking briefly over her shoulder at Meri with wide, excited eyes.

Thistle chose that moment to wander in, settling by Meri's knee with a soft sigh. He looked at her grandmother, his beetle black eyes shining interestedly.

"I knew a Kefithnath once," said Seraph.

Meri's head snapped toward her. "What?"

"You were barely older than a babe at the time, and I don't think your mother ever saw it." Seraph shifted in her chair just so, before she began to thread her fingers through Thistle's feathers. She chuckled as Thistle's eyes started to close in pleasure, and she moved to scratch him under the chin. "A creature came into my garden one night, larger than life. It had talons and a beak and the same piercing beetle black eyed stare as your Thistle here. It was sort of bird-like, but moved more like a snake, and had fur the color of purest desert sand.

"It came into my garden rather quietly. I remember one day picking you up — that day, you were fussing, and your mother was fast asleep, so I took you for a turn around the garden. That always soothed you, as it should. But we turned the corner, and there it was. It sat watching us, quietly. I felt as though it was measuring our worth. I had never seen such sober eyes on a creature."

"What happened to it?" Meri searched her mind for any memory of such a creature in her grandmother's garden, but couldn't pin anything down.

"It ultimately decided that I wasn't in need of a Thnathi, I suppose. I had you and your mother, so I was not alone."

"I didn't know that Kefithnathi could move from person to person like that." Meri considered Thistle quietly, wondering if he would ever leave her. The idea made her profoundly sad.

"As rare as it is to have a Kefithnath come to you, it is even more rare that one leaves before it has to. That one — I never learned its name — was older than me, I believe. Its beak was heavily scarred and damaged, and it was unable to close properly on one side. Most of its front left leg was torn asunder; I could see it limping. I sensed a great deal of sadness in it, too, as it moved around my garden, as though it was searching endlessly for something it would never find again."

"And then it was just gone," said Meri quietly. "I wonder where it went."

"Probably continuing its search, whether for the Keeper it lost, or where it wanted to call home. I do remember, the night that it left, it found you laying amidst blankets beneath my old willow tree — you remember the one?"

"Of course," Meri said, knowing exactly the tree her grandmother meant. That willow tree was much like its material realm counterpart; though in the fey realm, willows grew flowers thin as eyelashes instead of leaves, and when they fell, they fluttered on the wind like butterflies. The willow in her grandmother's garden was Meri's favorite tree growing up, and she would always sit beneath it with her books or a snack, or just to watch the garden around her.

"It found you there, because your mother went inside for a moment. It snuffled down low, peering right at you with its big, beetle eyes. You reached out, hand knocking its beak, before it blinked slowly, then backed away. I never saw it again after that."

Meri frowned, slowly running her hand over Thistle's head, tracing her fingers along the bumps beneath his skin that would one day be horns. "I wonder what it was looking for, exactly. Do Kefithnaths need to find another Keeper to attend to? Or do they just... wander until they return home, wherever that is?"

"Your guess is as good as mine, my dear." Seraph laid her hand atop Meri's and squeezed. "What a wondrous creature. To see one so young, freshly hatched into this world... and in the material realm!"

Meri smiled at her grandmother in response.

Seraph shifted back in her chair. "How has your leg been? Have you found anything that helps ease it?"

"Not any more than I could when I was a child," she said with a soft, tired smile. "Neither realms have anything to help heal all things, grandmother."

She sighed. "I just wish you didn't have to live with such pain."

Meri shrugged, stifling a sigh that contained the years of pain and grief. "I've been managing."

"I know you can handle it; I simply wish you had someone to help you out with things around here. For when you need it."

"I don't need any help."

Seraph eyed her in the way that reminded Meri of when she was eyeing Meri's work, preparing herbs. "Darling, yes you do. You may not *want* help, and I know you are extremely capable of doing things yourself, but it is a matter of *needing* help as a person."

"I have my friends now."

"I'm glad. Speaking of which, why don't we go find that friend of yours, and perhaps she can walk your mother and I into town so we can get a room at the local inn?"

"You can stay here," said Meri quickly, mentally running through how on earth she would be able to fit her mother and grandmother in her house, seeing as the only bed she had was her own.

Seraph *tsked*. "Absolutely not. I wish for my own bed by the sea."

Meri stifled a laugh and rose with her grandmother.

A little while later, Elestren walked alongside Meri to the periphery of the forest, letting her daughter lean into her. Meri's discomfort was too much to walk any further, becoming more apparent with every step she took. Wyn and her grandmother walked ahead, Wyn with Tiny in her basket, and Seraph with a long, beautifully wrought staff that she conjured out of thin air when they began to walk.

"He chose you, didn't he?" said Elestren.

Thinking she meant Thistle, Meri smiled down at the fey creature, who was striding along beside them. "Yes, he did."

"Not your Thistle. Of course he did. Your human."

"Zanve?"

"All of them, I suppose. That Wyn, she is quite lovely. I like the way she thinks, having multiple partners. You should consider that. A whole group of people to keep you safe and happy."

Meri nodded absently, knowing that unfortunately for her, one partner was quite enough for her. Even that had seemed impossible up until Zanve.

"It's rather fascinating, don't you think?" her mother continued. "All these mortals deciding you were the one they wanted to keep in their lives. They came around, poking and prodding with their questions, and then they decided they enjoy your company enough to stay. It's rather special, I think. I've only ever had one person that liked me enough to keep me around."

Meri blinked a few times, trying to parse through her mother's language. "Just the one? Mother, you have friends all over the realm."

"True, but none as special as your father was."

Meri's heart fell into the ground. "My father? Wasn't he fey?"

"No, not really." Elestren's expression softened. "He was fawn, of a kind. Tall, beautiful, strapping — his descendants were from the fey realm, but he himself had never stepped foot there. He was so mortal that you could practically smell the years and time on him, and how they leaked away almost as quickly as it does for most mortals."

"Where did you meet him?"

"Here, of course."

"Here? Do you mean the material realm?"

"No," Elestren shook her head and smiled sideways, gesturing toward the town. "Here, in Arrowmount. It's been a long time since that day. Feels like lifetimes, really."

Meri withheld her surprise, knowing that her father had once walked the cobblestones and forests of Arrowmount, like her. "I'm not that old."

"No, love. I mean first meeting him here. Everything about that day, the way the sea moved; it was as if everything was meant to be. He was here on a trip, of course, from the neighboring kingdom."

"He was a Scholar?"

"Of course, what other kind of mortal have you ever seen me take a liking to?"

"True," said Meri with a soft laugh.

"Your father was a perfect gem of a man," Elestren breathed. "You have his antlers, you know. With them, he stood seven feet tall, like a true king. In those few weeks, I knew I would never forget him."

"Only a few weeks?" Meri had always thought her mother and father had spent a lifetime together before they had her.

"Time is fleeting here, as you know. It was all the time we had, before I was off to Alieweth, and he was off home. But it was enough to last me until today, of course. And will last me forever, at this rate."

The thought was deeply sad, and sent Meri's heart into her throat. They only had a few weeks together. "Is he still alive?"

Elestren sighed heavily. "I don't believe so, no. I followed his life for a while, before you were born. But, my love, you know how time works in fey."

"I do," Meri answered softly. A hundred years could pass in this realm before ten in the fey realm, if it wished to. She also knew how fey aged compared to mortals. Only elves rivalled the fey in this realm with their expansive lifespans.

Her and her mother's relationship had never once been strained, despite being apart for years on end. Meri found that if she wasn't at her mother's side, adventuring, exploring, and learning, she went longer and longer without hearing from her. But she didn't resent Elestren for it; her mother had a life, and so did she.

"I've missed you," Meri said quietly, leaning into her mother's shoulder. "It's been far too long."

Elestren squeezed her hand tight. "I've missed you so, so much, my Meri."

They paused at the edge of the forest. Her grandmother tapped her cheek and talked of the ritual preparation in a few days, before she turned and started off toward town. The red roofs beaconed in the warm sun-shine, the lighthouse a far-off speck on the beautifully glistening ocean.

"I always knew you'd be back in Arrowmount," sighed Elestren, run-ning a hand down Meri's arm. "Home always finds a way to call us back."

"Mother—" Meri hesitated, biting her lip as her mother made to walk away. "I... I'm scared. Of what things are becoming with Zanve — could become with him. Does that... does that ever change?"

Elestren's smile grew slowly across her face. "That, my dear, comes with love. What is there to worry about?"

A surge of sudden, deep ending panic bubbled up in Meri's throat. All this talk of time and loss terrified her.

"What if he doesn't want me as much as I do him? What if he... mother, he is only human, and I am *me*. I will only be starting to age when he's long in the ground, and I... I do not want to lose him. I didn't realize that this is what becoming close to others would feel like, and every—" she laughed, feeling as though she was about to cry, the sound getting stuck in her throat, "—every moment is as though I'm about to tear my heart out at the thought of being without them. How can I stay connected to them, knowing that I will one day know what it is to lose them, though they will never know what it is like to lose me?"

Elestren squeezed her hands. "You are lucky to have found something so rare. Mortals form these kinds of connections every day, every hour of their lives, clinging to that feeling. It reminds them that they are alive. For, my love, don't you feel so desperately alive now? I can see it in your face. The last time I saw you, you were so stoic and soft. Now, I see my daughter that used to run around her grandmother's garden chasing the butterflies and pixies once again. You are *truly* living now, Meriwen.

"It is not about the ending," Elestren continued, "It's all about living in the middle of it. The everyday. We often lose sight of that, us fey. But you, you my daughter, are uniquely positioned to take that sight head on. Live. Love. Don't keep yourself hidden here in this cottage forever, alone."

Meri closed her eyes and laughed sadly, a tear escaping. "It's terrifying, though.'

"That is what being alive is for. Cherish it, because not many people get to experience it fully." Elestren wiped her thumb across Meri's cheek, stopping the tear. "You deserve this love, this life. Don't ever forget that."

"Thank you," breathed Meri, leaning into her mother's touch.

"Of course. Now, I must go, because I can already feel your grandmother's ire on my back for being slow." She winked, before taking a few steps away. "I will see you again tomorrow, my girl."

40

MONSTERS

Zanve

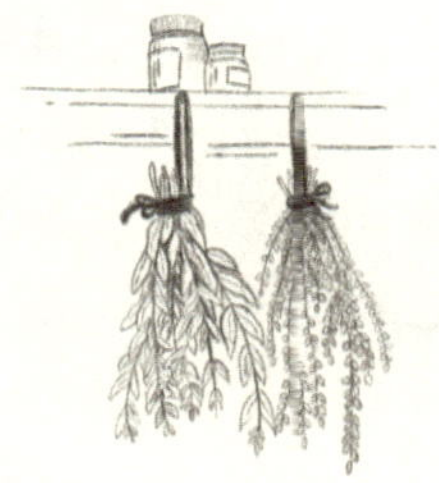

Zanve absolutely, positively, could not stand still as the crowd gathered on the beach in the weak morning sunshine.

For the past week, he'd been running up and down the cobblestone streets helping organize various groups and carrying heavy material help repair whatever was broken. It appeared that no matter what end of the town folks lived in, something had been damaged; from shingles being ripped off, to windows imploding, to wooden trim being torn clean off homes and buildings.

Zanve had passed by the Cobb's inn earlier that morning as they fretted over a wall that had collapsed inward, taking with it the front part of their inn. Chervil was out by the lighthouse, had gestured wildly as he explained something to Calian, who was looking up at the structure, concerned.

But now, after a day of movement and hard work for many townsfolk who had been up before dawn repairing, sweeping, and setting the town back into some sense of normalcy, everyone was tired and on edge.

They were all waiting and wondering what the Lord of Arrowmount was going to say in this sanctioned meeting. The majority of Arrowmount had come out to see what Lord Wymarc had to say.

Now that he was finally forced to stay still, Zanve couldn't keep his mind off of Meri. Her garden and cottage had been absolutely devastated by the storm, and he hadn't been able to go assess and help with the damage. It was driving him up the wall, to think of her dealing with the damage, let alone when she got the information from Sarrai.

Over the past few days, when Zanve wasn't hammering fences back into place or hauling sacks of sand, his mother was having him repair their own home and those of her friends. By the end of each day, he didn't have the energy to keep his eyes open and collapsed into bed, immediately asleep. He hadn't had the time or energy to think about anything.

But of course, being stationary now, his thoughts started to run rampant. He began to fully wrap his mind around the storm and what his friends had gone through that night. The questioning beforehand with Sarrai, and what Meri had said about an intruder—

The intruder.

The thought slammed into him almost physically. Meri had said the creatures of her garden were all out of sorts, having sensed some kind of intruder; that Thistle had sensed a stranger within the property line of the cottage. He had been pulled in every different direction, and hadn't given much thought to Meri's offhand comment, nor had any time to ask her if there had been any reappearance of the person.

Skies, and now he was here, waiting for this damned meeting to start, when he should be with her—

"Welcome, everyone, and thank you for coming," said a magically enhanced voice, casting out across the beach. Everyone turned toward the small stage that had been erected, where a figure now stood.

Zanve eyed Lord Wymarc. He was dressed rather plainly, which wasn't unusual; what was unusual was the distinctly uneasy, worried look on his face. Zanve couldn't pinpoint a single moment in his life where he'd seen the Lord of Arrowmount be anything other than rather happy and calm. To the side of the platform stood Sarrai and their assistant Argyle.

"I understand there have been some rather disturbing events happening of late," continued Wymarc. "With the odd magical storms, the unrest in the town center, everyone is understandably upset and worried as to what may be going on. Myself and my team, headed by Scholar Daruka that is visiting us from the Kingdom of Pralon, are trying to discover the heart of the matter—" he gestured to the Scholar and himself, "but for now, we have collectively come up with a plan to help keep everyone safe.

"We have worked tirelessly with Chervil over the past few days to implement a new alarm system that will run through the lighthouse and to various spots in Arrowmount," Wymarc explained as Chervil made himself visible off to the other side of the platform, lifting his rather impressive head of dark blue horns. "You'll probably have noticed a few of your fellow townsfolk running slightly more ragged; we have been testing out various systems that would work, and have finally settled on the best one we can think of for the moment. We are always open for suggestions, of course."

Lord Wymarc cleared his throat and looked around at them, as though making sure he was being heard, before continuing. "On rotation, we will have various volunteers who can wield magic stationed atop the lighthouse, watching for any sign of a storm. If they see one, they will alert the rest of the town by triggering the alarm system, which will wail.

Chervil, if you could demonstrate."

Chervil turned toward the lighthouse and waved. Everyone turned to look as a figure atop the lighthouse waved back, before a sound tore through the air around Arrowmount that instantly made hairs rise on the back of Zanve's neck. The gathered crowd around him all had various reactions; many ducked and tried to cover their ears, some swore loudly, and a few children started to scream.

The alarm, caterwauling off around the streets of Arrowmount, felt vaguely haunting. Zanve could hear the echoing of more alarm bells being set off at other ends of the town, ensuring everyone could hear it.

The moment the alarm cut, Wymarc clapped his hands together, drawing everyone's attention back to him. "As you could hear, there is no way anyone would miss that sound. If you hear it, get to cover as soon as you can; we will weather the storm the best way we know how. We are, after all, a seaside town and aren't strangers to large storms, are we?"

That caused a number of people to chuckle lightly, the tight mood breaking slightly.

"Are there any questions before we adjourn?"

"Can only magic users volunteer?" shouted someone from the front.

"We would like as many volunteers as possible," said Wymarc. "However, we will always need a magic user atop the lighthouse to be able to trigger the alarm. So we can pair a non-magic volunteer with a magic one, if it comes to that. The more eyes the better, I say."

There were more questions, but Zanve had stopped paying attention. He noticed a familiar head of black hair near the front, inching forward.

That can't be good.

Zanve shifted forward, glancing around, wondering if anyone else could see what he was seeing as Damian approached Lord Wymarc.

"Are there any further questions?" Wymarc cast a final glance over the crowd, and no one came forward. "Excellent. If you wish to speak to me after this meeting, feel free, but for now—"

"I have a concern I'd like to raise," said a voice that Zanve knew all too well. His heart dropped into his stomach as Damian walked up to Wymarc, getting on the platform with him, and half turned to address the crowd. He was wearing his uniform, pressed and starched so sharply he looked like a child's doll.

Damian placed a hand on Wymarc's shoulder as though they were comrades in arms.

"Uh, well, that's not quite what—" Wymarc tried, but Damian wasn't listening. Somehow, even though Wymarc's voice was the one that was magically amplified, Damian's voice cut clear across his.

"I come to report a sighting of a monster," he said, eyes travelling over the gathered crowd. The townsfolk of Arrowmount shifted, clearly intrigued, but no one really gasped or shouted out, which Damian seemed to have wanted as a reaction.

Zanve's whole body had gone cold.

"A... a monster?" Wymarc asked, looking baffled.

"I have seen it with my own two eyes," said Damian, nodding emphatically at the crowd. "I was out in the forest that wraps our home for a stroll and came across the beast — it is massive, black like night, and has eyes of purest evil. It did not see me; for if it did, I'm sure that it would have killed me then and there."

That got a bigger reaction. The noise of the crowd grew, anxious mutterings rising around them.

"My dear fellow, what are you talking about?"

"I come to warn the good people of Arrowmount of its presence, because we have to do something about it," said Damian, turning to Lord Wymarc, his voice pleading. "We must protect our town."

"I second this," said a second voice that shocked Zanve. Amalin, Captain Ludru's second, walked forward. Zanve glanced sideways at Captain Ludru, who was standing further off in the crowd; he looked just as baffled as Zanve felt.

Damian nodded to her as she stood at his side, her hands tucked behind her back, feet slightly apart. She looked the picture of authority.

"Briggs came to me with this issue first, to see if it should be addressed in a wider setting. After hearing what he has to say, I believe that whatever this beast is, it could sincerely be a problem for Arrowmount."

"We don't even know if it is a threat," said Wymarc quickly, trying to placate both the two guards and the crowd around him. "But, well. If you say..." Wymarc sighed, and glanced to a few of his servants who were standing off to the side, looking equally as uncomfortable.

"I can assure you it is," said Damian quickly. "Large beasts in the forest? It can only be a result of whatever the magical storms are coming from. We have to prepare ourselves for potential danger."

At this, murmurs of agreement started to ricochet around the gathered crowd.

"I suggest we do search parties, to try and locate where this beast is hiding," said Damian. "Then, we plan accordingly and take it out."

"Take it out? Good man, we don't even know if it is dangerous!" squeaked Sarrai, waving their arms as though to flag down a runaway carriage. There was a look of pure panic on their face, and their eyes darted around the crowd, as though looking for someone, before they looked back at Damian and Lord Wymarc. "We can find out more information about it, then make a rational decision after that."

Damian frowned at the Scholar as though they were nothing but a bug under their shoe. But before he could get a word out, Lord Wymarc jumped in.

"Yes, that is a good idea, Scholar Daruka. Let us all discuss this further at my manor, shall we? Whomever wishes to volunteer for these... uh, search parties, as this man — Briggs — and Lieutenant Reem, of course, say?"

Wymarc looked sincerely put out that his meeting had gone so off the rails. He opened and closed his mouth a couple times, shooting sharp glances at those around him before he ran a hand through his hair and shook his head.

"Right, anyone who wishes to volunteer for a search party and help with this, come forward. But as for the rest of you, I—"

"We want to know more about this creature!" someone in the crowd shouted. Multiple people cried their agreement.

"Yeah! What are you trying to hide, Wymarc? What do you know about this threat to our town?"

"Nothing, I can assure you," said Wymarc quickly, as the noise started to climb around him. He held up a hand, and after a moment, the crowd quieted marginally to allow him to speak again. "I assure you all that we will investigate this as thoroughly as we can. Lieutenant Reem, Captain Ludru, I ask you to organize your guards to help head the parties and report back what they find."

Captain Ludru emerged from the crowd and joined Amalin. "Yes, sir, we will."

Ludru eyed Damian as he came to stand next to the platform. Then, as though pulled by Zanve's stare, both Ludru and Damian looked directly at him. Damian's stare turned slightly smug, whereas Ludru's was relieved to spot him. The Captain motioned for Zanve to join him. "Let's get this organized, shall we? Einar, Briggs."

Zanve stepped up to them as Damian stepped off the platform at the Captain's behest.

"What exactly are you playing at?" Zanve muttered to Damian.

"Sorry? I'm not entirely sure what you mean."

Zanve caught a smirk breaking across Damian's face out of the corner of his eye as Zanve continued to survey the crowd, Ludru and Amalin starting to organize volunteers that were stepping forward. "All of this. There is no creature in the woods. Why cause panic?"

"Oh, there very much is a creature in the woods. A terrifying beast we know nothing about." Damian turned a self-satisfied smile on Zanve, his eyes shooting daggers. "It is our duty as town guards to keep the town safe, is it not?"

"Yes," said Zanve warily.

"Then, why are you opposed? Perhaps you know something of this monster in the woods." Damian leaned a little closer to him, dropping his voice. "Or rather, I should have said, this monster in a certain garden we both know quite well."

Cold shot through Zanve's veins. Damian. *Damian* was the intruder Meri's creatures had noticed in her garden. Zanve should have known; who else would have gone to spy on Meri like that? What had he seen?

"*No.*"

"Yes, in fact." Damian stepped away, moving toward Captain Ludru and Lord Wymarc. "I wonder what will happen when we pay your girl a visit?

"What exactly has she ever done to you?" Zanve practically growled, his hand lunging out and snagging on Damian's collar.

Damian shrugged, eyes glittering maliciously. "I've never liked you, or understood why everyone else does, Einar. Walking around here like you're better than everyone else. And that Witch is the same. But I know what you really are; nothing but blights on the town that need to be purged."

He stepped out of Zanve's grip before Zanve could question him further, and was replaced by Ludru, guiding Zanve to stand in front of a group of people he was now in charge of.

Skies. Zanve stared at the group, his heart beating fast. What was he going to do?

41

Blue Tendrils of Magic

Meriwen

Sunshine beamed into the greenhouse. Meri's mother stepped up beside her, and her grandmother had stationed herself in the fey realm room of the greenhouse, organizing and implementing the new plants and herbs that Meri had requested, the three of them preparing for the ritual that was to happen the following day.

It was finally time. Meri was properly relaxed now; she had help, and she was going to finally right the wrong she unleashed on Arrowmount. It was only under a day away, now.

They had been in her greenhouse since the morning, both Seraph and Elestren coming to her cottage bright and early, avoiding, as they said, the busyness of the town's repairs. There had also been a call for a town meeting along the beach; Meri assumed it had to do with the clean-up efforts of the town.

Elestren shifted on her feet. "Why haven't you shown Thistle the town, or shown Arrowmount Thistle?"

The question threw Meri off guard. She cleared her throat. "Because I don't want him to be feared. To be drawn and quartered, or whatever it is mortals do to beasts they are terrified of."

"Then it only makes sense for you to take the initiative and show him to them before they jump to conclusions. One thing that I've come to understand in my travels is that mortals are quick to judge, and even quicker to anger. But, most are quite reasonable beings."

"I'm... I'm terrified that they won't accept him," said Meri softly.

"Because they haven't accepted you?"

Meri put down the bundle of herbs she was preparing and frowned at her mother. "What exactly do you mean?"

"You aren't really a part of the town, are you, my love?" Elestren reached out and touched Meri's cheek softly. "You do all this incredible magic for them, keeping them safe, and yet, you live out here alone with your plants and your creatures. You said it yourself, when you were telling me of the mortals who have chosen you. You never knew what that was like before, to be chosen by them."

"No, but—" Meri shook her head. "The town never tried. When I arrived, they created rumors about me, and constantly stared whenever I went into town. I never felt welcome. I'm this oddity to them whenever I walk into town, so I assumed it was easier to keep to myself."

Elestren sighed. "My love, this is a seaside town. Ports like Arrowmount collect people from all walks of life. I have only ever seen the mix of people such that Arrowmount has in other port towns. You may be a unique person, but that doesn't make you odder than the giantkin that walks around with a bowtie around their neck, or any less deserving of a place here. You should let the people of Arrowmount into your heart, Meriwen. They deserve to know someone as exceptional as you."

Meri gazed at the herbs in her fingers, sighing.

"I never thought to," she admitted. "I thought at first that I would stay away, to let them get used to me. And then I simply stayed away, because it was more comfortable. I suppose you're correct, I should have tried harder."

"What is it that mortal mothers say?" Elestren tapped her chin softly, thinking. "Mothers always know best?"

Meri simply chuckled and shook her head, transferring the handful of meriwen in front of her into her mortar, before beginning to grind it up carefully.

"Tell them what Thistle is. Show them what he is. Show them what you are, go join them in the bar sometimes. There is so much life in this little town, you will drown in it."

Thistle pulled on the connection between him and Meri from outside.

Meri. Guest.

Meri ducked out of her greenhouse, listening for footsteps. Heavy footsteps sounded as Kaius emerged from the trees.

"Good morning," said Meri, trying to not sound too disappointed that it wasn't Zanve. "To what do I owe the pleasure?"

"I'm here to officially finish up work on your greenhouse, and also to bring you windows to fix up the back of your house." Kaius shifted, showing an incredibly large box strapped to his back.

"Already?" Meri let out a shocked laugh. "I can't believe the work is done on the greenhouse — and my windows, how did you get them done so quickly?"

"My family works fast when it's ordinary cottage windows," chuckled Kaius. "Plus, Wyn urged me to get this done as quickly as I could. I can see why." He turned to her cottage, the back of which was void of window panes. "We are testing out a new system that allows us to make them much faster than usual, since we've needed a lot of repairs to do across Arrowmount."

Kaius set to work quickly after Meri had introduced him to both her mother and grandmother in the greenhouse, officially sliding the last two panes of glass into place. When he stepped back, hands on his hips, Meri let out a soft, contented sigh.

"It's back," she said, taking a look around her familiar space, now made anew. She reached and opened up the top windows with a simple pull of a lever, letting in the fresh warm air.

"Let's get your house done, shall we?" Kaius turned to Meri and gestured out the door. She followed him, stepping into the sunshine. He ducked his head slightly. "Also, a lot of things are happening in Arrowmount, if you hadn't heard yet. As I left this morning, I—"

He cut off as a terrible keening wail sounded in the direction of Arrowmount, echoing through the trees. Meri winced as birds and creatures scattered around the garden, fleeing the unknown sound.

"What in all the realms is that?" asked Elestren, poking her head out of the greenhouse.

"That is a new alarm system that Lord Wymarc has had installed," explained Kaius. "They were having a town meeting on the beach, demonstrating it — something to help in case any more of those magical storms roll in."

"Clever," said Meri. "But hopefully unneeded."

"Hopefully." Kaius hefted a number of window panes up onto his shoulder. "Do you mind showing me where your ladder is?"

The day melted away as Kaius worked on her house and Meri lost herself to the ritual preparation alongside her grandmother and mother. Before she knew it, Kaius was finished and her cottage was back to normal, windows gleaming in the afternoon sunlight. He even showed her how to open a few of them that hadn't been able to open before; allowing for more air flow into her house, before he left, waving goodbye.

Thistle grew restless as the light began to fade from the sky, dusk approaching. Meri watched him with a frown as her mother and grandmother headed back into town for the evening, his attention on the forest around them.

"What is going on, Thistle?" she finally asked once they were alone once again. He chuffed at her, shifting in place uneasily.

People. In forest.

People in the forest? She listened hard, trying to make out any sounds other than the usual ones that the animals made. It took her a moment, but there, just there—

Boots. Heavy ones, and a lot of them. And voices.

Meri stood frozen in her garden, listening to the approaching noises of people getting louder and louder.

"Thistle—"

No.

"Please, I can't have them see you."

No. Not again. Not safe.

Thistle settled firmly in front of her, eyes tracking the forest. Through their bond, she saw images of Damian coming into her yard, and Thistle hiding away then. She got the message: Thistle wasn't going to leave her alone this time.

Lock jumped off of his spot on her garden chair and settled on her shoulders once more. "Mmm. Meri."

"I know, Lock," she whispered.

Then the men broke the line of trees.

"There it is!" someone shouted, pointing to Thistle. "That's the monster!"

Damian, the man who had shown up at her door uninvited weeks before, stood at the head of the group, an incredibly satisfied smile on his face.

Lock curled his nails into Meri's shoulder and hissed low, eyes locked on the man.

Intruder, said Thistle.

"This was the intruder?" she said quietly.

"Yes," answered Lock. "Him."

Meri's eyes shifted over the trees in a second, realizing that many of her usual animals were tucked back in the shadows, watching the group of people from a safe distance.

"What can I do for you?" Meri asked, raising her voice.

"We're here for your beast," said Damian. "Harboring such a monster is a danger to this town."

"He is not a monster," she said. "He is a fey creature."

Damian laughed, looking at the people around him. They were all shifting with an energy that unnerved Meri; she had never felt emotion like this pouring off of people, let alone the people of Arrowmount.

"That is obviously a dangerous creature," he said, gesturing to Thistle, who immediately set his haunches up and started to make an entirely unsettling sound in the back of his throat. The group drew back as one, as though inhaling in fear.

"Don't—" but her words were cut off as Damian shouted.

"*Seize it!*"

The group launched into movement, drawing out nets and makeshift weapons — though a few had actual wood axes and butchering knives. Thistle sprang toward the trees, drawing the mob away from Meri.

"No!" Meri hiked up her skirts and moved forward, but suddenly there was a deer in her path, crowding her, pushing her backward. "Root and ruin — I do not have — *move!*"

The deer simply stepped into her, until her feet were stumbling back. Lock slipped off her shoulders and onto the deer, tail thrashing.

"Thistle!"

The feathered creature evaded the group of buffoons rather expertly, before he disappeared into the trees.

Meri let out a scream of frustration and managed to side step the deer, pulling on a bit of the earthen ley lines for strength, before she, too, took off after him. Fear and magic pushed her faster than she knew she should have been able to run — she hadn't been able to run at all since she was a little girl, and now she was pounding her feet over the forest floor, trees whipping past.

She broke free of the tree line as the group descended on Thistle, shouting and jeering after him. Thistle was a blur as he kept ahead of them, darting here and there, sending them on a proper chase. He arced back toward the trees, but suddenly there were more people bursting forth, drawn by the shouts.

"Monster!"

"Catch it!"

"*Almost—!*"

"*—get it—!*"

Thistle was closed in now, back tracking toward the town. "No!" Meri yelled, her voice getting caught up in the wind as she raced after them. She had to reach them first. She had to make sure that they didn't hurt Thistle—

The sky was shimmering.

She caught it out of the corner of her eye; a tiny shifting of magic in the air. What had Caelynn said? They looked like ribbons, undulating in the sky? This — this glittering, odd magic, was what she must have meant.

The muscle in her leg spasmed, sending her to the ground in a heap of skirts, her shoulder jamming into the ground. The little bit of power she still had in her shuddered at the impact, immediately heading toward her aching limbs to try subduing the pain. Meri let out a soft sob and pushed off the ground, searching around for where Thistle had gotten to. She thought she heard her name, but couldn't fathom from where.

She pushed herself up, ignoring the throbbing as much as she could, and continued to shuffle forward.

Within moments, Meri watched as the small mob turned on her creature, someone running in with a pitchfork. Thistle's menacing form changed to one of immediate fear as he looked around, unable to see Meri. There was a pang of fear through their connection as Thistle realized he had no idea where he was, since he'd run so far away from the garden he'd lived his entire life in.

Terror, jagged and raw, shuddered through their bond as Thistle turned this way and that, trying to find a way out. Within moments, though, they had him cornered back against the wall.

"Stop!" Meri tried to push forward, willing her leg to support her weight, but instead, it simply shook and crumbled under her. The men paid her no mind; perhaps they didn't even hear her cries.

Meri! The one-word cry was audible only to her, slamming through her connection with Thistle. An image flashed in her mind's eye, seeing exactly what Thistle was seeing. He searched for her, desperate for her aid, as the mob converged on him.

As Meri tugged whatever strength she could from the earth, more than she ever had before, wrapping herself with it, she felt something change. One of the men had a rope, and they were trying to tie Thistle up, to restrain him. Thistle's fear was at a breaking point, an impending explosion of emotion through their connection.

She yelled incoherently, but it was too late.

There was a massive *CRACK* that shuddered through the ground, ripping at the seams of the earth. Meri watched as the men closest to Thistle were thrown back, bodies flying as a ball of vibrant blue magic exploded out from the center of their group.

It took Meri only a moment to notice the newly formed wound in the salt-worn wall wrapping around Arrowmount. It looked as though it had been hit with something so immense it had blown a hole clean through. A number of fissures spidered up and out from the point of impact, and, Meri assumed, into the ground where Thistle was standing.

This is what must have happened in her greenhouse, she realized. Though this was much, *much* more destructive than Thistle's power had been then. If he had had this amount of power, her greenhouse would've completely fallen to pieces.

Thistle ran toward her, terror leaking off of him in physical waves of magic. Blue tendrils of power spilled over him like ripples of water, dissipating into the air. She opened her arms, ready to pull him in, tears streaming down her face.

He never got to her.

As he leaped toward her, a spell snapped in the air like a whip, freezing him in place. Magic knitted itself around him, trapping him in a bubble. A magic user that Meri had never seen before stepped forward, triumph on their face.

The crowd of people cheered as Thistle was torn away from Meri, rising up above everyone, fear etched on his face.

"Meri!"

She turned to the voice, only to be gathered against a solid chest. Meri breathed in Zanve's warm scent as he pulled her into his arms. He knelt next to her, half cradling her as she sobbed.

"Meri, are you alright?"

"No," she breathed, agony radiating from her leg up into her back, but nothing, *nothing* compared to the ache splitting her chest in two. "They have him."

PART FIVE

Zanve of my Heart

42

HEALING DRAUGHTS

Zanve

Zanve held Meri in his arms, wishing beyond anything else that he had been there a few seconds sooner. She shouldn't have been alone.

Meri shook in his arms, tears streaming down her face as she stared at the crowd with rage.

"*Kill the beast! Kill the beast!*" someone started to call. The chant was picked up by a few people around. Zanve immediately stood, bringing Meri with him, holding her up.

Thistle was held aloft above the crowd as though he was a carcass being roasted over flames.

Then Zanve noticed the shimmers in the sky. They hovered low around the mob holding Thistle, flitting in and around their heads. Not a single one seemed to notice — but Zanve remembered the way the magic had done the same thing during the disturbance in the town center, warping people's emotions. He remembered the unnatural rage he had felt.

"Wait!" he bellowed, "Lord Wymarc specifically ordered we bring the creature to him if we found it and were able to capture it — do not harm him!"

"It is a monster," sneered one of the townspeople by him, looking up at Zanve with disgust on their face. "Just like that Witch in your arms. Monsters, both of them."

"BANISH THE WITCH!" someone else shouted, spitting at Zanve. Instinctively, Zanve held Meri closer to him, as though his arms would be enough to protect her. The crowd pressed in closer around them. He had to get Meri out of there.

"*Enough*!" yelled a magically amplified voice, rippling over the crowd. The mob separated begrudgingly as a figure walked through; Lord Wymarc being led by Captain Ludru. A servant dressed in purple hurried in behind, looking terrified.

Ludru glanced at Zanve as Amalin stepped up behind, her eyes tracking the crowd with an unreadable expression. "I'm afraid we're going to have to take her in, Einar."

"No," said Zanve, taking a step back. "She did nothing. All of these people are to blame, not her. Let her and Thistle go."

Lord Wymarc mouthed the word *Thistle* before he scanned Meri's face, then Zanve's, and followed Meri's line of sight up to Thistle, who was still frozen in the magical bubble over the crowd.

"Bring the creature to my manor," he said, his voice casting out. "We will keep it in my stables; I trust you're able to create something to keep it contained?" Wymarc looked at the magic user as they approached, holding Thistle aloft.

"Sir, yes sir," she answered, practically foaming at the mouth, her eyes bright with success. She wiped a strand of sweaty brown hair from her face, gazing up at Thistle like he was a prized ham.

Lord Wymarc nodded to her, then to his servant at his side. They cast a quick, neat spell directed at Lord Wymarc's throat, the magical effect banishing from his voice.

"I'm truly sorry for this," he said then, his voice hoarse but quiet, to Zanve and Meri. "Are you able to walk?"

"I will," said Meri, her voice shaking with effort as Zanve gently let go. "Don't hurt him."

"I will try everything in my power to see he is unharmed." Lord Wymarc sighed, looking at the crowd of people jeering and shouting around them, regular cries of 'kill the beast' and 'banish the witch' being started up. "Come."

"No, wait—" Zanve stepped forward, desperation fueling him. He *couldn't* let them take her. Who knew what this crowd, warped by the magic, would do to her?

Wymarc laid a hand on his arm. "All I am going to do is ask her a few questions, Zanve. I can promise you she will be perfectly safe in my hands."

"Let them take her, Einar," said Ludru, stepping between Zanve and Lord Wymarc. "We don't want any more trouble. Amalin!"

"Can't you see something's wrong here?" Zanve gestured at everyone as Meri took a trembling step forward, her hand extended toward Lord Wymarc. Amalin stepped up, sliding her arm around Meri's waist to steady her, Meri's arm going around Amalin's strong shoulders.

The energy of the crowd was starting to twist menacingly. Fear tucked itself right up against Zanve's throat. This whole situation was completely unpredictable; the smallest thing could set the crowd off even further, taking control right out of Lord Wymarc's hands. Then what would happen?

Sunlight flashed on the metal from the various makeshift weapons in the hands of the mob. The crowd surged as Wymarc started to move back toward Arrowmount, the magic user at the head of the party carting Thistle along.

"She and Thistle aren't at fault!"

"Einar, please, step back."

"No!" Zanve tried to push through Ludru's grip, tried to get to Meri once more. "Meri!"

She turned to look at him, her face a rictus of pain and sorrow. She mouthed something to him, but he didn't quite catch it as Ludru grabbed hold of his arm, yanking him around.

Sounding exasperated, Ludru barked out a command. "Briggs, hold him."

Damian's snarling, stinking breath came close to Zanve's ear as he grabbed hold of Zanve. Someone else from the mob stepped up, grabbing Zanve's other arm. "Got you and your little bitch too. What're you going to do now?"

Zanve let out a roar as the crowd churned around him, heading after Lord Wymarc, Meri, and Thistle. He couldn't see them anymore as Meri was swallowed up by the crowd.

"*Let me go!*"

"Calm down, boy," Damian crooned, tightening his grip. Zanve struggled as hard as he could, pulling both Damian and the other man holding him almost off their feet as he struggled forward. Zanve saw a glimmer of magic by Damian's ear, his stomach sinking. "Gods, you're like a rabid dog. Shut him up."

Zanve felt the panther in him rise up; his body trying to free him at any cost. But before his body slid into his more powerful cat form, pain shattered across the back of his head and darkness took him.

"Zanve? Oh, dear man, please wake up."

Zanve's whole world was a deep, painful throbbing as he blinked his eyes open. He was lying on his side in a room he didn't recognize, stone walls and stone floor covered in an age of grime.

Scholar Daruka was crouched in front of him, concern etched on their face. "Are you alright?"

"I don't think so," he answered, groaning. "Where am I?"

"Lord Wymarc's manor basement," Sarrai answered, sitting back. "They wouldn't let me bring in a healer quite yet, since they are currently seeing to your Meriwen. Oh, bother, this is all going so poorly."

"You could say that again."

Zanve pushed himself up despite Sarrai's protestations. His world swam and for a moment he felt as though he was going to lose his breakfast, then remembered he hadn't eaten anything more than a piece of bread and coffee all day.

"Careful! Oh, that wound looks bad." Sarrai winced as they inspected the back of Zanve's head. They rummaged around in their bag before they swore gently under their breath. "Argyle, do you have—"

"Yes, I do," answered a somber voice by the door. There was the gentle clink of a bottle out of Zanve's line of sight, before Sarrai was in front of him again, a tiny vial extended in their hand.

"Here, drink this." Sarrai brought it to his lips. "I don't always condone the use of healing draughts when one doesn't quite know the extent of the injury, especially a head injury, but this is all we have for now."

Zanve swallowed the draught down without complaint. After a moment, his vision began to clear, and the throbbing edged away.

"That's a touch better," said Sarrai, still examining the back of his head. "Don't move, alright? I will ensure that the healer comes down to see to you properly. I'm sorry I cannot do more."

"That's all right," answered Zanve, running a hand over his face. "What can you tell me of Meri and Thistle?"

"Lord Wymarc managed to get you all to his manor, where he instructed much of the crowd that has gathered to remain outside his gates. Unfortunately, that awful black-haired man who instigated all of this is somewhere, lurking as though he's waiting for something to bite his teeth into."

"That sounds like him." Zanve let out a long sigh.

Sarrai wrung their hands together. "Lord Wymarc wishes for me to identify what Thistle is. He believes that I can hunt down answers for him and the town; but I haven't told him yet. I don't know if he believes that I know what Thistle is, or whether Wymarc just believes that I can figure it out."

"Please, don't—"

"I will *never* tell them what he is. I don't trust these people with a creature like Thistle. That amount of power in their hands? Who knows what they'll try to do. And with the magic unbalanced in Arrowmount..." Sarrai shook their head. "It feels as though that there's some kind of last stand happening, growing, and building in the air."

Zanve nodded, then regretted the motion. "Find Meri, tell her that I'll figure something out. Keep her safe, please."

"I will." Sarrai grasped Zanve's hand and squeezed. "Her and Thistle. I will not let whatever power is running free through the streets of Arrowmount take either of them."

Zanve's head gave a painful throb, waking him up as noise sounded beyond the door to the room. Cell? He squinted around at the space, trying to determine what it was. He hadn't known that Arrowmount even had something like prison cells, but here he was, lying in a long-unused space that had been turned into some kind of storage room. There were crates of clothes in the corner, though they seemed far fancier than anything Wymarc would ever wear.

"Oh, Einar," called a voice that sent immediate dread into Zanve's stomach. Footsteps echoed before a figure approached, the door closing behind them. "What a sorry sight. Look at this, he's officially down where he belongs."

"Damian," said Zanve conversationally from the floor, unwilling to move or even open his eyes. "To what do I owe the pleasure?"

"Oh, we were told to come down and ask you a few questions." Damian's breath passed over Zanve's face as he bent closer to Zanve's prone form. "Be a good lad now and answer them nicely, alright?"

Zanve could hear the undertone of an *or else* behind that sentence. "Or?"

In response, one of the other figures — Damian must have acquired some new friends since Zanve was knocked out — kicked him hard in the ribs.

The air blew out of him and he curled away from the boot.

"Got it," said Zanve, his voice tight.

"Good boy," said Damian, his voice sickeningly sweet. He grabbed Zanve's jaw and turned Zanve's gaze up to his, forcing his eyes open.

Zanve wanted to slap him, but couldn't seem to make his hands move. "Now. Where did the Witch's beast come from?"

"I don't know," answered Zanve. Damian's fingers tightened painfully on his face.

That was followed by an answering kick to his lower back.

Damian laughed, the sound low and menacing. "Yes you do. Try again."

"The fey realm," he answered as another foot collided with his spine, the words practically flying out of him with spit.

"Much better." Damian stood then, starting to pace the small space. "So the Witch brought him here, then. Conjured him? Summoned him? What sounds better?"

"Summoned, I think," answered one of the cronies. "She summoned him to do her nasty business."

"Summoned him from the fey realm to exact her plans on the unsuspecting town," said Damian softly. "Something otherworldly, perhaps demonic we suspect; something to hurt the town. Pay for all the years she's lived outside of the town walls, watching and wanting to be part of us."

"You know that's not what she did," said Zanve, trying to sit up and failing, the room spinning around him. He got on all fours, trying to claw his way toward Damian, his back screaming in agony. "She would *never* do that."

"Oh, probably not, but who can really be sure?" Damian grinned, teeth long in the low light of the room. "Alright boys, I think Zanve has given us all the answers we want, don't you think?"

Matching snickers came from behind Zanve. He glared at Damian, who sneered back at him.

"Let's give that healer a run for their money. Have at him."

43

HALFWAY TO A PLAN

Meriwen

Meri wanted to get up and pace, but the healer had ordered her to stay seated. Sure, she wasn't entirely sure she could walk, with the pain radiating from her hip and leg, but sitting still was driving her mad.

She had no idea where Thistle was, or Zanve — or where anyone was, really. She had no idea if her mother and grandmother were entrenched in the chaos, or if they were currently having dinner somewhere, absolutely none the wiser to the fact that Thistle had been abducted and she was being held for questioning.

Meri hoped fervently that it was the latter.

So, she stayed seated, her fingers picking at her nail beds and her teeth making an absolute mess of her lips as she looked around the room Lord Wymarc had put her in. It was quite lovely, which felt entirely wrong in the current situation. She was seated on a plush sofa with beautifully embroidered pillows that matched the flowering design painted on the walls. Some of Lord Wymarc's servants had also brought in some food for her, which had remained completely untouched. She was on her second cup of tea, though, despite it not tasting quite as good as her own brews.

"Meri?"

She turned quickly, nearly sloshing tea out of her mug, as Wyn entered the door. Wyn shot a glance behind her, then shut the door as quietly as she could.

"Wyn!"

"Thank the gods you're okay," said Wyn, hurrying over. "I have been trying to get in for over an hour now, but they wouldn't let me."

"How are you there, then?"

"A carefully placed bit of bread and jam," she said, brushing hair back from her head. "A good distraction for anyone, even folks who are not in their right minds right now."

Meri sighed heavily. "It's the unbalanced magic again, isn't it? Affecting the townsfolk? I saw the shimmering in the sky."

"As much as I can tell. The energy around them is thick and choking, as though the magic is physically pushing them into doing what it wants. And if you stay too close to them for tooo long, you start to feel the same. It's contagious."

"Thank you for coming," said Meri, reaching for Wyn's hand and squeezing.

"Of course." Wyn squeezed her hand in return, her eyes wide and worried. "Do you know why it's like this? The magic? Why is it choosing to make the townsfolk angry and vengeful, rather than supremely happy?"

Meri simply shrugged. "It is so difficult to say what any kind of magic will do when it's let loose — but when the nexuses go off-kilter, the magic preys on high, sharp emotions. And when you have a group of people already a little afraid, with all the uncertainty going on with the storms…

poke at that, it becomes anger. Anything to make the fear go away."

Wyn sighed and leaned back in a plush chair, shaking her head. "It would be much better if the magic had picked festival time to break. That way everyone would be revelling a more, rather than going about with pitchforks trying to kill a completely innocent animal."

Meri's blood went cold, thinking of Thistle being carried away from her once again. She couldn't get the image of his terrified face out of her mind.

"Do you know anything of what's happened to Thistle? To Zanve?"

"I believe they're holding Thistle in a section of the stables, because there's an incredibly obvious bit of magic surrounding it," said Wyn, shaking her head. "Zanve, though, I couldn't say. I know that the healer was looking for him, though, which is concerning."

"Healer?" Meri's heart dropped into her gut. "What happened to him?'

"It's probably just a precaution," said Wyn quickly. "I don't know if anything happened to him. He's probably out there, trying to champion for you and Thistle to be let out."

Meri ran a shaky hand over her face. "I want to go home. I want this to be over, so I can go back to being in my garden with all the people I love."

"I know," said Wyn softly, before she pulled Meri into a warm embrace. "We're going to try everything to get you out of this, okay? Just hang in there. And maybe eat something, you look pale."

"Do you think you could do something for me?"

"Anything."

"Can you find my mother and grandmother and take them to my cottage? I want to make sure that they're out of the way, in case the magic gets them too. And, if I can't get out in time for the ritual tomorrow, make sure my grandmother can do it without me. See she has what she needs."

"I'll see if I can find them. They were staying at Cobb's, so if they're anywhere, I bet it's there. Cobb probably has your mother trapped in another one of his long conversations about the sea or something."

She let Wyn bully her into eating a small bite of a sandwich that she couldn't taste, chewing slowly and washing it down with tea. Meri only let her smile drop when Wyn left, shutting the door closed behind her.

Meri didn't have to wait long, though, before Sarrai opened the door and bustled in.

"Oh, Meriwen, how are you doing?"

"As well as I can," she answered. "Has there been any news? Is Zanve alright?"

"Ah, I believe they are holding Zanve in the basement in one of the rooms there. He got on the bad side of one of that awful black-haired man's cronies, I think, when he tried to follow you and Lord Wymarc into town. I talked to him though, and everything seems to be just fine. Superficial wound."

Nausea roiled through Meri. It was her fault he was hurt. He shouldn't be in any danger at all.

"Alright," she said quietly. "And Thistle?"

Sarrai's face paled. "That is a bigger issue at the moment. I fear that Lord Wymarc is losing control."

"Already?" The sky outside had darkened to night, but only a couple hours had passed with Meri stuck inside the room.

"He and his staff are trying to keep folks from breaking into the stables and pulling Thistle out. It's getting... worse out there." Sarrai let out a long breath. "I don't think that they are going to listen to Lord Wymarc. The magic is at a breaking point."

Meri put her head in her hands, covering her face, and groaned. "If only I could speed up time, I'd make everything okay. Then we could be out of here, Zanve would be alright, and Thistle wouldn't be in danger of being executed by a mob of angry townsfolk."

If only. Even if the magic was fixed and the emotions quelled from this dangerous precipice, who was to say what they would leave Thistle alone? Hadn't she been worried about how they would treat him long before the magical imbalance came in and swept away the emotions of the people in Arrowmount?

"I can't stay here anymore," she breathed, barely audible. Sarrai patted her shoulder nervously, not paying attention to what she was saying.

"Zanve is being held in the basement," said Sarrai. "First door on the left. I am going to go help out with Thistle's, uh, magical protection. You didn't hear from me — but there is a weakness from the right side, near the back."

Meri let out a long, slow breath, before she looked up at the scholar through her fingers. "What?"

"Thought perhaps you'd like to know. The magic user — I never actually caught their name, now that I think of it, oh dear — is quite the novice when it comes to casting larger spells. A little overzealous, and a bit punch happy, one would say. Very visible."

"Good to know," Meri said, nodding slowly. "Thank you, Sarrai, truly. When this is all over, I owe you a lifetime's supply of tea."

"I'll settle for a cuppa and a chat about ley lines in your wondrous garden," they said with a tired smile. "Now, if you were perhaps going to decide to take a little stroll down the hallway, you may want to stick to the right side, because there's a spot on the left that creaks slightly when the right amount of weight is placed on it — oh, and wait about five minutes, until you hear the guard outside cough."

Meri simply blinked after them as the Scholar slipped out of the room. She picked at the sandwich in her hand, before she stood shakily.

There was no way she was going to keep sitting here and waiting. She barely knew what she was waiting for; Lord Wymarc had set her up here and run off, probably to handle the mob that had gathered outside his gates, and left her behind with no idea when he was going to return.

Meri hovered at the door, listening to the guard outside. She looked around the room, wondering if there was anything she could use as a makeshift staff, but there was nothing more than soft pillows and furniture. She was going to have to do this using her own two feet.

The guard outside coughed, then shifted. Meri cracked open her door slightly, watching as the man turned from her, taking a few steps down the hallway. In that space, she slipped out of her room, listening to the man cough again, much harder and longer, into a handkerchief.

With his back turned, Meri slid down the hallway as carefully and quickly as she could, sticking to the right side, using the wall as much as she could for support.

The decent to the basement was smoother than Meri anticipated. With all the hubbub at the stables, the staff and whatever guards that were on duty were focused entirely on the outside; she didn't meet a single soul as she stealthily made her way through the halls.

Thank the skies she wasn't wearing shoes, she thought, her bare feet silent on the floors. She had to stop a number of times, listening for any sound, as she kneaded her leg, trying desperately to remain strong enough to keep going.

The healer meant well, but the poultices they had applied to her did absolutely nothing to appease the pain in her leg. Meri knew these treatments well from when she was a girl and healing from her accident; all they had done was repair the surface of her skin, leaving the muscle and sinew twisted beneath.

Now, they left the surface of her skin a little bit numb, but beneath that her pain raged like fire.

Still, she walked on.

She had to. She wasn't going to leave those she loved — her *family* — separated and alone.

There was a soft gasp as Meri's feet found purchase on the main floor of Lord Wymarc's manor. Her head bolted upright, coming eye to eye with one of Wymarc's staff.

"Please," Meri breathed. "I—"

"He's this way," the woman whispered, taking a few steps and extending her arm for Meri. "You'd be caught a lot quicker than if you're checking doors willy-nilly."

"You're... helping me?"

The woman laughed. "Of course I am. I don't want to see you locked up any more than Lord Wymarc wants to have you locked up. But of course, you didn't hear that from me."

She led Meri to a door tucked down a back hallway. Meri thanked her, and slid inside, leaving the door slightly ajar as she descended the stairs, carefully, painfully, one at a time. It left just enough light for her to see the first few steps, but whatever was beyond that was plunged in darkness.

First door on the left.

Running her hand across the wall in the dimly lit basement, her fingertips traced stone layered in grime and decades of dust. Finally, just when she was about to give up and start looking for a torch to light, her fingers grazed over a hinge, then wood, then a handle.

Inside, there was a tiny window that was letting in a wash of flickering torch light from outside; but it was enough to see by.

"Zanve," she gasped, immediately moving toward his crumpled form on the floor. There was nothing else in this room but boxes of what looked like clothing and some oddly shaped furniture. This was not a place to keep an injured man.

Whatever healer was looking for Zanve had never found him down here.

He was cold to the touch as Meri collapsed to the ground and gently cradled his head in her lap, drawing him to her. His nose was caked in blood, and there were bruises blooming on his cheek bones and jaw. Having only been here for a number of hours, his clothes and hair were already dirty, filled with grime and what Meri suspected to be blood, congealed and matted.

"Zanve please, wake up. Tell me you're okay," she whispered, stroking his face gently. "Come on, please. Wake up, Zanve. I can't do this without you. Please, we have to go."

He shifted in her arms, letting out a soft sigh. "Meri?"

"Yes! Yes, it's me."

"Am I dreaming?"

She touched his cheek, running her thumb across it. "I'm really here."

Zanve's eyes fluttered open, shining in the dim light. "Here I am, getting rescued by the woman that *I* was going to rescue. This should feel unfair, but I'm rather happy to see your beautiful face."

"We can't all be damsels in distress," she said, a tear escaping down her nose. She wiped it away furiously, and sat back to give him some room. "Are you alright?"

"Never better," he said, wincing as he tried to sit up. "Though I'm fairly sure I've got a number of cracked ribs."

"Who did this to you?" Meri gently ran her finger across his nose, tracing a line of a bruise there. If she ever had the displeasure of seeing the people who did this to her Zanve, she was going to rip them to shreds. The violent thought should have startled her, but right then, she could have spat venom at whoever dared to lay a hand on him.

Zanve shivered under her touch. "Take a guess."

"Damian."

"He didn't once lay a hand on me," he sighed. "But his cronies definitely had their fun." Zanve gazed up at her, before lifting a hand to caress her cheek. "You're okay? Did they hurt you?"

"No one touched me," she said, leaning into his palm. She hadn't realized until right then how much she craved it; the gentle caresses, the warmth of his skin.

Zanve breathed out, his face relaxing slightly. "What have I missed? Did they let you out?"

"I escaped, thanks to Sarrai. And I'm going to get you out of here — but we have to get Thistle first." she hesitated, throat tightening with fear. Zanve's eyes never once left hers. "They want to kill him, and I don't think Lord Wymarc will be able to stop them. We have to get back to the cottage, to safety, until I can perform the ritual. That way we can break whatever hold this magical disturbance has on Arrowmount, and hopefully deal with them as rational beings."

"That sounds halfway to a plan," said Zanve, sounding slightly impressed. "Something out of one of my adventure novels."

"You'll have to let me read one when we get out of here," she said quietly. "But for now, do you think you can stand?"

"My love, anything for you."

"Don't," she hissed.

"What?"

"Call me that." She shook her head. "Not right now. Not when we're in the middle of peril, in some dank storage room."

"But Meri," Zanve said, his voice low and smooth as he pushed himself to sitting, gently cradling the back of her neck. "You have to know how much I do—"

"Later. When we are safe, and I can smile and laugh and kiss you and won't hurt you when I do." She touched his lip gently, realizing that it had been split there. He smiled then, wide, which split the small scab that had been forming there.

His tongue lashed out and caught the blood before it fell down his chin. "I'm going to hold you to that, Meriwen."

Meri's whole heart felt as though it was going to implode. "I hope so."

44

WEAKNESS IN THE BARRIER

Meriwen

Meri and Zanve managed, somehow, to hobble their way out of the basement holding onto each other for support. The woman that had helped Meri before spied them from around a corner and lead them out through a back door, waving them off.

"Sarrai said that there is a weakness in Thistle's magical barrier," Meri said quietly as they crept around the side of Lord Wymarc's manor. Now that they were outside, she could hear the gathered crowd around the front practically roaring with noise.

"Could you break through it?"

"I've never tried to do magic outside of my garden, except when they took Thistle from me." Meri frowned, pausing in their slow walk to let her senses stretch out. It took a moment to locate a thread of the ley lines, but there it was, pulsing along beside them. "I could try."

"Let's see," said Zanve, squeezing her hand.

They crept along the side of Lord Wymarc's property, ducking along low brushes and beautifully flowered gardens. Meri realized something. "Zanve."

"Yes?"

"I have no idea where we are right now. I've never been to the Lord's manor before."

"Don't worry, I have," he nodded, gently tugging her arm along. "That woman was rather helpful, she let us out on the side that the stables are on."

"How do you know this place so well?"

"During my training days, they had me stationed here," he said in a hushed voice. "It was a long time ago, but sometimes they would have us map the grounds just to double check and ensure that the perimeter was safe. Thankfully, Wymarc has his own wall fencing him in from the rest of Arrowmount, and also—"

"We live in Arrowmount," said Meri, laughing softly. "When do bad things ever happen here?"

"If you asked me a year ago, I would have said absolutely never other than in ancient history."

The edge of the stables came into view, along with people and activity. Townsfolk gathered around the stables, including the magic user that had trapped Thistle in the first place, and one of the guards that Meri hadn't personally been introduced to. When she pointed him out, Zanve nodded.

"Quinlan. That's good, at least; he will help us if he can. But the others..."

"What if you shift?" asked Meri, stepping close to Zanve as they hid themselves close to the wall in shadow. "It's dark, it would be much harder to see a black panther than a man."

"That's an idea." Zanve started to work at the buttons of his uniform before he froze, frowning at her. "What about you?"

Meri cast her senses out, finding that thread of a nearby ley line once more. She pulled on the magic, drawing it in, before she hunted with her senses toward the magical barrier keeping Thistle captive.

"I will try to give you an opening," she said, eyes closed. She wasn't entirely sure how to navigate magic like this, how to push and pull it apart. The feel of it reminded her immediately of her tether with Thistle.

With a burst of clarity, she remembered their connection. She reached across their bond, searching for the familiar feeling of the fey creature.

Thistle? Meri pushed the thought through her connection to him, hoping he would hear her.

Instantly the reply came back. *Meri. Safe?*

I *am here,* she said back. *We are trying to get you out. There is a break, a weakness, in the magic holding you. Can you sense it?*

There was a tiny silence as she waited, Zanve still beside her.

Yes.

Can you break it? Push it open, enough to let Zanve in, and get you out?

A beat more, then, *Yes.* Along with it came images of the inside of his stable, the glistening, visible magical cage around him, and the spark near the bottom, catching his attention. Then there was the feeling of something expanding, stretching, and an anticipation.

"Okay," she said now to Zanve. "Thistle has a hold on the break in the cage holding him. He's going to break through and come out to you."

"Perfect. First—" Zanve pressed his clothes into her hands, and in the darkness, Meri caught only a flash of his skin as he leaned forward and kissed her gently on the cheek, right by the edge of her mouth. "Here is a promise that I will be back."

"Good," she said as the man vanished, and a sleek black panther took his place.

The injuries Zanve had endured transferred to this form too, she noticed. Though hard to see, she ran her hand over him carefully, noticing the matted blood on one side. He shivered under her touch, before he gently nuzzled into her hand.

"Be careful, my Zanve," she whispered, as he slipped off toward the stables.

Meri waited with bated breath, wondering if they would be able to sneak out without being seen. There were just so many people around.

Moments passed, stretching longer and longer. Meri tried to keep the weight off her leg, the pain throbbing like a second heartbeat through the lower half of her body. She needed to sit down, and soon.

Where were they?

A soft burst of frustration threaded through Thistle's bond to her as he showed her an image of the stable entrance, people standing guard right in the middle of the doorway. He and Zanve, it looked like, were out of the magical cage; but they weren't out of danger yet.

Meri watched from her angle, tracking the movement of the crowd. Then, a small figure popped into view, scanning the area. Meri recognized Sarrai in an instant, and gently shifted to show the Scholar where she was. They spotted her and nodded, before they shouted, pointing off in the opposite direction.

It worked a charm — the crowd of people gathered around the stables all rushed off to where the Scholar had pointed, leaving the path around the stables open. Sarrai stepped out of their line of sight and gestured at Meri to go.

"Thank the gods," she breathed for the first time she could remember — she wasn't one to really invoke any of the gods, let alone thank them, but when needs must — and watched two low, animalistic shapes approach.

"Thank you," she whispered to the Scholar as she passed them, Zanve and Thistle joining her, flanking her.

"My pleasure. Now's your chance — get going!"

The three of them crept out of Lord Wymarc's yard, slipping along the side of the property, sticking to the shadows and the bushes for cover. The crowd that had gathered on the property was loud enough that they didn't have to worry about making much noise, thankfully; all they needed to make sure of was that they weren't seen.

Which proved difficult, seeing as there was a large expanse of space between the gap in the high walls that surrounded Lord Wymarc's estate. A space that currently was crawling with people. People, she knew, that would recognize her on sight. The magic she held under her skin shivered with anticipation. Perhaps she could use it somehow, to create a distraction, and let Zanve and Thistle pass unseen.

Meri slid her hand over Zanve's warm, soft head, and gestured out. He looked at her and frowned — as much as a large cat could frown — and let out a soft, low grumble that clearly meant, *you first.*

"I'm right behind you," she whispered, nodding encouragingly.

Then, to Thistle, she thought, *keep him safe, okay? Get to the cottage.*

Thistle eyed her, but moved forward all the same. The fey creature was about the size of Zanve in his panther form now as he leaned up against Zanve, supporting him.

As they started to sneak out the front, Meri stepped into the line of sight of a few people. She walked as surefooted as she could toward them and the only way out of Lord Wymarc's property, hoping that she wouldn't slip or fall. She yearned for her staff for support; something to hold onto so that her hands would stop shaking.

"Witch!" someone called, and heads started to turn her way. She didn't stop; she kept walking directly to the gate as Zanve and Thistle snuck around the wall, their lower, pitch black forms unseen.

"Stop her!"

"She's escaping!"

Meri pushed on the ley line magic she held onto then, bringing it to the surface until her entire body was buzzing. She kept walking, letting the magic play along her skin and clothes. Any hands that tried to grab her jolted back, shocked by the magic she had wrapped herself in. She tucked Zanve's clothes up under her arm, and drew in as much magic as she could to keep her on her moving forward. It felt as though she was being encased in power; she had never pulled this much from the world around her and turned it back into support for herself.

In her periphery, she glowed.

She put as much strength as she could in her voice. "Let me pass."

The sight of her alone must have stayed most of their hands, for she walked out of Lord Wymarc's yard unbothered, despite the shouts and stares that followed her. No one had been able to touch her.

"WITCH!"

The shouts started to increase as she walked off down the cobbles, trying to keep her gait as steady as she could. But still, they didn't follow her. She wasn't the threat they feared; the thing they feared most was, they believed, still locked inside the stables.

She could barely make out Thistle and Zanve up ahead, passing between shadowy buildings. There was a beat — a moment when she thought they had got out, relatively unscathed, then—

"*She's taken the beast!*"

"Root and ruin," she swore, and started to lurch forward as fast as her injured leg would take her, pulling magic up around her like a shield.

45

FLASHES OF TORCH FLAME

Zanve

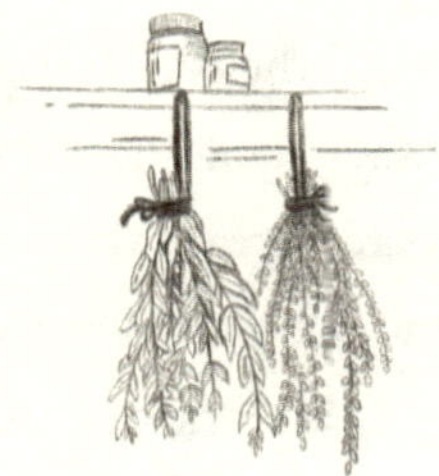

Zanve felt every movement of his broken and bruised ribs as he walked on all fours in his panther form beside Thistle, navigating out of Arrowmount. Thistle was now nearly shoulder to shoulder with him, more than large enough to support Zanve's weight as he tried in vain to keep himself steady. He hadn't been in this amount of pain in a long, long time. The last time was when he shifted as a young boy; when he would experience stinging torment as though needles were scraping along his bones and tearing at his muscles. This, the shifting shards of bone, was like a never-ending grind of agony.

Unsteady, shuffling footfalls came from behind them. Both Thistle and Zanve tensed, turning, but it was only Meri. She was running at them, her long skirt gathered in one hand, his clothes tucked under her other arm. Her hair streamed out behind her and her cheeks were pink

419

with exertion. Even in his pain addled state, Zanve could see the glittering of her eyes, determined and scared as she rushed after them. But, oddest of all, she was *glowing*.

"Go!" she shouted. "They're coming!"

With his enhanced hearing, Zanve could clearly hear the mob gathering in behind her, making their way down the cobblestones, shouting for blood.

Thistle nudged Zanve into motion once again. The three of them, injured, battered, and bruised, made their way through Arrowmount in a circuitous way. Thistle led the way, taking them down back streets and cutting between alleyways, avoiding the main streets Zanve would have taken. Instead, the fey creature led them around the perimeter, sure footed, as though he knew exactly where to take them. Zanve didn't question it, he was half paying attention as his sides throbbed with every step.

Thistle led them directly to the break he had caused in the wall; the crack big enough for all of them to squeeze through. Meri first, then him, and Thistle in behind.

The shouts of the mob were fainter now, as they squeezed through. Zanve wondered if the mob was hunting for them along the streets, or if they were heading directly out of Arrowmount, knowing there was only one safe place that Meri and Thistle would go.

He hesitated as Thistle moved forward, form staying low in the grass as the fey creature started to wind through the grass. Zanve glanced up at Meri, wondering how in all the hells she had been running the way she was, but when she got closer, he felt the magic leap off of her. She was coated in it; soft dancing lights illuminating every inch of her skin in swirling patterns. He followed her, trying to keep up.

Her legs and hips had the highest concentration of magic as it wrapped around her, illuminating her skirts. Her feet, too, were wrapped in it, as though she was wearing shoes made out of glowing, ever changing lace.

This close to her, Zanve could hear her panting, ragged breaths turn to sobs on every other inhale. She didn't stop and simply continued to run, tears streaking down her face.

Zanve couldn't imagine the amount of pain she was in.

Their small group started to ascend the meadow toward the tree line. Zanve's ears flicked toward the noise of the mob, suddenly louder in the night; the noise a rising cacophony of raucous laughter and chants of *kill the beast*. He glanced behind them and saw the growing mass of people, torches, and weapons exiting the unmanned front gates, heading their way.

Meri veered off slightly to the left as they approached the trees, which confused Zanve enough that he stopped and shifted back to his human form, dropping down to his knees in the long grass.

"Meri! What are you doing!"

"Drawing them away from you," she panted. She threw him his clothes, the fabric scattering out along the grass in front of him. "I'm visible, but you and Thistle can hide in the night. I can't stop the magic; without it, I can barely move. This is all I have. Let me keep you safe."

"Absolutely not," said Zanve, desperately dragging on his trousers before pushing himself painfully to standing before he caught up with her, wrapping his arms around her. "We stick together. I'm not letting them take you."

"Let me *keep you safe*," she ground out, making fists against his chest. "Please."

"And what, you're going to keep running until you drop, or they catch you?" Zanve shook his head. Out of the corner of his eye, he could see the mob advancing up the stretch of grass. "We stop, we face this, and them.

I've had enough of this crazed magical emotional turmoil or whatever it is that's going on."

"Only the ritual will stop that," she said quietly, her eyes soft and watery in the moonlight as tears continued to pour down her cheeks. "Please, Zanve. They want me gone. If I go, then my grandmother will fix the magic—"

"They tried to separate us." Zanve cradled the back of her head with both hands, tracing his thumbs along her jaw. "To keep you detached from the town. No longer. You belong here just as much as I do, or Lord Wymarc, or anyone else in Arrowmount. They will not force you out, because I won't let them. You have people here who will vouch for you, Meri, people who want you here."

"But—"

"Meri." Zanve lowered his forehead to hers. "Please trust me."

"I trust you more than I trust myself," she breathed, grabbing hold of his wrists fiercely. Then, as the angry, shouting mob echoed in the distance, she raised her mouth to his and kissed him with everything she had.

Everything stuttered to a stop. Zanve pulled her tighter to him on instinct, almost crushing the two of them together. Her hair caught in his hands, and she grabbed at his chest, hands trapped between them. She tasted of flowers and life and tea, and he never wanted to stop drinking her in.

They broke away, faces only a breath apart. His tongue snaked out, tasting blood as his split lip reopened, but he didn't care.

Meri's eyes shone in the moonlight. "My heart is yours, Zanve Einar. I hope you know that."

"And mine yours." Terror and love warred with one another in his chest as he held onto Meri, the pain throughout his body fading to the back of his mind. "Let's end this."

"Banish the Witch! Kill the beast!"

The mob's cries and awful, discordant laughter became clearer as the crowd of people ascended the meadow. Their torches cast long, menacing shadows through the grass as they trampled the freshly growing wildflowers.

Zanve stood in front of Meri, blocking her as they backed closer to the tree line. At the first opportunity, he was getting her through the woods and to her cottage. Not that it would do any much different than being out here with the mob encroaching on them, but at least there, she would be home.

Thistle stepped out of the shadows, pushing against Meri and Zanve, guiding them back into the trees as the fey creature growled and bared his teeth at the crowd.

"KILL THE BEAST!"

There was a snapping sound from nearby — Zanve flinched as the shadows around the tree trunks and long, overgrown plant life at the edge of the forest started to rustle and twitch.

"Mmmm Meri!" crowed a familiar, croaky voice, as a small figure launched itself up out of the grass and around Meri's shoulders.

"*Lock?*" Meri gasped. "What are you doing here? Get back to the cottage, get back to—"

"We are helping," he said, his tail twitching back and forth. "All help."

As Zanve watched, the shadows at the edge of the forest began to materialize into creatures of all shapes and sizes. It really was all of them, from the deer that had grazed in Meri's garden; to the cats perched on their backs, their tails fluffed out and postures rigid; to the badger, rabbits, and countless birds, and so many more creatures that Zanve couldn't name.

Thistle stepped in front of him and Meri then, readying himself as the mob crested the hill. Zanve felt the ache in his ribs acutely as he met the eyes of the man at the head of the line.

"We don't want to harm you, Einar," yelled Damian, his voice carrying. "We simply want to apprehend the dangerous beast and take the Witch back for questioning. Lord Wymarc's orders," he said, almost as an afterthought.

There was no way that this was under Lord Wymarc's orders — Zanve would never believe that, after the turmoil of the last few hours. The mob was clearly working for their own agenda now.

"Root and ruin," said Meri, reaching forward and squeezing Zanve's hands. "This is not going to be good."

"BANISH THE WITCH!" The mob cried. "KILL THE BEAST!"

"Hello, Witch," said Damian, tilting his head to see around Zanve.

"You ought to know my name by now," said Meri, stepping into view. "You must have an absolutely terrible memory."

"I refuse to use the name of someone so full of deceit and malice," he snapped back. "Someone harboring a dangerous creature — and is herself a danger to the town."

"He is not a danger — *I* am not a danger. In all my years here, all I have ever done is help this town."

"IT BROKE THROUGH OUR WALL!" bellowed someone.

"I SEE ITS HORNS," said another. "FIENDISH CREATURE!"

"It's just a babe," came a different voice, surprising Zanve. He at the crowd, trying to locate who spoke. The stable master was just off to the side, holding a large pitchfork and looking equally amazed at what he had just said. The shimmering magic clung to him less. Perhaps that meant that the magic only had so much power over the mob — influencing him less, letting his own thoughts break through.

Over the center of the mob, the magical, shimmering tendrils coalesced into a cloud so thick Zanve was surprised they could still see. It caught the light of the torches, flashing ominously.

No one seemed to acknowledge the stable master's comment. The crowd jeered and snarled, a beast waiting to attack.

"It attacked at least twenty of us when it broke the wall," said Damian, his voice cutting through the clamor. "Who knows what it will do as it grows. Something that can damage a symbol of Arrowmount that has stood, unmarred, for decades — nay, CENTURIES—!" He cried, fist in the air, and the sound was caught by the mob, "is a danger to all those who live in Arrowmount!"

"You cornered him!" said Meri, trying to be heard. "He was just trying to get away from you!"

No one seemed to hear her. The energy shifted, at a breaking point.

"Please!" shouted a voice from the back of the crowd. There was a soft struggle as a form pushed their way to the front.

Lord Wymarc, disheveled and panting as though he had run all the way here, put up his hand as though trying to quiet a class of twelve-year-olds. Zanve had to admire his effort, still trying to quell things, despite his lack of control over the situation.

"Please," he said again. "We are not violent people. Let us discuss this like civilized—"

"We will be whatever we need to be to protect Arrowmount!" bellowed Damian, his eyes catching in the flames of the torches around him, wavering menacingly. The emotions of the mob were too far gone — whatever spark had begun was now a full-fledged flame. "Take them!"

The mob moved, swallowing Lord Wymarc. The forest animals answered in kind, meeting the people head on.

Zanve pulled Meri close so she could hear him. "If you can find Arileas in this crowd somewhere, find him, and get him to quell the emotions of the crowd. He did it once before, maybe he can do it again."

Meri opened her mouth to respond but turned, distracted; five more figures appeared at the edge of the forest, materializing in one. Zanve immediately recognized his friends — Kaius, Jay, and Wyn stepped out, hands going up as though preparing to fight. Kaius' skin split as he started to grow larger, his large hands grabbing two mob members and slamming them together, knocking them out.

But the two figures behind his friends went to Meri. Zanve only caught their faces in the brief flashes of torch flame, but he saw the similarities immediately; Meri's grandmother and mother, had somehow arrived from the fey realm. Zanve saw their mouths move as they talked quickly among one another. Meri's mother took her arm, but Meri withdrew, shaking her head.

Around them, chaos reigned. For a moment, Zanve didn't quite know where to look. Everything was a maelstrom of people and creatures; fur, skin, teeth, and claws attacking one another.

Many folks in Arrowmount knew what to do when some*one* attacked them — but what was one to do when it was a badger, or a swarm of birds clawing at their faces? The mob was confused; one woman hightailed it back down the meadow as tiny birds dive-bombed her with their sharp claws and beaks.

But, there were so many of the mob, and so few of them.

Zanve backed up several feet, having lost sight of Meri in the chaos, but Thistle was still at his heel. He had to do *something*, but he was injured, shirtless, and without any weapons.

But, he *was* a weapon; for the first time in his life, Zanve transformed fully in view of the regular townsfolk of Arrowmount. His pants shredded around his legs, hanging off of him in sad flaps of material until he shook them off. He lashed out in his lithe, panther body, launching headlong into those around him.

He wasn't aiming to kill or seriously injure, but it was difficult to see what he was doing. Most of the people around him didn't even see him coming; a black shape the height of thighs weaving between them all, silently taking them down, one by one.

Zanve had no idea if they were winning or losing, but he hoped beyond anything that Meri could find Arileas if he was even in this crowd — the chances of that were slim to none, now that he thought about it.

But he had to hope they had a chance.

46

EVERY SINGLE ONE

Meriwen

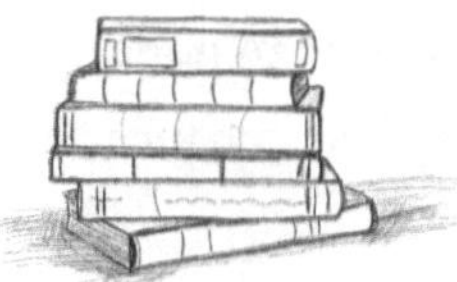

The ley lines' power continued to keep hands off of Meri as she pushed through the mob, trying to fight her way through the disjointed battle. Every so often she was shoved to the side as she tried to force her way through the moving bodies.

Lock had his nails in her skin, holding on for dear life as they hunted for Arileas, the bookstore owner. Why Arileas would be out here was beyond Meri, but if Zanve thought he could help…

This mob was *angry* — the blurred faces passing Meri were contorted with fury, far beyond reasoning.

As she got closer to the back of the mob, a few people turned to look her way, their faces more confused than anything. The glimmering magic hanging in the air, creating a blanket over the mob, was thinner on the outskirts.

Then Meri caught sight of Wyn helping Cecily Little stand. The market stall owner looked sweaty and determined, but not nearly as mad as anyone else. She only looked mildly miffed that someone had knocked her down in the first place.

The magic hasn't touched her, Meri realized, as she saw no shimmer around Cecily. Not everyone in this crowd was under the influence of the errant magic. Some were trying to help.

"Meriwen!"

She turned in time to see Lord Wymarc's hand outstretched toward her, stopping her in her tracks. She eyed him warily, but saw no magic around him either. "Sir?"

"Do you have any idea how to stop this madness? I have never seen the people of Arrowmount so…"

"Unstable?" she suggested.

"*Yes.*"

"If you can help me find Arileas, we may have a solution," she yelled, trying to be heard. Goodness, who knew battles were so *loud*.

"I think — yes, I believe I saw his partner just back there. Why does it feel like everyone in Arrowmount is out here? What is *happening* to my town?"

"I don't think it has a hold on everybody — I will explain everything, but we have to find Arileas first."

Lord Wymarc nodded and lifted his elbows up, starting to make way for her through the crowd. It was surprisingly effective.

At her slightly shocked look, he laughed. "I was once a young noble with nothing better to do than drink my way through bars, and let me tell you, when your friends get into fights, having a quick way to part the crowds was handy. Don't let my fancy shoes fool you, I can get down and dirty if need be."

Meri couldn't help but laugh. The sound bubbled up out of her, unexpected in the tumult of the evening.

It took them a few more heart pounding seconds of hunting before she caught sight of a bright flash of white; Arileas' hair whipping around as his fingers worked patterns in the air.

"Arileas!" she shouted, pushing through the crowd to his side. He looked distinctly worse for wear; his hair was tumbling out of a braid in thin strands and his forehead was smeared with something that glittered in the torch light. Shadows were playing with tricks with the hollows of his face, making him look haggard. A thin wisp of the errant magic swam toward his face, but he batted it away with a flick of his fingers.

"Meriwen? Are you alright?"

"I could ask you the same," she said. "What are you doing out here?"

"We felt the energy in Arrowmount, heard about the mob from one of our customers — and if I know anything about my husband, he will find himself in the thick of things in the blink of an eye." Arileas shook his head, looking concerned. "I don't know where he's got to."

"Zanve told me what you did for the crowd before. Can you do it again?"

Arileas frowned, picking up a little bag on his hip. The lining of the sack glittered in the torchlight. He dragged his fingers through it, as though hunting for something. "I don't have enough of my dragon scale left to do something that large. With the alarm system implementation and the repairs around town..." Arileas lifted his hands in defeat.

Out of the corner of Meri's eye, she saw Sarrai and Wyn standing next to each other, and an idea sparked in her mind. She started toward them, pulling Arileas with her. Lord Wymarc had lost once again to the mob, pulled in by its churning force.

"I think I know what to do. Come with me. Keep your elbows up."

Meri stumbled through the trees, followed by Arileas, Wyn, and Sarrai. They gathered up her mother and grandmother who were tucked back in the trees, the two of them bent over an injured rabbit, talking to it in soothing tones.

Meri led the way, shining like a beacon with her magically charged armor wrapped around her limbs. It was all that was keeping her upright, that constant pull from the ley lines around her.

They crashed through the path to her cottage as shouts and sounds of the struggle continued behind them. Yells echoed through the nearby trees as some of the crowd broke off and started to follow them.

"What are we to do?" asked her grandmother, rolling up her sleeves.

"Make a chain," Meri said, finding the spot in the middle of her garden where the nexus met. Lock leapt off of her and perched on a nearby garden bed. She breathed in, pulling even more power into her, and extended her hand to her mother. "Channel your magic through to Arileas. Give him everything you can."

Elestren grasped Meri's hand without hesitation. Meri exhaled and dropped her armor, holding onto her mother for dear life.

"I need my hands to cast," said Arileas, as Wyn and Sarrai fell into line, joining hands with her mother and grandmother.

"That's alright," said Seraph, putting her hand on his shoulder. "You will feel it all the same. Do what you have to do."

Arileas looked back at them all, warily. "Will this really work?"

"Trust me," said Meri, channeling the ley line magic through Elestren's fingers. Her legs began to shake, but her mother held her up, keeping her standing. "Please."

Arileas simply nodded and turned as the first figures burst through the trees and ran toward them, frenzied expressions on their faces. The elf's thin fingers worked fast, bright runes flooding the air in front of him, before he flicked his hands outward.

The spell practically exploded out from him in a burst of white light. It hit the few people coming through the trees in full force, knocking them unconscious. Light cut through the branches, leaving perfect slices in the leaves around them, as though tiny knives were carving their way toward the mob outside.

The noise from beyond her garden ceased. All was still. Meri held her breath, body trembling as her mother held her.

"Did it work?" said Wyn quietly, her hands clasping Sarrai and Seraph's fingers so tightly that Meri could see her skin pressed white around her knuckle bones.

"Let us hope," breathed Arileas. They waited a beat, looking at the unconscious people around them, before they all let go of one another.

Meri finally collapsed to the ground, no longer able to stand. She waved her mother and Wyn back, so exhausted that she couldn't put into words how little she wanted to stand up right then.

Something came crashing through the trees toward them then; they all stiffened, but it was just Thistle, leading the animals back to them.

"I will go check on them, see what happened." Arileas started back toward the path out of her garden. He rubbed a hand across the back of his neck, and continued on with a shaky voice. "I have never in my life held that much power in my hands."

Meri knew the feeling. Lock crawled down to her as Thistle rushed over, both of her creatures wrapping themselves around her.

What felt like only a second later, Arileas came hurrying back.

"They're all asleep. Every single one of them."

It took them a long while to gather the sleeping forms of those they loved, bringing them to her cottage and laying them in the long grass around Meri's garden, safe as they rested. Meri herself could only ask the others to help, forced to remain where she was. Wyn and Elestren helped her to her old garden chair, with Lock on guard to make sure she didn't move.

They brought Zanve to her, still in his panther form, but sleeping deeply; along with Kaius, Jay, and a number of others. Cecily Little, Gable, and a few half-orcs that Meri had never had the pleasure of meeting, were all laid carefully nearby. Even Firnean, Arileas' husband, was found.

"They'll hopefully be comfortable, at least," fretted Arileas, touching Finnean's head, wiping his hair off his forehead. "I have no idea what that spell did to them."

"My guess?" Wyn shrugged lightly, her eyes soft and pained as she looked at her unconscious partners. "You calmed them down so much they simply fell asleep."

Meri's grandmother made everyone tea. The darkness of the night was thick beyond her garden, as Meri sat with the battle-worn creatures shifting around her, half of her people unconscious and the other half murmuring quietly to one another. She felt as though she had slipped between realms.

"Meri," said Elestren, coming up to her. "You should go inside; you need to rest. We all do."

"Zanve—"

"Is asleep. As we should all be, resting."

"Yes," said Seraph, walking out after Elestren. "Let us all rest until sunrise, then we will figure out what to do next."

"The only fix is the ritual," said Meri, dragging a hand down her face. "We have no way to know if knocking them all out was enough to stop the magic from manipulating their emotions."

"We simply have to wait a few more hours, then. Tomorrow evening, everything will be set right." Seraph put her hand on Meri's shoulder. "You have done amazingly, my girl. You escaped, rescued the man you love and this marvelous creature from unknown fates, and you managed to come up with a solution that stopped much more pain and possibly death."

Meri blanched at the thought. "We don't even know who's seriously injured. We can't know until they wake — and we didn't check those still in the meadow."

"We've done all we can." Elestren crouched and wrapped her arms around her daughter. Meri sank into the embrace.

"Here," said Seraph, shaking back her long sleeves and moving out to Meri's garden. The tips of her fingers started to glow as she pulled on the ley lines. With quick movements, she shifted Meri's entire garden, her garden beds gently lifting and shuffling back a few feet to make space. Then, as though Seraph was conducting an orchestra, thick vines poured from the forest around them and sprouted from the ground, wrapping and contorting themselves into shapes as they moved closer.

Within the span of a few heartbeats, there were six beds laid out on the grass in front of them.

"I figure that most of you would rather not sleep inside Meri's house, seeing as your loved ones are out here," she said, gesturing to them.

"I'll get blankets," said Wyn, her eyes shimmering with tears as she hurried into Meri's cottage.

They all settled into beds under the stars, with each other and her animals as company. Meri didn't think she was going to be able to sleep, but the moment her head laid down on her vine-crafted pillow, she fell unconscious as though she had been hit with Arileas' spell.

Morning dawned, sunlight breaking bright through the trees. There was a brief moment of confusion as Meri opened her eyes, wondering how on earth she had come to be where she was, but then the previous night came back to her.

Those knocked unconscious by Arileas' spell were still sleeping soundly around her garden. Her companions, the five that had been protected by channeling their magic through Arileas, all slowly came to.

Thistle was curled at Meri's feet, with Lock wrapped in a tighter knot on top of him. They both woke as she shifted, trying to stretch out her legs.

"Well, good morning, I suppose," said Arileas, looking over the still sleeping people with concern written all over his brow. "I suppose we must simply wait for them to wake."

"Not for long," said Sarrai, pointing to Zanve who had transformed back to human and was starting to move in his sleep. Meri pushed herself to standing despite the deep, bone-tired ache spreading through her, and moved to his side as he started to move on the ground. She'd found him a new pair of trousers and a shirt, seeing as they'd lost his uniform last night somewhere.

One by one, their sleeping compatriots woke. They were all confused, but, as they received mugs of tea from Meri and her grandmother, they began to understand what had happened.

"That was the best sleep of my life," said Finnean, stretching and cracking his spine.

"I suppose that means everyone else will be waking," said Meri, her fingers locked with Zanve's. They had also bandaged his ribs with supplies Meri had in her cottage for the time being; but, they definitely needed to find a healer before the day was out.

"Let's go and see what's going on," said Zanve, bringing her knuckles to his lips. "Hopefully everyone got as good a rest as we did, and—"

A voice came from the tree line, interrupting them. "Excuse me, but what in all the realms are we doing here?"

They turned, noticing the few people who had fallen unconscious in the trees sitting up. Every single one of them had a look of absolute confusion on their faces.

"Good morning," said Meri, stepping forward with Thistle at her side. The few scattered folks looked at Thistle with unbridled surprise; but none appeared to have that malicious look to their eye from the previous night. "I think it's time we explained everything."

47

ZANVE OF MY HEART

Meriwen

Meri clutched her staff in one hand and Zanve's arm with the other, slowly making their way back over her well-trodden garden path out to where the rest of the townsfolk had been left the night prior. On her way, she collected those who had fallen unconscious in the forest, a line of people growing behind her.

Lord Wymarc walked up to stand next to her as she gazed at all the faces of the town she had chosen to protect so long ago. The early morning sunshine promised an incredibly warm day; and off in the distance, the ocean glistened like a hoard of spilled sapphires.

"Hello," she said carefully, drawing everyone's attention. "I presume a lot of you are very confused, and I was hoping to help clear that up."

"Why are we out here?" asked a woman to the right. "Does anyone else remember a... a mob?"

Slowly the others started to supply the story, and their memories came back; soupy, as though seen through the lens of a spell.

437

"Were we cursed?" asked an older man, looking distinctly worried.

"Not quite in the way you think. You see—" Meri stopped, trying to find the best place to start.

She looked sideways at Zanve, who gave her a reassuring smile. She supposed the best place to start, out of any, was the beginning.

"I don't believe I ever truly introduced myself to you all. My name is Meriwen, and I am a Keeper of the Lines."

Meri explained what she did for Arrowmount, explaining that the magical disruption that Arrowmount had been experiencing was her fault, but she was going to fix it; that very day, in fact.

"My grandmother, Seraph," she gestured to the High Fey standing nearby, "is a Keeper in the fey realm. She taught me all I know — and she is going to help me in this ritual, so we ensure that Arrowmount is once again as safe as it can be."

"Why haven't we ever seen you in town, doing this... this ritual?" asked the stable master.

"Because I didn't believe I needed to," she said. "I was scared, for one. I didn't know how you would all handle me coming in and performing magic you may not understand. Plus, it was easy enough to work from up here at my cottage."

"And it's not enough now?" asked Lord Wymarc.

"It may not be," said Seraph. "We believe that it is best to cover all our bases, to be sure. Both nexuses, balanced, and the strange events happening over Arrowmount — the storms, the manipulation of your emotions, and who knows how many other little things that have gone unnoticed — will cease."

A sigh went through the crowd, the tension easing.

"And the monster?"

Meri beckoned Thistle forward. He sat by her side, gazing at them all with an intense stare. The crowd shuffled uneasily.

"He is what the fey call a Kefithnath," she said. "He is a being of immense power, but his kind are here to protect. To bring peace, abundance, and help to Keepers. He is not a monster. He is just a creature, like any other of this realm."

"They are very rare," piped up Scholar Daruka, stepping up beside Thistle. "It is an honor that one chose Meri, and they both chose Arrowmount as their home."

Most of the townsfolk seemed unconvinced, but Lord Wymarc nodded. "Alright. Once this ritual is done, and magic is back in balance in our town, then we will come to a final decision about you and your creature, if that is alright with you, Meriwen."

Meri opened her mouth to agree, since that was perfectly fair, but a voice cut her off.

"Are you seriously just going to let her *go*?" Damian stumbled forward, his perfect hair askew. Meri could even see leaves and bits of twigs in it, as though he had a fight with a tiny bush. "After all of that? That's a *monster* at her side. And she herself isn't even from here. We don't need her here, balancing some magic none of us even know existed. How do we know it's true?"

"Let me prove it," Meri said, stopping Zanve with a soft squeeze of his arm as he surged toward the black-haired man. "If, after my ritual is complete, you all still wish for me to leave, I will go. Simple as that. I can return every seasonal change, to make sure that Arrowmount stays safe, but you will no longer see me here."

"That seems unfair," said Wyn. "You belong here, Meri. Just as much as the rest of us."

"Agreed," said Arileas. "Meriwen has done more for Arrowmount than most of us could dream of. Balancing such a force, all on her own?"

Meri simply shrugged. "It is my duty."

"I am willing to wait and judge Meriwen's actions as well as her words," said Lord Wymarc, nodding appreciatively. "Until then—"

"You're all hoodwinked by her," said Damian, his eyes bulging. "Every single one of you. How are we supposed to know that whatever knocked us out last night wasn't some fey spell that tampered with our minds?"

"It wasn't, because *I* cast it," said Arileas coolly. "It was the same spell that I used to calm everyone down in the town center during the last storm. Are you going to accuse me of being something, Mr. Briggs?"

Damian looked at Arileas as though seeing him for the first time. Even Meri felt a little unnerved at Arileas' hard glare and the tone that had come out of him. Meri was fairly sure no one in town had ever seen the usually soft-spoken bookseller like this. It was gently malicious, as though a hidden blade was waiting up his sleeve.

Not to mention Finnean at his side, with the actual blades in hand. Twin daggers spun absently along his fingers as he grinned at his husband.

Damian stammered incoherently until Captain Ludru came up behind him and put his hand on Damian's shoulder. "We are going to have a chat, Briggs. Come along."

Zanve couldn't contain his smile as he turned it on Meri. "This may just be the best day of my life."

"Give it a few hours," she said, letting out a long sigh. "We've got work to do."

Meri and her grandmother spent the day readying for their rituals.

Zanve, after much prodding from Wyn and Meri, finally conceded to seeing a healer. The healer ordered him to sit still for the day after they had checked his head wound and many of his broken ribs, because they couldn't heal the damage completely. Only time, and rest, would help.

Meri kept him in her kitchen, seated on a nearby chair, so she could watch him. She suspected that he was keeping a close eye on her, too; every time she passed by or leaned close, he found a reason to touch her or smile at her.

As the day descended toward evening, Meri and her grandmother hesitated at the same moment, their eyes connecting over the kitchen counter. The air started to change, tension tingling up her arms. She leaned against her counter as pain spidered up and down her leg like lightning.

Lock, who was asleep on the kitchen table, started to snore.

"It's time," said Seraph. "Meri, you'd best get to town."

Meri gathered her supplies and staff, looking back at Wyn, Kaius, Jay, Sarrai, and Zanve, who had all stuck around to help today. "Will you all come with me? I don't..." she breathed in deep. "I don't think I can walk all that way on my own."

Zanve took the basket of supplies from her and replaced it with his hand, lacing their fingers together. "I will follow you to the ends of the realm, if you asked."

"Bleurgh, were we like that?" Wyn mimed getting sick. "All this lovey-dovey stuff is too much for me."

"Oh, please," said Kaius in his deep rumbling voice, linking his fingers with Jay's as he teased Wyn. "You were the worst one. I remember when we first met Jay, you couldn't stop mooning over them for *days*, and then when they finally agreed to partner with us, you couldn't keep your hands off each other."

Jay's cheeks turned pink.

"Yes, well, at least I wasn't going around making grand statements like, *I will follow you to the ends of the realm if you asked,*" Wyn teased. She winked at Meri, and grabbed her staff that was resting by the kitchen door. "Come on, let's get you to town."

Meri smiled at her mother and grandmother, leaving them in her garden as she slowly made her way down her forest path, accompanied by her friends. Thistle lead the way, head held high.

Meri walked between Zanve and Wyn, each holding onto her arms, bolstering her.

Meri's heart was in her throat as they walked to Arrowmount. Adrias and Nisri were on guard today, tired but happy to see them all through. The anticipation of today, after months of not knowing whether or not she was going to be able to perform this ritual, was building up inside of her alongside the nerves of having to do this in front of people for the first time in her life.

The only other person who had ever witnessed her perform her ritual was her grandmother, who didn't really count, seeing as she was also a Keeper, and taught her all she knew.

All the people who would see her magic today would be witnessing something they never had before. And that in itself was terrifying — but more so was pondering what their reaction would be. Meri had no idea what they were going to do, or think, or say. Would they let her stay in Arrowmount after all this? Or was she going to have to find somewhere else to live after this, breaking ties with the town that had stolen her heart?

They made their way through town, Meri's bare feet making no sound on the cobblestones. For once, she didn't trip on the uneven surface; her feet found their way as she took her time. She let go of Wyn, opting for her staff on one side and Zanve's arm on the other, taking most of her weight.

Heads turned her way, watching as they made their way toward the town center.

When they reached the market, her friends quickly helped move whatever stalls were in the way. Slowly, a crowd began to gather as Meri planned out the ritual.

She made sure to say hello to everyone who decided to come out and watch. Lord Wymarc, Arileas, Finnean, Cecily and her partner Gable were all there. Caelynn strode over from her apothecary and stood with another giantkin, Calian, the two of them discussing something in hushed tones.

The space filled, everyone gathering in close, leaving just enough space for Meri to work.

They watched her with anticipation written across all their faces; some with excitement, and some with fear. She recognized a number of faces from the mob the night before; though today, they looked diminutive and apologetic as they hung back, trying not to be seen.

She had only minutes now. Her friends stepped back, joining with the waiting crowd. Thistle sat at Zanve's side, watching her with his beetle-black eyes.

"Alright," she said to herself. "It's time."

Meri cast her gaze up to the sky, watching the light around town dim. The multicolored flags fluttered daintily in the breeze as a few clouds started to creep over the sky.

With a soft sweep of her hand, she lit innumerable candles around the perimeter of her circle, casting those gathered in a soft glow as dusk fell around them properly. She paced around the cobblestones slowly, one hand still holding her staff, keeping her steady, as those around her watched in silence. Carefully finding each spot, she placed a bundle of herbs down at every point of a misshapen star, every point where the ley lines traveled through the streets around her and began to knot into one another, creating the nexus in the town center.

The moment the seasons started to change, she placed down the last bundle of herbs, and she heard those around her gasp.

The world around them was alight with tendrils of pure power. They ran up through the ground, around the onlookers' feet, and up into the air. The lines of power danced across her skin like a gentle breeze as she made her way to the nexus.

The townsfolk reached up, a few moved their fingers in the tendrils that had appeared, flashes of color erupting where their fingers interrupted the flow of power before turning back to blinding white. The ley lines curved and arced toward the nexus where they all converged, knotting and dancing with one another, before speeding off back into the world.

Meri settled both her feet right next to the brightest gathering of the ley line, her bare feet bracing on two separate cobblestones, staff on a third. It felt entirely different from the grass that usually tickled her feet during this ritual, but it didn't feel entirely wrong, either.

She got to work.

It wasn't overly complicated, her job. She began to recite lines she had learned long ago from her grandmother in a fey tongue so ancient that most High Fey only knew it from books; a language nearly lost to time. As she spoke, her voice like fluttering leaves and the feeling of waves breaking on a windy day, she reached forward and pulled at the tendrils of light. They didn't feel anything different from the power that she had grown used to pulling from the ground. The only thing letting her take them and manipulate them was the magic in her voice; the spell she wrought keeping everything in line.

The herbs at each point of the misshapen star around her anchored the ley lines in place.

With power in her words, in her hands, and channeled through the bundles of herbs lovingly prepared by her and her family, Meri began to unknot the nexus and realign the lines, all the while imbuing it with balance, prosperity, protection, and goodness.

Everything was going as planned; then, a rumble of thunder in the distance. Meri frowned as the townsfolk shifted uneasily around her.

That was when the new alarm system around Arrowmount chose to start blaring, and storm clouds gathered above the town, heavy and ominous.

After the chaos of last night, Meri felt entirely unbothered. She merely glanced up at the sky between phrases, and continued on. Nothing was going to shake her now, even as the clouds started swirling viciously fast, the sky turning purplish red.

She ignored the shifting crowd, all the while holding her ritual firm. It only took a few minutes; there was no way she wouldn't succeed now.

Meri was a Keeper, after all. This is what she was meant to do.

The sky opened up around her, rain cascading in a blanket of water, blurring Meri's sight until she could only see the wavering forms of her audience. For a heartbeat, she felt as though she was alone once again; performing her ritual at her cottage with no one watching.

She breathed out, speaking the last phrase.

The moment her ritual completed, the encroaching storm stopped; and with it, the last-ditch effort from the unruly magic to wreak more havoc on the town.

In a breath, the tendrils of light vanished, as did the storm around them. It wasn't as dramatic as the beam of light that Meri had done to vanquish the storms; but it was concrete and instantaneous. The storming clouds rippled apart above them, leaving a sky bathed in oranges and pinks as the sun set. The alarm stopped and silence descended on the town.

Meri drew in a breath, and smiled. She had done it. Her ritual had succeeded, and the magic was balanced once more.

"Well, Meriwen, that was quite something," said Lord Wymarc, coming through the quietly murmuring crowd and taking both her hands. "If I don't say so myself, that was completely concrete proof that your magic worked. I have never seen a storm... vanish, quite like that."

"It was gorgeous," said Caelynn, moving over and smiling at Meri, her ears and nose dripping wet. "I have wanted to see your ritual for years now — and to finally witness it?" Caelynn shook her head, tears in her eyes, unable to say more.

Slowly, one by one, the townsfolk all came over to shake hands with Meri or exchange a few words of wonder. She met them all, trying to remember their names, to put them somewhere in her mind so she would never forget them.

Zanve came up to her when most of the town had gone, leaving a few members behind to put the town center market back to its proper place. He smiled, sliding a hand into hers, before he turned to meet Lord Wymarc's eye.

"Sir, if you don't mind me asking, but what is your final decision on Meri and Thistle?" He squeezed Meri's fingers gently. "Because we would rather like her to stay."

"After a show of magic like that, I can certainly say we need you here," said Wymarc, beaming at her. "I would never want to evict anyone from their home, especially one that they do so much for."

"I owe you the biggest mug of tea," said Meri, the words tumbling from her.

"Tea?" Lord Wymarc's eyes sparkled. "Tea would be lovely."

"Just wait until she lets you try one of her resilience teas," said Zanve. "You'll be going for *hours*, no exhaustion in sight."

Lord Wymarc looked at her curiously.

"I imbue teas, tinctures, and the like with magic," said Meri, blushing slightly. "It's nothing as showy as all this ley line business, but it's something. By all means, you should come around to give it a try."

"Her tea helped me with my back pain," said Caelynn as she helped Wyn gather Meri's herbs and candles from around the square. "I have never felt younger than after I have a cup!"

"I'm sure many here in Arrowmount would be glad to hear of remedies like that," said Wymarc.

"Why don't you sell them, Meri?" called Jay, listening in as they helped Kaius move Gable's stall back into place. "It could help you get to know the town better. And them, you."

Meri tilted her head at the thought. Doing what she loved, curating remedies and teas for various ailments, and also meeting the town through it?

"I could never sell them," said Meri, "but I would be more than happy to give them away to whoever needed them."

"Think on it," said Wymarc. "A little bit of something for the town to give back to you after all you've done."

Meri nodded as a feathered head nudged her hand. "And Thistle?"

Wymarc looked at Thistle, who was seated by Meri's side. A delighted smile split across his face. "Honestly, I never once believed that that creature was a monster. He is as welcome as you, Meriwen. And I'm honored to have a creature of such power, if Scholar Daruka is to be believed, as our town protector."

He bowed to Thistle, who very clearly lowered himself in a bow to the Lord of Arrowmount.

Relief flooded through Meri as Lord Wymarc stepped away, leaving them finally on their own. She laughed, giddy, turning toward Zanve, who was grinning as wide as she was.

"We did it," she said.

"*You* did it, Meri," he answered, picking her up and spinning her around, before wincing slightly and putting her back down, one hand on his ribs. Meri laughed again.

"Whenever you do that, it feels like I'm flying."

"I will do that better when I don't have a couple of still-healing ribs. You deserve to fly, my Meri."

What felt like hours later, Meri and Zanve said goodbye to Wyn, Kaius, Jay, and Scholar Daruka as they all made their way home. They carried exhaustion with them as they went; the ordeal over the past twenty-four hours drawing them toward the comfort of their beds.

Meri and Zanve kept their fingers entwined as they walked, Meri leaning on her staff for support, worried about hurting Zanve more. He was walking a little stiff now, which made Meri anxious.

"I'm fine, Meri."

"You have broken ribs, Zanve. I'm going to worry about you."

"*Healing* ribs, they're healing."

Meri smiled and brought their joined hands to her lips, kissing his knuckles. Her chest felt lighter than it had in months. She laughed, the sound bubbling up out of her. "You are wonderful, you know that?"

"Am I?"

Meri stopped at the edge of the forest, looking out over the meadow as the sky darkened around them, the first few stars glittering above them. A couple of firebugs flickered in the grass around their feet, swirling up around the trunks of trees.

"Completely, unerringly wonderful. Without you, without that day when you came to my rescue, I wouldn't have had my entire life changed."

Zanve cupped her cheek. "All because I wandered into the woods following a bright light."

He drew her close, pulling her up against him until she could feel the bandages beneath his shirt pressing into her. His eyes traced her face, going soft in the fading light. "Is now the right time to do this?"

She smiled knowingly. "Do what?"

"I recall someone telling me not to declare anything in the middle of a dark basement."

"I didn't want it to feel like we had to say those things because we felt like we were in danger," she said softly, leaning into his touch. "I wanted when we said those things to one another to be just another day, to make that day special."

"That makes sense," he answered, his voice barely above a rumble. "Too bad today is not like any other day."

That didn't matter anymore. Meri couldn't go another moment without saying it.

"I love you, Zanve Einar. More than anything." Meri turned her face to kiss the palm of his hand. "You came into my life and totally upended it, in the most perfect way. I was not alive before I met you — I am yours for as long as you will have me."

His mouth opened slightly, surprise breaking across his face.

"Meriwen of the Garden," he whispered, gently sliding a bit of Meri's hair behind her ear and cupping her jaw, gazing at her with such adoration that Meri couldn't help but gasp a little. "You beat me to it."

"Zanve of my Heart," she answered, and pulled him closer. "You could say it a thousand times, and I would never tire of it."

His purple eyes crinkled at the sides as he smiled. "You have utterly changed my world. I thought I was happy before all this; but nothing compares to how I feel now. You've brought so much color into my life, Meri. I love you more than words can say."

Zanve bent his head to her, then, and Meri met him halfway. Their lips met, both of them sinking into one another. Zanve tasted like tea and warmth as Meri let herself melt in his arms. She wound her arms around his neck as his hands threaded back into her hair.

They kissed slowly and sweetly, hidden from the world along the tree line that wrapped around Arrowmount, knowing it was only the first kiss of a lifetime's worth.

AFTER

Meriwen – A few weeks later

Heavy, dripping summer heat clung to the world outside as Meri stirred a fresh batch of cooled tea for her visitors. She'd set out a batch in the sunshine to brew all yesterday, and it was finally ready to serve. Today, she had a married couple in her kitchen, requesting one of her remedies to help with aches and pains.

"He has been a craftsman for most of his life," explained one spouse, holding onto their partner as though they were worried that he might run away if they didn't hold them in place. "He complains often of this ache in his back."

"It's nothing more than age and what this job does," said the man, frowning. "I don't see why we need—"

"That's exactly why we need it," said his partner, shaking their head. They were a brilliant blue water elemental, their skin undulating with every expression that crossed their face. "Because every cleric we've gone to, even those in Pralon when we went to visit family several months ago, couldn't do anything about it long term."

Meri knew very well what they meant.

"Do you have anything for dealing with those kinds of pains?" they asked, turning to her. "The ones that plague you regularly?"

"I do, but you must remember that it will not cure the pain, it will simply help alleviate it somewhat. My magic is not a cure-all. No magic is." The couple nodded to her. "Let me grab the right ingredients — I will have it ready for you momentarily. It will be enough tea to try and see if it will help; if you do find it helps, feel free to come back or send a messenger for more. I will make you a larger batch to last you the season." She passed them glasses of the cooled tea. "Here, to help beat the heat while you wait."

They sipped curiously, before both their eyes lit up in pleasure.

Meri vanished into her greenhouse and gathered the proper herbs, before grinding them a number of times with her mortar and pestle, imbuing the familiar meadowsweet and valerian tea with her usual pain relief and calmness, before filtering the bundle into a small linen bag.

She returned to the couple and handed them the bag. "One cup in the morning or at night, whenever you feel the most pain. I usually take mine in the morning, to get me through the day, but my friend Caelynn told me she takes hers at night to help her sleep. If that's the case, let me know, and I will add in a few extra bits to help you sleep more soundly, too."

"Th-thank you," stammered the man, taking the pouch. "What do we owe you for this?"

"Nothing," said Meri with a kind smile. "If you come back for more we can speak about payment; but for now, simply try it out and let me know what you think."

"We can't just leave here without giving you something for your time, your magic," said the water elemental. "Isn't there something we can do?"

Meri tilted her head and smiled. "If you come across any wild dandelions on your property, cut them and bring them to me. That will be payment enough."

"Dandelions," said the man with a frown, before pocketing the small bag.

"That we can do," said his partner. Before the two of them left, they paused to give Thistle a pat, who was laying by the path in a well-loved patch of long grass that was no longer tall enough to hide him in.

The couple vanished down the pathway back to Arrowmount, waving goodbye. Zanve came around the corner, his shirt sleeves rolled up past his elbows, and his pant legs rolled up above his knees.

He grinned at her and leaned in for a kiss.

"What has got you all happy?" asked Meri, smiling.

Beyond him, Meri caught sight of a small gnomish boy that had appeared in her garden. He must have brought a message from Arrowmount when she was speaking with the couple. The boy scratched Thistle between the ears, reaching up on his tiptoes, even with Thistle laying down.

Thistle had grown immensely in the past few weeks since the solstice. His two sets of horns were a good few inches long now, standing proud on his head. The feathers around his face had started to thin out, revealing a strong leathery hide. Along his body, the feathers were thick and shone in the sun.

Zanve held up a roll of paper. "I just received news."

"Hmm?"

"You're going to have to prepare a bit of anti-nausea tea," he said, his eyes positively shining. "Because we're going to have a set of tiny feet running around soon."

Meri froze. "Wyn?"

"Yes!"

She let out a delighted shout, jumping into Zanve's arms.

"I'm going to be an uncle," said Zanve, his eyes shining with unshed tears.

"I will have that batch ready in just a moment — you can take it to her. No, actually, let's both take it to her. I want to see how Jay's latest project is going with the tree in their backyard. I'll also have to tell my mother — she is going to be so excited for Wyn."

Her mother had taken an immediate liking to Wyn. After the solstice, Elestren had stayed in town for a week visiting Meri, and invited Wyn along to Meri's garden every chance she got.

After her grandmother had gone back home to the fey realm, the Keeper who had completed Seraph's ritual for her had come out to place a looking glass in Meri's cottage. Keeper Arthie had installed it right above Meri's kitchen counter. Whenever Meri wanted to talk to her grandmother, she would say a small phrase in High Fey, and the mirror would connect to the adjoining one in her grandmother's kitchen.

Elestren had a small pocket mirror to keep with her on her travels that connected to both Seraph and Meriwen. It was an elegant solution, and Meri often found herself talking to her mother and grandmother long into the night, discussing news and recipes.

Zanve scooped Meri up with one arm, spinning her around. Meri squeaked, clinging to him, her skirts trailing out around them as he kissed her. He tasted like sunshine and fresh flowers.

"What was that for?" she said, slightly breathless. He put her down gently, but did not let her go.

"Because I wanted to," he answered. "And I could."

"Careful, or I'll have you shoveling out a new patch in your garden," she teased. A mischievous grin spread across Zanve's face.

"I love it when you say that. *My garden.*"

"Of course it's yours," she said, laughing. Zanve had begun his own garden to the side of Meri's cottage, where the ground soil was rich and the plants would receive enormous amounts of sunlight, perfect for a vegetable patch.

"You never answered me about turning one of the rooms on the second floor into a guest room," he said, picking up a watering can to deposit it by the kitchen door. "Now that Wyn is expecting, I want her to be able to have a place to sleep in case she ever stays too late."

Meri chuckled to herself. She could already see what kind of an uncle he would be; loving, ever present, and absolutely obsessed with the little one. "Yes, love. We can make it a proper guest room, large enough for all of them if they wished. Though you'll have to be the one to bargain with the pixies to move my mother's journals."

"We could expand the cottage at the back, make a proper library room for the journals," he suggested. "I'm sure the pixies would like that."

"That's an idea." She turned to gaze up at her little stone cottage, wondering what they could do to it. "With space for your books, too. We'll have to do something about our room as well, it's the size of a broom closet."

"I like it, it's cozy," he said, pressing a kiss into her temple. "But we can do whatever you'd like."

A while later, after she and Zanve had delivered Wyn her anti-nausea tea, Meri traced her fingers over one of her mother's journals. It was one of only three she kept down in her kitchen now, having returned the others to the pixies on the second floor.

The journal was propped open to the storm quelling spell, one that she hadn't used in months. Thankfully, she didn't anticipate it happening anytime soon, either; since the solstice, the magic in Arrowmount had completely remained steady and balanced. With the fall equinox approaching, too, she felt confident she would keep it that way.

Outside, Zanve was inspecting the handful of sprouts growing in his patch. He smiled at the tomato plants, reaching out and touching one of its tiny, young leaves.

Thistle, resting behind Zanve, began to play with a bright blue beetle that had landed nearby, the beetle unafraid of the growing fey beast, like it knew, somehow, that Thistle would never hurt it. Instead, it seemed to almost goad Thistle on as they played, flying up higher out of the fey creature's reach.

Lock wound his way up onto the counter next to Meri, a content swirl of steam curling from his nostrils.

Zanve came into the kitchen smelling of churned earth and growing things. He wrapped his arms around her, placing a kiss against her temple. "What are you thinking about?"

"Just how odd and wonderful it is, that this cottage feels more like home to me now than it ever has before," she answered. "With you here, and our friends visiting more and more."

"Home," he said, the word rumbling in his chest. "It really does."

"Even for you? Outside of the town you know so well?"

He kissed her, long and deep. "My Meri, anywhere with you is my home."

She smiled, despite herself.

The past few months had been some of the strangest and best in her life; but, as Meri knew very well, strange things often happened around her. That was par for the course, being the Keeper of the Lines in a town such as Arrowmount.

ACKNOWLEDGEMENTS

And with that, the Arrowmount Books trilogy has come to a close.

Through the writing process, it can be so tricky to know whether or not your brain is going in the proper direction and that your story isn't absolutely unintelligible. Thankfully, I've been incredibly lucky to have found many people who have given their time and knowledge to help me make this story the best it can be. My lovely beta readers, you were all absolutely invaluable to this story, and I cannot thank you enough. Ally, Julie, and Phoebe — you three are incredible, and I can't thank you enough for helping me shape this story into its best form. Not only did you help me shape this story, I can call all three of you friends as well.

To my lovely (in real life) friends who have offered support and excitement from day one: Yelani, Sophie, Sofia, Hannah, Alexander, Tess, Kait, Tamsen, Danny, Taylor, and SJ. And specially Cass, who has been with me the longest and has always been the best cheerleader to all of my endeavors. I love you all so, so much.

To Tess Brenan, for once again, being both an incredible friend and SUPREMELY talented artist. I think this is my favourite cover of the three in this trilogy – you captured everything about this story's vibe and Meri and Zanve's energy together. Thank you endlessly.

Thank you especially to all my friends from my online life who have been excited for this book even before *A Second Story* (Arrowmount

Books #1) came out into the world. I am so glad I have you all as part of my life everyday. My lovely friends, you are all the best, and I adore you all endlessly.

Thank you especially to the hosts of the Writing about Dragons and Shit podcast, who not only have created my favorite podcast ever – but are some of the loveliest people as well. Erin M. Evans, Treavor Bettis, and B. Dave Walters, you are forever inspirations!

A special thank you to my amazing friend AND editor, Yelani! I cannot imagine what this book would have been like without your expertise helping guide it to its final product. You took my story and elevated it exponentially; taking my sentences and ideas and making me sound SO much better than I do in actuality. I cannot put into works how much I appreciate your work and dedication to this book.

There are so many more people in my life that have added fragments to my writing life and love of books, but I think the biggest contributors have to be my parents. Thank you, Mom and Dad, for supporting my love of reading and stories from day one. I know I don't say it enough, but thank you for letting me run wild with whatever stories were burning in my head, and I love you.

What a ride it's been, but I'm so glad that you, dear reader, have found your way through Meri and Zanve's story. Thank you for visiting Arrowmount in these pages; and thank you for reaching the end of the road with me for the Arrowmount Books trilogy.

CHARACTERS

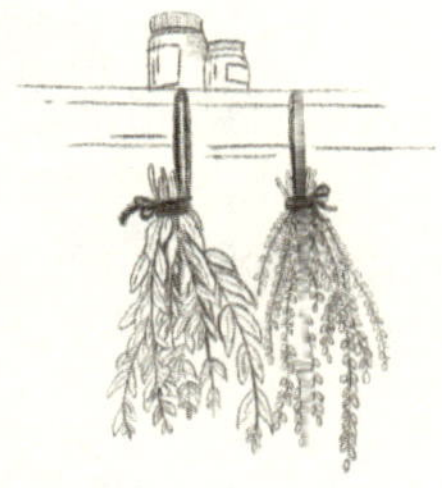

- **Aeric**: (pronounced: Ar-ric) Worker at the Old'n Narrow bar, elf.

- **Adrias Waylan**: Town guard. Dwarf.

- **Amalin Reem**: Lieutenant, Second in command to Captain Ludru of the Town Guard.

- **Andrew**: Teenage gnome, helper at May's Cafe.

- **Argyle**: Scholar Daruka's assistant. Human,

- **Ariawyn**: (goes by **Wyn**) Elf, baker/confectionist. Best friends with Zanve, partnered with Kaius and Jay.

- **Arileas Damaris**: (pronounced: Arr-ih-lee-ass Dam-Ahr-iss) Owner of the bookstore A Second Story, elf.

- **Briar**: One of the owners of the Old'n Narrow bar, human.

- **Cadoc**: Town guard, newbie. Human.

- **Caelynn**: (pronounced: kay-lynn) Giantkin who runs an apothecary in Arrowmount.

- **Calian**: (pronounced: Cal-ee-an) Mysterious giantkin who seems to live around Arrowmount.

- **Captain Ludru**: (pronounced: Lud-rue)The captain of the Town Guard.

- **Cecily Little**: Magic Goods stall owner and Lottie's sister, earth elemental.

- **Chervil Tealeaf**: (pronounced: shh-er-vill) Lighthouse runner and owner, blue fiendling.

- **Corwek**: Cook at the Old'n Narrow bar, goliath.

- **Damian Briggs**: Town guard. Zanve's nemesis. Human.

- **Della**: An elderly gnome who lives on Fetterly Place, wife to Neema.

- **Elestren**: (pronounced: El-ess-tren) Meri's mother, High Fey. Sometimes goes by Elestren Fair. Realmstrider.

- **Finnean**: (pronounced: Fin-ee-an) Owner of the bookstore A Second Story, human.

- **Gable**: Owner of the bakery stall in the market square, dating Cecily Little, elf.

- **Healer Bryndis**: Healer in Arrowmount.

- **Hemlock**: (Goes by **Lock**) Bottle-green wyrmling. Lives in Meri's kitchen cabinet, often worries like an anxious grandmother.

- **Jay**: Humanoid from the Manid Empire. Race never specified; cursed dragon sorcerer. Partnered to Wyn and Kaius.

- **Kaius Miirthgrove**: (pronounced: k-eye-us) Earth elemental, lava/magma based. Partnered to Wyn and Jay.

- **Kirandir Dulra**: (pronounced: Keer-ann-deer Dull-rah) Our lovely local bard, half-orc.

- **Lottie Luck**: Suspected thief, earth elemental. Sister to Cecily Little, girlfriend to Kirandir Dulra.

- **Lord Wymarc**: The Lord of Arrowmount, human.

- **Marin Miirthgrove**: Head glass smith at the Glass Forge. Kaius' father.

- **May Camire**: Owner of May's Cafe, half-elven druid.

- ***Meriwen***: (pronounced: merry-when) Our lovely Keeper of the Lines. High Fey.

- **Nisri Frosthelm**: Town guard. Dark elf.

- **Neema**: An elderly gnome who lives on Fetterly Place, wife to Della.

- **Percival**: (Usually called Tiny) Wyn's ancient cat.

- **Quinlan**: Town guard. Human.

- **Scholar Sarrai Daruka**: A scholar from the Kingdom of Pralon, in Arrowmount to study a mysterious fey-related event. Gnome.

- **Seraph**: Keeper Seraph, Meri's grandmother. High Fey.

- **Thistle**: Fey creature.

- **Vena Einar**: Zanve's mother. Human.

- ***Zanve Einar***: (pronounced: zan-vee) Our brave Arrowmount Town Guard, human shifter.

GLOSSARY

- **Arrowmount**: A coastal town, where our story takes place.

- **Blackshell Forest**: A thick, often (magically in places) impenetrable forest to the north-west of the continent of Ravaryn.

- **Caspasian Isles**: A series of tropical islands located in the Caspasian Sea, to the south east off the coast of Arrowmount (refer to map for more).

- **Centurion**: A godly war that occurred centuries ago in the history of Ravar.

- **Dragon Scale**: a magical component so potent that it acts as conduits to spells that need components to create. Dragon scale is mined out of the Nerian Empire's mountains, and is a highly sought after commodity in the northern empire. It is rarer to see in the Brenem Empire, but of course like all commodities, it makes its way where gold will take it.

- **Druid**: A class of magic users that are nature based, and find

463

their magic through the force of nature itself or natural deities.

- **Eldar's Wall**: An ancient wall gone to ruin on the outskirts of Arrowmount (refer to map for more).

- **Elementals**: Humanoids that take on aspects of their elemental lineage. Most commonly there are air, fire, water, and earth elementals, but as there are many different aspects to each element, you'd be hard pressed to find many elementals who resemble one another, even if they were of the same element.

  - Notable elementals: Cecily Little and Lottie Luck, earth elementals.

- **Feycross**: A small village in the Brenem Empire. Reportedly has a portal to the fey realm.

- **Fiendling**: Humanoid beings that have fiendish blood running through their veins, which gives them their often unique colouring, horns, tails, and occasionally sharp teeth. Along with average humans, they can range from about five feet to just over six feet tall.

- **Giantkin**: A broad term to refer to races of folk who loosely resemble humans, in a way, but are related to giants in a distant, second or third or tenth cousin fashion. In this work, this term is used to refer to giantfolk that occasionally have large drooping ears and wide faces with a slightly snout-like shaped nose. They're very tall, often reaching well over seven feet tall, and range from having tough, grey skin with no fur to slightly softer, more furry beings.

- ○ Notable giantkin: Caelynn, the owner of the apothecary in town.

- **High Fey**: A branch of fey beings that are akin to elven folk in the material realm; they populate the fey realm and run it through various kindoms.

- **Keepers of the Lines**: Sometimes referred to as "Keepers," these are the fey beings that choose to devote their life to the upkeep and balancing of the magic in nexuses of ley lines.

- **Ley lines**: Powerful "lines" of energy that run through every realm, occasionally crossing or knotting in places called nexuses. These are the spots that Keepers tend to in the fey realm, and our Meri tends to in the mortal realm.

- **Maigsir**: The Goddess of the Sea and Sky.

- **Manid Empire**: A southern empire on the continent of Ravaryn.

- **May's Cafe**: A local cafe on Fetterly Place, beloved by locals of Arrowmount.

- **Narakami**: A city in the Manid Empire.

- **Narveil**: A small town in the Nerian Empire.

- **Nerian Empire**: Northern empire on the continent of Ravaryn.

- **Old'n Narrow**: The local bar in Arrowmount.

- **Pixies**: A fey realm creature with long, spindly limbs, that often are compared to branches. They are very verbose, and take offence when people forget (or don't know) that they can read and speak. They often take up residence in any realm's best archives and libraries.

- **Pralon**: Also known as the Kingdom of Pralon, a city in the Brenem Empire.

- **Quharian Meadowsweet**: A breed of the meadowsweet plant, specifically grown in the Quharian region of the Manid Empire (refer to map for more).

- **Savras**: The God of Knowledge, Divination, Fate — often believed to be all seeing.

  - Mighty Savras, or other creative expletives, have been often heard throughout Arrowmount as a favoured curse.

- **Scumbrlwrengigelu**: A common herb found everywhere in the fey realm.

- **Tanju Violets**: A rare breed of the violet flower, specifically grown in the Tanju region of the Manid Empire (refer to map for more).

- **Thnathi**: Sometimes called The Rare Ones, the Thnathi are an incredibly rare fey realm creature.

  - The Kefithnathi are a branch of Thnathi that are in reference to a specific creature that brings positivity, protection, joy, and a positive force to wherever they decide to go. They are connected to Keepers of the Lines.

- **Wizards**: A class of magic users who learn to do magic through a spell book and lots and lots of practice.

  - Notable wizard: Arileas Damaris

- **Wyrmling**: A small dragon-like creature that grows to about the size of a small child in length. They generally have thin leathery wings, not used for flying but used for gliding around. Four legs, clawed hands, often have scaled snouts, but can be as varied in colour and textures as their cousin, the dragon.

- **Zidien**: Also known as the Kingdom of Zidien, a city in the Brenem Empire.

ABOUT THE AUTHOR

J. A. Collignon (AKA: Jenna, but you can call her Jenn) is a Canadian author based out of the prairies who loves everything fantasy. Fantasy books, movies, TV shows, and TTRPG podcasts; you name it, she loves it. Most often, she can be found on her couch with a thick fantasy book in hand, listening to fantastical music playlists.

Jenn is an avid member of the bookish internet community through her Youtube channel, TikTok, Instagram, and Bluesky. Follow her to keep up to date on future book releases.

Youtube: Jenn's Bookshelf
Tiktok: @jennsbookshelf
Instagram: @authorjacollignon
Bluesky: https://bsky.app/profile/jacollignon.bsky.social

www.ingramcontent.com/pod-product-compliance
Lightning Source LLC
Chambersburg PA
CBHW031732180726
48283CB00005B/1470